FLASH POINT

KENNETH ANDRUS

This novel is dedicated to those I had the privilege to serve with while on active duty and those currently serving our country in the armed forces.

"Organized force alone enables the quiet and the weak to go about their business and sleep securely in their beds, safe from the violent without and within."

Alfred Thayer Mahan

Prologue

USNS IMPECCABLE T-AGOS-23
THE SOUTH CHINA SEA
THURSDAY 12 DECEMBER

"United States Naval Vessel, you are operating illegally in Chinese territorial waters. You are endangering Chinese fishermen in violation of international law. Take immediate action to clear the area or suffer the consequences."

Anthony Carlson, Master of the *USNS Impeccable*, scowled. Whatever those consequences might be were not yet apparent, but he was in no position to argue the point. He fixed his eyes on the Chinese ships just four hundred yards from his own, considering his options. There weren't any.

A People's Liberation Army-Navy Y-12 patrol plane harassed them for almost an hour the day before. The plane flew as low as his mast top buzzing them like an angry hornet before disappearing over the horizon. He knew it would only be a matter of time before the Chinese ships arrived.

Sweat inked dark circles on his shirt. The *Impeccable* drifted in the current making two knots. A PLAN ocean surveillance ship and a Bureau of Maritime Fisheries patrol vessel were keeping station off either beam. Two fishing trawlers were maneuvering to assume a blocking position dead ahead. He felt the eyes of his first mate burning into his back. He ignored him and continued to stare at the Chinese ships, wondering how in hell he would get everyone out of this mess without somebody getting hurt.

He was more frustrated than angry. Politics had won over common sense. Still he could accept the Pentagon's approval of his mission, but he couldn't reconcile the decision and putting his ship and thirty-seven-man crew at risk. The other reality? He would gain nothing by dwelling on events out of his control.

He turned to his first mate. "Bob, have the guys charge the forward fire hoses. We'll be needing them shortly."

"You think they're planning on boarding us?"

"That would be ill-advised." Carlson picked up the headset of the bridge-to-bridge radio. "We are operating in international waters under the protection of the provisions of the United Nations Conventions on the Law of the Sea."

The response cracked over the bridge speaker. "Your actions are a grave contravention of international law. They are unacceptable to the People's Republic of China."

Carlson shrugged. The response confirmed the futility of following his guidance on how to respond if confronted by the Chinese.

The trawlers closed to within fifty feet, pitching in six-foot seas. A large swell heaved the nearest boat's bow free of the water, exposing its barnacle-encrusted keel. The Chinese captain wouldn't be able to control his vessel. The next surge would send it careening into the *Impeccable*.

"Are they bluffing, Captain?"

"Not this time."

"How do you think this will play out?"

Carlson glared at the fishing boats. "We'll find out soon enough."

He knew the Chinese could make a case for their actions. The fact was that, while the *Impeccable* conducted legitimate hydrographic surveys of the sea floor, she had another task. Equipped with a towed-array acoustic system to detect and track undersea threats, the *Impeccable* kept tabs on the People's Liberation Army-Navy's nuclear-powered attack and ballistic-missile submarines deploying from the Yulin Naval Base seventy miles to the north.

Their course followed the fiber-optic cable carrying Chinese military communications between their installations scattered across the South China Sea and those on Hainan Island. He didn't know how the information obtained by mapping the seafloor topography would be used, but he suspected someone planned to tap the cable.

"Your provocative actions endanger fishermen within the People's Republic of China's Exclusive Economic Zone."

The Chinese fishing trawlers crossed the *Impeccable's* bow.

"Damn, them. Bob, sound the collision alarm."

"Skipper, the —" The blaring of the *Impeccable's* klaxon drowned out the rest of the first mate's sentence.

Carlson gripped the sill of the bridge window. "Emergency stop. All astern. Brace for impact."

The *Impeccable's* twin screws bit into the water. The ship shuddered in response, the ocean boiling at her stern. She went dead in the water, her massive hull looming above the fishing boats.

He shouted over the din. "Wilson, can you see what they're doing down there?"

"They're reading to throw a net over the side."

"What?"

"It's a fishing net. They're trying to foul our props."

"Knock 'em off their feet."

Battered by twin columns of saltwater from the *Impeccable's* fire hoses, the Chinese dropped the net and retreated out of range. Once safe, they yelled obscenities and waved Chinese flags in defiance. One of the fishermen expressed his displeasure in another way. He mooned the Americans.

"Well, that's a first," Wilson remarked.

Carlson nodded. He may have won this round, but their position was untenable. "*Yuzheng* 311, our intention is to leave the area. Request a safe pass. Over."

A burst of dirty-brown smoke from the trawlers' stacks signaled the Chinese's next move. Picking up speed, the ships circled around to the *Impeccable's* stern. Carlson's eyes stung from the acrid stack gas enveloping the bridge.

"What are they up to now, Skipper?"

"Damned if I know."

The first mate started to ask another question when the look on Carlson's face stopped him.

"Adams? You documenting this?"

"I'm getting it all on my recorder, Captain."

"Wilson, get a couple guys aft. Now. And charge a couple more hoses."

The situation was deteriorating and two fire hoses wouldn't stop the Chinese for long. That would take considerably more persuasive power than his vessel possessed. "What's the status of the Navy?"

"The *Chung-Hoon* just raised us, Captain. She's making thirty knots."

Carlson wondered if the Chinese would appreciate the irony of having a Navy destroyer named after a Chinese-American Admiral charging toward them. What he did know? The Chinese wouldn't back down. Not this time. He surmised the Chinese commander received his orders directly from the People's Liberation Army Chief of the General Staff, General

Li Xiao, to force the *Impeccable* out of the area. He had to buy time.

"*Yuzheng* 311. You are required under international law to operate with due regard for the rights and safety of other lawful users of the ocean."

The Chinese captain ignored him. "American Naval Vessel, your size threatens the safety of our fishing vessels. The cable you are towing could ensnare their propellers. They have been forced to take evasive action."

"Threatened my ass," Carlson muttered. He checked his watch. *Twilight in another forty-five minutes.* "Where the hell is the Navy?"

"Sir?"

"Bob, tell the crew to prepare for an emergency destruct. We need to secure the cryptology gear."

"Do you—?"

Carlson anticipated the question. "Reel in the 'Fish.' There'll be hell to pay if they get their hands on the gear."

"Skipper, we just raised the *Chun-Hoon*. They've launched their helicopter. It's a long shot, but they're thinking when the Chinese see it, they'll disengage."

"You got a satellite fix?"

"Yes, sir. Seventeen degrees, eighty-one minutes north. One hundred ten, thirty-nine east."

"Get those out."

"Captain? This is Wilson. We've got a problem. A couple Chinese are swinging grappling hooks. They're trying for the array cable."

"Is the Fish secured?"

"We've got another thirty feet."

"Get an ax."

"An ax?" Wilson stared uncomprehending at the bridge. "Captain, we should be able to hold them off with the hoses."

"You may have to cut the cable."

"Oh, got it."

"Adams, get back there and settle them down. Bob, get on the horn and alert engineering to stand by. We can't wait for the Navy. I'll be needing max revolutions."

"What are you planning on doing, captain?"

"Getting the hell out of here."

"But our top end is only twelve knots."

"Yeah, that could be a problem."

Chapter One

"I shouldn't be learning about this from the newspaper."

Randall Stuart's hands tightened around the copy of *The Washington Post*. "We've got enough problems with the Chinese without them trying to hack our computers at Commerce. The *Impeccable* last month and now this?"

Stuart was angry. Angry at the winter storm raging outside. Angry at the Chinese. Angry at being caught off guard by the *Post*'s headline.

He dropped the newspaper and glared at Dan Lantis, his Chief of Staff. "What do we know?"

"There's more than what's being reported, Mr. President."

Stuart's eyes hardened. "Did they breach our firewalls?"

"No, sir. Security held."

"Then what happened?"

"The contents of John's laptop were accessed when he was in Beijing for the G-20 Economic Summit. Cyber Security believes the Chinese used what they downloaded to try and hack Commerce's system."

"We have proof?"

"The FBI has a trace to the Chinese Academy of Military Sciences in Jinan."

Stuart's shoulders tightened. "Same outfit that penetrated Google's accounts. How did John let this happen? It violates every tenet of security—"

"He left his computer unattended in his suite."

Stuart snapped. "He did *what?*"

"He thought one of his aides would secure it."

"Wasn't it encrypted?"

Sleet slashed against the bulletproof windows of the Oval Office. The glass protected him against the frigid onslaught. The windows didn't shield him from this latest assault.

He grasped his pen and drew a spiral on a notepad. "What do I need to do?"

"With John or the Chinese?"

"John."

"He's pretty upset."

"At the moment, his feelings aren't at the top of my list of concerns. I'll ask for his resignation."

"I wouldn't do anything until the FBI completes their investigation."

"Do we know what they were after?"

"John believes they were targeting information relevant to punitive tariffs."

"You'd think Beijing would understand the tariffs are being driven by our friends on The Hill."

"I doubt they believe Congress operates without us pulling the strings."

"If only." Stuart tapped his pen on the spiral. "Have we approached their embassy?"

"Their spokesman said something to the effect of we shouldn't be so paranoid. They feel any implication against the government of China is guilty of cybercrime is not conductive to fostering mutual trust and friendship between the People's Republic of China and the United States."

"They can't be serious. Who do they think they're dealing with? Some banana republic? The sheer arrogance of that statement..."

"Their response did reflect a certain lack of finesse," Lantis finished for him.

"My read is they could care less what we think and that, my friend, is a dangerous position. You think anyone at State would care to explain how all of this fits with their policy of engagement?"

Lantis had heard all the arguments. Following the mid-air collision between a Chinese fighter jet and a Navy surveillance plane in the first month of Stuart's administration, the Pentagon had pushed for a containment strategy. The Secretary of State, Richard Valardi, had countered, recommending a policy of engagement as the most pragmatic approach.

"You didn't agree with my decision."

"Circumstances have changed."

"We need to reconsider. Their actions represent a clear and present danger." Stuart blackened the center of his spiral. "We have to push back."

"That should make the Pentagon happy."

"This isn't about the military, although we could take the stance that Beijing's penetration of Commerce's computer system could be construed as an act of war."

"Pretty extreme," Lantis said.

"Perhaps. Their verbal posturing at the Stockholm China Forum suggests they're positioning to retaliate in kind if we impose tariffs."

"They wouldn't come out very well. Our economies are too interdependent," Lantis replied. "That, and they're projected to have their first trade deficit in eight years."

"We're just as vulnerable to rising commodity prices. Pull that National Intelligence Estimate from a couple of months ago, will you? The one addressing the impact of Beijing's modernization programs."

"What's the connection?"

"Oil, our trade deficit, international shipping, the flow of hard currency to Beijing. They're using their currency reserves to buy U.S. Treasury Bonds. These cyberattacks are coordinated and targeted. They're part of a broader plan of economic espionage."

"So they —"

"They're supporting our national debt."

"Beijing would intentionally drive us to bankruptcy?"

Stuart massaged his forehead to ward off a headache. "They could if they chose to."

"What's our next move?"

"Who's Richard's lead at State?"

"Adrian Clarke, Assistant Secretary for East Asia and Pacific Affairs."

"I want his analysis."

"I'll call."

"Anything else?"

"No, sir. That's it."

Stuart thought a moment and managed a wry smile. "Just another day in the office?"

"I suspect there's more to come. You going to watch the game?"

"That's the plan. So, how about getting out of here? You need to spend some time with your kids before something else happens to screw up our day."

Stuart waited until Lantis left before opening the top right drawer of his desk. He felt around for his stash of TUMS. He selected a green one, popped it in his mouth. He glanced at the Rembrandt Peale portrait of George Washington displayed over the fireplace and set to work.

Ten minutes later, he completed typing several annotations to the prepared remarks he was going to deliver at the State

Dinner that evening. He hit the print button and headed for the door of the adjacent office.

The pile of correspondence overflowing his secretary's in-basket elicited a pang of guilt. He searched her face, concerned she might not get home for several more hours. She had followed him from Ohio where she served as his personal secretary when he was governor. He considered her to be part of the family. "I made a few changes, Mary Allus."

She reached around to pull the speech off the printer. "I was just getting a head start on next week's work. It won't take more than a minute to clean this up and close the shop."

Her answer eased his conscience. He left Mary Allus to her work and walked to the breezeway connecting the executive offices with the White House residence. Slowing, he turned to the Secret Service agent who had fallen in behind him. "What do you say we call it a day?"

Their feet crunched on small drifts of salted ice as a gust of wind pushed the men past the dormant rose garden toward the living quarters. Taking the stairs to the central hall of the residence, they saw the Chief Usher approach with a welcoming smile.

"I see it's time to pass the baton," Stuart said.

"Thank you, sir. Will there be anything else?"

"No, I'm good."

"Good afternoon, Mr. President," said the Usher. "Mrs. Stuart is still out."

"The homeless group?"

"Yes, sir."

"She keeps my priorities straight on days like this."

"We're all proud of her, sir."

"Thank you, Jim," Stuart said, handing over his suit coat.

The Chief Usher draped the coat over his arm and studied Stuart's face. "Would you care for something to eat, sir?"

"Could I just have a soda?"

"It's a long time to dinner, sir."

Stuart craved a couple of grilled hotdogs, but resisted. "I'll be fine."

He settled down in his recliner and clicked on the TV. It wasn't unusual for the station to be preset on ABC, but as he prepared to change it to ESPN, the words of the anchor stopped him.

"At the top of the hour our correspondent in Manila, Marie Lynne, is reporting the President of the Philippines has accused the Chinese of illegally detaining Filipino fishermen and breaking international law by building military installations in the disputed Spratly Islands. The Chief of Staff of the People's Liberation Army, General Li Xiao, countered those claims, demanding an apology for an illegal Filipino incursion into Chinese territory and the harassment of its fishermen. The Philippine government is vigorously denying any wrongdoing and is appealing to the international community for support."

"Now what?"

The remainder of the report did not provide any further information, so he clicked over to FOX. Nothing. Exasperated, he flipped back to the Super Bowl, hit the mute button, and picked up his secure phone. He scrolled down until he located the number of his National Security Advisor and pressed the speed dial. Three rings later, a familiar voice came on the line.

"Brown residence."

"Justin?"

"Mr. President. How are you, sir?"

"I could be better. I'm not interrupting anything, am I?"

"No, no, of course not. I was just collecting myself for the dinner tonight. What can I do for you?"

"Did you happen to catch the segment about the Spratlys on ABC?"

"Yes, I've got the TV in the bedroom on. The embassy

alerted me about a statement the Foreign Ministry was going to release. They're protesting the boarding of a Filipino fishing boat by Chinese navy personnel. The report didn't say anything about the military installations or President Montalvo going on national TV. Something else must have happened we don't know about."

"You think it's unusual that Xiao responded?"

"Makes me wonder if the civilian leadership even knew."

"Who's setting the agenda? Xiao or Zhu? I'm thinking Zhu's got a problem holding his government together."

"If Xiao's becoming the dominant player, we've got a problem."

"When will you get the next report?"

Brown glanced at his bedside clock. Several more hours. "It's four in the morning there, sir."

"How did that reporter—"?

"Lynne?"

"Yes. How did she get her report on the air so fast?"

"The embassy believes she has back channel access to someone in the Foreign Ministry."

"What do you think is going on?"

"I'm hesitant to venture a guess without more details. I wonder if Manila and Beijing haven't just blundered into this confrontation."

"Whatever the cause, I don't want us getting dragged into the middle of it."

"I can't see that happening."

"I'm not so sure." Stuart stared out the window. The sun had set. "Justin, the rules are changing. We're not positioned well if we have to intercede. State's initiatives in Southeast Asia are losing traction. I don't want Admiral Lawson's Pacific Command to be our only option if this situation between the Chinese and Filipinos worsens."

Brown pulled off his glasses and chewed on the stem. "Understood."

"We'll talk tomorrow. There's not much we can do about it right now."

Stuart hung up. The football pregame show flickered on the TV, unseen.

"Randall?"

Stuart turned at the sound of his wife, Dianne's, voice. "In here."

She flicked on the overhead light. "What on earth are you doing sitting there in the dark?"

"I was talking with Justin."

"Is there a problem?"

"Something's going on between the Chinese and Filipinos. We'll know more tomorrow. How was your event?"

"You're changing the subject."

"Yup."

"It's serious?"

"Could be."

"Anything I can do?" she asked, reaching for his hand.

"No, I'm fine. We've just got some damage control to attend to next week."

Chapter Two

HEADQUARTERS COMPOUND
UNITED STATES PACIFIC FLEET
PEARL HARBOR, HAWAII
06:20 MONDAY 27 JANUARY

Mike Rohrbaugh dropped his razor and raced around the corner to the nightstand to silence his telephone. He snatched it off the cradle before the second ring. His wife stirred but didn't wake.

"Commander? This is Mac."

"Dang, Chief, couldn't you use my cell? Kate's still asleep."

"No, sir. It's best I use the land line."

Rohrbaugh dabbed at the shaving cream dripping down his neck. "Something up?"

"There's traffic on the board you need to read before morning formation."

"Be there in a few."

There was no sense asking for details. Rohrbaugh picked up his cell and carried it to the bathroom, finished shaving, and dressed in his summer white uniform. He paused in front of the mirror to check the alignment of his service ribbons. The blue and white of the Navy Cross, the nation's second highest award for bravery, topped the five rows.

Rohrbaugh preferred to wear his working khaki uniform with only the pin identifying him as a Navy SEAL, but his preferences accounted for little this morning. The Commander of the Pacific Fleet, Admiral Anthony Morey, had ordered the staff to wear their whites and assemble in front of the headquarters building for an awards ceremony. Unit cohesiveness.

"Mike?" his wife murmured.

"Did I wake you?"

"Who called?"

"Mac."

She relaxed. When Rohrbaugh had transferred to Hawaii from San Diego, they'd had no choice but to place her mother in a nursing home and she lived in fear of any unexpected call.

"Could you ask him to use the cell?"

"Will do. How do I look?"

"Dashing."

"I'm off." He leaned over and kissed her on the forehead.

Rohrbaugh exited the kitchen door and strode up Makalapa Drive making for the windowless operations building a short distance from his home. *Damn, did the Impeccable run into more trouble?*

He crossed the narrow pedestrian bridge leading to the back entrance of the building and commenced the sequence of actions necessary to gain access. Inside, he acknowledged the Marine security guard and proceeded down the hall to his office space.

"Here ya go, Commander," Senior Chief Boson's Mate "Mac" Mackenzie said handing him a red-hashed top-secret folder. "The first page is operative. The report also has an interesting quote from General Medeiros, the AFP Chief of Staff."

"Armed Forces of the Philippines?" Rohrbaugh asked more of himself than Mackenzie as he took the report.

Rohrbaugh flipped open the folder, passed over the routing codes, and read the intelligence summary of the recent Sino-Philippine confrontation in the Spratly Islands.

"Mac, this incident fits a pattern going back to the end of the Vietnam War. There's bound to be more trouble. The only positive I see is that it's not as bad as when the PLAN opened fire on those Vietnamese soldiers back in '88 mowing them down when they were wading ashore. Sank a couple of their ships too."

"'Slaughtered' would be a better word. Guess they figured nobody would know until a video turned up on YouTube a couple months ago."

Rohrbaugh's jaw tightened. "The Vietnamese commander should never have put his men in that situation."

Mackenzie inwardly cursed. He'd touched a nerve. He changed the subject. "From the looks of it, they're not stopping with the Vietnamese and the Filipinos. They're going after the Japanese. The PLAN sent one of their destroyers to shadow several geologic survey vessels conducting hydrographic studies in support of the Japanese Maritime Self Defense Force."

Rohrbaugh looked at a map taped to the wall. A black line delineated the maritime boundaries Beijing had established for itself; the Nine-Dash Line. "Interesting."

"Makes sense, Skipper. That report says the People's Congress tossed out a manifest called the 'Law on the Territorial Waters and Their Contiguous Areas.' Hell, they're using the damn thing to lay claim to the entire South China Sea."

"I don't like the sections pertaining to Freedom of the Seas and the Rights of Navigation."

"Crap," Mackenzie said.

"Crap pretty well sums it up," Rohrbaugh said. "And, we have a trigger."

"Oh?"

"The AFP Chief of Staff is deploying his naval forces to patrol the waters surrounding the Spratly islands to prevent intrusions by foreign elements, including fishermen."

"Nothing unusual there."

"Uh, oh."

"Skipper?"

"The general says part of the Navy's mission is to investigate maritime markers in waters claimed by the Philippine government. He also accused Beijing of building a military installation on some place called Mischief Reef."

"The Chinese said they're shelters for their fishing fleet."

"That's pure B.S., Senior. Did you see the paragraph about the special weapons bunkers? Those don't sound like fishing shelters."

"Seems to me, Skipper, that Mischief Reef has got an appropriate name. If the AFP pushes this, there's no way we're going to be able to remain on the sidelines."

Rohrbaugh dropped the Intel report on his desk. "That's what I'm thinking. I need everything we have on the South China Sea and the Spratly Islands. And could you pull the draft of OPLAN 1729?"

"You looking for something for us to do, Commander?"

"Sure am, Mac, but we need to secure this stuff. Protocol calls. Time to assemble for colors."

———

Rohrbaugh's eyes shifted from the American flag whipping in the trade winds and turned his attention to the Pacific Fleet band playing "Anchors Aweigh." He scanned the other members of the staff arranged in a neat semicircle around the flagpole set in front of the headquarters building. Like him, they appeared anxious to get back to their offices. His feelings were mixed.

He'd completed his sixth month on the staff and was still adjusting to the change following his command of SEAL Team One in San Diego. Like other post-command officers at COMPACFLT, he chafed at the restraints of a shore staff tour. Harder to accept was the knowledge that any future operational deployments as a SEAL Team leader were over. That was for the younger guys.

He turned his attention to the ceremony listening to Admiral Morey complete his remarks and lead the other flag officers into the headquarters building. When the admirals were out of sight, he called out to Mackenzie. "Time to saddle up, Senior. Let's get on it."

It didn't take long for the two SEALs to focus on several potential Chinese targets. The weapons bunker Rohrbaugh had noted in the Intel report could easily contain a Seersucker anti-ship cruise missile. That would make sense if the PLA intended to lock down the sea-lanes. Intelligence also verified the PLA had acquired long-range surface-to-air missile systems from the Russians and constructed an early warning radar installation on Fiery Cross Reef.

"Damn."

Mackenzie looked up from his keyboard. "Sir?"

"We've got some serious trouble brewing."

"How's that?"

"The PLA has bases scattered all over the place. These will sure as hell make things difficult for our carrier strike groups. They're looking to gain reaction time with these new installations. And that airfield in the Paracel Islands."

"Su-30s?"

"No doubt."

"I thought their fighters didn't have the legs to intercept the carrier strike groups as long as we stayed clear?"

"Affirmative, but the Intel guys reported Iran provided them in-air refueling technology."

Mac clenched his fists. "Another gift to the Chinese from our buddies in Tehran. That's a bunch of thugs I really want to take out."

"You got any good news?" Rohrbaugh asked.

"Nope. The PLA is focusing on their rapid reaction forces and just concluded another war game near the Strait of Taiwan. Their objective was to prepare their forces to attack and occupy an outlying island and fight off an aircraft carrier."

"Not much doubt about who they've got in their sights."

"No, there isn't."

Chapter Three

CAVITE NAVAL BASE
MANILA, REPUBLIC OF THE PHILIPPINES
08:00 TUESDAY 28 JANUARY

"So, Admiral, what you're telling me is you have no idea about the fate of our fishermen?" Medeiros was incredulous.

General Antonio Medeiros, Chief of Staff of the Philippine Armed Forces, studied the faces of his senior leadership. He summoned them to their Western Military District headquarters to address the latest threat to their country. Like him, they were livid with impotent rage.

They had been preoccupied with the Muslim insurrection in the Southern Islands and now had to contend with a Chinese violation of Philippine territorial waters. Beijing had established a military presence on Mischief Reef despite their protests. Exacerbating the crisis was the fate of seven Filipino fishermen detained by the Chinese seventy-two hours earlier.

The Chief of the Philippine Navy stiffened. "That is correct."

"And you have no idea of what transpired and what

actions, if any, by the fishermen could have led to their detention?"

"No, sir. No suitable explanation has been provided by Beijing. There can be no doubt the fishermen were in our waters."

"It's been three days. President Montalvo demands answers."

"The Chinese persist in claiming they spotted our fishermen near one of their support installations, but saw them leave the area."

"Their duplicity is breathtaking. Has the Foreign Ministry given us anything?"

"Nothing useful. They've just quoted the Chinese embassy spokesman saying these 'shelter structures' have been erected by the Chinese Fisheries Administrative Department for the sole purpose of guaranteeing the lives of fishermen working the waters of the Nansha Islands, the Chinese name for the disputed islands."

"Yes, I know what the Chinese call them," Medeiros responded through clenched teeth. Calming, he relaxed his jaw. "Let's review the bidding."

"There are several realities underscoring Beijing's actions," the Admiral said. "The first of these dates to 1999 when China refused to sign our Manila Declaration adopted by the Association of Southeast Asian Nations. As you know, the declaration's intent to commit the six countries claiming portions of the Spratly Islands into refraining from any destabilizing actions has gone nowhere."

Medeiros slapped table. "I do know. Zhu stated that reaching such an agreement would be 'long and hard and difficult.' And, that vague diplomatic pronouncement means, 'Never.'"

The Admiral ignored the outburst. "The second reality is the absence of the American military."

"And we advised the government, did we not? As we

predicted, the Chinese moved into the vacuum created when the United States relinquished control of its naval base at Subic Bay and Clark Air Force Base."

"Yes, they did," Medeiros said, irritated at the Air Force Chief of Staff for wasting their time by re-stating the obvious.

While the average Filipino had approved of this development, the response of the AFP had been muted. All of them understood the importance of America's protective umbrella. Making things worse was their government's recent rebuff of a naval logistics agreement with the United States after opponents claimed it would be in violation of Philippine sovereignty.

"It is no secret the PLA has been emboldened by the withdrawal of the Americans from their Asian military bases. They are intent on claiming the entire South China Sea now that their Seventh Fleet is out of the way."

"Judging from the Foreign Ministry's lack of success, it's apparent the Chinese aren't about to negotiate away their options to assert their territorial claims," the Deputy Chief of Staff said.

"At least the Chairman of the Senate's Armed Services Committee is speaking out," the Admiral replied.

A dubious look crossed Medeiros' face at the mention of his cousin. The Chairman was never at a loss for words. "What did he say this time?"

"That the Chinese are putting up structures throughout the entire South China Sea like a dog urinating on trees and posts to mark its territory.' And that we should not allow ourselves to be used as a doormat."

"I'll be sure to thank the Senator," Medeiros said. "Now, on a more rational note, I've been informed the Foreign Ministry is preparing an *aide memoir* for Beijing's ambassador. The communication expresses serious concern regarding Beijing's incursion into our Economic Exclusion Zone. I doubt it will have any effect, so let's address the task at hand."

Medeiros looked across the table at the AFP Deputy Chief for Operations. "General, would you review the surveillance data?"

"We still don't have a clear idea what assets the Chinese have deployed. Aerial photography has identified two 1,200-ton supply vessels and a Dazhi-class survey/submarine support ship."

"Anything else?"

"Our aircrew was at the end of their search pattern, but managed to image the airfield on Fiery Cross Reef. They identified heavy construction equipment the analysts surmise will be used to complete upgrades. The strip will soon be capable of handling large transport aircraft and Su-30 interceptors."

Medeiros tapped the chart in front of him. Even with the upgrades, it would be months before any Su-30 squadron deployed from Fiery Cross. "Admiral, what's the status of your forces?"

"The few serviceable vessels are committed to patrolling the Southern Islands supporting our counter-insurgency operations. The only realistic long-term option we have is diplomacy."

"Regrettably, I must agree. But a short-term response to Beijing's actions is another question altogether." Medeiros looked at of his colleagues in turn. "Isn't it?"

The senior staff nodded their heads. To a man, they understood there could be no further delay if they were to prevent the PLA's actions in Philippine waters from becoming a *fait accompli*. They had to move decisively with whatever assets they could mobilize if they were to deter the Chinese.

"Thank you, gentlemen. Shall we review our options and put muscle in our government's protests?"

Medeiros' eyes focused on a map of the Pacific. "Perhaps we can also find a way to involve the Americans."

Chapter Four

MANILA
19:40 TUESDAY 28 JANUARY

"Hello? Yes, this is Ms. Lynne. Yes, certainly. Twelve thirty tomorrow afternoon? I'll be there. Thank you. Good night."

ABC's Manila correspondent, Marie Lynne, topped off her glass of chardonnay. She took a sip, reflecting on the unexpected call and the events of the past week. It would have been helpful to know why she was extended the invitation, but her caller gave no hint about what to expect. She surmised the meeting had something to do with the Chinese.

———

She was no closer to an answer when she pulled into the portico of the Manila Hotel the next afternoon. She set the brake, exchanged her car key for a parking receipt, and entered the lobby. The click of her heels on the marble tile caused a few heads to turn in mild curiosity, changing to active interest as she walked to the dining pavilion. She was conscious of the effect her entrance caused, but her mind remained focused on the meeting with the Foreign Ministry's representative.

There existed a *quid pro quo* between the Ministry and their resource in the press. The arrangement offered distinct advantages to both parties; the tradeoff of access to exclusive inside information by the reporter for the dissemination of a favorable viewpoint for the government.

The Minister of Foreign Affairs considered Lynne a reliable source for channeling the government's viewpoints to Washington. Her worth was not lost on him. He would tune into the network to check the pulse of the world, and he understood the value of the American broadcasting giant's global reach.

Lynne saw her friend Raul Atencio rise to greet her, delighted the Foreign Ministry had sent him.

"How are you, Raul?" she said, offering her hand.

"Very well. And you?"

"Couldn't be better. It's great to be back in Manila after Mindanao. The situation there is still very dangerous."

Taking advantage of President Montalvo's cease-fire with the main separatist rebels on the island of Mindanao, Lynne had leapt at the government's invitation to interview the leader of the Moro Islamic Liberation Front.

The MLF leader had provided her a synopsis of his negotiating points and warned her to stay clear of the more radical separatist group, the Abu Sayyaf. A fact known to Atencio, but not Lynne, was that the day she left Mindanao, Abu Sayyaf attacked the unit of the 104th Infantry Brigade that had escorted her during her visit to Barira town. The ambush killed four soldiers and wounded six in a rain of mortar rounds and machine gun fire aimed at disrupting the plebiscite set for the following week.

Southern Command had learned the Muslim splinter group planned to take Lynne hostage while she accompanied an International Red Cross mission to the remote area. The government ushered her out of danger's way, offering the excuse that coordination with the town authorities was not complete.

"We were worried about your safety," Atencio said. "But now we have a new concern—Chinese expansion in the Spratly Islands."

Atencio led her toward their favorite table. Placed by a large palm, the table afforded a panoramic view of the gardens and dining pavilion. He waited until their waiter was out of earshot.

"President Montalvo is most concerned about the latest intrusion into the Panganiban Reef area by units of the Chinese military and the detention of our fishermen. These actions are unacceptable. Our government is developing a plan to deal with it but we are concerned Washington may not be fully cognizant of the danger to the stability of the region."

Lynne ran her fingertip along the edge of her butter knife. She knew the U.S. embassy in Manila was swamped with inquiries from the anxious Philippine press. The majority of these inquiries where framed within the context of the Philippine-American Mutual Defense Treaty. The reporters wanted to know what the United States intended to do about the Chinese.

The official U.S. position remained firm. The treaty did not apply to the Spratlys. Washington would not take sides on the rival claims of the Philippine and Chinese governments and had signaled it preferred to see any dispute settled peacefully on a bilateral basis.   .

Atencio followed Lynne's finger. "Are you aware an unauthorized trip to the area by thirty-nine local journalists was turned back by the Chinese this morning? We had no prior knowledge of the journalists' action and first learned of the mishap when an official protest was delivered by the Chinese embassy to the Foreign Ministry. The gist of the note was that the incursion was considered provocative.

Lynne's eyes narrowed as she began to formulate the story she'd submit.

"It would be beneficial to have an impartial observer. I'm afraid the aborted effort of our journalists was well intended, but without coordination with the appropriate governmental agencies and adequate security, they were bound to fail. As it is, the only result was to further complicate the issue."

Lynne recognized her cue. "My network has already aired reports of the Chinese actions and President Montalvo's statements from Malacanang Palace. I could provide additional depth if I was afforded the means to travel to the disputed area."

Atencio smiled. "I believe something could be arranged that will prove most beneficial for all of us. I can reach you at the regular number?"

"Certainly."

Lynne collected her car and made the right-hand turn onto Roxas Boulevard intent on returning to her office to prepare for the trip. The road ran parallel to Manila Bay and in front of the American Embassy several hundred yards away. She thought about stopping, but changed her mind and continued past the compound.

Chapter Five

SOUTH CHINA SEA
PALAWAN ISLANDS
14:26 THURSDAY 6 FEBRUARY

L ynne exited the cramped military aircraft that had flown her to Palawan Island and came to an abrupt halt, pounded by the heat radiating in rippling waves from the empty tarmac.

She gathered her gear and began walking toward what appeared to be the terminal building. She had covered half the distance when a jeep careened around the corner of the adjacent hangar and screeched to a stop at her side.

"Toss your stuff in the back. The captain is anxious to get underway."

She interpreted this curt greeting as all the introduction she was going to get and scrambled in.

The driver gunned the engine and took off with a roar, barreling down the runway without waiting for her to get settled.

Thrown off-balance, she grabbed the seat frame. "How far is it?"

Her wide-eyed attention was riveted on near-misses of trucks, buses, various farm animals and pedestrians. She doubted they would survive the short trip.

Twenty harrowing minutes later, they slid to a stop enveloped in a cloud of dust and exhaust. The driver pointed out her destination, a small naval station set within the clutter of the port. He bid farewell without a hint of irony, "Have a safe trip."

Lynne looked in the direction the driver indicated and set off for the ship that was to be her home for the next week. An officer detached himself from a group of sailors loading supplies and walked toward her.

"Ms. Lynne? I am the executive officer, Lieutenant Santos. If you will please follow me?"

Santos motioned for a sailor to pick up her gear and led the way while providing a brief description of his ship. "The *Emilio Jacinto* is considered to be the most capable patrol boat in the Philippine Navy. She displaces 710 tons and is armed with a 76mm cannon and four 7.62 machineguns."

He completed his narrative as they boarded and led her aft before descending a ladder leading to a tiny room. "You will be using my stateroom. Now, if you will excuse me, my presence is required on deck. The petty officer will help you get settled."

Lynne found her way to the bridge after unpacking and found a spot out of the way to observe the crew. The patrol vessel's bow swung away from the quay and sailors were coiling the dripping forward lines on the deck. No longer tethered to the shore, the vessel's freedom was announced by a shrill whistle over the ship's speaker and a loud voice proclaiming, "Underway. Shift colors."

Lynne felt the *Emilio Jacinto* come to life with the gentle lift and fall of the ocean swell as they headed toward the open sea. A green channel marker slipped by.

Satisfied all was well with his vessel, the ship's captain motioned Lynne to join him. "Ms. Lynne, I am Captain Reyes. I trust you have found your quarters to your liking?"

"Yes, thank you."

"Excellent. I will be on the bridge for the next several hours, but if you would join me for dinner, we will review the particulars of our mission."

A look of consternation crossed Lynne's face. At a loss at what to do next, she didn't move.

Reyes turned to face her. "You are welcome to stay if you wish. Our destination is First Thomas Shoal, 248 miles from our current location."

———

FIRST THOMAS SHOAL
06:35 FRIDAY 7 FEBRUARY

Lynne secured the watertight door and stepped out on the weather deck just as the morning sun broke the horizon. The faint odor of diesel fumes greeted her and she could taste the salt in the air. The ocean, royal-blue tipped with white where waves broke over the barrier reef of a small horseshoe-shaped atoll.

There was already a great deal of activity on board. A knot of sailors clustered near the stern were preparing to launch the small boat she'd seen yesterday.

The unmistakable whopping sound of an approaching helicopter prompted her to look in its direction. She recognized the aircraft. A Vietnam-era Huey. The muzzle of a machine gun poked out the starboard door. Below the helicopter, two patrol vessels and what appeared to be an ancient World War II ship, an LST.

Now that's interesting. I wonder what's up?

Lynne turned her attention to the activity around the small boat. Reyes stood watching several Marines load satchels of explosives. He motioned her to join him.

"Good morning, Captain."

"Good morning Ms. Lynne. How are you this fine Navy day?"

"I couldn't be better, thank you. I see there is about to be some action?"

"Ah, yes. The ship's boat and Marines. We are approaching an illegal maritime buoy the Chinese placed in our waters. It is a hazard to navigation and could endanger our fishermen by leading them onto the reef. I have been ordered to remove it."

"And the Huey and other ships?"

"We are not anticipating any difficulties, but they are accompanying us to prevent any unfortunate accidents if an unsuspecting vessel should approach. We wouldn't want someone to stumble into harm's way as we dispose of this marker."

"I see," Lynne said, taking note of the scripted response.

"The smaller patrol boat is the *Romblon*, a gunfire support ship."

Lynne studied the vessel, thinking Reyes use of 'ship' a bit overstated.

"And there. The ship coming abeam of us, the *Salvador Abcede*. Her displacement is only 147 tons, but she is our fastest and armed with one 40mm and two 20mm cannon. The amphibious ship is the *Kalinga Apoyo*. She is transporting reinforcements for our garrison on Pagasa Atoll north of our location."

Reyes shifted his feet, anxious to resume supervision of his command.

"Captain, I apologize for keeping you from your duty."

"Yes, if you will excuse me. Our small boat is rigged out ready to be lowered."

Reyes took his place on the bridge and maneuvered the *Emilio Jacinto* to a safe distance while Lynne watched. Her excitement mounted, anticipating the fate of the Chinese channel marker.

She didn't wait long. A thunderous explosion rocked the air. The buoy disappeared in a fountain of white water and swirling dirty-brown smoke. The boom of the explosive charge sent a flock of loitering sea birds scattering in disarray. They wheeled in the air, adding squawking protests to the din.

The sea birds had just settled down when the solitude of the isolated atoll was shattered again. This time, the roar of jet aircraft approaching at wave-top level punctured the quiet of the morning.

Lynne whirled, seeking the source of the ear-piecing noise. She spotted approaching planes, tensing in fear.

"They're ours. F-5s," the sailor standing next to her volunteered. "Judging from their markings, they're from the 6th Tactical Fighting Squadron flying out of Villamore Air Force Base. Nothing to worry about."

The jets roared overhead, splitting the air with a pair of sonic booms. They vanished to the north as quickly as they had appeared. Only a thin cloud of exhaust and silence remained. Despite their impressive display, Lynne learned that these vintage planes represented almost the entire operational jet aircraft of the Philippine Air Force.

———

The few curious Chinese who occupied the island were also watching the activity of the new arrivals. Their first reaction to the morning's events was pleasant surprise, relieving the tedium of their daily existence. As awareness dawned, their good humor was replaced by shock, then anger, as several more buoys were blown out of the water.

They ran to their command building, jolted into action by the Filipinos. The message the garrison commander sent to his superiors at the PLAN headquarters on Hainan Island was not nearly as positive as the one a chuckling Captain Reyes sent to Cavite Naval Headquarters.

———

His primary mission complete, Reyes turned his attention to his next goal, the reinforcement of Pagasa Atoll laying one hundred and sixty miles to the northwest. He left the astonished Chinese behind and guided his small flotilla between the PLA installations on Johnson Atoll and Mischief Reef. The PLA forces were now on full alert and itching for a fight.

———

AT SEA
17:35

That evening, Lynne stood on the bridge observing the navigator plot the ship's course. While the Spratly Islands appeared tightly grouped on her small map, she realized they covered a substantial portion of the ocean. "There are so many islands."

"Very few people understand this," the officer responded. "There are over one-hundred islands and atolls in the South China Sea oriented southwest to northeast, all scattered within this oval-shaped area two-hundred fifty miles wide by five-hundred miles long."

Lynne noted a seamount defined by a deep slash crossing the chart. "What's this?"

"The Palawan Trench." The navigator traced his index

finger across the chart. "The deep water is contiguous with the Ryuku Trench extending from the Southern Japanese Islands. American attack submarines …"

"Oh?" Lynne said in response to the navigator's mention of the U.S. ships.

"Captain on the bridge."

The navigator gave way to allow Reyes access to the ship's compass and chart table.

"Good evening, Ms. Lynne. I trust the navigator has been informative?"

"Thank you, Captain, he —"

"Sir, we were just going to talk about Pagasa Atoll," the navigator interrupted, afraid he would be reprimanded for mentioning the submarines.

"Yes, we have occupied the atoll for almost thirty years. It lies barely fifty nautical miles north of the nearest Chinese occupied island. We believe the Chinese moved our missing fishermen to this area."

———

Lynne retired to her stateroom armed with Captain Reyes' insights and the images of what she had witnessed still vivid in her mind. She began to enter meticulous notes on her laptop, beginning with the evening's discussions dealing with the geopolitical and military significance of the Spratly Islands.

Reyes had made a point to address the provisions of the United Nations Convention on the Law of the Sea. He emphasized that international law gave the Philippines the legal right to contest the occupation of their islands by the Chinese. However, with so many overlapping claims by the six principle countries involved, it was impossible to establish clear boundaries.

The next piece of the puzzle was the Manila Declaration. The ASEAN countries wrote the document in an effort to prevent the very confrontation that had occurred this past week. It was a futile gesture. Beijing took a divide and conquer approach and refused to sign the accord. They would only participate in bilateral discussions.

From her research, Lynne knew this point wasn't lost on the diplomats gathering in Manila. The Philippine Undersecretary of Foreign Affairs spoke for the assembled nations: "You can't *discuss* multiple conflicting national claims on a bilateral basis. The nations must *negotiate* on a multilateral basis to reach our common goal for peace in the region."

Lynne recalled that particular quote. *Well, gentlemen, at the moment nobody appears to be talking; bilateral or otherwise. Unless something happens real soon to turn things around out here, we're headed for serious trouble.*

With those concerns, Lynne opened a new file and began to compose her story.

"Tensions heightened this week between the Philippines and China over territorial rights in the strategic Spratly Islands following the destruction of maritime marker buoys by units of the Philippine Navy. The center of controversy between these two Asian countries lies in an unlikely scattering of barren coral atolls in the South China Sea that stand over suspected reserves of oil and natural gas. This is not the first time armed confrontations have occurred in this region..."

Her fingers froze on the keyboard, her mind wrestling with the wording of the next paragraph. She closed her laptop.

———

PAGASA ATOLL
11:23 SATURDAY 8 FEBRUARY

Any thoughts Lynne had entertained of Pagasa Atoll being a tropical paradise were driven from her mind when the patrol boat tied up alongside the small stone jetty. She adjusted her floppy hat to cut down the glare and stepped out the shade of the ship's superstructure. She was slapped by a wave of heat supercharged by humidity.

The heat intensified as she walked down the prow onto the quay. The sun's rays blasting off the bleached coral of the adjacent runway pounded against her body. She glanced at her watch. Not even noon.

A C-130 Hercules cargo plane was parked in front of her. Several men were taking refuge from the torrid heat in the slip of shade beneath its wing. Behind the plane, sat an army Huey helicopter. Adjacent to the runway stood a whitewashed concrete structure with a corroded tin roof. In front of the building, the Philippine flag hung lifeless from a short flagpole. Several yards away, a rusted ladder led up to an open observation tower topped by a thatch of palm fronds. Hidden by coarse grass and patches of scraggly bushes were several empty gun emplacements and a scattering of battered fifty-five-gallon oil drums.

Lynne turned back to the cargo plane stunned by the thought this desolate atoll could be the site of Armageddon. Two officers in sunglasses and flight suits emerged from the C-130's cargo ramp. They looked in her direction, spoke a few words to each other, and sauntered over.

"Good morning," the taller of the two said. "You must be, Ms. Lynne, the correspondent. We were told to expect you."

"Yes, thank you."

"I am Major Villanueva, the aircraft commander of the Hercules. You will be riding my aircraft back to Manila. This is Captain Baptiste, pilot of the Huey. He has been directed to fly you over several of the disputed islands to observe the Chinese activity. Captain Reyes has urgent matters to attend to and declined our invitation."

The real truth behind the latter statement was Reyes didn't trust the airworthiness of the Huey. The assurances given him by Captain Baptiste, who remarked with a straight face that all of the unsafe helicopters had already crashed, had done little to change his opinion.

Captain Reyes did have work to do, though. He had received a report from his superiors at the Western Military Headquarters. The PLAN was preparing several of their destroyers to get underway for the Spratlys. He was to locate and free the missing fishermen before the Chinese could intervene.

Lynne's tour of the atoll's primitive facilities took little time and she was soon airborne in the Huey. Afforded a bird's eye view of the island, she noted its shape reminded her of a very large snail. The bulk of the island comprised the shell while the runway extending over the shoreline on either side of its base represented the head and foot. A concrete barrier at the far end of runway, stuck forth like the creature's antennae. She doubted the small garrison could hold off a determined foe.

The atoll soon disappeared over the horizon and Lynne leaned forward in her canvas seat. All she could see was an empty sea. Their destination, Subi Reef, was twenty-six nautical miles to the north.

A slowing of their airspeed signaled their arrival fifteen minutes later. She studied the facility in the distance as Baptiste hovered at a safe distance to avoid antagonizing the Chinese.

A three-story concrete structure topped with a large communications dish perched on the small island. A narrow causeway jutted out from the main structure connecting to a helipad.

"There's no sign of our missing fishing boat and the place looked pretty quiet until we showed up. There's nothing we can accomplish here but invite trouble. We're going to proceed northeast and check out several other islands before heading back."

No sooner had these words been uttered than Lynne noted bright flashes twinkling from several corners of the building. She wondered if the garrison was trying to signal them and watched with detached curiosity the graceful flight of red and orange balls reaching out toward her. Curiously, they appeared to get bigger as they approached.

Baptiste's reaction was much faster. "We're getting the hell out of here."

"Oh." Lynne gasped as she collapsed back into her seat. *Someone just tried to kill us.*

"Hey, look over there. What in hell are they doing there?"

Lynne scanned the island in the direction Baptiste indicated. Covered with mangroves and coconut palms, nothing appeared remarkable. Then the open door of the Huey framed a fishing boat riding at anchor in a small cove. Lynne craned her neck, trying to keep the boat and two frantically waving fishermen in sight while the pilot maneuvered the helicopter to get a better view.

"Those look like PLAN patrol boats by the shore," Lynne heard Baptiste tell his co-pilot. "Get plenty of shots of them and the fishing boat."

Lynne pressed her back into the seat. She had seen all she cared to and prayed Baptiste wouldn't press his luck. "How are we doing, Captain?"

"We've seen enough. Time to get these pictures back."

———

The blades of the Huey hadn't stopped rotating before Lynne and the digital photos of the three vessels were hustled aboard the C-130. The Hercules lifted off the coral runway and set a course to the northeast.

"Ms. Lynne," Villanueva said, "Look out your window. Just forward."

Lynne did as she was told. Below her, the ocean was cut with a long white arc scribed by the *Kalinga Apoyo*.

"Judging from her course change, the LST has received orders to return to Pagasa. I suspect she will be involved in the rescue effort of our fishermen. You know it was in these same waters in 1944 that Admiral Kurita was defeated in his attempt to destroy the American invasion force during the battle of Leyte Gulf. At the time, your Seventh Fleet was composed of over seven-hundred ships. It's unfortunate your Seventh Fleet is not so large now."

Lynne considered this statement. Villanueva had just pointed out, without a great degree of subtlety, a much smaller Seventh Fleet represented American interests in the region.

"Smaller doesn't necessarily translate into weaker, Major. I suspect President Stuart is viewing the security issues in the South China Sea within a much broader context."

"So how do you think he will respond to the Chinese threat in the Spratlys, Ms. Lynne?"

Lynne didn't have an answer to his provocative question.

Villanueva spoke to her silence. "Things are different now, aren't they?"

Chapter Six

CAM RANH BAY
SOCIALIST REPUBLIC OF VIETNAM
18:20 TUESDAY 11 FEBRUARY

Commander Nguyen Tran Thang stood at the end of the pier jutting into the protected waters of Cam Ranh Bay. He enjoyed the evening breeze coming off the ocean and often came here to clear his mind. Tonight his executive officer, Lieutenant Ly Tien Doung, stood by his side.

Nguyen picked up a rusted bolt and rolled it in his hand. "Ly, there is much to ponder in these strange times."

"Sir, are you referring to the fishing boat incident?"

"No, while the incident is another example of Chinese aggression, that is not our concern. We may become the chosen field of battle for a proxy war between the superpowers. And the irony? Our leaders are turning to the Americans."

"Is that bad, sir?"

"Not necessarily." Nguyen threw the bolt into the bay. A proponent of the Arab philosophy of 'An enemy of my enemy is my friend,' he contemplated the ripples expanding beyond the point of the bolt's impact. "Playing the Chinese and Americans off each other makes eminent sense if it provides balance to our policy. Of course, this strategy will only be effective to the extent we can maintain this act."

Nguyen knew the Chinese could not be trusted even though his government had accepted Beijing's support during the war with the Americans. The most glaring example of Beijing's duplicity had occurred in 1979 when China sent its army across their common border. The confrontation with Vietnam's battle-hardened army proved disastrous for the PLA and they were sent reeling back across the border in defeat.

While the Vietnamese army prevailed in their confrontation with the Chinese army, the Navy had not fared so well in a battle for control of the Paracel Islands in the northwest quadrant of the South China Sea. The annexation of these strategic islands by the PLAN was the opening move in a series of calculated actions by Beijing to dominate the region.

"But sir, the American Seventh Fleet did nothing to stop the Chinese."

Nguyen paused before answering. He could understand the Americans' position, but it was shortsighted and, in the long term, a mistake. "Ly, I suspect the Americans took great pleasure in seeing their former enemies fighting amongst themselves."

He considered himself a pragmatic man and his feelings of ill will toward the Americans had long since disappeared. The Americans' fixation on their loss in the War of Unification meant little to him. "Lieutenant, the Americans are a strange people, honorable and generally well-meaning, but often misguided."

"Perhaps they will do better when their interests are threatened."

The deep growl of diesel engines interrupted their conversation. A patrol boat was returning from its patrol of the Con

Son Basin, site of Vietnam's major oil exploration and production facilities to the southeast.

"Sir, it's the 371."

Nguyen grunted his approval and watched the vessel complete its approach. The HQ-371 was the last of four Tarantual-1 missile combatants ordered from the Russians, a powerful addition to Vietnam's fledgling navy.

Lost in thought, he lost track of the time. The sun dropped below the horizon sending flashes of red across the wave tops. Nguyen's subconscious recoiled, as his mind was driven back to a November night in 1988.

———

CON SONG BASIN
NOVEMBER 1988

Nguyen braced his feet to counter the pitch and roll of his vessel scanning the horizon with his binoculars. *There*. He could just make out the silhouettes of the other two boats of the squadron.

Eight hundred meters abeam and slightly astern, their presence was betrayed by white water breaking over their bows. Smaller than his ship, the two Komar missile patrol boats mounted Styx anti-ship missile launchers provided the real punch of the squadron. The capability of the two missile boats did nothing to deter his confidence in his own warship. The *Dien Phan* was a Shanghai II class patrol boat brisling with four 37mm and four 25mm cannons.

Nguyen gave voice to his feelings and addressed the Officer of the Deck. "It would be foolish for them to challenge us."

The OOD answered with a note of caution. "We have not done well predicting their intentions. We must be vigilant and be prepared for the unexpected."

"But —"

The OOD held up his hand. "Captain, the enemy vessels' bearings remain constant. Distance four point seven kilometers, closing at twenty knots."

"Very well. Has there been a response to our hails?"

The OOD looked to Nguyen for confirmation. "No, sir."

"Try again. If there is no response, alert the others to prepare for a course change to two-seven-zero. Our orders are to keep them away from the oil platforms."

The OOD keyed his microphone. The clicks resounded like shots in the charged atmosphere. "Unidentified ships, this is the Vietnamese Naval vessel *Dien Phan*. You are entering restricted waters. Identify yourself and state your intentions."

Silence followed. Nguyen glanced at his watch. 21:35.

The horizon erupted in multiple white flashes illuminating the undersides of the distant clouds. The rumble of thunder followed within seconds. Nguyen's first thought was it must be a storm.

The Captain recognized the danger. He spun toward the OOD. "Evasive action. Target the lead ship. Commence firing."

The first salvo from the Chinese destroyers bracketed the patrol boat to Nguyen's left, throwing up huge fountains of water. He saw his sister ship emerge from the cascade, twisting and turning in the eerie light cast by a bursting star shell. The missile boat evaded the salvo while attempting to bring its missile launchers to bear. His own forward cannon began to roar.

The *Dien Phan's* four diesel engines added to the cacophony. Jammed to full throttle, their 4800 horsepower drove the patrol boat to her maximum speed of thirty knots.

"Nguyen, contact headquarters. Give our bearings and tell them we're under fire."

Nguyen stumbled toward the radio. The muzzle flashes of their cannon had ruined his night vision.

"Cam Ranh, Cam Ranh. This is the *Dien Phan*. We are under attack by Chinese destroyers. I repeat, under attack by Chinese destroyers. Our present location is twenty-two kilometers north-north east of the Con Son oil fields. We are returning fire and taking evasive action. Do you copy? Over."

A near-miss lifted the port bow out of the water. The patrol boat shuddered in response, lurching to starboard.

Nguyen saw a streak of white cross his bow. The streak terminated in a thunderous flash just as other shells converged on the *Dien Phan*. He was thrown off balance when the helm was thrown hard over. He grasped for a bundle of electrical cables. The bridge windows exploded into thousands of shards.

Someone was down, screaming. Another bent over the chart table, his head centered within an expanding black pool. A sailor still manned the helm amidst the carnage.

Nguyen's lightly armed vessel was no match for the radar-controlled heavy guns of the Chinese destroyers. A shell tore through amidships and exploded. The concussive wave and blast of heat from the detonation threw him into the bulkhead. He slid to the deck, stupefied. The bridge filled with dense smoke.

The *Dien Phan* pounded over the waves, trying to evade the deluge of shells. Another near miss lifted the patrol boat's stern out of the water. Nguyen's horizon tilted with a nauseating spin

He slammed into the dark outline of the chart table and tumbled to the deck. He braced himself to stand and gasped as pain pierced his shoulder. He rolled to his side, trying to push off with his other arm. He rose to one knee, but fell again as the *Dien Phan* heeled in a starboard turn.

Abruptly as it had begun, the assault ended. The Chinese flotilla disengaged and retired to the northeast. Nguyen starred at his watch. His vision cleared. He could just make out the numbers on the dial. 21:52. Seventeen minutes. An eternity.

He was dazed. His eyes burned. His ears rang. There was a coppery taste in his mouth. His tongue hurt.

Must have bit it, he concluded. He became aware of his surroundings, the lingering smell of gunpowder, the distinctive acrid odor of burning electrical equipment. He sensed movement.

He stood and took an unsteady step, then another. He stumbled over the contorted body of the OOD and crashed to the deck, his arms flailing in a futile attempt to break his fall. He stared at the ruin around him in disbelief. There were muffled sounds. Someone speaking to him.

"Lieutenant, can you hear me?"

Nguyen nodded.

The Captain offered his hand and pulled him up. "Good. Check with damage control. See what they need."

Nguyen completed his assessment and reported back. "Captain, there is no immediate danger to the boat. The crew extinguished several small fires in the plotting room."

"The engine room?"

"Fully operational."

"Take the con. We haven't been able to raise the 302. Her last bearing was to the northeast. Use that to set your course."

It wasn't difficult to spot the 302, bow canted in the air, settling by the stern. The glare reflecting from the fires still burning on the destroyed patrol boat illuminated the sky. The flames cast rippling vermilion arms across the waves pulling them to the stricken ship.

Nguyen couldn't answer the questions in the unseeing eyes of his dead shipmates. The billowing smoke pouring from the stricken ship compounded his feeling of dread. The smoke carried the spirits of his twenty-two comrades toward the heavens.

When Nguyen and the *Dien Phan's* crew could do no more, they abandoned the hulk of their sister ship and commenced their search for the second patrol boat.

The *Dien Phan* was barely making headway when they reached the last known position of the remaining vessel. They drifted through the flotsam as the crew swept their searchlight across the water. The dull rumbling of the patrol boat's idling engines filled the void in Nguyen's mind.

"There. There's someone in the water. Over there."

He responded to the lookout's cry and peered into the darkness. They were approaching the remnants of their sister ship. Nguyen stared at the wreckage trying to make sense of the carnage strewn across the sea.

"Lieutenant, Lieutenant. Survivors."

Nguyen rushed to the man's side. Several exhausted men clung to an oil-drenched piece of wreckage. "Throw them a line. I'll get a boat hook."

Together they pulled in the wreckage and heaved the injured men up over the side onto the deck to join their rescued comrades. Some of the injured lay on the deck retching, vomiting from the fuel oil they'd swallowed. Others lay pale in shock from mutilating wounds that curiously had little blood flowing from them. Those without visible injuries stared vacantly into the night.

It was then that Nguyen's eyes caught a glimpse of something else in the water. He leaned over the railing. *There it is, what is ...*

The emotions of the night flooded over him as recognition came. He felt detached, alone. His country's ensign, just visible, rippling beneath the surface of the oil-stained water. Hate filled his soul.

———

Nguyen's trance was broken by the sound of footsteps. A hand on his shoulder brought him back to the present.

"Commander, I hate to intrude, but we have unfinished work."

"We do indeed," Nguyen replied in a flat voice. He cast a final glance at the dark waters and turned toward the headquarters building silently repeating a vow to his old shipmates:

I will be patient and bide my time, but I will have my revenge. Honor will always be yours, my fallen comrades. Though your bodies rest forever beneath the restless waves, I witnessed your souls ascend to the heavens on an ethereal cloud. I will assume your mantel of bravery and continue the struggle so, I too, may honorably join you and our ancestors.

Chapter Seven

THE STATE DEPARTMENT
WASHINGTON, D.C.
08:25 MONDAY 10 FEBRUARY

Adrian Clarke timed his arrival to provide a few minutes of preparation before the start of the morning brief. The Assistant Secretary of State for East Asia and Pacific Affairs, he would take the lead in crafting State's response to the recent Sino-Philippine confrontation in the South China Sea.

A career diplomat in his 26th year, he knew how to turn such unforeseen events to an American advantage. He was also one of the few at State who appreciated the significance of the Spratly Islands.

Despite his familiarity with the area, he too had been caught off-guard by the confrontation between the Chinese and the Filipinos. No indication had crossed his desk of the confrontation and he wondered what, if anything, the Pentagon knew.

He'd been in continuous contact with the Embassy in

Manila since the incident, and had communicated the official American position to the Ambassador:

'The United States did not view the dispute between the Chinese and Philippines as something warranting direct American intervention under the mandates of the American/Philippine Mutual Defense Treaty.'

Clarke snapped closed the latches of his briefcase. *If it were only that simple.*

With that admission, he rose to acknowledge the arrival of the Secretary of State, the honorable Richard Valardi. "Good morning, Mr. Secretary."

Valardi nodded a curt reply and strode five measured steps to the head of the table. He took his seat and scanned the highlighted sentences of his briefing book. Without bothering to look up, he began. "What do we have on the Spratlys?"

"It's quiet at the moment, sir."

"Well, I suppose that's a start."

"I'd like to begin by summarizing the latest messages from the embassy."

"Proceed."

"In his weekly address from Malacanang Palace, President Montalvo said his government views the actions taken by elements identified with the People's Liberation Army as inconsistent with international law and the spirit and intent of the 1992 Manila ASEAN Declaration."

Valardi popped the lid off his fountain pen, a sure indication he wasn't happy.

Clark ignored the gesture. "Montalvo went on to say he has received assurances from the civil authorities in Beijing there would be no need for mediation by a third country.

"Or intervention by a third country," Valardi said. "My

read is Zhu is looking for a way out. He's implicated the PLA. By throwing Xiao under the bus, he's provided Montalvo an opening to negotiate the release of the fishermen."

"The Chinese are pushing for more."

"Yes, sir. We know they're constructing a series of strategic outposts that will soon dominate our sea lanes of communication. And this brings us to the present developments in the Spratlys. The embassy confirmed yesterday's reports on ABC. General Medeiros issued a statement saying his forces are conducting sea and air surveillance to deter any further illegal activity."

Valardi snorted. "I doubt the Chinese navy feels particularly intimidated."

"No, sir. Manila understands military intervention is not a viable option. Montalvo is looking to counter Beijing by seeking to leverage regional and maritime security issues."

Valardi looked up from his notes. "Judging from their reaction, the Chinese were surprised by his response. They've proposed exploratory talks."

"Beijing's buying time. They're trying to assure the ASEAN countries they have no intention of escalating tensions in the region and are willing to discuss a peaceful resolution of the dispute with the Filipinos."

"While the Chinese are making these pronouncements, our intelligence reports the PLAN is readying a task force to deploy to the Spratlys," Valardi said.

"Their offer to open exploratory talks is most considerate," Valardi continued. "They're the ones stirring things up. The National Security Advisor and I are of the same opinion. The Chinese incursion into the Spratlys has as much to do with domestic politics as it does foreign policy. Zhu and his supporters have their hands full jostling with General Xiao for political dominance."

"Yes, sir. We must frame the execution of our policy for

the Spratlys within the context of the PRC's involvement in Taiwanese affairs."

Valaridi's voice rose in anger. "Taiwan? What in hell do the Nationalists have to do with this?"

Clarke cursed under his breath. He should have known Valardi would be irritated if presented too many variables. "Taiwan is the unknown in the equation, sir. Any move on the Nationalists' part to take advantage of the current crisis will not be tolerated by Beijing. Xiao will jump on this crisis to strengthen his power base."

"Do we have any indication the Nationalists are contemplating any such action?"

"No, sir."

"What are you saying, then?"

"We should not challenge Beijing by bringing Taiwan into any deliberations pertaining to this latest Sino-Philippine confrontation."

Valardi leaned forward. "I have no intention of doing so. Are you suggesting we should avoid direct involvement in the present dispute between Beijing and Manila?"

"Yes, sir. My recommendation is to echo Montalvo's statements and encourage both parties to work toward a collaborative settlement while providing what support we can to Manila."

"And Zhu?"

"It's crucial we avoid placing him in an untenable position vis-à-vis the PLA and their change in senior leadership this fall."

"What else?"

"We need to respond to the overtures from the Philippine and Vietnamese governments to expand our commercial and military ties."

"The end point?"

"Strengthen our overall position."

"What assurances can you provide?"

"None. We have to balance our approach. A zero-sum calculation in our relationship with China is a non-starter. Neither of us can be in a position if one of us succeeds, the other must fail."

"I'm not convinced we should assume a passive posture in this affair. Beijing's intent is clear. They want to create a Sino-centric Asian block and drive us out. But, that said, we may not have much of a choice, Valardi said. "Beijing has no incentive to stop, unless—"

"I'm not suggesting we assume a passive posture, sir."   .

"Fair enough." Valardi checked his watch and pushed away from the table. "I will present my recommendations to the President."

Chapter Eight

HEADQUARTERS, U.S. PACIFIC FLEET
HAWAII
07:30 MONDAY 10 FEBRUARY

Mike Rohrbaugh wrote the date at the top right-hand corner of his green ledger: 10 February. There was nothing auspicious about the date, but this day, like so many others he'd encountered over the years could hold the unexpected. He completed his page by drawing a vertical row of small boxes on the left-hand margin. He would place a check mark in each of these after he had addressed each task.

Next to his first box he wrote, 'Power of Attorney.'

With things heating up in the South China Sea, he had to be prepared to deploy at a moment's notice even if there was zero probability of being given orders for a mission. Even so, he figured it would be prudent to verify his Power of Attorney.

He rested his pen on the ledger and sorted through the open questions concerning the recent events in the Spratlys, then wrote 'M. Lynne—ABC' by the second box.

She was the variable in his contingency planning. He'd read her reports pertaining to Pagasa Atoll. The events she described were accurate. How she managed to get on that island remained an unknown. And how much did she know about the U.S. actions to counter the Chinese?"

He didn't trust reporters and suspected she wasn't divulging everything she knew. And that could cost lives. He stowed the thought and moved down to the third box: AFP.

He flipped open the routing folder that held the weekend's message traffic. The first thing that caught his mind's eye was actually something he didn't see. There wasn't anything new from the Philippine military.

Blowing up those channel markers at First Thomas Shoal wouldn't exactly go down as one of military history's most audacious acts, but for the Filipinos it was mighty significant. So, what were they up to? He made a note to ask the Ops boss during morning report.

Next up? Box four: PLAN. There was precedent for the PLAN taking offensive action in the region. Sin Cowe Island in '88 and the Parcel group in '74 were cases in point that went unchallenged by the international community. The Intel on their warships being readied at their South Sea Fleet base on Hainan Island was solid and meant trouble. All the Chinese needed was a pretext.

So, what where the Chinese going to do? Worst-case scenario; mount a pre-emptive strike on the Philippine garrison on Pagasa Atoll–and entangle U.S. forces in the process.

Best case? The PLAN ships remained in port while the diplomats worked a solution. Rohrbaugh grunted. Given the recent history in the region, the odds of that outcome were low.

Rohrbaugh's thoughts were interrupted by the appearance of Mackenzie. "Morning, Mac. What kind of deal did you get on your wheels?"

"Four Michelin XLT's. Two-twenty including mounting.

The hardest part of the whole evolution was finding the damn phone number for the Exchange's new tire shop."

Rohrbaugh smiled at the memory of Mac swearing his way through the military phone directory. "Yup, another mystery of life. We can build a carrier, but not design a functional phone book. Pull up a chair."

"What's up?"

"Working the variables. The Filipino military isn't saying anything, but the Chinese are on the move. Got a whole flotilla including amphibs readying to get underway. Since we don't know the intent of either the Chinese or the AFP, we're going to be reacting to events if things turn south."

"You think something can be worked?"

"If you mean a diplomatic solution, I wouldn't hold my breath. The message board has a paragraph about the Chinese harassing the Vietnamese north of the Bach Ho oil rigs. Got pretty intense, but nobody was hurt."

"What do you think the odds are that field is the next flashpoint?"

Rohrbaugh thought a moment, and wrote, "Bach Ho oil rigs' next to block five. "I'd give them at better than one in four. Of course, those could change depending on the Vietnamese."

"I don't like it," Mac replied before changing the subject. "Anything new on those PLAN bases?"

"Yeah, they're feeling a bit feisty."

Mac pulled on his chin. "You think the Chinese are considering neutralizing the AFP base on Pagasa?"

"It'd make sense."

"Take them out before we could get our forces to the area and leave us holding the pieces."

"That's crossed my mind. If I were the Chinese, I'd have that option on the table."

"It's anybody's guess at this point," Mac said.

"One thing for sure, we can't permit those anti-ship missile sites to go operational."

"Could we stage a team to create a little mischief?"

"That'd be my call," Rohrbaugh answered. "But those decisions are way above my pay grade. A key piece would be linking with a sub for the insertion. That's best done out of Pearl or Guam to simplify our planning factors."

"Think we should run the idea up the flagpole?"

"Wouldn't hurt, but let's wait until we run a few details to ground."

Rohrbaugh stood. "I'm off to morning report. Maybe I'll learn something."

Chapter Nine

THE WHITE HOUSE CABINET ROOM
14:03 TUESDAY 11 FEBRUARY

Stuart's arrival was heralded by a small armada of aides bursting through the door ahead of him. He paused at the threshold and caught the eye of his National Security Advisor, Justin Brown.

Brown was an intense man who never approached anything in half-measures. A man of extraordinary intellect, he earned his Ph.D. at the Harvard School of International Relations, and joined the State Department before retiring to a prestigious chair at Stanford University. Stuart had lured him from his academic post with an offer to become a member of his cabinet.

"Good afternoon, Mr. President."

"Ready to launch?"

"Yes, sir."

Stuart acknowledged the naval officer standing beside Brown. "I trust the Joint Chiefs are keeping the Ship of State afloat?"

"We've had fair seas, but there's turbulent air ahead, Mr. President."

Stuart sized up the officer's response. During the first Gulf War, then-Commander Robert Mahan Lawson commanded the Clansmen of VA-46 flying close combat missions in the kill boxes of Iraq. Lawson understood the nature of war and, like other combat veterans, would do everything within his power to avoid conflict.

The two men also shared a common bond. Both were naval aviators. The Chairman taught Stuart how to fly at the Naval Air Station in Pensacola, Florida. Lawson had been an instructor pilot and Stuart, a newly commissioned Ensign.

"Stay the course, Bob."

Lawson was the latest of a long lineage of Naval officers to serve his country and he enjoyed Stuart's complete trust. His middle name was taken from a distant relative, Alfred Thayer Mahan whose writings over a century ago foretold of an inevitable confrontation with China in his treatise titled 'The Problem of Asia.' Lawson had reviewed the work in preparation for today's meeting. He'd highlighted a quote from the renowned theorist Sun Tzu: 'Every battle is won before it is fought.'

Stuart took his seat and pulled out a note pad. "We have a full plate this afternoon gentlemen, so let's get going. Bryce, what's your estimate of Beijing's intentions?"

Bryce Gilmore, the Director of National Intelligence, was the zealous guardian of the nation's secrets and the grand inquisitor of its enemies, one Stuart could count on not to hold his punches.

"Xiao has recovered from his surprise at the audacity of the Filipinos' response. The PLAN's readying a flotilla at their Hainan Island base and will be ready to deploy within several days."

"What are we looking at?"

"Besides the combatants, surveillance identified combat

support personnel and construction equipment staged on the pier. These assets suggest intent to accelerate development of their various outposts in the Spratlys. That said, we have a bigger problem."

Stuart's jaw tightened. "Let's have it."

"The AFP has located the detained fishermen."

"And?"

"They're planning a rescue attempt."

"When?"

"Within the next twenty-four hours."

"Bob, what does the Navy have in the region?"

"The Lincoln Strike Group. They'll be transiting the Strait of Malacca Friday."

"Bryce, does the National Reconnaissance Office have coverage?"

"We'll need to reposition one of the birds. I'll work with Sheldon."

Stuart studied the faces of the DNI and Secretary of Defense, aware of the acrimony that would bubble to the surface between the two. "Sheldon? You on board?"

He'd nominated Sheldon Payne to be part of the administration because of his reputation of designing and implementing the strategies required to execute large corporate mergers. His intent was to provide a new direction at the Pentagon. Payne's six years of military service, including a tour in Vietnam as an Army infantry platoon commander, helped cement him in the position. His basic operating premise in international affairs and their link to the foreign policy of the United States was that America's policy should be guided by the pursuit of the country's national interests and not misdirected by the application of abstract moral principles. A 'foreign policy realist' were the kindest words his detractors could find to describe him.

"We'll coordinate NRO's and NSA's input."

Stuart read Valardi's fretful look. "What's your take, Richard?"

"I can't see what Beijing would gain by deploying their fleet and escalating tensions. There's a disconnect. Zhu has extended diplomatic feelers to discuss a resolution."

"Perhaps Xiao got wind of the AFP's intent and they're working both angles," Stuart said.

"Let's hope Montalvo doesn't miscalculate," Brown said. "We can't afford to get drawn into a confrontation with Beijing."

"Mr. President?"

"Yes, Richard?"

"I should meet with the Philippine ambassador. They cannot be allowed to use force to free their fishermen before all diplomatic efforts have been exhausted."

"Set it up."

Valardi looked over his shoulder to catch the eye of his senior staffer and gave him a nod.

Stuart waited until the aide gathered his notes and exited the side door. "Bryce, you have something?"

"For argument's sake, what if that Chinese captain acted on his own volition?

"That's improbable. Xiao—"

Payne tapped his pen on his water glass. "This is all about oil."

Stuart leaned forward so he could look past Valardi, whose jaw had dropped. "Say again?"

"Oil. It's the common denominator," Brown affirmed.

"That's been my contention all along," Stuart said. "What's also driving Beijing's response, be it Zhu's or Xiao's, is the off-shore wells being exploited by Hanoi and Manila."

"Exploited? Aren't those wells in their territorial waters?" Valardi said.

"That's a moot point," Gilmore said. "The PLA's declared Hanoi's and Manila's actions as tantamount to theft of a

Chinese natural resource and a direct threat to their sovereignty. This ties into the Chinese cyberattacks on the oil companies working with the Vietnamese and Filipinos."

"Night Dragon?" Brown asked.

The reference of the code word for Beijing's cyberattacks caused Stuart to look up from the notes he'd been scribing. "Bob, where are the flash points?"

"The words, 'theft,' 'threat,' and 'sovereignty,' are operable. If we take Taiwan off the table for the purposes of this discussion, the biggest danger lies in the Spratlys."

"It's also important for us to understand how the Senkaku Islands fit into the equation," Gilmore added. "They define the northern edge of the South China Sea."

Stuart cast a sideways glance at Valardi who was now popping open and closed the top of his fountain pen, a sure sign of distress. "Richard, do you have a handle on where the Japanese will come down?"

"Tokyo's urged restraint."

"So, the answer is no."

Valardi stiffened, but Stuart didn't give him a chance to respond. "Bryce, what else do you have that's germane?"

"Hanoi submitted a complaint to the United Nations about PLAN ships harassing their survey ships in the Con Song oil fields."

"This more of Xiao's doing?"

"Don't know," Gilmore answered. "Perhaps their intent is to destabilize the region. It could be a rogue operation by a consortium of generals looking to line their pockets."

Stuart rubbed his forehead. "Is this stuff connected?"

"No question. Beijing's objective is to seize control of the South China Sea. They'll play for time. Their classic 'Push, then pull back' strategy. That said, there's no telling how they'll react if their hand is forced."

"Such as this confrontation with the Filipinos."

"Exactly."

Stuart noted Valardi set his pen on the table. "Richard?"

"A Chinese Foreign Ministry official met with our ambassador."

"What do they want?" Gilmore prodded.

"I'm getting to that, Bryce. They want to pre-empt our involvement. They're blaming the seizure of the fishing boat on the overzealous actions of a local district official enforcing a Fishery's Department policy of a two-month fishing ban. The ban only applied to contested territorial waters and there was a 'misunderstanding.'"

"Then why haven't they released that damn fishing boat?"

"The key word is 'contested.' Implicit in its use is the implication the Filipino fishermen were in Chinese waters."

Stuart sensed Valardi was back on firmer ground. "We're sure of this?"

"Yes."

"Have the Japanese said anything about Beijing's position?"

"No, but this does introduce another variable. That said, I don't feel Japan will be a player unless they're drawn in."

Brown shook his head. "I wouldn't be surprised if Beijing doesn't apply some diplomatic arm twisting to keep the Japanese on the sidelines."

Stuart drew wet circles on the mahogany table with his glass watching the water swirl up the sides. "Will Beijing remain content with just bullying?"

Payne filled in the silence that followed. "Richard, what's the impact on our Okinawan bases and Yokosuka?"

"I can't give you a definitive answer. We'll need to work with the Japanese."

Stuart let go of his glass. "What's Defense's view?"

"We're reviewing our contingency plans for a low intensity conflict," Payne said.

"You're not implying this confrontation between Beijing and Manila can't be contained—are you?" Valardi asked.

"Just bein' pragmatic, Richard," Payne replied choosing to use his southern accent.

Valardi popped off the top of his fountain pen. "I'm not comfortable with the idea of any level of conflict."

"I share your concern. I've never been comfortable with the term, 'low-intensity,' when applied to the Spratlys," Payne said.

"Care to elaborate?" Stuart asked.

"The history of conflict in the South China Sea has shown it to be unpredictable, of limited duration, and violent. With the notable exception of the Chinese, the claimants in the region have limited capability to project force beyond their coastal waters. What we all need to consider is the close proximity of their forces. The potential of a limited conflict providing the spark for a broader confrontation is significant."

"Bob, you care to comment?" Stuart responded.

"It's best to put the geography in context, sir. We're dealing with an operational area the size of the Gulf of Mexico."

"And not the open Pacific, which comes to mind."

"Yes, sir. Our forward deployed assets in the region are adequate to cover any foreseeable contingency."

"What haven't you said?"

"We have to exercise Freedom of Navigation and increase our surveillance and intelligence activity while we sort things out."

"Just so it's on the table," Gilmore said, "The Agency has been looking at a range of possibilities which could provide us a presence in the Spratlys."

"Care to enlighten us?" Payne asked.

"I'm not prepared to offer specifics at this time."

Finding an opening, Dan Lantis caught Stuart's eye and tapped his watch.

Stuart took his cue. "Justin, you have anything?"

"No, sir. I believe we've covered the salient points."

"Let me summarize. The actions taken by the Philippine government are well within their rights as a sovereign nation. I do not want to get dragged into this mess, but if we must, it should be under circumstances of our own choosing. I want to take every measure to support Zhu while taking those actions necessary to protect our national interests.

"Richard, make it clear to the Philippine ambassador that Manila must not take overt action against the Chinese to secure the release of their fishermen. And direct our ambassador in Beijing to request a follow-up meeting. I want to see who shows up."

Stuart saw Valardi's nod of affirmation, and turned to Gilmore. "Bryce, get back with me with your intelligence requirements.

"Sheldon, develop the contingency plans in case we can't keep a lid on this mess. I'm afraid our friends in Manila may need our help. And Bob?"

"Yes, sir."

"Alert the *Lincoln*. Her presence may be enough to dissuade the Chinese from doing anything stupid."

"Yes, sir."

"Justin, I'll need a Presidential Review Directive with the decision analysis and tasking for my signature."

Stuart crafted his actions to set the foundation for resolving a pending crisis, but his gut told him he was already playing from behind. He chose not to voice his concerns. "Good meeting, gentlemen. Let's get moving."

Chapter Ten

PAGASA ATOLL
SOUTH CHINA SEA
07:28 WEDNESDAY 19 FEBRUARY

"Captain?"

Reyes looked up from the pile of messages scattered across his desk. His executive officer, Lieutenant Lenny Santos, stood in the doorway.

A little-used cot was set up in the corner of his improvised office ashore, but his fatigue was only in part from lack of sleep. A new reality had replaced the euphoria from the destruction of the Chinese navigation buoys. It was one thing to surprise the Chinese with a single audacious act. It was quite another to rescue the detained fishermen.

"Enter."

"Good morning, Skipper. I have the readiness report."

Reyes motioned to a rickety chair. "I never thought we'd be attempting an eighteenth-century cutting out expedition right out of the exploits of Horatio Hornblower. You are familiar with the books, yes?"

"No, sir." Santos was accustomed to his commanding officer's fondness of sea stories and waited for him to explain.

"Ah, well then, I have taken a page from Mr. Forester's books to formulate the plan to rescue our fishermen. His Captain Hornblower was a bold English tactician whose tactics confounded his enemies."

Reyes brightened at the thought of emulating one of his heroes. "What is our status?"

"The *Abcede* completed her reconnaissance of Likas Island and *Romblon* fired ranging rounds to calibrate their mortar."

"Excellent. Have *Abcede's* tanks topped off. I want her made ready for a rapid turnaround."

"They have their orders, sir."

"And the *Emilio*?"

"We'll be ready, Captain. The crew completed gunnery practice and the Special Ops detail set up a one-kilometer course to simulate the run-in."

"Very well, XO. I'll be onboard in short order. You may attend to your duties."

Reyes took a sip of stale coffee and began to shift through the pile of paper in front of him. Near the bottom of the stack he located the Western Military District's latest intelligence report. The contents were sobering.

All indications from the PRC's ambassador confirmed Beijing had no intent of releasing the fishermen despite communications with the Americans to the contrary. The Chinese were seeking unacceptable concessions from the government. These would entail acknowledging Beijing's illegal occupation of Mischief Reef and their other outposts constructed in Philippine waters as legitimate.

He knew there would be no turning back. Manila's Washington Ambassador met with Valardi and thanked the Americans for their support. He then informed Valardi that while Philippine government understood the American position, President Montalvo would do whatever was necessary to ensure the nation's security and the safety of the detained fishermen.

He placed the intelligence report in the folder containing his other messages and set off for his ship. The C-130 was parked at its accustomed place on the grassy tarmac after delivering the photographs of the missing fishing boat to Cavite. A working party was moving cargo stacked around the loading ramp so the aircraft could make the return trip.

The transformation on the island was incredible. The old gun emplacements were being cleared and topped with camouflage netting while new ones were being constructed for the 40mm cannons the LST had delivered. Enveloped in a cloud of coral dust, a small truck loaded with munitions set off for the new bunker constructed near the center of the island. Reyes approved the moves. If the Chinese chose to attack, they would have a fight on their hands.

LIKAS ISLAND
05:30 FRIDAY 21 FEBRUARY

"Captain on the bridge."

Reyes strode through the watertight door and joined Santos. "What's our status, XO?"

"Likas Island is dead ahead, sir. We are making five knots. Course zero-six-zero."

"Very well."

Reyes turned at the sound of a crewman behind him. His communications officer delivered the message they all expected. The message read: EXECUTE

Reyes made his way to the bridge wing and frowned at the light reflecting off the waves. A figure standing to his left sensed his displeasure and stepped away.

"Excuse me, sir."

"You're fine, Lieutenant."

Reyes changed his focus to a wisp of clouds beginning to cast a veil over the moon. Their approach would not be compromised.

Santos called from the bridge. "Captain. Slack tide in thirty minutes."

"Very well."

Reyes addressed the officer from Naval Special Warfare Group 91 positioned at his side. "Lieutenant Torres, I'd say it's time for you to join your men."

"If I may take my leave, sir?"

"God speed, Lieutenant."

Reyes followed Torres onto the bridge and watched him disappear into the darkness before speaking to Santos. "XO, we are fortunate to have such men. Now it's our time. What's the distance to our objective?"

"Three kilometers."

"Slow to three knots. Assume course one-two-zero. Alert the boat crew to launch the Zodiac and embark the team. When you have confirmation the raiders are underway, do a COMM check and send Torres a bearing for the lagoon."

"Yes, sir."

"We'll assume our station at two kilometers. Order the *Salvador Abcede* to remain on station and be prepared to escort the Zodiac. *Romblon* should close to one kilometer in case we need her for fire support. If Torres has a hot reception, he'll signal with a red flare."

———

THE LAGOON
LIKAS ISLAND
05:45

Torres looked at his compass verifying their course. "We'll begin our run-in in two minutes. Check your gear, clear your weapons, and click on the safeties. There will be no chambered rounds going off."

He continued through his checklist. He tucked it in his pocket and addressed the man carrying the team's grenade launcher. "Gunner, look to your weapon."

"Aye, aye, sir," Gunners Mate Second Class Ramirez responded, double-checking the bandoleer of grenade rounds crossing his chest.

"Montanong, secure the engine. We'll paddle the rest of the way."

The raiders bent over and dug their blades into the water, gaining momentum before settling into a steady rhythm born of hours of training. Torres slipped on his night vision goggles when they neared the mouth of the lagoon and swept the anchorage. He focused on the halo of greenish light from their objective.

That's her. Reyes' timing was perfect. The incoming tide had swung the fishing boat around so it lay stern-on to the shore. There would be no need for time-consuming maneuvers to escape.

They made their way into the lagoon and drifted by the thick hemp anchor line angling down from the bow of the vessel. Torres let the zodiac's momentum carry them far enough to observe the transom with the vessel's name: GLORIA.

"Hold fast. Be alert for anyone sleeping on the deck. Maintain strict noise discipline until we crank up the engine. It won't matter after that."

"Boats, when you hear the engine, get out of here. Boarding team: Go, go, go!"

Torres lead the way. He threw his right leg over the gunwale and rolled onto the fishing boat's deck landing on a sleeping fisherman. He clamped his hand over the startled man's mouth and pointed to the Philippine flag sewn on his sleeve.

"Shush."

The fisherman froze. Three other raiders dropped around him, deploying to either end of the pilothouse. Two of them peered around the corners of the structure and motioned to Torres they'd secured their objective.

"Where's your captain?" Torres said.

The fisherman pointed to the pilothouse.

"How many are there?"

The man held up seven trembling fingers.

"Are you the engineer?"

The fisherman shook his head.

"I want you to get in my boat."

The man hesitated, afraid to move.

Torres stood. "You'll be safe. I'm going to find the others."

The man didn't move.

"Mantanong."

"Sir?"

"Help this man, then join me on the bridge. I'm going to find the captain."

Torres slid open the pilothouse door and stepped into the cramped space. He spotted a man snoring in a hammock slung from the overhead.

"Captain?"

The sleeping form stirred.

"Captain."

"Huh?" The man bolted upright. "What... Who—?'

"I am Lieutenant Angelo Torres. Philippine Naval Special Forces."

"What are you doing on my boat?"

"Getting you out of here."

"But..."

Torres lowered his weapon. "There is no time for discussion. Move your crew to my boat. You stay. I'll need you and your engineer. My men will assist."

"We—"

"Move it, Captain."

The fisherman rushed off to gather up his confused crewmates and usher them over the side to join their comrades.

"Lieutenant, we're ready to go," a voice called from the Zodiac.

A loud splash resonated in the dark just as the raiders pushed off. Torres jerked his head toward the sound. "What the hell was that?"

Mantanong peered over the side. He lifted his palms upward accompanied by a shake of his head.

Torres addressed the captain. "We gotta go. Are you ready?"

The captain looked toward the Chinese warships.

"Once the Chinese figure out what we're up to, things are going to get mighty exciting."

Torres could not have anticipated just how exciting things were to become. If he had been a student of history, he might have appreciated how often the course of events of a nation or the world turned on a quirk of fate. One of those moments was unfolding.

A Chinese sailor had woken early and walked down to the narrow beach bordering the lagoon to relieve himself. He cupped his free hand over his eyes and focused on the *Gloria* searching for the sound of the splash. "What? What are they doing?"

The sailor stumbled up the beach trying to button his pants. "They're escaping! The fishing boat is escaping!"

Torres reacted to the shouting. "Ramirez, you and Flores take position on the stern. Provide covering fire. Mantanong, go forward and cut the anchor line."

He cupped his hands and roared across the water. "The outboard! Use the outboard. Get out of here!"

When he heard the sound of the Zodiac's engine, he yelled toward the bow. "Mantanong. You got the cable?"

"On it."

The *Gloria's* captain did not require coaxing and pushed the ignition button. The engine turned over with a belch of stack gas. He engaged power to the shaft. The boat stirred, the bow veering to port.

"The anchor's dragging us around," the captain screamed. "We're still anchored."

Torres bolted out of the pilothouse. "Chief, we're going to run aground. Cut the damn cable."

Muzzle flashes winked along the shore. Three rounds thunked into the wooden superstructure of the pilothouse.

The thick anchor cable began to slide across the deck. The bow pivoted further. The boat gave a jerk when the cable caught on the corner of the deckhouse. Mantanong rushed to free it. The weakened line parted, the free end whipped through the air.

The *Gloria* responded with an uncontrolled surge propelling it toward the opposite shore. The captain felt the pull of the wheel in his hands and spun it, countering the turn. The unexpected movement of the boat ruined the bead drawn on them from an AK-47.

Torres ducked into the pilothouse to place a call to Reyes. "Mako, Mako. Cutlass."

"Cutlass, we copy."

"Mako, we have a hot reception. Repeat, a hot reception."

"Roger that, Cutlass. You have a hot reception. What is your status?"

"The Zodiac has cleared the lagoon. The fishing boat is underway. We are . . . Hold one."

"Cutlass, we have lost your transmission. Repeat your last."

Torres would have preferred to continue his update, but the evolving situation aboard the *Gloria* and the Chinese patrol boats demanded his immediate attention.

The random automatic rifle fire was now more deliberate and numerous rounds were impacting the pilothouse. One bullet struck the compass, shattering its glass cover. The other two bullets of the three-round burst splintered the instrument panel. Slivers of metal and wood flew across the wheel.

The *Gloria's* captain cried out in pain, blood welling from his hands. "Take the wheel."

Torres grasped the spokes and corrected their course. Spotting his Chief, who had moved from his exposed position on the bow to seek cover behind the superstructure. "Mantanong, the captain's wounded. Get in here and bandage his hands, then take the wheel. Keep the bow aimed at the center of the channel."

No sooner had Torres completed his order than he saw the forward 37mm gun mount of the nearest patrol boat swing in their direction.

"Oh, shit. Gunner. Gas. Gas. Gas. Put a round on the bridge."

Ramirez shouldered the launcher, adjusted his aim, and lobbed a grenade.

Yellow-white tongues of flame erupted from the twin cannons of the patrol boat. Torres gripped the sides of the doorframe and heard the shells whistle overhead. They impacted on the distant palms sending a cascade of fronds to the beach.

Torres focused on the shattered palms, astonished that the Chinese had missed. They couldn't depress their gun barrels low enough to hit the fishing boat without blowing holes in their own ship. He also realized that when the *Gloria* closed the mouth of the lagoon, they would be in point-blank range.

The second patrol boat's turret traversed in his direction. He stared wide-eyed at the open mouths of the dual cannon pointed at him, suppressing the reaction to duck. "Ramirez. Two rounds on the near boat."

"Will do." Ramirez sighted his launcher and fired. The tear gas canister exploded with a whitish puff. The Chinese sailors abandoned their gun in a panic, scrambling to escape the toxic cloud.

"Hey, Ramirez, Torres hollered. "We just may pull this off."

———

"Mako, Mako. Cutlass."

Beside himself at the loss of contact and the sound of heavy gunfire, Reyes managed to respond with a steady voice. "Cutlass, we copy."

"Mako, the Zodiac should be nearing your location. We're closing the mouth of the lagoon and receiving small arms fire. The captain is wounded."

"Roger that, Cutlass."

"Captain, we have the Zodiac in sight twenty points off the starboard bow," Santos confirmed.

Reyes looked to his right, spotting the blinking red light in the distance. "Cutlass, we have the Zodiac."

Before Torres could respond, the Chinese guns erupted; 14.5mm shellfire churning the water around him.

"Ah, Mako, we have a situation."

Chapter Eleven

CHINESE PATROL BOAT, SHANGHAI 1331
06:10 FRIDAY 21 FEBRUARY

The captain of Shanghai 1331 was no longer rational, his judgment clouded by rage and loss of face. Their prize was being stolen from under his very nose. Headquarters would be infuriated. They would never accept any excuse for failure. His career was over and the sting he felt was only due in part from the tear gas. He screamed his orders with uncontrolled fury.

The deck crew re-manned their stations and cast off the lines tethering the patrol boat to shore. The pressured gunners rammed home their shells into the automatic feeder and fired their first rounds. The shells landed long and wide of their target. Correcting their aim, the next rounds walked up the lagoon. Fountains of water chased down the stern of the fishing boat.

Ramirez and Flores dove for cover. The 37mm rounds impacted the transom, demolishing the entire stern quarter. Splinters and shrapnel sprayed in all directions, wounding both of them.

Ramirez reacted first, ignoring his own pain, and crawled to Flores. Blood stained his friend's utility jacket.

Torres reached them a moment later. "How is he?"

Ramirez rolled his friend over searching for the wound. "I don't know, Skipper. Maybe not too bad."

Torres saw the jagged splinter protruding from Flores' back and gave it a tentative pull. "This has to come out. Hold him steady."

"Arghhh."

"Hold on, buddy. It's out," Ramirez said while he held pressure over the wound and fumbled for a battle dressing with his other hand. He looked at Torres, "Looks like things are getting pretty hairy, Skipper."

"Time to call the cavalry. Throw me one of your flares."

Ramirez pulled a signal round from his bandoleer and pitched it underhand. Torres grabbed it with his right hand and fed it into the breech of the launcher. He aimed skyward and squeezed the trigger. The red signal flare arched across the sky.

————

Two kilometers seaward, Reyes spotted the flare. "*Romblon*, close the lagoon. Provide covering fire. Barracuda, execute Operation Retrieval. Repeat, execute Operation Retrieval."

Romblon's gunner's mates were standing by their weapons. Hidden by the darkness, they waited in ambush just beyond the mouth of the lagoon. Several muttered prayers when the *Gloria* passed.

"The Chinese are right behind us."

The gunners disengaged their breech locks and charged

their weapons. Their eyes were riveted on the black expanse between the white water breaking on the shore defining the channel. They wouldn't have long to wait.

"Mako, Mako. Barracuda. We have a hostile exiting the lagoon. Permission to fire."

"Barracuda. Mako. We copy. Engage."

Reyes competed his transmission, a grim smile crossing his face. The squat gunboat's maximum speed of eighteen knots and lines didn't match those of the sleek barracuda, but the comparison with the predator's rows of razor-sharp teeth did.

———

First to fire were the Barracuda's 60mm mortar crew. They fed their tube from the pile of shells stacked near the ammunition ready locker and lobbed a cascade of high-explosive rounds over the palm trees.

The *Romblon's* gunners gripped the handles of their weapons holding fire, waiting their turn.

Barracuda's commander anticipated his gunner's first instinct would be to sweep the Chinese vessel with their weapons. He directed their fire to the bridge. "We will first decapitate the serpent, then cripple it."

A withering hail of lead ripped into the patrol boat. The Naizhu's bridge disintegrated in a cloud of smoke, flashes of exploding shells, and flying metal.

The Filipinos turned their 20mm cannon and .50 caliber machine guns on the stern. They were certain that nothing could have survived their initial fusillade. The results were no less lethal. The patrol boat went dead in the water, black, acrid smoke pouring from the engine room.

The *Romblon's* guns fell silent, smoke curling from their muzzles. An eerie silence permeated the air following the sheer violence of the preceding minutes. Stunned, the Philippine sailors tried to sort out what to do next.

Their answer came when the Huey appeared and began circling overhead. Operating from the LST, the squadron's helicopter had just finished inserting a Marine rifle squad on the island. It now had the second Chinese patrol boat under observation.

"Barracuda. Proud Eagle."

"Proud Eagle. Barracuda."

"Barracuda, you've got trouble headed your way."

Reyes listened to the communications between his two units with increasing concern. *Romblon* was in significant peril. His plan to keep the Chinese bottled up in the lagoon had failed. "XO, have we recovered the Zodiac?"

"Yes, sir. The fishermen have been escorted below."

"Very well. Order the *Abcede* to close and provide supporting fire for *Romblon*. The situation for our small barracuda will become ugly unless we stop the Chinese. We'll hit them with triangulated fire."

The exposed mortar crew on the forward deck of the *Romblon* couldn't have agreed more with their squadron commander. The second Chinese patrol boat was emerging from the lagoon. The boat was so close they could read the hull number. When its forward gun mount began to traverse in their direction, they scrambled for whatever cover they could find.

———

In the cramped engine room of *Shanghai* 1331, the Chinese engineer was unaware of the evolving battle. His world was enveloped in noise. The pair of cruise diesels were at full throttle and he had just brought the two boost engines on line when the four 25mm antiaircraft guns overhead added their percussion to the din.

He listed to the pitch of his roaring diesels over the hammering cannons. He throttled his engines to full power.

The first hint of trouble caught his eye. A wavering needle on the number-two booster diesel fuel injector gauge. The engineer stared at the gauge as it swung further to the right. The inner casing pressure of the engine swung past the red line.

The vessel's age and lack of yard time to perform required maintenance had caught up with him. A crack in a fuel line buried deep inside the diesel was spraying vaporized fuel directly onto the red-hot engine.

A thunderous explosion ripped through the engine room turning it into a blazing inferno. Water cascaded through the twisted plates of the hull and the patrol boat began to settle by the stern. Black, oily smoke billowed from gaping hole in the deck where the antiaircraft guns had been. The gun's high-explosive shells began detonating in the fires adding to the carnage.

Those sailors who could swim struck out for the Naizhu. Their comrades could offer them no assistance. Their sister ship had been pushed by the waves of the approaching storm onto the coral reef and was now hard aground.

———

Reyes spun at the sound of the distant explosion. "What the hell was that?"

The overhead speaker provided the answer. "Mako, Mako. *Abcede.* Over?"

"*Abcede.* Mako."

"Mako, we have secured our weapons. The Naizhu has grounded on the reef. The Shanghai is on fire and sinking.

Romblon is standing by to rescue any sailors in the water. We have not approached because of the secondary explosions."

"Do what you can without endangering your vessel."

"Roger that, Mako. It's going to be tough maintaining station off this lee shore. I'd prefer not to join the Naizhu on the reef."

Reyes pulled his eyes away from the amber glow illuminating the horizon. "Do not endanger your command." He turned to Santos. "XO, you have the con. I must get a message to headquarters."

———

While Reyes gave his report, others halfway around the world listened in. Intelligence officers from the NSA were eavesdropping on the Philippine captain, his communications intercepted from a satellite positioned hundreds of miles above the South China Sea.

These men shared Reyes' surprise when the Chief of the Philippine Armed Forces' voice came over the radio:

"Mako, this is General Medeiros. We have something in mind."

Chapter Twelve

THE WHITE HOUSE
08:15 SATURDAY 22 FEBRUARY

Stuart slammed down the report containing a formal protest from the Chinese. "Damn it, Justin. Why does this stuff always happen on a weekend?"

Brown shifted his weight from his right leg to his left.

"Have our experts at State had a chance to analyze the wording in this thing?" Stuart didn't wait for a response. "How could Beijing possibly believe we had anything to do with sinking those two ships?"

There was not much the administration could do to defuse this latest crisis, but this fact did little to blunt Stuart's displeasure. Brown stole a sideways glance at Dan Lantis hoping to find some support. None was forthcoming. Lantis appeared to be focusing his full attention on a large scuff marring the shine of his left shoe.

Brown ventured a guess. "Mr. President, the Chinese may have caught word of Richard's meeting with the Philippine ambassador and concluded we received advanced notice."

Somewhat mollified, Stuart replied, "That would make sense."

"We're querying PACOM to see if there has been any contact with the AFP."

Stuart relented. "Take a seat. When I get a better feel for what's going on, I'll convene the NSC to consider our options."

THE PENTAGON
08:35

The briefing officer came to rigid attention when Payne entered the room. "Good morning, Mr. Secretary. I have just presented the status boards to Admiral Lawson. With the exception of the Pacific theater, activity in the rest of the world is low. The Gulf remains quiet and the Iranians haven't challenged any of our aircraft for several days."

Payne looked over the LAD screens in the Pentagon's command center displaying the deployment of U.S. forces throughout the world. "I understand our friends in Manila have gotten the Chinese stirred up."

"It'd be safe to say Beijing's not real happy at the moment," Lawson replied.

"Let's see what we're up against," Payne said. "Major, you may begin."

"Yes, sir."

The Major's assistant typed a series of keystrokes on her laptop. Three separate images were projected in response to her commands: a map of the South China Sea, a naval base, and a small island with several vessels scattered about.

"Mr. Secretary, we highlighted several islands to provide an overview of the contested areas. Those occupied by the Chinese are in red, Philippines in blue. Those claimed by the

Vietnamese, green. Hainan Island is at the upper left. The star represents Likas Island where the confrontation took place."

"How bad?"

"The Chinese took a beating, Mr. Secretary," the Joint Staff's Chief of Intelligence answered. "We don't know the casualty count, but the combined crews of the two patrol boats total around eighty. The Filipinos have picked up a number of survivors."

"What do we have on surveillance?"

"A Naizhu class patrol boat is grounded on the reef. There is no sign of the second vessel, a Shanghai-II. We presume it sank."

"Any idea what they're going to do with the survivors?"

"No, sir," the Chief of Naval Operations said. "If we can take anything from the absence of back channel diplomatic communications or public pronouncements from the Foreign Ministry in Manila, they don't have any idea either."

"And the Chinese?"

"We have strong indicators they're preparing a retaliatory strike."

Payne twisted in his seat to address the Chief of Naval Operations. "Admiral?"

"The PLAN's rapid deployment squadron is ready for sea."

"Their base?"

"Hainan."

"Composition?"

"A mix of frigates and destroyers. The *Fu Zhou*, a Sovremmenny class guided missile destroyer, two Luhu class destroyers, and two Jianghu class frigates."

"Can they cause a problem for us?"

"No, sir. As configured, the flotilla presents only a minimal threat. I can't say the same for the Filipinos."

"Submarines?"

"We've accounted for all of them except a new diesel boat.

It put to sea several days ago and is believed to be conducting routine training off the mainland."

"What else?"

Lawson flipped open his briefing book. "Major, would you please put up the other shot of the harbor?"

"Mr. Secretary, this is a view of another part of the base," the CNO continued when the picture appeared. "I would like to point out the activity around the three ships clustered in the center of the image. The three from top to bottom are a replenishment oiler, a fleet supply ship, and a repair ship. If these auxiliaries join the combatants, the Chinese plan an extended deployment. What caught our attention was the two amphibs at the top of the picture. They're completing an onload of combat troops."

"Well, that's just great."

Payne's retort reflected his growing exasperation with Manila. The administration could be dragged into this mess whether it wanted or not. He recognized his comment didn't contribute anything positive to the analysis and posed a pertinent question. "Bob, do y'all have any specifics on what they're up to?"

"No, sir. But we have some ideas based on the characteristics of these two vessels. The ship with the helicopter pad on the stern is a Yuting class amphibious assault ship. It's capable of embarking two-hundred and fifty troops. The other is an older Yukan class with essentially the same capability. It just returned from delivering heavy construction equipment to their installation on Fiery Cross Reef. The Chinese are lengthening their runway and building the infrastructure to handle a broad range of combat and support aircraft."

"None of the Philippine garrisons in the Spratlys will present the PLA much of a challenge except the one on Pagasa."

"Pagasa is an obvious source of irritation. It's where the Philippine Navy sortied for their attack. It's strategically situated to threaten the Chinese outposts on Mischief, Subi, and Johnson Reefs. I'm sure the Chinese would like nothing better than to eliminate it."

Payne frowned. "Any others?"

"Nanshan Island, just north of Mischief Reef. It's claimed by Manila, but not occupied. Major, would you please point it out?"

Payne glanced at the postage-stamp-sized island before dismissing its significance. "I'd say we've missed our chance to cool this affair off."

"Manila hasn't done us any favors," Lawson affirmed. "They've just provided Beijing a legitimate opening for a counter strike."

"We can't permit that."

"I agree, Mr. Secretary."

"Major, can we have the previous slide showing the disposition of our forces? Run lines from the PLAN base on Hainan Island and the *Lincoln* to a point just west of Pagasa Atoll."

"What am I looking for?"

"The Strike Group is transiting the Strait of Malacca. They should pass Singapore today."

The CNO referred to the two intersecting lines on the screen. "The distance the *Lincoln* will have to make up to be in a favorable position relative to the Chinese is approximately two-hundred fifty miles. It's 1915 hours on Hainan. The surveillance photos were taken at 1600. Our next satellite pass in daylight will be at 0720. Their flotilla should be underway at first light. I fully expect to be looking at an empty anchorage. If my assumptions are correct, we have eleven hours."

Lawson closed his briefing book. "We need to issue an immediate warning order to PacFleet."

Payne turned to the CNO. "Admiral, please see to it. Bob, would you join me in my office?

·   ·   ·

Payne and Larson were seated in Payne's oak-paneled office when the phone on his desk rang.

"Sheldon?"

"Good morning, Justin. I have Bob with me. We were expecting your call. How's it going in your neck of the woods?"

"The boss was in rare form this morning."

"I can imagine. What's up?"

"The President wants to meet this afternoon. I'll have to get back with you on the exact time. Will you be ready?"

"Already working it," Payne said.

"See you this afternoon."

Payne replaced the receiver. "Bob weren't y'all planning to split off a destroyer from the *Lincoln* group to conduct a Freedom of Navigation op through the Taiwan Strait? The timing isn't good."

"I agree, we shouldn't be stirring that particular pot right now. I'll make sure it's canceled. No sense in provoking the Chinese."

"I'd say with the way things are developing, we'll have ample opportunity to do that next week."

———

UNITED STATES NAVAL BASE
YOKOSUKA, JAPAN
23:47

International crises are not considerate of the time. It was almost midnight on Sunday when the commander of the Seventh Fleet was startled out of a sound sleep by the high-pitched ringing of his bedside phone.

He fumbled for the receiver of his secure line, managing to stop the noise. "Triebull."

"Admiral, this is Lieutenant Wallin, the Watch Officer. We have an 'Immediate-Eyes Only' message from PacFleet."

There was no point in asking questions. He would learn soon enough what prompted the message. "Thank you, Lieutenant. I'll be right in."

Triebull threw on his khakis wondering what would trigger a message at this hour. He snatched his car keys off their hook in the kitchen and drove down the short winding road to his flagship, the USS *Blue Ridge*. He parked his sedan by the prow and stepped into a cold drizzle.

The quarterdeck was backlit with diffused light. There was no sign of activity, the only sound, the patter of rain on the accommodation ladder. *Best to make a little noise.* He grabbed the railing and clomped his way up the steps of the access-tower. The noise had its desired effect. He returned the salute of the startled Officer of the Deck and disappeared through the watertight door leading to his office.

The quarterdeck watch rang out the three-paired bells of a Vice-Admiral. "Seventh Fleet, arriving."

Wallin heard the bells and popped out of the flag mess just in time to intercept Triebull. He handed him a message folder. "Admiral, I've taken the liberty to call the Chief of Staff and the Three. They're on their way."

"Good thinking."

Triebull settled behind his desk and scanned the message for content, then re-read it. He pulled out a pen and began jotting notes in the margins formulating his response. As the supported commander, the responsibility fell on him to analyze the tactical situation and submit his recommendations back to the Pacific Fleet in the format of the Commander's Estimate.

A metallic knock announced the arrival of his two senior staff officers.

"Good morning, gents. It appears Washington has given

us something to jumpstart our week. Have a seat and take a look at our tasker."

Triebull looked up a moment later. "Going over the probable scenarios, the only force we have available to interdict the Chinese is the Lincoln Strike Group. Judging the relative distance, they'll have to transit compared to the Chinese flotilla, it's going to be tight getting her in position to offer a credible deterrent.

"Our variable is the intentions of the Chinese commander. We won't know those until he's well underway. Bearing in mind the constraints outlined by Washington, we'll provide Admiral Gireaux as much leeway as we can. That said, let's take a look at the chart and calculate some timelines."

Chapter Thirteen

THE WHITE HOUSE
15:00 MONDAY 24 FEBRUARY

Stuart tapped his fingers on the Beijing embassy's latest report. The communication concluded with the observation that the Chinese government spokesmen remained silent. The notable exception was a curt statement issued by a low-level Foreign Ministry official: "Beijing will take measures necessary to counter any threat to its national sovereignty." Not a good sign.

Damn, Manila has miscalculated—or have they? What could they …?

Dan Lantis popped his head in the door. "Excuse me, Mr. President. The staff's assembled."

Stuart looked up just long enough to reply. "Thank you, Dan. I'll be there in a moment."

He turned his attention to his yellow legal pad and jotted down a final question. Stuart considered the conflicting agendas of the PLA and the civilian authorities in Beijing. These two antagonists were drawing his administration into the morass they were creating. Frowning, he followed Lantis into the cabinet room.

"Good afternoon, gentlemen," he said. "You've all been working this problem with your staffs. It's time to pull it all together. Sheldon?"

"All our indicators point to an imminent deployment of elements of the Chinese South Seas Fleet," Payne responded. "Five combatants, two amphibious ships, and supporting auxiliaries. Our analysts are basing their probability estimates on the amphibious ships. They've embarked their full complement of troops, which leads us to believe they plan to occupy one or more islands."

Stuart turned to Lawson. "Any idea where they're headed?"

"There are several possible scenarios each framed by the degree of risk they're willing to assume. Beijing may wish to confine their response to executing a limited retaliatory strike to extract a price for the destruction of their patrol boats. On the other hand, their intent may be to use the AFP's actions to justify a larger action."

"Sheldon?"

"The scenario that would cause the least amount of diplomatic fallout would be for the Chinese to simply chase the Philippine Navy out of the area, reinforce their existing facilities, and increase their gray-zone ops to further destabilize the region. This would effectively put Manila on notice that no further military action on their part would be tolerated. Furthermore, it would serve to consolidate their position in the Spratlys."

"Mr. President, I have something."

Jarred by the sound of Valardi's voice, Stuart clenched his jaw. He was tired, and something in the pitch annoyed him. "What?"

"We have indications from Beijing's latest diplomatic rhetoric that this is exactly what they're contemplating."

"This?"

"Sheldon's three points."

"Continue."

"We notified their ambassador that we would not look favorably upon any further escalation of military action by either party. This statement was prefaced by our expectation that the two principles should resolve this crisis bilaterally. Beijing is aware of our broader interests in the region, but may have concluded they can continue to advance their own agenda without provoking us."

Stuart bit his lower lip. Sheldon might be onto something. "I'd like to explore this line of reasoning. Justin, what's your cut?"

"We've been looking for means to pressure Manila."

"I'd look to our basing and logistics negotiations," Brown said.

"You're suggesting we link the two?" Payne asked.

"We don't want to leave the Filipinos hanging out on a limb," Stuart answered. "That said, our response must be tailored to not encourage Manila to come running to us every time they get in over their heads."

"Like they've just done," Payne observed.

"I would expect reciprocity," Brown added.

Stuart wrote down LEVERAGE in bold letters, underlining the word twice. "Bob, I'd like to hear the remainder of your threat assessment."

"Mr. President, there are two islands the Chinese might be interested in. The first is Pagasa, site of the largest Philippine base in the Spratlys. The second is an island claimed by Manila some sixty miles north of their installations on Mischief Reef with a rudimentary airstrip."

Payne leaned forward. "Bob, are you referring to that

postage stamp you pointed out in the Tank? Nanshan Island, wasn't it?"

"Yes. And if Beijing were to occupy that postage stamp, they could neutralize the garrison and airfield on Pagasa."

"It's barely above sea level for God's sake," Payne said.

"True enough, but the line of approach for the Chinese flotilla to both of these potential targets from Hainan Island is the same. We won't be able to ascertain their intentions until they are almost on top of Pagasa. If they choose to target the Philippine garrison, the PLA would not have sufficient force to occupy or reinforce any other islands."

Stuart noted Valardi's mouth open and pre-empted him. "Bob, could you venture a guess on the probabilities?"

"If I were the Chinese, I'd be tempted to take out Pagasa. In the final analysis, though, I'd say the risks are too great."

"Caveats?"

"I'd add one," Payne said. "If the PLA is provoked further. Having said that, I believe the Chinese will choose to strengthen their current outposts."

"I concur," Gilmore added, "but we have another variable to consider."

Stuart picked up his pen and wrote down 'variable.' "And what would that be?"

"The NRO passed us an intercept between AFP Naval Headquarters in Cavite and the commander of the Philippine flotilla. The message indicates they may be considering action against another Chinese installation."

"What the hell!" Payne cried. "Why didn't I know about this? Do we have time to stop them?"

Gilmore held up his hands in supplication. "I just heard about this as I walked out the door. I've asked for any intercepts that can clarify the situation."

Stuart ignored them and turned to the one man he could count on to keep his head. "Bob, we've got to consider inserting the Lincoln Strike Group between these folks to keep the peace."

"Yes, sir."

"Richard, you know where you fit?"

"I'll draft a confidential note and deliver it to the Philippine embassy. I'll word it in such a way as to convey our 'grave concern' about escalating the crisis and include implicit language that we have knowledge of the Cavite communications. I—"

A Navy captain entered the room, approached Lawson, and handed him a folder.

All eyes were now on Lawson. His grim expression conveyed the contents.

"Bob?"

"More trouble, sir. The Philippine navy has reportedly taken action against a small Chinese outpost on Scarborough Shoal."

"Scarborough Shoal?"

"It's some one-hundred and forty miles west of Luzon. They've destroyed another maritime marker, evicted the Chinese, and raised the Philippine flag."

"Does the report mention casualties?"

"No, sir."

"When did it occur?"

Lawson touched his thumb to his fingers counting off the time zones. "Two hours ago, our time."

"What else?"

"We can expect the PLAN flotilla to be underway within the next three hours."

Stuart digested the unwelcome news. "Well, gentlemen, it appears we've been overtaken by events. Can *Lincoln* get there in time?"

"It's going to be close," Lawson replied. "We sent the alert message to PacFleet just after noon concurring with Seventh Fleet's recommendations. We've received the confirmatory message. With your approval, sir, we'll send the execute message."

"Timelines?"

"*Lincoln* should be completing her transit of the Strait of Malacca as we speak. The escorts topped off their bunkers before entering the Strait, so fuel will not be an issue. Based on our estimate of the PLAN's probable course, the Strike Group will be in position within twenty-eight hours. The Chinese have less than half the distance to travel, but we have a four-hour jump."

"How soon can the Chinese be there?" Brown asked.

"We believe their flotilla will be making, at best, eighteen knots. That will place them near Pagasa in twenty hours. If the combatants break off and proceed ahead of the slower vessels, they could be in position in as little as fifteen."

Stuart shook his head. "That's cutting it close."

"We've diverted an Air Force E-3C and the ready P-8 from Kadena is airborne. Even if *Lincoln* is several hundred miles away, she can make her presence known in a number of ways that may be enough to unsettle the Chinese."

Stuart spun his wedding band with his thumb. "Get them moving. Sheldon will fill you in on anything you need to know."

Lawson gathered his notes and stood to leave. "Yes, sir."

"Richard, what's your take?"

Valardi appeared immersed in his own thoughts and didn't respond.

"Richard?"

"Ah, sorry, sir. What did you say?"

"I asked for your opinion."

"The Pentagon's operating premise is the mere presence of the Lincoln Strike Group will be enough to dissuade the Chinese from taking any precipitous action. I'd like to know the specifics of the Rules of Engagement."

"Sheldon?"

"Our tasking order to PacFleet states that under no circumstances shall our forces engage the Chinese. Furthermore, we have provided the Strike Group commander guidance that if his force is faced with a potentially hostile act, he is to disengage."

"It's imperative we convey to Beijing our intent is to prevent the crisis from escalating," Brown said.

"Understood."

"Richard, draft a communiqué that addresses our desire to ensure the safety of the international sea lanes. Beijing understands this issue holds significant importance. It shouldn't come as a surprise."

"We may be able to defuse future confrontations in the Spratlys if we play to the Chinese sense that they are the aggrieved party."

"I hardly get the feeling China is the aggrieved party," Gilmore said.

Stuart had heard enough and cut off any further discussion. "Sheldon, what can you tell me about Scarborough Reef?"

"The Chinese occupied the atoll under the guise of establishing an outpost for their fishing fleet. It's an approach similar to what they used late last year on Mischief Reef. Satellite imagery has identified a radio transmission tower and several rudimentary structures. We've also confirmed Manila's contention that an alleged 'survey ship' the Chinese Foreign Ministry claims is supporting their fisheries department is the *Xing Fenshan*, an intelligence vessel."

"Well, that shouldn't come as a surprise to any of us. Sheldon, have Admiral Cortez provide a Position Statement. Coordinate with Richard to ensure there is no ambiguity."

"I can dispatch my Assistant Secretary, Adrian Clarke, to conduct personal consultations with Manila and Beijing. He can facilitate negotiations if both parties agree."

"Send him. Make sure he understands I want our response

to be firm, but evenhanded. I do not want any of our actions providing an advantage to Xiao and the more extreme elements within the PLA."

Valardi cleared his throat. "Addressing the specifics of our relationship with Beijing beyond the present difficulties with Manila, we must focus on keeping open the lines of communication and pursuing confidence-building measures."

"Can we accomplish those without undercutting Montalvo?" Stuart asked.

"Possibly."

Brown considered the various options to cover Gilmore's clandestine operation on Blue Horizon. "Richard, we have a plan?"

"We're working the details."

Stuart closed his notebook. "Keep it at that. We'll know soon enough how this plays out."

Chapter Fourteen

USS ABRAHAM LINCOLN CVN-72
THE STRAIT OF MALACCA
01:30 TUESDAY 25 FEBRUARY

R ear Admiral Bud Gireaux, Commander Carrier Strike
Group-12, surveyed his world from the flag bridge
towering five stories above the *Lincoln's* flight deck. He needed
to reflect. He'd spent the better part of several hours in the
Tactical Flag Command Center working a warning order
from Seventh Fleet. The order came as a complete surprise
after CSG-12's six-month deployment to the Persian Gulf.

The ear-piercing thunder and roar of flight operations
were on hold until the *Lincoln* transited the Strait of Malacca.
He listened to the rushing sound of the bow wave as the
massive carrier split the ocean. Paradoxically, the absence of
noise on a warship was a cause for alarm, signaling an engineering casualty. There was nothing wrong on the *Lincoln* this
morning.

Over one-thousand feet long, the Abe displaced 95,000
tons. The carrier's size commanded respect from those sharing
the Strait with her. That fact did not lesson the dangers she

faced. Gireaux would have preferred making the passage through the congested ship traffic off Singapore during the day.

Navigating the shipping channel clogged with hundreds of vessels from fishing boats to supertankers was a test for any captain. He did not envy the commanding officer of the *Lincoln* conning his ship through the narrow waterway separating the Malay Peninsula from the Indonesian Island of Sumatra.

Darkness and distance prevented Gireaux from seeing all the ships of his command. He knew they were there—stretched over four miles, in line-ahead formation. The destroyers *Stout* and *Forrest Sherman* led the formation. The cruiser *Gettysburg* trailed the Abe at 1500 yards. The fast replenishment ship *Supply* and destroyers *Kidd* and *James E. Williams* brought up the rear.

This was the *Stouts's* last WestPac deployment for several years. She would be in the yards after returning to the States. With that in mind, Gireaux eased her skipper's disappointment at having his freedom of navigation operation canceled by providing him with new orders.

The nuclear-powered attack submarine, USS *Honolulu*, cruised point unfettered by the congestion of vessels navigating the strait above her. She was well ahead of the surface ships seeking out any Chinese submarines that might pick up and trail the Strike Group as it transited the South China Sea.

Stalking enemy submarines was standard operating procedure for American attack boats, but there was an added import to *Honolulu*'s mission. The Chinese must not know what the *Lincoln* was about. The carrier was heading into harm's way.

The *Lincoln's* commanding officer was seated on the bridge, surrounded by a bank of computer screens. One of these provided input from his ship's primary surface-search/navigation radar. In very short order he was going to be shutting the system down along with all other equipment emitting a signal that could identify the *Lincoln* and fix her position.

Gireaux's plan had raised the eyebrows of the navigator. The Abe would be blind except for the passive input of the wide band receiver. They would rely on the receiver and the low-tech human eye for the next several hours. The risks they would take to complete their transit past Singapore and past the Riau Islands guarding the mouth of the strait would be great.

Gireaux acknowledged the danger and made a provision for another navigation aid to assist his captains until they reached the safety of the open water.

The Strike Group executed a course change to the northeast after the lights of Singapore dropped over the horizon. Satisfied all was well, the *Lincoln's* commanding officer left the bridge for the ship's Combat Information Center

The senior watch officer rose to meet his captain. "Good morning, Skipper. We have a 'Go' order."

"Well then, shall we get on with it? We'll execute as soon as I have confirmation *Kidd's* helicopter is in position."

While they were speaking, a MH-60R Seahawk lifted off the destroyer's flight deck to scout the way for the Strike Group. The aircrew of the antisubmarine warfare helicopter was intrigued by this unusual assignment. By any measure, it beat the planned run of movies and mail from the carrier.

———

Gireaux returned to the TFCC at dawn, waiting for word from the MH-60 flying ten miles ahead of the Strike Group. Refreshed from a nap, he had just polished off a donut when the helicopter reported. Their projected course remained clear of hazards and, to his surprise, there were no Chinese flagged vessels.

He turned to his operations officer. "Anything from *Honolulu?*"

"No, sir. She's running silent."

"Very well. I believe it's time to give our Chinese friends a little surprise. Order the *Stout* and *Supply* to detach. Inform the Captain he is to assume course 045 and increase speed to twenty-five knots. We'll impose EMCOM alpha when *Stout's* ready to transmit."

The *Lincoln's* captain was on the bridge when he received his orders. He issued a cautionary warning. Despite her huge size, the carrier's two Westinghouse nuclear reactors providing power to her steam turbines allowed her to accelerate at an astonishing rate exceeding that of her escorts. It would not do well to run up the stern of the *Gettysburg* before the cruiser could assume her station off the *Lincoln's* port beam.

He swiveled his chair to watch the *Stout* and *Supply* steer north-northeast assuming the Strike Group's original course. The two ships were soon to play an integral role in the deception of the Chinese.

Supply was a trusted friend, always there when you needed her, providing fuel and sustenance to the ships of the Strike Group. The replenishment ships like her didn't possess the glamour of the warships, but the Navy couldn't execute its mission without them.

Many years had passed beneath the CO's wings and he now conjured memories of VF-1's 1977 deployment to the Indian Ocean on the USS *Enterprise*. Escorted by the nuclear powered cruiser, USS *Truxtun*, they had spent much of their time steaming in empty circles. This mindless task called for a

change in the acronym for the battle group from Nuclear
Powered Task Group, NPTG, to "No Place to Go."

The tedium of the long deployment had been relieved by
a symbolic exercise with the Iranian navy, who were allies at
the time, and a brief port call in Mombassa, Kenya. Those
three days of liberty in Africa were crazy, but those stories
were best left untold.

What fascinated him nearly forty years ago was watching
the two nuclear powered ships racing at twenty-eight knots to
push the Soviet navy cruisers shadowing them to run out
of gas.

They waited until the Russians stopped to refuel their
"coal burners," then the U.S. ships tore over the horizon. In a
cold war version of hide and seek, the *Enterprise* and the
Truxtun vanished. It was with great mirth they tracked the
Soviet Bear reconnaissance plane flying around trying to relo-
cate them. Now as captain of the *Lincoln*, he was about to give
the Chinese a taste of this old Cold War tactic.

"Captain? The escorts are on station. Admiral Gireaux
has ordered us to set EMCOM alpha."

"Very well. Shut her down."

At that, the *Lincoln* and her escorts ceased all radiated
emissions from her radars and communications equipment.
For all intents and purposes, the Strike Group vanished in the
vast expanse of the Pacific Ocean. The *Stout's* electronic
warfare specialists completed the deception. They turned on
their own set of emitters and acoustic simulators to mimic
those of the Strike Group.

Chapter Fifteen

PLAN MARITIME PATROL PLANE, RED STRIKE
THE GULF OF TONKIN
09:34 TUESDAY 25 FEBRUARY

R ed Strike searched the horizon from the command seat of his PLAN Y-8MP maritime patrol plane. He'd been in the air several hours approaching its assigned station off the coast of Vietnam. Its mission: to intercept the Lincoln Strike Group. The distant solid bank of dark clouds portended trouble. Would he be able to visually confirm the presence of the American battlegroup?

He straightened in his seat, honored that he'd been selected for the mission. General Xiao and the senior leadership of the PLA understood if they were to realize their goal of controlling the South China Sea, they would have to neutralize the American Seventh Fleet.

Red Strike dismissed the rumors that more thoughtful voices within the government wished the generals would consider the other outcomes. Xiao ignored their concerns, swept caution aside, and advanced his timelines. The success of his intercept mission was deemed critical to the PLA's strategy to counter the American carriers.

The integral component to be evaluated in today's live-fire exercise was an experimental over-the-horizon targeting system suspended below the patrol plane's fuselage, a knock off of the American C-130. The heart of this system was a modified version of the British Rascal Searchwater Radar capable of guiding a KR-1 anti-ship missile launched from another aircraft toward a target over two hundred miles away.

The PLA abandoned an earlier effort to install a less sophisticated system on their aging IL-76 bombers, opting instead to pursue an integrated system consisting of the radar carrying patrol plane working in tandem with the new Xian JH-7 and Sukhoi Su-30 fighter-bomber regiments.

Red Strike's aircraft was configured to validate new targeting technology. His success would further the PLA's goal of achieving over-the-horizon targeting for the Moskit anti-ship missile.

The patrol plane also carried the new M400 reconnaissance system suspended in a second pod. This system would provide the targeting and guidance required for the Moskit. This weapons system would be a powerful deterrent to the American Strike Groups.

There was another top-secret piece of the Chinese deterrent being deployed to support the Spratly strike force. Known only by Xiao and his inner circle, one of the new Kilo 636 class diesel submarines had received orders to head east. The submarine incorporated the latest stealth technology with an advanced targeting system for the Klub anti-ship missile and would soon give the unsuspecting Yankees fits.

The small group of PLA generals sharing tea with Xiao this morning had ample reason to exchange expressions of optimism with one another. Their ambitious plans to confront the Americans and rectify their recent political setbacks resulting from the embarrassing debacle in the Spratlys were underway.

Red Strike Actual could not permit himself the luxury of dwelling on the motivations of his superiors. His instruments were registering the first hits from the American Strike Group and the weather wasn't cooperating. He pushed his misgivings about firing a missile in the direction of an American warship to the back of his mind.

The cold front moved in, bringing clouds and slashing bursts of rain. Visibility deteriorated. He couldn't see the ocean surface. He'd have to rely on the aircraft's upgraded navigation and avionics suites.

Red Strike knew there would be breaks in the clouds. There had to be. He would descend and take pictures of the American ships when they emerged from the leading edge of the front.

Red Strike reached the intercept point in another thirteen minutes. He tensed. The surface search radar hadn't registered the expected signals to account for all the American ships.

He dismissed his technician's concerns. "The Strike Group's course and speed are exactly as I predicted. Check your system."

He spotted a break in the cloud cover and put the patrol plane in a slow glide. Two wakes popped into view. A destroyer and a supply ship were at the head of these telltale markers.

"See, aren't the Americans just where I said they would be?"

"Yes, comrade," his copilot replied. "We have visual confirmation of several of the escorts and we have clear electronic intercepts from the carrier, but where is it? We must update headquarters with the course and speed of the American Strike Group."

"Yes, yes. I know."

"But "

"We'll retrace our steps. The carrier must be hidden by the clouds."

Silence greeted this order, compelling him to provide amplification. "We are being tracked by the American air-search radars, are we not? Place your call."

"Yes, sir."

The copilot did not want to join his commander and stick his neck out in this ruse, only to have it lopped off by the squadron commander. "Hainan, this is Red Strike. We have visual confirmation of several elements of the American Strike Group. We are expanding our search pattern to confirm the presence of the carrier."

The co-pilot's wording earned him a sharp look from Red Strike.

"Where is that damn carrier?" Red Strike muttered under his breath. They had sighted the *Stout* and *Supply*, but otherwise the sea was empty. Time was being lost and his next check-in was due. Taking a deep breath, he made the call himself. There was no sense dragging the others down with him.

"Hainan, this is Red Strike Actual. We cannot confirm the presence of the carrier."

Dead air greeted his call. This came as no surprise to Red Strike, though he had wished for better.

The response came through his headphones a moment later. "Red Strike, confirm your last."

"We have not seen the carrier."

"Say again, Red Strike. You cannot confirm the carrier's location?"

A different voice came over the speaker, an angry one Red

Strike recognized as his commanding officer's. "How's that? Where is it?"

Sweat beaded on Red Strike's forehead. "I don't know, sir."

"What have you been doing up there for the past hour, scratching your butt?"

This rhetorical question was followed by one demanding an answer. "What have your sensors shown?"

"Comrade Colonel, we have electronic verification of the carrier, but no visual sighting."

"What of your surface search radar?"

He felt compelled to lie. "It reads two signals, but I can't validate them. We have experienced difficulty with its calibration."

"There are only two ships, you fool. The Yankees have duped you. Not only have you failed in the test of our targeting system, you have lost the Americans. There is nothing wrong with your instruments. The carrier is nowhere in the area. Have I taught you nothing?"

"I will find the carrier, Comrade Colonel."

"We will have ample time to discuss your failure after you return to base. In the meantime, I will calculate the Strike Group's possible location and vector you accordingly. We must assume the Americans are heading toward our flotilla. Your lack of attention to duty has compromised our mission to avenge our comrades."

Red Strike gripped the yoke, striving to suppress the tremors racking his body. He knew his fate.

Chapter Sixteen

USS ABRAHAM LINCOLN CVN-72
SOUTH CHINA SEA
05:10 WEDNESDAY 26 FEBRUARY

Gireaux made his way to the darkened flag bridge. The solitude provided him the opportunity to collect his thoughts. He'd just issued his orders setting in motion the actions necessary to locate the PLAN flotilla. Time would tell if he would succeed.

The first of his messages had gone to Admiral Triebull on the *Blue Ridge,* requesting real time surveillance support. This would provide the coverage he needed until one of his own planes was in position to track the Chinese ships. Triebull, in turn, had forwarded the request to the Commander, Patrol and Reconnaissance Wing One at Kamiseya who scrambled his ready P-8 Poseidon from Kadena Air Force Base on Okinawa.

He took a sip of dark-roast coffee from his personal mug and focused on the flight deck. A shadow in the 'Junkyard' located aft of the island caught his eye. A squat, beetle-like tractor, part of the assemblage of yellow painted vehicles used to service the carrier's aircraft detached itself from the stationary objects surrounding it and set course for the 'Hummer Hole'. A rapid series of chops from a crewman's flashlights signaled the tractor had reached its destination, a tow bar projecting from the forward landing gear assembly of an E-2D Hawkeye.

Satisfied, Gireaux set off for the Combat Information Center.

The primary mission of the E-2D was airborne early warning. The plane also served the fleet in multiple other roles, including command and control, and targeting. Nicknamed the Hummer because of the distinctive noise created by its turbofan engines, the Hawkeye was an ungainly looking bird with a large saucer-shaped radar rotodome perched on its back. Its appearance, though, was more than compensated by the aircraft's value to the Strike Group. Defenseless, it would be provided an escort by two F/A-18E Super Hornet fighters from the Black Aces of VFA-41.

———

US NAVY EP-3E ORION, SEA BIRD
PATROL SQUADRON TWENTY-TWO
06:45

"So far, so good," Sea Bird commented to his copilot as he completed a course change to the southeast. "We'll see if we get any reaction from the Chinese."

"Sea Bird. Raven."

The Navy pilot recognized the voice of his Air Force teammate. Swiveling his head, he scanned the sky.

"Raven. Sea Bird."

"Sea Bird, I have two contacts lifting off the PLA airfield

near Fuzhou vectoring for intercept. Their signatures identify them as J-7s."

Not much escaped Raven. He piloted an E-2C Sentry, the big brother of the Navy's Hummer. The 961st AACS squadron's moniker, "Eyes of the Pacific" was apt. The electronic eyes of the surveillance plane could identify and track with precision anything within hundreds of miles.

"Roger that, Raven. We copy two J-7s. Appreciate the heads up."

The J-7 was the designator given the PLA Air Force's version of the Soviet Mig-21 jet interceptor. The crew of the P-8 Poseidon knew them well. The Navy pilots were even able to recognize the faces of several of the Chinese pilots, who had distinguished themselves from their comrades by flashing hand-written signs from their cockpits at the Americans.

The signs were not flattering, but they did provide a diversion. Their hot-dogging behavior had also resulted in a midair collision with another P-8 just over a year ago. The Chinese pilots had exercised sounder judgment after the incident, but their shadowing of the Navy patrol planes was still a hair-raising experience.

Sea Bird completed his transmission, banked his aircraft, and set a course to the PLAN ships. Distancing himself from the J-7s, the crew of the Poseidon focused their attention on finding their quarry.

———

Ninety miles away, the crew of the E-2D Sentry kept tabs on the J-7s until the Chinese reversed course to their base. His mission complete, Raven altered course to the northeast as the rising sun pierced the horizon off their starboard wingtip. He only had a moment to relax before a voice came over his headset.

"Major?"

"Yes, Levinson?"

"Sir, we just picked up three aircraft taking off from Luishing."

"Luishing's the PLAN's airfield on Hainan Island. Wonder what they're up to?"

"You get an ID?"

"No, sir. They're at the edge of our range."

"Okay. Pass on what you have to Kadena."

Tired from the long mission, he relinquished the yoke to his copilot. "Doug, take us home."

———

USS ABRAHAM LINCOLN CVN-72
SOUTH CHINA SEA

"Admiral?"

Gireaux turned at the sound of his Chief of Staff's voice. "Yes, Sandy?"

"Sir, we just heard from Sea Bird. They've picked up the Chinese. They'll have them visual in forty-five."

"Do you have their current position?"

"Yes, sir."

"Let's take a look."

The Strike Group's and the Chinese's projected courses at sequential points of time were marked with a series of arcs representing the forward edge of Gireaux's E-2D's 350-mile electronic search capability.

From these, he deduced the flying time the Hawkeye would need to acquire and maintain contact with the Chinese flotilla. He then made a quick estimate of the refueling requirement for the F-18s. The fighters were going to be airborne longer than the standard mission cycle from launch to landing.

"Admiral, looks like we'll make it."

"So, it appears. Let's get the birds aloft and line up refueling."

"My money is on the Chinese splitting their force. They'll bypass Pagasa and send most of their combatants to chase the Filipinos from Scarborough Reef. They can deploy the remainder of their force to their installation on Mischief Reef."

"Let's see if we can change their plans."

The Hummer, manned by a five-member crew from the Wall-bangers of Navy Carrier Airborne Early Warning Squadron, VAW 117, took to the air first. The three tactical data systems operators took little notice when the catapult flung their aircraft off the forward edge of the flight deck as they set up for the mission.

These specialists were now monitoring the computer consoles of their APS-145 antennae array. An integral piece of Sea Shield, the nation's new missile defense system, the array represented a quantum leap in capability. The electronically steered design provided Gireaux with continuous 360-degree search capability for target tracking. For today's mission, the system provided the Sun Kings a robust mechanism to monitor mundane objects such as ships and airplanes.

The senior petty officer pressed his intercom button. "Skipper, we're up and operational."

Aboard *Lincoln*, the swirling cloud of steam created by the launch of the E-2D had not yet dissipated before the flight-deck crew sprang into action. Under the critical eye of the catapult officer, two F/A-18F Super Hornets were positioned for takeoff.

The pilot of the starboard fighters completed his pre-launch checklist and gave the plane captain a thumbs-up to start turning the aircraft's engines. His name and rank stenciled just below the canopy rail identified him. Lieutenant Commander Marc "Diego" Koch, the squadron's executive officer.

All was ready. The crew disconnected the engine start cart. The catapult officer stood to attention and rendered a crisp return salute.

Koch advanced his throttles, powering them to a full crescendo. Verifying their performance from the digital readouts of his instrument panel, he kicked in his afterburners. A gut-wrenching roar consumed the air.

The catapult officer lunged forward, throwing his left arm downward until it touched the deck. The F-18 leapt off the forward edge of the flight deck driven by the duel forces of the catapult and the twin blue-white cones of fire from its engines. Fifteen seconds later, the second fighter was in the air. The entire choreographed launch sequence for the three planes had taken one-hundred and sixty seconds.

Moments after they were airborne, the Lincoln's commanding officer secured from EMCOM alpha. The Chinese would soon know his ship was in the area and there was no reason to go in blind.

Koch watched his wing mate, Lieutenant "Pele" McCormick, join up and did a communications check. "Merlin Two. Merlin One. How copy?"

Flashing a thumbs-up to Koch, McCormick responded. "I have you Lima-Charlie, Merlin One."

"Roger that, Merlin Two. We'll assume station off the Hummer."

Koch had been briefed on the rules of engagement in the event of trouble. You could never predict what might happen on a mission such as this, but as the carrier receded in the distance, he felt confident they would only have to be alert for a surface-to-air-missile threat.

Confident there was no way the Chinese could have any

aircraft in the area, he nonetheless alerted his Weapon System Operator, seated behind him.

"Wizzoes, let me know if you see or hear anything weird."

"Anything in particular?"

"No, man. We just don't want to be surprised."

"Roger that."

"You ready to run through the weapon and navigation systems?"

"Yeah, let's do it."

The two aviators completed their systems checks in short order and were talking about the new movies the Osprey delivered when a transmission interrupted.

"Merlin One. Virgil."

"Merlin One. Go Virgil."

"Merlin One, we have a contact zero-three-zero. Three bogies. Two closing Sea Bird. One appears to be falling back."

"Got an ID?"

"Negative, Merlin. No one's supposed to be out here but us. CIC has requested a Kill Track. I'm refining my beam."

"Affirm. Keep me posted."

Several minutes later Virgil provided his update. "Merlin One, we have confirmed two bandits descending through fifteen-thousand closing Sea Bird at four-hundred knots. They'll have her in their crosshairs in fifteen minutes."

"Roger that, Virgil. You have Sea Bird?"

"Working it."

"Copy. Patch me through when you do. We're calling the carrier."

"Home Plate, Home Plate. Merlin One. We've got two bandits closing Sea Bird at four-hundred knots. They'll be on them in less than fifteen minutes. There's a third contact that's fallen back. Virgil's raising Sea Bird. We'll patch the call."

"Merlin One, Umpire. Join with Sea Bird and provide escort. Stay on your toes."

"Aye, aye, Umpire. Wilco."

"Wizzoes, you pick up on the voice?"

"Yeah, the Admiral's calling the shots."

————

"Sandy, we on the same page?" Gireaux asked his Chief of Staff.

"Yes, sir."

"Get the tanker and Ready-5 in the air. It's time to let the Chinese know we're in the neighborhood. Confirm the strike package and place the aircrews on alert in case things turn south."

"Admiral?"

Gireaux pivoted to face his intelligence officer.

"Sir, those are J-8s. The third is their tanker."

"What's your confidence level?"

"High. The PLAN's 25th Regiment of their 9th Air Division has accepted delivery of the new J-8Ds. These aircraft have air-to-air refueling capability giving them a six-hundred-mile combat radius. Intelligence indicates they began limited extended range intercept exercises this past November."

"What else?"

"An hour ago, we were copied to a message from Raven. At the end of their mission they reported three aircraft lifting off from Luishing Airfield. Sir, that's the 25th Regiment's base."

Gireaux didn't need any more. "Sandy, draft a flash message for my release to Seventh Fleet and please inform the Captain I'd like to have a word with him. We're going to have a busy day."

Chapter Seventeen

F/A-18F SUPER HORNET MERLIN ONE
SOUTH CHINA SEA
07:20 WEDNESDAY 26 FEBRUARY

"Merlin One, Virgil."

"What's up, Virgil?"

"We've got Sea Bird. Figure you'd want to introduce yourselves. We'll patch you through."

"Roger that, Virgil. Standing by. Wizzoes, you working the frequencies?"

"On it. The P-8 guys must be feeling the sky's a bit crowded with all the company."

"Merlin One, Virgil. You should have them now."

"Thanks, Virgil," Koch said. Keep our comms open with Home Plate. Sea Bird, Merlin One. How do you copy?"

"Loud and clear, Merlin One. It's getting pretty interesting up here."

"What's your status?"

"We've got a couple of J-8 Finbacks bracketing the aircraft. They want us to follow them."

"Copy that. What's their —?"

"Whoa!"

"Sea Bird?"

"Merlin, we just had a near miss. I've got turbulent air."

"Affirmative, Sea Bird. On our way. Wizzoes, bring up Virgil and get a vector for intercept. Home Plate? Are you copying?"

The Carrier Air Group Commander came on the line. "Merlin One. You've got a bunch of guys sitting at the edge of their seats. Get those bandits out of there. Umpire is standing by to authorize weapon release if the situation warrants. We're launching the Ready-5."

On cue, the flight leader of the two VFA-251 Hornets on standby to launch in five minutes, checked in. "Merlin, Shotgun. How copy?"

"Shotgun, we have you Lima Charlie. Glad to have the Black Aces on board. We're coordinating the intercept with Virgil."

"Merlin One," Sea Bird broke in. "Our sitrep is shitty."

———

Gireaux leaned forward and pressed his hands over his earphones. *Damn.* "Sandy, the Chinese are desperate. They can't have much fuel. Let's hope they don't do anything stupid."

"I wouldn't count on it, sir."

"We'll—"

Sea Bird cut Gireaux off. "Tally ho, Merlin. They just went weapons hot. Rolling into evasive maneuvers."

Koch didn't wait for guidance. "Pele. Drop your auxiliary tank. Stay with me."

Two resonating booms sounded as the F-18s broke the sound barrier. Racing toward Sea Bird at six-hundred and seventy knots, the fighters were gulping fuel from their internal tanks.

Virgil needed no reminder the F-18s would need recovery tanking to make it home. The F/A-18E, Sea Wolf, with a refueling pod slung under its port wing was standing by to provide that service.

"Sea Wolf One Three Seven. Virgil."

"Virgil, Sea Wolf. We're on heading three-five-five, four-hundred fifty knots, climbing through four-seven-zero-zero feet."

"Sea Wolf, continue your present course and speed. Level at ten. We'll direct you to the rendezvous point for Merlin."

Virgil took control of the airspace and brought the fighter escort up on the net. "Shotgun, Virgil. How copy?"

"Solid copy, Virgil. You going to get us in the action?"

"Affirm. Stay tuned. Same Bat time, same Bat channel."

"Admiral, Merlin should have a visual on Sea Bird in eight minutes."

Gireaux nodded affirmation to the CAG and addressed the CIC watch officer. "Commander, do we have any indication those J-8s know we're closing?"

"No, sir."

The CAG filled in the details. "Admiral, Virgil is circling outside the effective range of their radars. Merlin is making his approach on the deck. We should surprise them."

"It's still a crap shoot," Gireaux replied. "We'll know soon enough if Koch can convince the Finbacks to break off."

A broken transmission from Sea Bird silenced the room. "W..er..aken..its!"

Virgil responded first. His call, much closer to the truth than he could have imagined. "Say again, Sea Bird. You are breaking up."

A different voice, strained but controlled, answered. "Virgil, we've taken rounds. Nobody's hurt. I've got damage outboard the port wing and a fire warning light for number two engine."

"Roger, Sea Bird," Virgil affirmed. "Do you have visual on the J-8s?"

Sea Bird scanned the sky before answering. He didn't see the Chinese jets. What he did see caused his ass to tighten—a silver vapor trail streaming behind his battered left wing.

"Virgil, we're losing fuel. We may not have enough to make it home. I'm switching tanks to seal it off."

"Sandy," Gireaux said, "I'm not willing to take the risk. That's a long way home over open water for those kids flying a damaged aircraft."

"The strip on Pagasa may be long enough."

"We don't have a choice. Divert them. Eagle Flight can provide escort."

"Admiral, they'll have to announce their intentions in the clear and hope the Filipinos are listening."

"Get'em movin'."

"Sea Bird, Home Plate. You have a BINGO. Broadcast an in-flight emergency over the international band and divert to the AFP airfield on Pagasa Atoll. Virgil will provide range and bearing."

"Roger, Home Plate. Affirm, Bingo. Diverting to Pagasa."

"Virgil? You copy?"

"Lima Charlie, Home Plate."

"Clear those J-8s out of the area," Gireaux ordered. To the CAG he ordered, "Get a FLIR in the air. This is no time to be blind with one of those Kilos lurking around. Coordinate the ASW effort with *Honolulu* and the surface screen. Sandy, get the watch officer at Seventh Fleet on secure."

Gireaux removed his headset and turned his attention to a

bank of monitors. The F-18 carrying an AT-FLIR would soon provide real-time visual to the command center.

"Home Plate. Merlin Lead."

"Merlin Lead. Home Plate," Gireaux answered.

Sea Bird recognized the Admiral's voice, "Umpire, we have Sea Bird."

"Copy that, Merlin. At my mark, commence your run at four-five- zero feet. Give the bandits a minute, then light them up with your targeting radar. Stay alert. Virgil will direct Sea Bird to decrease her airspeed and make a gradual turning descent to the north. Do you copy?"

"Wilco, Umpire," Koch replied repeating the orders.

Gireaux contacted the Hummer. "Virgil. Update Sea Bird's status."

"Umpire, Sea Bird at two-hundred fifty knots, heading zero-six-zero, altitude four thousand."

"Virgil. Umpire. Execute."

"Aye, aye, Umpire."

Gireaux flexed his fingers. "Merlin Lead, stand by for my order."

"Wilco."

"Merlin Lead, Umpire. Execute." He turned to the CAG. "You have tactical control."

"Home Plate, Merlin Lead. Confirm we have an execute."

"Affirmative, Merlin. Go weapons red."

Koch gave the order to arm their AIM-120 AMRAAM and AIM-9 Sidewinder air-to-air missiles. "Go hot."

Wizzoes engaged the Fire Inhibit Switch. "Master arm on. Weapons hot."

"Merlin Two hot," McCormick said.

"Pele, follow me in," Koch directed. "I'll take the guy on the right. You have his wingman."

"Roger that."

Koch pointed the F-18's nose up and confirmed his digital readouts. "Wizzoes, take us in. I'll level at four-six feet and light'em up."

"I have them straight in. Three miles."

Before he could respond, Koch observed a flash of sunlight off the canopy of one of the Finbacks. The two Chinese jets were breaking left in pursuit of the fleeing patrol plane. He only had an instant to react. "Damn, they're going after Sea Bird. The lead guy is lining up for another firing run."

"We've too close for the birds," Pele said.

"Roger that. Change of plans."

Koch pushed his throttles forward and began his turn to close the Chinese jet. "Pele, I'll take him. Cover my six. We're positioning for a deflecting shot."

Listening to the exchange, Gireaux came up on the net. "Merlin Lead. Umpire. Pop the J-8 with your radar. Fire a warning burst if he doesn't break off. If he goes weapons hot, take him out."

"Wilco, Umpire."

––––––––

The Chinese pilot pressed home his attack under orders to cripple the American spy plane. He centered the P-8 in his gun sight and squeezed off a short burst from his cannons. The missile warning tone in his headset went off before he could send another stream of 30mm shells at the fleeing plane. He was being targeted. Undeterred, he fired again. His rounds sliced through the thin skin of the American aircraft.

––––––––

Sea Bird's aircraft shuttered from the impact of the J-8's cannons. "Merlin, we're taking fire."

"Sea Bird. Merlin Lead. I'm on him."

Koch switched channels. "Umpire, Umpire. The bandits have gone weapons hot." He didn't wait for a response. "Engaging now."

Koch adjusted his angle of attack and focused on his heads-up display. *Good. A little more to the center. All right, just a little more. Gotcha.* He depressed the trigger of his Vulcan cannon. A stream of high explosive 20mm shells walked along the fuselage of the Finback.

The effect was immediate. The Chinese jet began to smoke and lose altitude. Flames winked from the fatal wound to its engine.

Koch voiced his feelings on the result. "AMF."

"We splashed the bastard," Wizzoes added.

Koch called the carrier. "Umpire. Merlin One. We have a confirmed kill. The pilot has blown his canopy and ejected."

"Merlin—"

McCormick's voice cut off Gireaux. He had seen the stricken J-8's wing mate maneuver behind Koch. "Sponge, he's on you."

Koch pulled back on his stick and executed a vertical climb. His missile warning alarm went off. "We're painted."

He hit his rudder and rolled into a hard-right diving turn. Forced into his seat by the maneuver, his G-suit inflated keeping blood flowing to his brain. He heard McCormick's voice over the blare of the missile alarm. "Vampire. Vampire. You've got a heater. Evade."

"Chaff," Koch reacted, initiating a series of jinks to evade the Chinese air-to-air missile. He craned his neck around and spotted the missile. The heat-seeking homing device in the Chinese missile's nose had ignored the chaff and was guiding on his engines.

Koch had one chance. "Bat-turn. Execute." He turned into the pursuing missile with a tight, high-G, one-hundred-eighty-degree turn.

The missile whizzed by his canopy at a combined closing speed of one-thousand miles per hour.

"Whoa! How you doing back there?"

"Are you nuts? I've gotta check my pants."

McCormick concentrated on the remaining J-8, too engaged to observe his wing mate. He confirmed a lock on the Finback.

He depressed the red firing button and felt a slight jolt as the missile left the rail. "Fox-3."

The AMRAAM's engine ignited when it fell clear of the aircraft. McCormick watched in fascination as it sped in a graceful arc toward the wildly maneuvering Finback.

"Merlin Two, you have a launch?"

"Affirmative, Umpire. Fox-3."

The Chinese pilot was either good, lucky, or both. Diving for the wave tops, he caused the missile to lose contact and plunge into the ocean behind him.

"Umpire, Merlin Two. The Sparrow splashed."

"Merlin Two," Koch answered, "Let him go. Form up."

"Pele, I owe you one."

"You can buy me a beer when we get home."

"You're on. How you set for fuel?"

"Running critical."

"We'll check in with Sea Bird, then gas up before we're left sucking fumes."

Koch keyed his mic to raise the patrol plane. "Sea Bird, Merlin Lead. Can you make it to Pagasa?"

"Yeah, think so. We're shot up, but airworthy. I don't like the feel of the rudder, though. Can you give us a visual?"

"Wilco."

Koch eased up to the damaged plane. What he saw shocked him. "Sea Bird, your vertical stabilizer and rudder are shot all to hell. They may hold together if they're not abused."

"Roger that. I'll take it easy."

Virgil's voice came up. "Merlin Lead, Shot Gun will assume escort. You are being vectored to Sea Wolf for refueling."

––––––––

PHILIPPINE ARMED FORCES BASE
PAGASA ATOLL

"Major, Major," the air control officer shouted as he burst through the open door of the command center. "We have received an emergency distress signal from an American patrol plane. They want to land here."

"What?"

"An American plane. They want to land here."

"Are you sure?"

"Yes, sir. Their call came over an open channel."

"ETA?"

"Less than ten minutes."

"Oh, shit." The Major leapt out of his chair, knocking it over, and sprinted out of the building. "Clear the airstrip. Get those things off the runway."

A confused knot of soldiers stared at him in response.

"A plane is coming!"

The men's consternation was not misplaced. After several hours of work, they had just finished positioning six concrete barriers across the runway to discourage any attempt by the Chinese to land troops on the island. The soldiers managed to remove all but two when they heard a low flying aircraft.

The major looked in the direction of the sound. He could just make out the distinctive silhouette of the American plane. A P-8. "Shit."

He cupped hands and yelled to the control tower. "Wave them–"

A F-18 thundered over the island cutting him off in mid-sentence. Undeterred, he screamed over the noise. "Wave them off. The runway's not clear."

———

Eagle Flight confirmed the warning. "Sea Bird, you have a fouled deck. Repeat, a fouled deck."

Sea Bird tightened his lips. He had no options other than acknowledge. "Affirm."

He lined up his aircraft and began the approach to the tiny island. His arms ached from wrestling with the sluggish controls of the damaged plane. He took a deep breath and lowered the landing gear.

Sea Bird shot a glance at his co-pilot.

"Gear down and locked."

They would have one chance. "Here goes."

———

The soldiers froze in disbelief, then scattered like quail. They just made it to safety before the plane impacted the coral landing strip.

Sea Bird cleared the first obstacle. He wasn't so lucky with the second. The right landing gear assembly clipped the barrier and the plane careened sideways down the runway. The P-8 slammed into the airstrip's wave barrier, enveloped in a cloud of swirling dust and smoke.

The crewmembers of the wrecked patrol plane were shaken, but alive. They began to stir. They checked themselves for injuries. Several peered at the island's control tower through what should have been the aft compartment of their aircraft. Their limited vista of the island was framed by jagged aluminum and dangling wires created when their aircraft's weakened tail section broke off.

Sea Bird stared at the water lapping against the leading

edge of the cockpit window. The two escorting Hornets of Eagle Flight snapped him out of his trance as they roared over them at treetop level. He blinked and watched the F-18s complete a starboard turn away from the island. He released the clips of his chest harness and looked at his co-pilot. "I guess we'll be needing to find another way home."

———

COMBAT INFORMATION CENTER
USS ABRAHAM LINCOLN

Gireaux listened to the reports coming in and addressed his Chief of Staff. "Sandy, the next move's up to them. Maintain the strike package on ready standby and confirm one of the Hornets is carrying the FLIX pod."

"Yes, sir."

"Now, who can update me on the threat to our aircraft?"

The CAG answered. "Admiral, The *Anyang* has a thirty-two cell VLS for their HHQ-16s. Max range, forty nautical miles. The rest of their ships carry HQ-7s."

"Keep'em circling out of range. Direct Sea Wolf Two to locate and drop survival gear for that downed Chinese pilot. The gesture may help cool things off."

"Home Plate? Vigil."

"Vigil, Umpire copies."

"Umpire, Sea Wolf Two reports a Chinese warship, hull number 112, has detached and assumed a course to pick up their downed pilot. The remainder of the PLAN flotilla has turned northwest."

Gireaux looked at the live images of the main body of the Chinese ships sent from the AT-FLIR equipped F-18 shadowing the PLAN flotilla. He had visual confirmation the Chinese had broken contact.

"Umpire affirms your last. Carry on."

"Admiral, it appears we've come out on top."

"I wouldn't count on it, Sandy."

———

What Gireaux didn't know was that one of the Chinese navy vessels had not turned for home. Stalking her prey, Kilo 636 trailed the *Lincoln,* undetected by the Strike Group's ASW screen.

Chapter Eighteen

THE WHITE HOUSE
WASHINGTON D.C.
05:10 WEDNESDAY 26 FEBRUARY

Stuart pulled on his pillow debating whether to give up and get dressed or try to go back to sleep. The bedside phone rang, making the decision for him. He focused on the blurred digital readout of the alarm clock. 0510. He reached for the phone almost dropping the hand-set. "President Stuart."

"Mr. President? Justin. I'm sorry to wake you, sir, but we've received an OPREP 3 PINNACLE/FRONT BURNER."

The code words swept the cobwebs away in an instant. "OPREP- 3" was the designator for a message requiring immediate action; "PINNACLE," a national emergency. "FRONTBURNER," an attack on U.S. forces.

"Ah, give me a sec. I'll take it in the study."

Looking over his shoulder to make sure he hadn't woken Dianne, he slid off the bed and made his way to the adjacent room. "What's going on?"

Stuart didn't interrupt as Brown explained.

"And there were no U.S. or Chinese casualties?"

"No, sir. Just the two aircraft."

"Does Richard know?"

"Not yet. Defense has been informed. Sheldon is expecting Bob's call."

"Would you call Richard and bring him up to speed?"

"Will do."

Stuart replaced the telephone and watched the secure phone light blink out. *Crap, here we go again.*

"Randall?" Dianne called from the bedroom.

"I'm sorry. I tried to be quiet."

"What's happening?"

"The Chinese. There's been an incident in the Spratlys."

"Is it serious?"

"They fired at one of our patrol planes. We shot down one of their fighters."

"Dear God. Is the crew safe?"

"I don't know. I need to go to the office."

———

Stuart looked at the yellow legal pad covered with his distinctive scrawl. He had completed the basic outline of his response in just over half an hour. His head throbbed. There were still a few holes to fill, but all in all, he was satisfied.

He removed his reading glasses, rubbed the bridge of his nose, and swiveled his chair to face the expanse of parks fronting the White House. His eyes came to rest on the Washington monument.

Fatigue washed over him. Light-headed and hungry, he grasped the arms of his chair. He pushed himself up and sauntered off to the small galley adjacent to the Oval Office where he found some granola after rummaging through the pantry and a container of milk in the refrigerator, then returned to his desk.

He took a slurpy bite of cereal and leafed through a pile of position papers in his inbox. He settled on one that addressed a Social Security reform package. Several drops of milk dribbled from his spoon and landed on the report creating a scatter of gray-white circles. *Well, that wasn't very Presidential.*

He wiped off the wet spots with his sleeve and commenced to read. He was deep in thought when the door to the outer office opened.

"Good morning, Mr. President," Mary Allus said. She handed him a folder of news clippings. "Your morning paper."

"How is it out there?"

"Nasty." Her face clouded. After all the years caring for her boss, nothing escaped her.

Stuart felt her gaze on his unshaven face and puffy eyes. "Couldn't sleep."

"That's pretty obvious. May I?" she replied, snatching away the cereal bowl and replacing it with a single sheet of paper with his schedule. She didn't expect him to elaborate. She would learn soon enough what new crisis had forced him into the Oval Office at this hour.

She gestured to the schedule. "We're going to need to change this."

"Can you squeeze in a meeting of the Principles later this morning?"

"I'll have the kitchen fix something for a working lunch."

He picked up the news clippings and responded without looking up. "That would be good. Thank you."

Mary Allus didn't move.

He set the papers down. "What?"

"Mr. President, I can fend off the hordes while you get cleaned up. It's now or never."

He ran his hand over the stubble on his face. "I'll be out of here in a minute. I wouldn't want to appear disheveled for my adoring public."

———

Stuart walked down the narrow hallway leading to the Oval Office feeling a bit more human after a shower and shave. He spotted Gilmore and Brown standing in the doorway of his Special Assistant's office and motioned them to follow.

"Let's get the day going."

Gilmore took a seat and waited until Brown closed the door. He flipped open his copy of the Presidential Daily Brief. Six minutes later, he finished.

"Thanks, Bryce, that'll be all. Justin, stay a minute, will you?"

He waited until the door clicked closed before handing Brown the legal pad with his notes. "You don't need to read those now. There isn't anything that should surprise you. The only change I've made is stepping up our timelines. We'll discuss the major points at eleven."

Brown peeked at the second page. "The Deputies Committee has been working the decision analysis for the issues outlined in the Presidential Review Directive you signed on the twentieth."

"I want an update on each of my numbered points. Their integration will be critical. If we do this right, we'll have the foundation to support our interests in the Pacific for years. If we don't, well…"

"We will get through this."

"There are a couple of variables we'll need to address."

Brown ventured. "The reactions of the Chinese and the press?"

"We'll have an easier time with Beijing."

Brown pulled on his chin. "We need to construct a cover

story for the loss of the P-8. I'd prefer not to go down this path, but we have no choice if we want any chance of containment."

"And the Chinese?"

"My guess is the Chinese will elect to keep their latest setback under wraps while they lick their wounds and nurse their anger. Richard believes they'll put on a conciliatory face to Manila to calm the ASEAN countries while they prepare to play hardball."

Brown set Stuart's notes on the coffee table. "It's time we bring in Bob. He needs to know what the Agency has going."

"Valid point, but Langley's piece should be handled offline. I've spoken with Sheldon and Bryce. I told them we have to keep the operation within the Agency. It has to be kept clean without any links to the military. I directed Bryce to work up the Memorandum of Notification to authorize the project."

Brown paused. "You know, those guys still have their contacts in Vietnam."

"I trust Bryce has nothing going on we don't know about."

"Nothing that I know of."

"Make sure."

———

THE ROOSEVELT ROOM
10:55

Brown dropped his notes on the conference table and looked at the portrait mounted over the fireplace at the far end of the room: Teddy Roosevelt storming up San Juan Hill with his Rough Riders. The portrait represented another piece of White House trivia. This picture of the Republican president was replaced with that of President Franklin D. Roosevelt when the Democrats held office.

He pondered these men's different approaches to governance. TR was known for his philosophy, 'Speak softly and carry a big stick.' FDR recognized that the war with Japan was as much about economics as it was territorial ambitions and nationalism. Placed within this historical context, the room and its representative portraits was an apt place for the NSC's deliberations.

"Hey, Justin, how you holding up?" Valardi asked to Brown's back.

"Oh, pretty well, considering," Brown replied. "I was just wondering how TR and Franklin D would deal with the Chinese."

Valardi slipped off his jacket and hung it on the back of his seat. "You think it's hot in here?"

"No, I'm fine," Brown said as Lawson and Payne entered the room. He handed them each a copy of Stuart's notes. "Bob, he'll want to know what you have on the aircrew."

Stuart strode in before Lawson could reply. "You read my mind. What's the latest?"

"Aside from some bruises and stiff muscles, they're fine, sir. We dispatched a C-130 to fly them back to Kadena. They're being examined and debriefed, then will be put under wraps. The P-8's a total loss, but they secured all the TS gear and took it out with them."

"Keep on top of it."

"Yes, sir."

"Richard, what do you have?"

"There's been no reaction from Beijing. For the moment, it appears they're content exchanging diplomatic protests with the Filipinos. A spokesman from the Chinese embassy in Manila issued a statement stating the raising of a Philippine flag by local fisherman on Scarborough Shoal was a serious violation of Chinese sovereignty and that a repetition would strain relations. If you will excuse the pun, that raises a red flag."

Valardi referred to his notes. "The release went on to say the Philippine Navy sent ships to the area to disrupt amateur radio activities on the island that had been organized by a non-governmental organization of China. That, of course, is just complete hogwash."

"Your interpretation?"

"My sense is they're trying to legitimize their position that they're the aggrieved party. The significant piece is General Xiao and his supporters in the Central Military Commission have suffered a series of embarrassing setbacks. The end result should result in a loss of credibility within the government for their entire agenda. That should weaken their influence at the 17th Party Congress meeting this fall."

"That's a lot of 'shoulds,' Richard. Who's calling the shots? The Foreign Ministry or Xiao?"

"I can't answer with certainty."

"You must have an opinion."

"The problem we're facing with the Chinese government is this: the political, fiscal, and social mechanisms that should allow them to manage this transition don't exist," Brown responded.

"Where does this leave the PLA?" Payne asked, ignoring another 'should.'

"I was about to get there. The CCP's Central Military Commission and the General Staff of the PLA view all of these developments with alarm in part because the General Staff's Department of Logistics controls thousands of factories and an immense workforce. With the CCP at risk of losing control and relevance, the PLA may well be positioning itself to fill the vacuum."

"Just terrific," Stuart said. "So, what you're telling me is we have no idea who will be in charge in China or what direction the country's going to take?"

"Not with certainty."

"What's the outlook for the People's Congress?" Stuart prodded.

"They'll follow the party line."

Stuart rolled his eyes. "Tell me something I don't know."

"The People's Congress should provide us some sense of the balance of power within the government, but it's just too far in the future."

Not placated, Stuart looked at his watch and cut off any further discussion. "That's another 'should.' We need to move on. Sheldon?"

"Mr. President, the PLA has not moved to a heightened alert status. Military communications remain at normal levels and surveillance has not detected any increase in activity at their air or naval bases."

"What about their flotilla?"

"The ships are returning to their home port with the exception of an auxiliary and a destroyer escort. Those two remain forward deployed. The AFP has informed our military attaché in Manila they are working with the Chinese to arrange for the transfer of the surviving crewmembers of the two patrol boats. Both sides aren't saying anything publicly about their negotiations."

"Working to cool things down?"

Valardi took a sip of ice water. "Presumably, but they're still taking jabs at each other."

"What are they saying?" Stuart asked.

"A spokesperson for President Montalvo said Manila will look into Beijing's protest over Scarborough Shoal," Valardi said.

"At least that's a start."

"Yes, but in the same breath they requested China provide a response to a protest submitted months ago concerning Beijing's occupation of Mischief Reef. The statement concluded by saying there was no need for protest and counter protest if each party followed the Code of Conduct proposed in the Manila Accords."

"That's a subtle dig," Brown said. "The Code's provisions for maintaining the status quo was signed by every regional country with a vested interest, except China."

Payne referred to his briefing book. "Precisely. I'm sure that's why Montalvo issued a press release from Malacanang Palace stating he ordered General Medeiros to strengthen the navy's presence in the Kalayaan Island group and intensify aerial surveillance of Panganiban Reef."

"Bob, what do they have? It can't amount to much."

"They're pretty much at the bottom of the barrel when it comes to deployable assets. Medeiros ordered two more patrol boats to sea in an essentially a symbolic gesture."

"Anything we can do to assist?"

"Besides leaving the *Lincoln* in the area for a few more days, we can put together a military assistance package that will marginally increase their capability over time,"

"But the Philippine military is in such a sorry state, it'll take years and an infusion of billions of dollars to build an effective force."

"True enough," Payne said.

Stuart glanced at TR's portrait. This wasn't the time to debate outcomes, they needed to charge the hill. "What do we need to do to push this foreword?"

"I'd suggest we frame our policy around the Status of Forces Agreement and Mutual Defense Treaty. I'd like to have my Assistant Secretary for Internal Security Affairs, Jim Crenshaw, begin working these with PACOM."

Stuart redirected Payne's suggestion. "Richard?"

"I'll hook him up with Adrian Clarke. Adrian's working the draft for a new approach, the Enhanced Defense Cooperation Agreement."

"Work the details and get them on the road. Richard, have we heard anything from the Japanese?"

Valardi jotted down a note as he answered. "Yesterday their Foreign Minister met with our ambassador. He expressed his government's concern about the implications for regional stability and appealed for calm. He made it clear Tokyo would not view with favor the use of our bases on Japanese territory as staging points for any action against the Chinese."

"I don't like the tone of those remarks," Gilmore said.

"We need to put them in context," Brown replied. "They have any number of economic agreements in the works with Beijing that will be jeopardized if the Chinese wanted to put the squeeze on them."

"Keep the Japanese in the loop and add Tokyo to Clarke's itinerary," Stuart said. "Bob, you're up."

"Short term, the *Lincoln* has to remain in the area. We tasked Seventh Fleet to look at CTF-70's upcoming deployment in case the *Washington* has to relieve her on station. Long term, we need to take a hard look at our OPLANs."

"I concur. What else?"

"We stood up the Joint Task Force 519 at Makalapa. The augmentation requirements for the command and control element have been identified. PacFleet is bringing in their analysts and planners."

"Any problems?"

"A few turf issues to resolve with the special ops component."

Stuart cocked his head.

"Nothing we haven't seen before."

"Bryce, you're up," Stuart said.

"We have intelligence from our sources in the Philippine Department of Foreign Affairs linking both the diplomatic and military assistance issues. There's also considerable interest in renewing the RP-US joint military training exercises on the scale of those in the past. The AFP wants to tie these to the Mutual Logistics and Support Agreement negotiations. Sheldon, you have anything to add?"

"The MLSA is structured as a continuance of the executive agreements negotiated in support of the war on terrorism. These provided the framework for the military equipment brought in by our forces for the Balikantan 06-1 war games in Basilan a couple of years ago."

Valardi's eyebrows knotted. "The Philippine government hasn't approached us on any of these issues."

"I suspect there are any number of reasons," Gilmore said. "For starters, the opposition by the Foreign Affairs Secretary, Florencia Cruz, and key opposition members of the Senate."

"I understand the Senate, but isn't the Secretary on our team?"

"We have a well-placed national who says he's angling to make a run for the Presidency."

"Who's your source?" Valardi asked.

Gilmore ignored the question. "The Chief of the Philippine National Police informed us he has unequivocal evidence the Chinese have their hand in stirring up the public demonstrations against a renewed American presence."

"Oh?" Valardi sputtered. "This explains their ambivalence to our overtures. Is the Secretary tied to this?"

"Not that we know of."

"Then he may rethink his stance. In any event, Malacanang should be more receptive to our proposals."

Gilmore looked at Stuart. "We can exert some subtle influence on the key players."

Stuart kept his face expressionless, but his brain was spinning. *Now what in the hell else is going on that I don't know about?* Instead of pursuing an answer, he ended the conversation.

"One more thing. The Foreign Ministers of the ten ASEAN countries met in Kuala Lumpur this past week and delayed signing the draft document, 'The Declaration on the Conduct of Parties in the South China Sea.'"

"What's its significance?" Payne asked.

"The document provides the framework to resolve disputes in the region. The meeting broke up with a press release stating it couldn't be signed. Numerous changes in the wording couldn't be resolved."

"Why doesn't that surprise me?" Stuart said.

"Par for the course, sir."

"We'll deal with it. Justin, you're up."

"There are two venues where we can exert our influence to get the Declaration untracked; the Council for Security Cooperation in the Asia-Pacific and the Asia-Pacific Economic Cooperation summit."

Stuart placed his hands on the table. "We need to wrap up. Justin, what haven't we covered?"

"We'll need to brief the Congressional leadership. It won't take much to stir up the House International Relations Committee when this gets out. They're already raising hell about the trade deficit."

"Dan has that," replied Stuart in a tone that was much calmer than he felt. "I'll be meeting with them this afternoon. I'll want you and Sheldon there. Set up a minimal notice press conference with the leadership. I want them standing at my side."

"Mr. President?"

Stuart couldn't conceal the fatigue in his voice. "What's on your mind, Justin?"

"We haven't had enough time to gauge Beijing's reaction."

"What do you suggest?"

"I'd take our lead from Manila."

"Is State comfortable with that?"

"We told Manila to put a muzzle on anything pertaining to the P-8 incident," Valardi replied.

"What about the press?"

"Malacanang announced the repatriation of the Chinese sailors they rescued. We can build on that," Brown answered.

"Interesting choice of words," Payne said.

"Yes," Valardi answered. "They reflect the tacit agreement Manila and Beijing reached to defuse the situation."

"And the press?" Stuart persisted.

"I'll take that," Brown said. "We should acknowledge the public statements made by the Chinese and Philippine governments. Our official position remains the same."

Payne spoke. "The press release should state the United States 'views with concern' the crisis in the South China Sea and that we will take those measures we deem necessary to maintain our interests in the region consistent with our long-standing position regarding existing treaties and freedom of navigation."

The harshness of the language alarmed Valardi. "My office can craft the appropriate language."

"Work the press release with John. I want to review the draft this afternoon."

"Yes, sir."

"Gentlemen, we're going to push forward on four fronts: diplomatic, economic, military, and covert. Justin has the lead and will prepare a National Security Policy Directive for my signature. Bryce will brief each of you on his operation. It is classified Top Secret - Eyes Only, code word: BLUE HORIZON."

Chapter Nineteen

PEARL HARBOR, HAWAII
06:38 WEDNESDAY 26 FEBRUARY

The morning sun highlighted the crater rim of Diamond Head and, across the island at Pearl Harbor, the soft trade winds stirred the fronds of the coconut palms. A solitary runner shattered the serenity of the new day.

Mike Rohrbaugh pounded across the wooden planks of the narrow pedestrian bridge spanning a listless stream. He entered a curve in the pathway and eased his pace to a comfortable jog before pulling up across from the Pacific Fleet boathouse.

His morning run had taken him along the narrow path paralleling the shore of East Lock, past Pearl Ridge, and beyond the power plant to his turn-around point three miles out. He would have caught a glimpse of the new Advanced SEAL Delivery System facility situated on the Pearl City peninsula had he gone a little farther.

Rohrbaugh clasped his hands behind his head, took several deep breaths, and dropped to the ground to pump out the first of several sets of pushups. He flipped over to stretch his legs. Things were beginning to look up.

At least for this morning anyway, he cautioned himself. On tap to conduct a site visit to SEAL Delivery Vehicle Team One, he had a follow-up Action Officer meeting scheduled later in the day at SubPac.

The thought elicited a self-deprecating snort. *Action Officer. Yeah, right.*

He was not a great fan of meetings, considering most of them monumental wastes of time. More often than not, he would find himself sitting on his butt listening to endless blather about somebody's inconsequential pet project.

He smiled at this assessment. *Boy, you're on a tear this morning.*

He recalibrated his attitude, reminding himself that this particular conference actually held promise. The brief was hosted by the Commander, Submarine Forces Pacific and would be his first opportunity to review the operational lash-up of the Advanced SEAL Delivery System with the Expeditionary Strikes Groups. He was curious how those efforts would pan out. The ESG concept of operations held real possibilities, and he was already working details on how they'd integrate with OPLAN 1729.

He jumped to his feet. *Up and at it. The day isn't getting any younger.*

―――――

DRY-DECK OPERATIONS FACILITY
SEAL DELIVERY VEHICLE TEAM ONE
07:45

"Hey, Skipper. You're sure a sight for sore eyes."

Chief Hull Technician Dante Vasquez strode across expanse of the dry-deck operations facility, delighted to see his old team leader. "I didn't know you were coming over, sir. Hell, nobody tells me anything around here."

"No secret, Chief, just early," Rohrbaugh replied, gripping Vasquez's outstretched hand. "I'm here for the hot wash. Rumor has it you're part of the team. You behaving?"

"Oh, as much as I can, sir, considering everything. Have you heard from the guys?"

Rohrbaugh sized up his former teammate. "Nope, nothing lately."

Vasquez had been injured in a training mishap while they were in the field together. He'd barely made it out. A further blow came when a medical board failed to clear him to return to a SEAL team. He took a new tact after the decision and targeted the Deep Submergence Program Office of the Naval Sea Systems Command. The Directorate program officer overseeing the ASDS project relented under Vasquez's onslaught and assigned him as a supporting chief for the two-member crews performing the tests and evaluations of the new mini-sub.

Rohrbaugh looked over Vasquez's shoulder and cast a professional eye at the sub. "Give me a tour after the brief?"

"Yes, sir. She's a great piece of gear. None finer. The teams love it. We'll need to take you out."

"Roger that, Chief. Right now, I need to know the heading for the conference room."

"Aye, aye, Commander. If you'll follow me to the break in the bulkhead, sir."

Rohrbaugh returned to the dry-deck shelter an hour later. He caught sight of Vasquez near the bow of the ASDS. His path took him along the full length of the submersible.

Stern planes and prop look pretty much like a fast attack boat. Lighter colored rectangle centered in the hull. Side-looking sonar? Smaller panel? A bow thruster? Gull wing access door presumably for the crew. Humm, no sail like a regular submarine. Wonder how you see out of the damn thing?

Vasquez looked up at the sound of approaching footsteps.
"Hey, Commander, how was the brief?"

"You ought to know the answer to that."

"Yes, sir. I do, sir. I stand corrected, sir."

"Right answer."

Vasquez smiled and waved his arm in the general direction
of the ASDS. "You like her?"

"How about you tell me?"

"Aye, aye. I'll start with the basics. Displaces fifty-five tons
on the surface, 65 feet long, 8-foot diameter. The two-man
operating crew is situated in a forward compartment. Eight-
man team rides dry in the pressurized compartment aft.
Plenty of room for mission-configured cargo. Lockin/Lockout
from the hyperbaric chamber allows egress at considerable
depth. Speed, max submerged depth, range and endurance
classified top-secret. All 'Need to Know,' sir."

"Yeah, right."

"Roger that, sir. Actually, there's a little more to the story."

"So, I've heard."

"Yes, sir. The acceptance trails set us back. We had to wait
until the new lithium ion technology was perfected. Another
piece was the propeller. The cavitation gave us an unsat
acoustic signature. Damn near anyone could have heard us
coming. At any rate, we looked at the number of blades and
configuration of the cruciform vortex dissipaters and got a
good fix. The redesigned propeller system has eliminated the
noise and given us a top end of eight knots submerged.

"Matter of fact, you wouldn't believe what we went
through to find the ideal type of steel for blast/shock hardening. The engineers had to…"

Vasquez's voice trailed off when Rohrbaugh's eyes began
to glaze. "Ah, sorry for the dive into the weeds."

"No problem, Chief, but you were leaving me behind. Do
we still have those two subs configured?"

"Yes, sir. Both the *Greenville* and *Charlotte* are fitted with latching pylons. Better yet, the *Carter* is on her way. She's a real force multiplier. Say, Skipper, you got a minute for me to show you the ropes?"

"Lead the way."

"Step lively, sir."

Vasquez climbed up the ladder leading up to the open gull-wing door of the control room and eased into the right-hand co-pilot's seat. Rohrbaugh followed and settled in beside him.

"Welcome aboard Boat One, Skipper. I'll let you drive."

"Fine, and just how would I go about doing that?"

Vasquez pulled a set of car keys out his pocket and jangled them.

"Alright, knock it off."

Rohrbaugh tapped the joystick set before him. "This have anything to do with it?"

"Roger that, sir. The joystick's a great idea. Gives you a real feel for the boat."

"How do you see where in hell you're going?"

A non-hull-penetrating periscope is paired up with the snorkel. That unit and the radio/ESM mast fold back on the hull for stowage. Our inertial guidance is outstanding. Sure beats our old open water navigation system. All we have to do is plug in our predetermined course, speed and depth into the computer. The navigation system guides us hands-off through the entered waypoints."

Rohrbaugh whistled. "Impressive."

"The boat commander pilots the sub from your seat. Delicate maneuvering is executed by retractable bow and stern thrusters."

"How's he selected?"

"All the pilots are department head tour submariners selected from a pool of volunteers. Before they start training, they complete the five-week Navy Dive School course in Panama City."

"Makes sense. The copilot?"

"Post platoon commander, SDV qualified."

"Good to have one of our guys up front."

"Yes, sir. The copilot handles lockin/lockout, sensors, comms, and life support. Skipper, I can't begin to tell you how much better this vehicle is. The stress and fatigue when we had to ride wet in the old MK VIII is eliminated."

Rohrbaugh couldn't discount Vasquez's enthusiasm and from all appearances, the ASDS was a neat piece of gear. "You're a believer, Chief?"

"Yes, sir. I'd trust my life on her."

"When can you get me a ride?"

"I suspect you may be getting more than a ride, sir."

Rohrbaugh cocked his head. *More? What's that about?*

———

FLEET INTELLIGENCE CENTER, COMPACFLT
10:17

Mackenzie checked his watch. Under ordinary circumstances, it wouldn't have mattered if Rohrbaugh was running late, but the Ops Boss had called an unscheduled meeting to review the crisis in the Spratlys. The scuttlebutt was the situation could go critical any moment.

He frowned and turned back to thumb through the pile of reports and background information he'd gathered on potential targets.

Rohrbaugh drew up short when he entered the room. Prepared to share his visit to SDVT-1, he stowed the thought. "What's up, Senior? You've got that look on your face that spells trouble."

"Nothing good, Commander. We've got a situation in the Spratlys. Captain Lane's set a meeting for 1100."

"What the hell happened?"

Mackenzie handed him the message folder containing Gireaux's flash messages. "Be easier if you read these."

Rohrbaugh set the folder down after reading the messages and pointed to the pile of paper on Mackenzie's desk. "What you got there?"

"Stuff off the internet," Mackenzie replied spreading out a pile of pictures. Commercial satellite imagery. Not too different from those our Intel guys provided, but there are some shots providing a different perspective of the Chinese installations."

Rohrbaugh looked over Mackenzie's shoulder. "They don't seem particularly threatening stuck out in the middle of the ocean like that, but we'd have to take into consideration there's no cover for an insertion. Where are they?"

"The first images show two structures on an atoll named Mischief Reef. It's reported to be an observation and communication post with a garrison force of four hundred. The strategic significance is its proximity to Palawan Island and the Malampaya offshore gas fields. These are Johnson, Subi, and Fiery Cross Reefs."

Rohrbaugh picked up one of the photos.

"Subi reef."

Mackenzie pulled a chart from the open drawer of his file cabinet and slid it across the table. "Here, Skipper, this should help. I've been running down anything I can find on their installations and set up a corresponding database.

"They've got stuff scattered all over the damn place. Marker buoys at Sabina, First Thomas Shoal, and Pennsylvania Shoals. Installations of various sizes on Fiery Cross, Cuarteron, Johnson, Subi, and Mischief Reefs as well as Woody and Rocky Islands in the Paracels. All told, we're looking at some one thousand troops scattered over seven islands."

Rohrbaugh scanned the data base. "Is there a Second Thomas Shoal?"

"So happens, there is. The place has an interesting history. The AFP grounded one of the landing ships on the shoal back in '99 after the Chinese occupied Mischief Reef. They've got a platoon of Marines living on board to establish sovereignty."

"Eight Marines hardly constitutes a deterrent," Rohrbaugh said.

"I wouldn't be so sure, Skipper. The PLAN has devoted a lot of resources blockading the place. The Marines are resupplied by air-drop."

"Maybe 'irritant,' would be a better characterization."

"Gotta hand it to them. The didn't roll over."

"Solid work, Senior. Wouldn't be good form if we took down the wrong island." He tapped the chart over the location of Mischief Reef. "This the site of their command and control network?"

"I'm thinking that'd be Fiery Cross."

"History?"

"The Chinese grabbed the island from Vietnam in 1988 after the PLAN blew two Vietnamese ships out of the water. Four years later the Chinese began to explore for oil in the same waters after landing troops on Da Loc Reef. Wherever the hell that is."

Rohrbaugh screwed up his lips. "No kidding."

"I've got more homework, but I've found an island called Dao Ba Loc. It has a couple names, West York and Likas could be the same place."

"Likas is where the Filipinos took out those Chinese patrol boats. We're beginning to see a common thread."

"Everything's in a neat package. Oil and the right of free passage through the international sea lanes. Easy to see why Washington is so spun up."

"Solid work, Senior."

"Thanks, but you've gotta get outa here."

Rohrbaugh reappeared two hours later to find Mackenzie populating his database. "Senior, we've got our marching orders. We're to flesh out 1729 and lash it up to JTF-519's C3I structure."

"Anything new?"

"Nope, nothing for us. But we're tracking in the right direction. The JTF guys will develop the Flexible Deterrent Options once we provide them our Joint Warfare Capabilities Assessment. They'll plug that into the CONOP."

"Straightforward enough."

"Think so? I haven't had the time to give you the skinny from my SDVT-1 visit. First things first, though. It's time for a couple of old dogs to learn some new tricks."

"Oh, Lordy. Now what are you cooking up?"

"We're going to pay Intel a visit and tap into the NGA. You up for a little network-centric warfare?"

"The what?"

"The National Geospatial-Intelligence Agency. Use to be called the National Imagery and Mapping Agency."

"Can't say that helps much, Skipper. Can you tell me without having to shoot me?"

"Senior, I just can't help giving you a hard time."

"Yes sir, and I can't help saying how much I appreciate the time and effort it must take to develop this lowly subordinate."

"We're going to build this database of yours from the bottom up. The NGA can provide their imagery and analysis as-well-as precise mapping and charting, then we can send some of our people in for special recon," Rohrbaugh said.

"Whether we'll have a role in Direct Action remains to be seen. Precision-guided munitions will accomplish the quick strike stuff. Our role will be working with Intel to identify specific targets."

"Works for me, Skipper. I'd say we could pull off the entire operation without the PLA even knowing what hit them. Suddenly their outposts are just off the air. In and out.

Launching a wave of Tomahawks with those electromagnetic pulse warheads will fry their electronics and conventional warheads will take out the hard targets. Matter of fact, I've heard the CBV-107 Passive Attack Weapon is being redesigned to be compatible with our cruise missiles. Figure the PAW can take out the PLAN aircraft and radar on Woody Island without killing too many of their troops. Not too messy."

"I like your tactical mind, Mac. Fits right in with building our CONOPs around *Carter* and *Ohio*. We'll put a straw man together for the CINC proposing a link to 1729. Be easier to secure the resources and funding lines."

"Roger that. I'll start putting it together for your chop."

Chapter Twenty

DEPARTMENT OF FOREIGN AFFAIRS
MANILA
13:00 MONDAY 10 MARCH

"Good afternoon, Mr. Clarke. It's a pleasure to see you again." The Under Secretary for Foreign Affairs, Florencia Cruz, extended his hand in greeting. "It's good of you to travel to our country on such short notice. I trust your trip went well?"

"Thank you, sir," Clarke responded, continuing with the pro-forma diplomatic niceties. "It's a pleasure to be in Manila again. Secretary Valardi asked that I pass along his best wishes."

"I believe you know everyone here?"

Clarke scanned the faces in the room. "All but a few, thank you."

He recognized the Special Assistant to the Under Secretary, Raul Atencio, standing to one side. "Raul, good to see you again."

"Mr. Clarke." Atencio didn't extend his hand.

Clarke turned to his host. "Shall we get started?

"By all means."

Clark took his seat and poured himself a glass of water while listening to the men around the table rattle off their names and positions. An impressive assembly and presumably, all strong Montalvo allies.

"You do not believe the actions taken by our government were of our own choosing?" opened Congressman Estrada. "They should not be considered as ...what were the words used by Secretary Valardi with our ambassador in Washington?"

"Precipitous."

"The Chinese provoked us," the Congressman continued. "They have infringed upon our rights as a sovereign nation. Would you have done anything different? We are all waiting America's response to the downing of your P-8 reconnaissance plane, the remains of which, I need not remind you, lie wrecked on Pagasa?"

Clarke waited until he was sure the Congressman had finished before speaking. "Congressman Estrada, are you aware we destroyed the Chinese fighter that damaged our patrol plane?"

The AFP Deputy Chief of Staff's eyebrows arched. "Huh?"

"Two weeks ago, an American carrier strike group intercepted and turned back a PLAN flotilla underway in the South China Sea. This Chinese force, including troop carrying amphibious assault ships, was to seize your installation on Pagasa Atoll."

"Wha—"

"General, we have chosen not to address these events in a public forum."

The Presidential Security Advisor responded. "Mr. Clarke, I must, too, be frank and address the possibility of a hidden agenda on your part. Do you intend to propose the reintroduction of American forces into our country?"

"No, sir. However, there may be mutual benefit for both our countries to explore the renewal of joint military training exercises on the scale we conducted in the—"

"I must object—," Cruz said.

"Please permit to continue, sir." Clarke interrupted. "The scope of these would be predicated on bringing to fruition our current negotiations for the Status of Forces Agreement."

Cruz seethed with anger. "Perhaps…sir. You do understand my government will engage Beijing in discussions to promote outcomes in concert with our long-term national objectives …. Yes?"

"That, of course, sir, is your prerogative." Clarke replied evenly.

Alarmed at the confrontational tone the discussions had taken, the Senator spoke. "Mr. Clarke, I have just introduced Senate Resolution 443. In doing so, I enunciated our country's need for a strong alliance with the United States."

"That would be most helpful," Clarke said while trying to figure out what was going on in the minds of the Filipinos.

The AFP general listened with one ear to the acrimonious discussions. He cleared his throat. "But the United States cannot ignore Chinese infringement on our territorial waters."

"I believe our actions speak for themselves, sir."

"Indeed. Then you will understand we will take those measures necessary to protect our interests."

"Certainly."

"General," Cruz said, "would you please elaborate on those measures the Department of National Defense is taking to ensure compliance with the President's directive?"

"Of course, sir," the officer replied with more bravado than he felt. "We have already repositioned the *Emilio Jacinto* squadron and flown additional surveillance and attack aircraft to our airfields on Palawan."

At this point the Congressman inserted himself into the discussions. "I have before me House Resolution 944. It is titled, 'Resolution Condemning Chinese Intrusion into The Country's Economic Exclusion Zone, Commending The Philippine Navy And The Rest Of The Philippine Armed Forces For Gallantly Protecting Our Territorial Integrity In Connection With the Latest Incident At Scarborough Shoal And Fully Supporting President Montalvo On The Spratly Issue.' We the —"

Cruz reacted to the incredulous stares of the Americans. He halted the Congressman in his tracks. "Why thank you, sir. Perhaps you could provide us with the written text?"

The General dropped his head to avoid Clarke's eyes. *Mother of God. All I have is my bare ass sticking up into the wind at the Chinese and all he can do is offer a speech? Give me something to fight with. Here I am trying to enlist the help of the Pentagon and the Department of Foreign Affairs seems to be operating off a completely different page. This isn't what we had discussed this morning.*

Before the General could respond, the Congressman spoke. "I recommend we send our Navy after any Chinese fishing boats."

"And what do you propose we use to implement such a course of action? Rowboats?" the General muttered under his breath.

Clark nodded to Crenshaw.

"I believe we are positioned to assist your government in its present difficulties."

'Difficulties' might be one way to characterize an ill-advised military strike against the Chinese, Atencio thought. *There may be some rationale for dragging the United States into this issue with Beijing, but we run the risk of becoming a pawn in a confrontation between two goliaths. There must be a way to extricate ourselves from this parasitic dependence on the Americans...Perhaps I can enlist the unwitting assistance of Ms. Lynne?*

———

AMERICAN EMBASSY
15:30

The Deputy Chief of Mission opened the debrief. "How'd it go, Adrian?"

"Brutal."

"That bad?"

"I underestimated the degree of resentment remaining about our old bases at Subic and Clark. We've got a ways to go before we can even consider fashioning any permanent basing agreements. Fortunately, the Senator stepped up. He may well be the man we approach to broker a deal."

"And Cruz?"

"He was downright obtuse. I'm not convinced the Under Secretary or his Special Assistant, Atencio, are on board with President Montalvo. I smell a rotten fish."

"That's our read," the Charge d'Affairs said. "What about the military?"

"The General remained focused on the AFP's requirements. It's safe to say the military remains in our court."

"I wish it were that simple," the DCM said. "From my experience, you never know who is positioning themselves for the next election or, for that matter, a coup. Based on past history, if the AFP perceives the country is not headed in the correct direction, they will take measures into their own hands."

"On a positive note," Clark said, "once we got through the preliminaries, the discussions went well enough. What was your read, Jim?"

"I concur, but I don't believe we need to push the basing agreements," Crenshaw said. "The path of least resistance is through the Vietnamese. Colonel, you spent the day at WESCOM, what's your take?"

"I'm not hopeful."

"What about Subic Bay?"

"Our approach has been 'hands off' in keeping with the commercialization of the facilities and name change to Subic Bay Freeport."

"Do you think there's any possibility of requesting limited access for our warships under a new SOFA?" Crenshaw asked.

Clarke covered his mouth, stifling a yawn. "We've received some feelers from the Vietnamese on the use of our old base at Da Nang. Jim and the Colonel are on tap to meet with them during our trip to Hanoi."

The Charge d'Affairs picked up the yawn. "Let's call it a day. I've got enough to brief the Ambassador."

Chapter Twenty-One

DIRECTOR NATIONAL INTELLIGENCE
MCLEAN, VIRGINIA
06:10 THURSDAY 13 MARCH

B ryce Gilmore took a thoughtful pull of his Marlboro. He had started smoking them when he was twelve. *Come to Marlboro country—to where the flavor is.*

The brand fit with his self-image; rugged, self-reliant, taming the West despite the fact that he had gained thirteen pounds over the past year and his chin was beginning to sag. He set down the intelligence report on the South China Sea and picked up the morning copy of the *Wall Street Journal.*

He tapped the ash from his cigarette and turned the pages of the paper scanning each one in turn. The marketplace was not what held his interest this morning even though he owned several million dollars- worth of stock.

His search stopped on page A-6. The article he searched for: an insignificant four-inch double column. He uttered a grunt of satisfaction when he finished reading.

There were no changes or additions from the draft he had approved for release. Truth be told, he wouldn't have objected if *The Journal* had seen fit to add some of their own analysis. That piece of inadvertent obfuscation would have added another layer of legitimacy to the activation of Blue Horizon.

The story read:

'Yesterday a new startup joined the ranks of offshore oil and natural gas exploration ventures intent on meeting the world's increasing demand for petroleum products. Horizon Offshore Exploration [HOE] based out of Houston will not be listed on the NYSE or the NASDEC and there are no immediate plans for an initial public offering. Hoping to exploit the potential of undeveloped fields ringing the South China Sea, a company spokesman for HOE announced the company would soon join with PetroVietnam to begin exploratory drilling in the Con Son Basin's White Tiger Field. An extension of the Sunda Shelf landmass that was above sea level at the peak of the Ice Age, the basin is reported to have huge deposits of crude oil.

Engineers have said Vietnam has also renewed drilling in the Wan Bei-21 block in the Blue Dragon field approximately 200 miles off the tip of southern Vietnam. PetroVietnam's

General Director said—'

"Morning, Bryce. Did you see it?" Gilmore's Deputy Director, Ralph Cox, asked as he strode into the room.

Gilmore waved him toward an upholstered chair. "Just now."

"For better or worse, we're in the oil business." Cox replied eyeing the cigarette with disapproval.

Gilmore relented and snuffed out the butt. He knew the rules on smoking in Federal office buildings. He viewed them as just another bureaucratic irritant. *It's none of their damned business if I want to kill myself.*

"At the moment, I'm not exactly feeling like a tycoon. Coffee?"

"Thanks," Cox replied wondering if all ex-field agents had this self-destructive streak.

Cox poured himself a cup from the carafe on the side table hoping Gilmore hadn't brewed it. He took a tentative sip and settled in the chair. "We haven't seen a reaction from Beijing yet——"

"They don't have much to go on. The PLA sent a couple of reconnaissance flights over Platform Four, so they know it's been reactivated."

"They're going to be pissed with HOE and PetroVietnam for setting up shop in their backyard."

"Tough shit."

"You'll get no argument from me," Cox said.

Gilmore peered over the top of his glasses. "We're going to have to stay alert for Beijing's counter moves."

"Understood."

"So, where are we?"

"Right on target. The Director of Operations has the A team working this one. The roughnecks they recruited are a real rogue's gallery. I've seen some pictures. They look like a bunch of damn pirates. Tattoos, earrings, hair down to their shoulders."

"Salt of the earth."

"Last I heard they were pumping 9,000 barrels a day. That represents most of Hanoi's production."

"I thought it was a dry well."

"Surprised everyone."

"What's it costing?"

"The Vietnamese estimate it's going to run near three-hundred and fifty million annually. Hanoi is providing the bulk. We've guaranteed their development loan through HOE."

"We're covering a good percentage of our long-term outlay."

"It's probable the projected startup costs will run less than expected if you sign off on the team's new recommendations."

Gilmore pressed his back against his chair. He didn't like surprises. "And those are?"

"The major piece is modifying Platform Ten instead of new construction."

"How'd they come to that decision?"

"Revisited their plan."

"You've seen it?"

"They ran the strawman by me a couple of days ago."

"Can I sign off on the product?"

"They'll have the final draft to me this afternoon. I've got the team penciled in on your schedule day after tomorrow."

"Is BLUE HORIZON in this morning's brief book? I don't want to tell the President one thing, then have to change my story."

"No, but it's possible it could come up."

"Give me the short version."

"In the original agreement, the Vietnamese were to lease exploration blocks 121 and 123 to HOE for joint development. Our plan was to build a new rig in 123 and set up our surveillance team. The specifics of this agreement weren't released, and as far as we know, Beijing has no knowledge. The tricky part, 123 overlaps zones claimed by the PRC. This is bound to touch a nerve since the Chinese National Offshore Oil Corporation leased these same areas to an American company, Lakeland Energy Corporation."

"Where the hell did they come from?"

"They have a corporate office in Denver."

"Where's the linkage?"

"We've traced Lakeland's affiliation to a Hong Kong listed

company, China National Offshore Oil, Ltd. That's the State-run parent of CNOOC. The kicker…"

Gilmore shifted in his chair. He didn't like to play 'Guess What I'm Thinking.'

"This week, our China analysts came across a transcript posted on the Foreign Ministry's website detailing Beijing's position on their claims in the South China Sea. What got our attention was a statement saying they would protect Lakeland's activities by force if their interests were threatened."

"They're serious?"

"It's credible."

Gilmore reached for his package of Marlboros, then pulled his hand back. "You're telling me we could get drawn into a war between China and Vietnam over the activities of some damn American company?"

"I wouldn't dismiss the possibility. Beijing can position itself to cover their actions by appearing to protect the interests of an American company."

"I don't think I'd care to try to explain the logic of this to the President."

"For openers, I'd explain Beijing's intent is to box us in and limit our options to interfere. Of course, there's also a reasonable explanation for going with a U.S. firm."

"I don't want to go there. Did we know any of this when I signed off on Blue Horizon?"

"No. Lakeland kept their negotiations with CNOOC secret until they signed their agreement."

"What about Commerce? They were sure as hell all over us when we were setting up our venture with PetroVietnam. And what about the Caspian Sea negotiations with Yukos Oil? Lakeland had to jump through the same hoops to get their deal blessed, didn't they?"

"We're checking."

"Lakeland's a shell for a Trojan horse?"

"Unknown."

"We have to do better. Does Lakeland have any big donors tied to Commerce?"

"We—"

"Don't answer that. Just give me the final report. We'll have to sort this out later. Anything solid on Lakeland?"

"We're infiltrating one of our people."

"I'm thinking we should exert a little gentle persuasion on Lakeland and convince them to take their business elsewhere."

"I'll look into it."

"Be discreet. We can't get caught snooping around a domestic company. We'll have to coordinate our investigation with the FBI if you come up with anything suspicious."

"It must be great to be king."

"Not even close, so don't feed me that crap. I get enough from our friends in Congress."

"More flack on the re-org?"

"Yeah. Endless, but give me the rest."

"Beijing was edgy enough before Manila stirred the pot. Now they've been put on guard by a new rig PetroVietnam constructed in the Thanh Long —"

"The Blue Dragon oil field?"

"It's a platform some two-hundred miles southeast of Vung Tau scheduled to tap into the producing strata by May."

"How's this fit?"

"I've brought a map."

"You're kidding."

"Nope. You don't pay me enough."

"I'll take that under consideration."

Cox spread out the map on Gilmore's desk. "This is the general area we're talking about. CNOOC granted drilling rights to Lakeland to the same block."

"I see."

"This is another rig that caught our analyst's attention. It's what prompted us to reconsider our plan. This platform wasn't even on the table when we began our negotiations with the Vietnamese. Construction began years ago in collaboration with the Russians. When Moscow pulled out, Hanoi opened the area to foreign bidders. Even Mobile sunk several test wells."

"Lord, don't tell me they're involved?"

"No, thank God. It appears PetroVietnam decided to go it alone."

"This could escalate," Gilmore said.

"Exactly."

Gilmore ran his finger over the chart. "This will put us just to the west of the Lakeland concession. Hasn't Hanoi put together a multinational consortium to develop a natural gas field in the same area?"

"They have. British Petroleum has the lead for a two-billion-dollar project that includes building a pipeline connecting the field to a power plant at the Phu My Industrial Center."

Gilmore sorted through the implications. "What's Beijing saying?"

"They're raising hell and putting the squeeze on BP. They're saying the project constitutes an infringement on China's sovereignty."

"I don't want our guys caught in the middle."

Cox brushed his hand across his chin.

Gilmore recognized his deputy's mannerism. "What's on your mind?"

"Before the VietSovPetro joint venture dissolved, Petro-Vietnam and the Soviet company, Nestro, built ten drilling platforms in the Bach Ho oil field. It's our recommendation HOE take sole possession of Platform Ten and plant the flag. We can then team up with Hanoi and draw our line in the sand."

"Why Ten?"

"Our engineers tell us it's in the best structural shape. Its design is such that it can readily be retrofitted to meet our needs."

"How close to the Chinese will this place us?"

"Seventy-five miles from the Kan Ton-III exploration vessel. CNOOC just deployed the ship to sink test wells."

Gilmore looked at the map. "Damn."

"Yeah, the rig is almost equidistant between Da Nang and Hainan. You can see why everyone is so spun up."

"Both of them appear to have valid claims if you take into consideration the two-hundred-mile EEZ."

"Possession is nine-tenths of the law. I'd say a real horse-race is developing."

"So it seems."

"We'll need to maintain the appearance of an oil-producing platform to secure our cover."

"And how do you propose we do that?"

"That was my question. The easiest solution would be to reactivate the drilling and after an appropriate amount of time, announce a dry well. We can then move everybody off the rig but our guys. We're checking with the geologists to see if that scenario would have validity with CNOOC's engineers. Fortunately for us, but not the Vietnamese, there has been a notable lack of output from the majority of wells in the Con Son basin. With the exception of Platform Four, most haven't even covered their development costs."

"You're telling me I shouldn't invest any of my retirement fund over there?" Gilmore said looking to wrap up the conversation.

"You'd find better odds in the gold market. Without forcing the metaphor, the silver lining in all of this is, we'll save millions and be able to stand up our operation months earlier if we use Platform Ten."

"Passes the reasonable man test."

"There's something else."

Gilmore checked the time. "I don't need to point out that

the more convoluted this becomes, the greater the risk of something spinning out of control."

"Acknowledged, so you're not going to like this piece."

"I'm already sitting. Go ahead."

"Hanoi has obtained a line of credit with Tokyo."

"So?"

"They want to lease several of their offshore fields to the Japan Offshore Petroleum Exploration Corporation. Hedging their bets."

"I wanted the short version."

"It's convoluted."

"No doubt. I'll have to take a scrubbed version to the NSC. Get State and Defense in the loop. That said, it'd be the President's call."

"Yes, sir."

"What else?"

"The National Reconnaissance Office spotted a Chinese cable-laying ship in the South China Sea. The PLA's expanding their network of sub-ocean fiber optic cables to harden communications between their various installations in the South China Sea with their command center on Hainan."

"Can we tap it?"

"DIA's exploring the idea. The NGA has pinpointed the cable's location. Matched it with *Impeccible's* seabed topography before the PLA chased her off."

"The Navy's done it before in the Sea of Okosk. Our subs tapped the Soviet's Northern Sea Fleet's undersea cables off Murmansk."

"The *Parche?*"

"She's the most notable. After her decommissioning, the *Jimmy Carter* assumed the mission. She's the third and last of the Seawolf class. Based out of Bangor, Washington. Her construction was delayed to allow for the installation of a one-hundred-foot hull extension aft of the sail providing naval special warfare and Intel capabilities way beyond anything previously available."

"And those are?"

"*Carter* has berthing and equipment storage to support fifty SEALs and a dedicated command suite. She also has a large ocean interface storage area called a 'Moon Well' incorporating a wasp waist."

"Wasp waist?"

"The cargo compartment narrows to a four-foot diameter fore-aft passageway for the crew, hence the name. What provided the step up is that the compartment can be configured for mission-specific equipment to support littoral operations."

"What can she do for us?"

"Beyond inserting special op guys for tactical and strategic surveillance, the Navy can deploy pods capable of tapping into sub-ocean laser communication trunk lines."

"We can't pass this up."

"Our guys can barely contain themselves."

"Those Navy divers had guts. Have they asked for anything?"

"They've dropped a hint they want to stage from Platform Ten to run ops with their new submersible."

"How about the *Carter*?"

"Nothing."

"Any risk of blowing our cover?"

"Minimal. If the Soviets didn't intercept our guys right outside Murmansk, I doubt the Chinese could."

"We need to modify the platform?"

"No idea."

"Find out."

"Listen, boss. You gotta go. There aren't any surprises in the briefing book. We're right on the mark regarding the Philippine Foreign Ministry's position on the MLSA. There's a note on the Chinese Ministry of State Security's activity in Manila, and some info on ABC's resident correspondent."

Gilmore folded Cox's map. "Touch base with me this afternoon."

———

GEORGE WASHINGTON MEMORIAL PARKWAY
06:45

Gilmore's armored sedan turned right onto the G-W Parkway for the short trip to the White House. His security detail followed, ready to race into a blocking position if the situation warranted.

He peered out the side window at the stark outlines of the trees lining the parkway. "How's the traffic?"

"Advance says we have clear sailing, sir. You'll arrive with time to spare."

The driver and escorting agent didn't expect an answer and got none. The morning run provided Gilmore a respite from the constant onslaught of meetings, calls, and crises he faced each day.

Gilmore turned from the window and pulled the red leather binder containing the President's Daily Brief from his attaché case. The binder's cover read: "Director, Top Secret – Contains Codeword Material."

He flipped to the first tabbed section that summarized the new developments in Somalia. He wrote a note to contact the French and see if the agency could get collaboration from their counterparts in Djibouti.

The next section summarized the latest information from the station chief in Manila. There'd been a significant increase in communication with the Chinese ambassador following the Clarke visit.

Manila appeared to be considering rapprochement with

Beijing and had taken under review several proposals submitted by the Chinese. His analysts felt Beijing's proposals represented the initial moves to woo the Philippines into their sphere of influence.

The PRC was implementing a number of political and economic measures that would be difficult for Manila to ignore. The proposals were structured to guarantee certain territorial claims by Manila and to strengthen the position of the Philippines within ASEAN. If implemented, they would upset the balance of power in the Pacific.

Gilmore wondered where Montalvo fit. The report suggested all of the activity was emanating from the Foreign Ministry, not Malacanang Palace. *And what about the military?* He couldn't imagine they'd have a hand in this. Any scenario implicating the AFP's acquiescence couldn't be taken seriously.

He swayed in his seat as the sedan turned onto the Roosevelt Bridge. They would be at the White House in minutes. He pulled out his iPad and jotted down a cryptic 'to do' list.

(1) validate/collaborate
(2) intelligence/analysis
(3) Montalvo visit
(4) mtg with Richard
(5) BH
(6) NSC presentation
(7) WHY??

Gilmore stared at number seven. *What forces were at play that would so alter the allegiance of a long-term ally? Have they been cowed by their confrontation with the PLA? Were they using this opportunity to position the Philippines to benefit from the changing dynamics in the South China Sea? Or were they looking to wrestle concessions from the United States?*

He picked up the secure telephone and selected a number from autodialing.

"Cox."

"Ralph? Bryce. I just went over the Station Chief's report. We need a better handle on the Foreign Minister's agenda."

"You think Cruz's positioning to replace Montalvo?"

"What do we know?"

"For starters, there are elements within the DFA and a few influential Senators who will block any agreement that would open the door for a renewed American military presence."

"We have anything on the Ministry of State Security?"

"They have someone in the DFA on their payroll. We're chasing the leads."

"What about the military?" Gilmore asked.

"The senior leadership is in our camp. The National Police appear to be aligning with the generals. Public statements issued by a Presidential spokesman have been noncommittal. Our source confirms Montalvo remains on the fence. At this point, there isn't an immediate threat."

"I don't agree. What happens if the Lincoln Strike Group gets sucked into another confrontation with the PLA?"

"Shit."

Cox's reaction elicited a chuckle from Gilmore. "Well, that's a succinct summary of my thoughts. In any event, that falls into Richard's and Sheldon's court. We'll let them sort it out."

"I'm thinking it's time for us to spin up our contacts in Hanoi and Manila. Get the hard data and set up our countermoves in case this thing spins out of control."

Gilmore replaced the receiver, picked up the iPad, and typed: (8) counter moves.

With Montalvo's visit to Washington two weeks away, he began to formulate a plan. He set the foundation with the essential question: *Who is this insider and what can we do to neutralize him?*

Gilmore's sedan came to a stop at the White House's security gate. He glanced out the window, noting a cluster of people milling around a satellite feed van. He studied their faces while he waited for the guards complete their checks.

He placed another call to Cox. "We've got an ABC van. Any idea what going on?"

"No."

The security guard waved them through. "Have a good morning, Mr. Gilmore."

The news team passed out of sight as his car passed through the gate and pulled into an empty stall. His secure phone rang.

"Gilmore."

"We've got something hot," Cox said.

"Anything to do with that van?"

"Yeah, they're about to break the story on the P-8 incident."

"Any surprises?"

"Don't appear to be any."

"Wonder what took them so long? Do we know their source?"

"A reporter in Manila."

"Got a name?"

"Lynne. First name, Marie. She was the lead on the series detailing the rescue of the Philippine fishing boat."

"Her background material was deeper than anything we had. We have anything on her source?"

"She's not about to divulge, but our resident agent suspects someone in the Foreign Ministry."

"Our mystery man?"

"Could be."

"It's time to find out more about Ms. Lynne."

"I'll notify the embassy."

"Stop by this afternoon."

Gilmore terminated the call and added another bullet to his list:

(9) Marie Lynne

Chapter Twenty-Two

QUEZON CITY FARMER'S MARKET
MANILA
08:40 FRIDAY 14 MARCH

L ynne began to run. She chanced a look over her shoulder and stumbled over a child playing in the dirt. She caught herself and darted into a narrow aisle between two ramshackle buildings.

Where is he?

She caught a fleeting glimpse of the man stalking her. He averted his eyes, turning away in a furtive attempt not to be noticed.

"Whoever you are, buddy, that's not going to work."

Few Westerners bothered to come to the Quezon City farmer's market and he couldn't have been more obvious. Tall, blond hair, wearing a white button-down shirt...with a tie? *Really?*

Time to ditch this asshole. She made a feint to the right, then pressed her way down a narrow alley, blending in with the milling shoppers. At the end of the block, she made a quick left and ducked into a side stall, slipping behind a stack of slatted chicken coops.

Her eyes flicked around the shop. An ancient woman perched on a stool in the corner plucking the feathers off a scrawny chicken. The woman looked up with mild curiosity and resumed her work on the lifeless bird.

Lynne took several deep breaths and parted the bamboo screen that served as the door. She scanned the alleyway. There was no sign of her pursuer.

She took a tentative step. A pit bull mix snarled, baring its fangs. Lynne yelped and stumbled back into the safety of the shop. She lost her balance and fell into the coops, prompting loud squawks of protest from the feathered occupants imprisoned inside.

The old woman looked up, eyeing her with annoyance. Lynne uttered an apology and backed out the door trying to control the trembling that racked her body. She willed herself to walk, sidestepped the dog, and set off for her car.

———

"Crap. Lost her," the stalker said to his partner. "Think she found another way out?"

"There she is."

The stalker swung his head around. "Where?"

"Over there. By the fruit stands. See her?"

"Took her sweet time getting back. Think she paid a visit to a drop point?"

"Hard to say, but that change in her routine this morning sure as hell is suspicious. We'll need help. Do a sweep and set up surveillance in the area where she ducked out of sight. Damn, she sure knows her way around that rabbit's warren."

———

Lynne fumbled for her car keys and managed to unlock the door. She slammed it shut and slumped against the steering wheel, trying to collect her wits.

She flicked her eyes to the side mirror. *Nothing.* Assured, she turned over the ignition and eased her rusted Toyota into traffic.

A street urchin ran up gesturing he wanted to wash her windshield. She waved him off and continued through the traffic light. The omnipresent poverty of the barrios was one thing that never changed. Today, this familiar incident provided Lynne a fragment of reality.

———

"She's moving," the driver said. "The scanner up?"

"Yeah, we're good."

They had already collected a good deal of information intercepting the signals from Lynne's wireless Internet in the apartment and counted on her making a call to her boss. The driver tapped the steering wheel waiting for several vehicles to pass, then hit the accelerator, pulling behind the Toyota.

———

Lynne shot a glance at the rearview mirror. A gaudily decorated jeepney minibus lurched to a stop in front of her. She slammed on the brakes and pounded on the horn. "You crazy son of a bitch."

The burst of anger was cathartic. She swung around the bus and back into traffic. *I've been in that market a hundred times and nothing like this has ever happened. Never even come close. Why now?*

She gasped. *He must have been waiting outside my apartment. Why would someone want to watch me? I'm not exactly a national security risk. Who could possibly think...?*

With that insight, the realization hit. *The story.* Her boss had warned her about an entanglement with Atencio. *He's been reliable in the past, but then, the pictures of the wrecked P-8. Weird. He took them back saying they were very sensitive and no one should suspect I've seen them.*

Her gut churned. She felt violated. *Who's doing this to me? The embassy? Why would they suppress knowledge of the incident?*

She recalled the events following the broadcast of her report. A Defense Department spokesman had issued a rebuttal denying the confrontation. The Pentagon's explanation? The P-8 made an emergency landing due to mechanical failure and was destroyed after hitting a concrete wave barrier.

While the public affairs officer acknowledged the *Lincoln* had been in the South China Sea, he noted the Strike Group was merely transiting on the way home after six months in the Gulf. And the two F-18s? They'd been dispatched to conduct a visual inspection of the damaged P-8. Those statements were, of course, completely true—up to a point. They just excluded several critical pieces of information.

Perhaps Washington and Beijing are trying to avoid a repetition of last year's international confrontation and are going back-channel to defuse the crisis. If that were true, then what could Raul hope to gain by telling me? He had to know I'd break the story. What's missing?

She picked up her cell and punched the autodial. "Ron?"

"You're running late. Anything wrong?"

"Plenty. Someone's been watching my apartment. He followed me to the market."

"Where are you?"

"I just crossed Valencia."

"You still being followed?"

"I don't think so."

"Be careful."

"Ron? Could they know about my meeting with Raul? He's been acting really strange and not returning my calls. That's not like him. He even used an intermediary to set up the meeting. There's something else odd, too. We met in some hole-in-the-wall and he kept looking around as if he was afraid someone would see us."

"Any idea what's driving his behavior?"

"None. He even offered to help me set up a cover story and a way to pass more information so nobody could trace him. This is nuts. We usually meet at noon at the Manila Hotel. I should have known something was up. I was focused on the story and not thinking. What have we stumbled onto?"

Ron cut her off. "Wait till you get to the office. Okay?"

"I'm scared."

"I know. We'll work it out."

———

Across the city, Lynne's tail commented to his partner, "Appears we've got our mark."

"Think that's his real name?"

"No reason to think otherwise. Sounds like she knows him real well. Maybe too well. My guess is we're dealing with that midlevel guy in the Department of Foreign Affairs."

"We've got enough. We gotta get back and brief the boss."

———

AMERICAN EMBASSY
15:00

"Mr. Ambassador, we have a break in the ABC case. We've identified the source. Earlier this week we narrowed our list to four probables and—"

"Jack, please just tell me who it is."

The CIA station chief's shoulders slumped, deflated by the Ambassador's response. "He's a midlevel bureaucrat in the DFA."

"I don't suppose he has a name?""

"Raul Atencio."

"Never heard of him," the Ambassador said. "What's he do?"

"Special Assistant to the Under Secretary for Policy."

"Doesn't help."

"I'd be surprised if you'd recognize him, sir," the Deputy Chief of Mission said. "Like most SA's, he performs his job behind the scenes. At least until recently."

"Enlighten me."

"What placed Atencio on our short list was his change of behavior over the past few months. The Under Secretary has allegedly been sick with an unspecified illness. We attributed Atencio's actions to standing in for his boss."

"The problem is, we can't confirm the Secretary's illness," the Station Chief commented. "Atencio has gone from standing in at various functions to participating in the decision-making process. What caught our attention was when he showed up at the table for the policy discussions with Clarke. He's fronting for Cruz. My cut is the Secretary's purported illness is a masquerade."

The Ambassador frowned. "What's in it for them? All this palace intrigue is making me nuts. I want something solid."

"Atencio and Cruz are members of the opposition Lakas CMD party. By leaking the story, they're planting the seeds to weaken Montalvo's government in anticipation of this fall's general elections. The CMD, National People's Coalition, and Liberal Party along with several smaller ones, have banded together to promote what they're calling the Government of National Unity."

"Have any polls been conducted? They would give us something."

"Nothing formal," the DCM answered, "but there appears to be significant grass-roots support for their coalition. Much of our analysis is based on the average Filipino's fear of further military confrontations with Beijing. The coalition has never supported the renewal of the MLSA and they're linking the U.S. military presence with the difficulties with China."

"That's utter nonsense."

"But that's the risk we took by not exposing Beijing's actions," the Station Chief said. "We lost points with Montalvo when we didn't come out in full support of his government in the fishing boat hijacking."

"Can we turn things around?"

"Possibly. They intend to address the country's foreign and budgetary crisis by establishing closer ties to regional and political powers."

"The Chinese?" the DCA asked.

"Exactly."

The Ambassador's eyes narrowed. "Do we know Montalvo's countermoves?"

"I've got that," the DCM said. "He was preparing to release details of a comprehensive plan of his own, but he pulled the announcement after the flap caused by the ABC story. Malacanang is exercising spin control while Montalvo revamps his Ten Point plan. He's dropped rumors to the press that he may announce a wholesale reshuffling of his cabinet."

"He going to remain in our court?"

"My read is he will, but he's hedging his bets."

"In other words, Montalvo will initiate talks with Beijing."

"The tricky part is, he doesn't want to lose the support of the military."

"What do you suggest?"

"The AFP remains our strong card. We need to maintain a firm commitment to them."

"I'm not so sure," the Station Chief responded.

That statement caught the Ambassador off guard. "Excuse me?"

"The AFP's been accused of conducting a dirty war against leftist activists."

"Collaboration?" the Ambassador asked.

"Human Rights Watch."

"The U.N. looked into similar accusations and implicated the army in the killings," confirmed the DCM.

The Ambassador massaged his temples. "That's not helpful."

"No, sir."

The Ambassador stood, clasped his hands behind his back, and began to pace. "We'll need to get a read from the Palace to determine if we have to move back our timetables for negotiating the MLSA and related issues. We might get a better return on our investment if we focus on economic assistance to strengthen the government without stirring the pot over basing."

"Should we pull the plug on the *Truxtun's* visit to Subic?"

"Too strong a signal," the DCM answered. "Considering the lead time to complete negotiations, I'd leave it on the table."

"Makes sense," the Ambassador said. "Let's get our plan together. We've got a week before Montalvo leaves for Washington."

"I'll have our analysis and recommendations to State ready for release tomorrow morning," the DCM responded.

The Ambassador's eyes hardened. "Now what about that damn reporter? Lynne, isn't it?"

"Yes."

"Should we bring her in for a little chat?"

"Not yet, but we can use her to link Atencio to the Chinese Ministry of State Security. We need to take him out of circulation."

"Do it."

Chapter Twenty-Three

THE WHITE HOUSE
14:00 TUESDAY 18 MARCH

Stuart cast a cursory glance through the arched windows lining the north wall of the cabinet room. Under different circumstances the Rose Garden would have beckoned him from across the colonnade. He took his seat and called to order the Principles Meeting of the National Security Council.

"Justin, what's your read on the ABC story?"

"As much as our friends at *The Post* wanted to keep the story alive, it's been pushed off the front page by the leadership changes in Tel Aviv."

"What else?"

"Malacanang is backing our version of events. The Chinese have remained silent except to say they couldn't comment on the loss of an American plane over international airspace."

"Richard?"

"I'm concerned about the leaks."

"I've that covered," Gilmore said. "Last Friday, I received

a Field Appraisal from our station chief in Manila identifying the source."

Stuart's lips tightened. "Who is it?"

"The Special Assistant to the Undersecretary for Policy. Guy named Atencio. Our information is credible, but not yet actionable."

"Understood."

"There's evidence he's fronting for his boss. Both of these men belong to the governing coalition partner, Lakas CMD Party."

"How's that significant?"

"They've been working with the new National Coalition Party to unseat Montalvo in this fall's elections."

"Montalvo must know Cruz is trying to undercut him," Valardi said.

Gilmore ignored Valardi's body language. "Presumably so. We believe Montalvo is buying time until he can announce a reshuffling of his cabinet. Having said that, there's something sinister at play. We uncovered evidence that Cruz is on the payroll of the Chinese Ministry of State Security. If Montalvo's aware, he's not showing his hand."

Valardi's pen rolled off the table. "What?"

Brown retrieved it. "Surprised me too."

Given the moment to regain his composure, Valardi nodded a 'thank you' to Brown. "Should we inform Montalvo?"

"I'll do that," Stuart said.

Gilmore blinked. There was no mistaking Stuart's tone. "We're working on substantiating the details of his contacts and payoffs."

"When will you have proof?"

"Thirty-six hours. In time for Camp David."

"Cutting it close," Stuart said. "I've got to have that package for Montalvo. You have the evidence of collaboration from your Philippine sources. Surveillance photos, copies of bank statements?"

"Yes, sir."

"Richard, this would be a good time to share what you have."

"A pattern emerged when we looked at the actions of the DFA. A case in point is a report we received from our embassy in Brazilia that's been substantiated by a story in today's *Manila Bulletin*. Their banner reads: 'RP, China Considering Joint Gas Project in Spratly Islands.'"

"What the hell?" Payne said. "After what just happened. They can't possibly be serious. Why would they drop this on us before Montalvo's visit?"

"Leverage," Brown replied.

"Pretty damn inconsiderate considering we just saved their sorry asses," Payne said.

"Does it matter if China and the Philippines pursue joint development of the natural gas fields in the South China Sea?" Brown mused. "Would this represent a potential short or long-term threat to us?"

"If this agreement was taken as an isolated event, it would not warrant the characterization as a threat," Valardi said. "In fact, I believe a persuasive case can be made that a bilateral agreement between Beijing and Manila would be a positive development."

"Go on," Stuart said.

"If we give our tacit support to bilateral negotiations, we'll be sending a positive signal to Beijing."

"What's going on?" Brown asked. "This more of Cruz's doing?"

"It's consistent with actions he's orchestrated within the DFA," Valardi replied flipping over a page of his notepad. "I'll quote the article:

'Following informal talks between DFA officials and a Chinese delegation led by Vice Foreign Minister Yang Po at the sidelines of the Forum for East Asia-Latin American Cooperation meetings held in San Palo last week, the Philippines and China are eyeing joint projects such as natural gas exploration and development of the fisheries industry in the Spratly Islands in a bid to build confidence and trust between the two countries to make way for a possible resolution of border issues in the South China Sea.'"

"That was one sentence? Long-winded, just like their diplomats," Payne said.

Those observations earned the Defense Secretary a look of disapproval from Stuart. "Do we have any evidence of any off-line discussions at the conference?"

"No, sir. But we did tell Manila they should handle the Spratly issue with Beijing. I'm not sure how much we should read into this development."

"The context then was different," Brown countered. "We were talking about the release of a fishing boat crew and trying to keep from getting dragged into a war with the Chinese."

"That turned out well, didn't it?" Payne said.

"Gentlemen," Stuart interrupted. "We've left some broken glass on the ground, but let's press on, shall we? Richard, what exactly did the Chinese say?"

Valardi extracted a sheet of paper from his briefcase. "The Chinese ambassador in Manila said that, for the time being, Beijing would put aside differences with Manila on the exploration of natural gas to set an example of dispute settlement.'"

"Natural gas. Not oil. Everyone note that detail?" Payne asked.

"There's also a subtle threat woven in," Brown said.

Stuart urged, "Please elaborate."

"Nine years ago, China negotiated an agreement with Manila to develop natural gas deposits in the Reed Bank sea mount. That was all well and good until the Filipinos went behind Beijing's back and issued a drilling permit to an American consortium."

"There you have it in a nutshell. The genesis of China's move to occupy Mischief Reef and Scarborough Shoal," Payne said

"Exactly. Taken within this context, the wording 'set an example' is ominous. So is the ambassador's next statement: 'China would urge the other claimants to enter into similar agreements while territorial disputes remain unsettled.'"

"Pretty tough," Gilmore said. "I doubt Hanoi is thrilled."

"They aren't," Valardi answered. "Their Foreign Minister has already been in touch with our ambassador."

Stuart drew a spiral on his notepad tapping his pen on the center point. "Bob, is there anything new I should know about Exercise Balikatan?"

"No, sir. The advance team is already in-country. Expeditionary Strike Group Five is operating with elements of the Philippine navy off Luzon. It goes without saying, the AFP wants to push through our military assistance package."

"No surprise there, Sheldon, but in the interest of time, let's skip the details. What else?"

"I'd like to provide a synopsis of the progress we've made with the Fleet Response Plan."

"Go ahead."

"By the end of the summer, we'll have in place the components enabling us to surge fifty-percent more combat power to the Western Pacific."

"This increased capability will not escape the notice of the Chinese."

"No, sir. We've validated JTF 519 with our Terminal Fury exercises. Those exercises focused on identification and mobilization of the command staff and worked C4ISR. We're ready to plug in the various operational components."

"The broader question is: how will the Chinese react?"

Stuart said. "The last thing I need right now is for the Law of Unintended Consequences to come into play."

"We should expect some saber rattling."

"Such as?"

"Making another move to strengthen their position in the Spratlys. Less likely would be a move on Taiwan."

"The PLA's defense strategists' goals are to secure their borders and establish a protective zone extending hundreds of miles into China's surrounding seas. If threatened, they may act before we've strengthened our capabilities," Lawson cautioned.

"Bob, where would you focus?"

"If there's a flash point, I'd expect the oil platforms in the Con Song Basin."

"What's behind your reasoning?"

"The PLA's setback in the Spratlys will not deter them for long. Since they were rebuffed in their attempt to push eastward toward the Philippines, we shouldn't be surprised if they don't turn south to test the resolve of the Vietnamese. There's a smaller chance they'd look to the Senkaku Islands and challenge the Japanese."

"Your best guess?"

"They'll go south."

"Anyone disagree? Bryce?"

"It fits. Xiao has made it clear he's losing patience with countries taking advantage of his restraint to the theft of crude oil in waters claimed by China."

"Beijing's biggest club is not the military option. It's their economic power," Valardi said.

Brown threw another opinion out on the table. "I don't believe we should reverse our position to oppose bilateral agreements between China and the nations of ASEAN. We can't approach these discussions between Manila and Beijing as an isolated event. There are other avenues we can pursue to establish common ground with Beijing."

"I'd suggest you propose to Montalvo he continue to stress the importance of the Manila Declaration," Valardi said.

"That's my intention," Stuart replied.

"The PLA has sustained a series of embarrassing setbacks that should strengthen the influence of the moderates supporting Zhu," Payne said. "The time's opportune to advocate complete acceptance by all parties of the terms of the declaration."

"I concur," Valardi said. "Now is not the time for Manila to get cold feet. They have an advantage even if their window of opportunity is closing."

"My guess is that's Manila's thinking. They have to exploit what little advantage they still have," Gilmore observed.

"There's trouble on the horizon if Montalvo insists on going it alone."

"I don't believe he will," Stuart said. "They're other points we shouldn't lose sight of. The Filipinos are bringing their Malampaya natural gas fields online. When they do, they will have secured their national energy needs for years to come... which the Chinese haven't."

"We're back to oil."

"Indeed, we are. We can discuss alliances, terrorism, regional security, military deterrence, and economic growth, but in the end, the single strategic issue that underpins all of these is oil. Bryce, why don't you summarize the National Intelligence Council's report?"

"The bottom line: The world will reach its maximum crude oil production capacity within the next two years. No new substantial deposits have been discovered and the existing reserves will not meet surging worldwide demand."

"Where do we stand?" Payne asked.

"Our strong suit is natural gas and fracking."

"But we still have to secure the world's crude oil supplies," Payne added.

"And that, gentlemen, is ultimately what the South China Sea is all about," Stuart said.

He looked around the table to signal he wanted everyone's undivided attention. "While we must take these into consideration, there is one Montalvo doesn't have to contend with. With no meaningful industrial or financial base and cheap labor, the Philippines can't be economically influenced by China."

"Coerced is the more applicable term," Gilmore said. "That and they're buying folks like Atencio on the cheap."

"For starters, we all need to understand the degree to which our two economies are interdependent. Raising our national debt limit was necessary, but it comes with risks. China has helped support our currency, but the Chinese Central Bank may well sell off U.S. Treasury notes because of a weakening dollar against the yuan."

"Even the rumor of such an action sent the dollar plunging against the yen last year," Valardi said.

"And that in turn, negatively affected our trade balance with Japan and resulted in a panicked sell-off in the New York Stock Exchange."

"What do you propose?" Valardi asked.

Stuart seized the moment to re-exert control and cut off any further discussion. "Bob is on the mark when he identified the Con Song Basin as a flash point. I want a balanced approach that contains Xiao and the hardliners of the PLA while providing every opportunity for Zhu's moderates to retain control of the government this fall. Am I understood?"

Stuart confirmed the affirmative responses. "Richard, I've reviewed the Deputies Committee's point paper on foreign policy initiatives for the Asia-Pacific. I want you to float the proposal for a forum for energy cooperation to the principals. Japan, Korea, Russia, and China."

"If the overtures are received favorably, we'll be able to

develop them further at the upcoming APEC meeting, Mr. President."

"There will be no 'ifs' in these negotiations."

"Yes, sir."

"Good. Our plans for dealing with the Chinese will be flexible and capable of responding to unanticipated events. Be alert for subtle signs that represent a threat to our long-term objectives in the region. I expect you all to have contingency plans in place for us to review and execute on a moment's notice. Tomorrow and Thursday we'll take those measures to keep our friends in Manila from wandering off the path."

"Be reasonable—do it my way?" Lantis summed up to Stuart after the room emptied.

"That's the intent."

"You don't think you were too hard on them?"

"No. I appreciate their passion, but they do have to remain civil. I'll talk to Bryce and Sheldon."

"By the way, I've got another item. I couldn't find an appropriate place to work it in," Lantis said, pulling a newspaper clipping out of his coat pocket. "I doubt this made it into Bryce's Intel brief."

Stuart scanned the header: *China Tackles Toilet Summit.*

"Dan, it's apparent I don't keep you busy enough," he quipped, then sobered. What's this all about?"

"An example of multilateralism?"

"Spare me."

"How about a three-day international commode conference with delegates from nineteen countries discussing such pressing issues as toilet technology, lavatory management, and the causal relationship between toilets and tourism development."

"Who comes up with this stuff?"

"It's on a need-to-know basis, Mr. President."

"Please tell me we were not represented."

"Sorry, sir."

"Oh, Lord." Still grateful for the respite, Stuart smiled. "Would you please remind me again why I asked you to be a member of my personal staff?"

"I serve at the convenience of The President, sir."

Chapter Twenty-Four

SPRATLY ISLAND
THE SOUTH CHINA SEA
07:45 FRIDAY 21 MARCH

N guyen Tran Thang stood at ease on the bridge of his patrol boat, HQ371, watching a frigate bird wheel and dip a short distance away. He took a sip of his morning tea, savoring the strong flavor of the Oolong blend. It was one of his few indulgences and he could feel the stress of the previous night's mission drain from his body.

He shifted his gaze to an awkward vessel tied up off his starboard side. He'd escorted the transport ship three hundred miles from Da Nang to this isolated outpost on Spratly Island.

A satisfied smile crossed his face. The first contingent of troops assigned to the garrison had disembarked and were lining up in a loose formation on the pier.

Labeled 'tourists' by the Foreign Ministry, these men represented only a single component of his country's complex plan to counter Beijing's expansion into Vietnamese waters. When completed, the installation on the three-square-kilo-meter island wouldn't amount to much, but it would be a persistent thorn in the side of their enemy's outposts scattered across the Spratly archipelago.

For the past several months the Army Air Force had been working to extend the island's 2,000-foot runway last used by South Vietnamese forces in 1975. The strip was being prepared for commercial flights by Vietnam Airways. Or so they wanted the media to believe. In point of fact, the new airstrip would expand the country's defensive perimeter.

He studied the soldiers. The Ministry's ruse would be exposed soon enough. After that, any further pretense of secrecy would be self-deceiving. But no harm would come from continuing to claim the island was a resort.

While he pondered Beijing's possible responses, his executive officer, Lieutenant Tien, joined him. "XO."

"Yes, Comrade Commander?"

"Prepare to get underway for Amboyn Cay. I want to weigh anchor within the hour."

Nguyen took a final sip of tea. The tea's name, Fu Shou, was auspicious, meaning Buddha's hand. He wondered if he should heed the urgings of the monks and devote himself to the peaceful teachings of this master, but dismissed the thought. Perhaps in another lifetime. Not after the events on Cuarteron Reef that had led to his assignment.

The sandy cay lay just to the northwest of his current location and had played a much larger role in the recent confrontation with the PLAN than its size would suggest.

The island was claimed by Hanoi in 1988, but no one had even bothered to step foot on it except a few enterprising souls mining guano. The barren island had none-the-less become part of the strategic initiative to counter Chinese expansionism in the region—a pawn in an escalating game of international chess.

The Foreign Ministry had even provided Beijing several proposals the year before to resolve claimancy issues and establish Vietnam's right to explore oil deposits in the Blue Dragon and White Tiger fields.

The areas were of particular importance to the government because of the recent agreements PetroVietnam had signed with the American company, Horizon Offshore Exploration.

Regrettably, China denounced as impertinent the Ministry's offer to submit the issue to the International Court of Justice for arbitration. The government erected a stone marker on Cuarteron Reef and several other atolls in the immediate vicinity following the collapse of this initiative.

Beijing countered by claiming irrevocable sovereignty over the entire area and increased its naval presence to back up its privilege.

The Chief of the General Staff, in turn, countered the PLA's actions and ordered his forces to begin patrolling the islands that defined the southern border of Vietnam's claims in the South China Sea.

The bulk of these contested islands formed a scattered chain extending east from Nguyen's current location and terminated in Pigeon Reef one-hundred and forty miles away.

While he thought the characterization overstated, the army had fortified two of them. The garrisons on Amboyna Cay and Barque Canada were each manned by a single platoon of soldiers. These small outposts southeast of Spratly Island were his next destination. Any further effort to establish an agreement on demarcation lines delineating maritime sovereignty was a complete waste of time.

Nguyen made note of a dotted line on this chart representing Beijing's alleged maritime boundaries. 'The 'Nine Dash Line.' He marveled at the sheer audacity of the Chinese. He traced his finger over the map stopping at the strategic Balabac Strait separating the southern Philippine Islands from Malaysia.

"Is something wrong, sir?" Tien asked.

"They are seeking to assert their dominion over an expanse of ocean that defies comprehension."

"The Chinese?"

"Yes."

"They cannot enforce their claim, can they?"

"Not without difficulty, XO."

"Will we encounter trouble at Ambyon Cay and Barque Canada?"

"Our mission will proceed as planned unless we run into an unexpected entanglement with the Filipinos. They've negotiated agreements with Beijing's Ministries of Fisheries and Geology and Mineral Resources to pursue aquatic and seabed exploration. Using those agreements as pretext, the Chinese have begun a construction project on Commodore Reef to support their fishing industry."

"Should we divert and update our intelligence? It's not far from our research station on Pigeon Reef."

Nguyen paused. "Commodore Reef has become a source of consternation for the Foreign Ministry in their dealings with Manila."

"Filipino fishermen are thumbing their noses at us, dragging their nets around the atoll with impunity," Tien added.

"Their actions can no more be tolerated than Beijing's. Since the Ministry's complaints to Manila continue to be met with indifference, we've been ordered to put some bite into our diplomatic protests."

"Do you have a plan, sir?"

"I have the latitude to escort out of the area any Filipino boats illegally fishing near Pigeon Reef."

"And the Chinese?"

"Our guidance in dealing with them is less precise."

"That could be to our benefit."

Nguyen tired of the questions. "What are the potential

risks and planning factors required to conduct a reconnaissance of Commodore Reef?"

Tien straightened. "Sir, if the Chinese have established a
presence on Commodore Reef, the advantage the PLA will be
intolerable. Even if the Chinese were there under the auspices
of a collaborative effort with the Filipinos, it's probable they
would twist the partnership to their advantage. Beijing will not
have forgotten their betrayal by Manila under similar circumstances several years ago."

"Very good, XO. The Chinese failure to grab the Reed
Bank natural gas fields caused them considerable loss of face."

"But didn't the PLA turn the balance of power in the
South China Sea by seizing Mischief Reef?"

"Indeed, they did. With that in mind, the Chinese will find
a way to evict the Filipinos from Commodore Reef. The PLA
will have then established a flanking position extending south
along their self-proclaimed territorial line from First Thomas
Shoal and Mischief Reef."

"They could sweep up our small outposts."

Nguyen made his decision. "We will do exactly that."

"Sir?"

"We are going to use the Filipinos and Chinese to bait our
trap."

"How?"

"Patience, Lieutenant. You will soon see how to apply the
tenets of asymmetric warfare and turn America's interests in
the region to our advantage. That is, if the Ministry is clever
and acts on the advantage I am about to give them."

"We are going to bait a trap?"

"Precisely. Now, see to your duties."

Nguyen scanned the open water beyond the harbor. At
this hour, Ladd Reef would just be visible. A wisp of color
caught his attention. He concentrated on the spot. A thatched
hut stood in the middle of the lagoon perched on a cluster of
spindly bamboo poles.

He pulled his binoculars from their bulkhead rack and lifted them to his eyes. A slender staff planted in front of the shelter came into focus. He followed its course upward.

His country's flag still flew. Tattered and bleached a pale red by the sun, it was a testament to the determination of his countrymen to stand defiant before any adversary.

The voices began to call. "Avenge us. AVENGE US. Do not forsake our sacrifice."

Louder now, they imposed their will: "Avenge us, AVENGE US."

Nguyen broke into a cold sweat. He tried to suppress the horrors of that night so many years ago, but they were seared into his mind. The smells of charred flesh. The mutilated bodies. Helplessness, rage, the guilt of surviving when so many others had lost their lives. They all haunted him.

———

PIGEON REEF

The HQ371's launch cleared the channel leading from Pigeon Reef's sheltered lagoon, encountering the first breaker rolling over the barrier reef. The small vessel slammed into a second. They plowed through the wave-top, a shower of seawater drenching its occupants.

Nguyen was far from annoyed. He welcomed the deluge.

His visit with the officials of the small research station had gone well enough, but the discussions left him with a lingering sense of frustration. He had tried in vain to turn the topic of conversation from a discussion of the intricacies of fisheries research in the South China Sea.

"Have you had any contact with the Chinese or Filipinos from Commodore Reef? While you were surveying and setting out your nets and buoys, did you see any PLAN or Philippine naval vessels?"

Despite his prodding, the officials hadn't been able to provide any useful intelligence to supplement what he had seen.

Nguyen pulled off his sunglasses and wiped off the salt spotting the lenses. He balanced them on his thigh and rubbed his temples to massage away the throbbing headache he'd been contending with for most of the day.

Any further concern about his headache vanished when the launch rammed into another breaker. The impact forced the boat's bow skyward, its momentum carrying it up the face of the wave. The launch paused at the wave's apex, then pitched downward.

At the bottom of the trough, it buried its bow into the base of another oncoming wave sending a torrent of water cascading into the boat. The water disappeared through the deck gratings, sloshing angrily around in the bilge. Jarred off course by the collision, the launch was struck a quartering blow by the next breaker, almost broaching.

The blow flung Nguyen off his seat. He grabbed the gunnel to break his fall. "Mind your helm. Bring her straight into the breakers. If you present our quarter, we'll swamp."

He twisted in his seat to look at the retreating island. The vista was in stark contrast to what he had seen earlier in the day at Commodore Reef.

Commodore Reef held no resemblance to a quiet backwater research station. It was being transformed into another Chinese bastion. Through his binoculars, he'd seen two oceangoing barges, both flying the Chinese flag. The largest, with a huge earth-moving scoop, was dredging the lagoon. The second, rigged with a pile driver, was pounding in the foundation supports for what was going to be a very substantial building. Nguyen counted numerous PLA engineers, but no Filipinos.

·   ·   ·

"Captain?" The Petty Officer held out the headset for ship-to-ship radio. "Excuse me, sir. Lieutenant Tien requests to speak with you. He says it's most urgent."

"Nguyen."

"Captain, the watch has heard explosions."

"What? Where?"

"They are infrequent and appear to be coming from the east."

"It appears we have our illegal fishermen. They're using dynamite. Are you ready to get underway?"

"Yes, sir. We've shortened the anchor."

"Do we still have that Chinese ensign?"

"I'll have to dig for it, sir."

"When you find it, hoist it at the peak."

"Sir?"

"The Filipinos will see the Chinese flag and report this to the authorities at the AFP's Western Military Command Center."

The pitch of the launch's engine changed. They were slowing to approach the stern of the patrol boat. The coxswain reversed his engine and eased the boat up against the hull of the larger vessel.

Nguyen didn't wait for the launch to come to a full stop. He leapt for the chain ladder and was pulled aboard by Tien.

"Has there been any status change of the contact, XO?"

"The explosions have stopped, sir."

"They're probably scooping up their haul. There is no art in the way they fish."

Nguyen looked at the masthead. The Chinese ensign fluttered in the breeze. "Good, you located the flag."

"Yes, sir."

"What's the distance and bearing?"

"Three kilometers. One hundred degrees true."

"Find Petty Officer Phuong and have him report to me. Then I want you to make stencils to change our hull numbers

to match one of the PLAN's Houjian class patrol boats.
And, XO?"

"Sir?"

"You're going to have a chance to practice your Tagalog.
You will command the boarding party."

———

THE FISHING BOAT
DILIHA V.

Intent on sorting through the stunned mass of fish piled on
the stained deck of their trawler, they had not seen the boat
approach. The first indication of trouble for the fishermen of
the DILIHA V. was a foreign voice hailing from across the
water. They jerked their heads around searching for the source
of the sound.

"There!" yelled the first man to see the unknown vessel.
"Over there."

The others looked to the area indicated by their mate. A
patrol boat raced toward them, white water foaming at
its bow.

"What do they want?" the Captain worried to no one in
particular. "We've done nothing wrong."

Any question the seamen had about the intent of the
intruders vanished when a burst of gunfire erupted from the
patrol boat. The 76mm cannon rounds tore a ragged line of
waterspouts across their bow. The fishermen stood paralyzed
in disbelief. Even though they couldn't comprehend the
dialect, there could be no misunderstanding the message
being conveyed. This was dead serious.

They watched with mounting trepidation as the warship
slowed, coming to a stop off their beam. The patrol boat's
forward gun mount remained trained on them while an
armed boarding party readied itself.

The ship's ensign signaled its identity. Chinese. The captain recovered his wits sufficiently to read the vessel's hull number below the bridge.

The fishermen could only stare when the boarding party swarmed onto their deck. They were herded into a tight knot by bayonet-tipped rifles. No words were needed. The cold look in their captors' eyes and the rifle barrels leveled at their chests conveyed their intent. "Do not disobey. Follow our orders."

Tien stepped forward, certain the cowering crew would not resist. He glared at the dead fish. "Chinese fish. Chinese water. Understand?"

He spotted a shovel on the deck, picked it up, and thrust it into the nearest Filipino's hands. "Chinese fish." He motioned for the man to shovel the mound of dead fish over the side.

He directed his anger at the captain. The fisherman could not be allowed to alert the Philippine Navy. At least, not yet. Tien knew his captain's intent—to proceed undetected to the north and deal an equally unpleasant surprise to the Chinese garrison on Sin Cowe Island.

"Radio?"

The captain didn't respond.

Tien pulled his pistol from its holster and took aim at the man's head. "Radio."

The petrified man shook his head. "No. No radio."

"Good. You leave now. Chinese water."

"I go."

Tien uttered a satisfied grunt. He'd set the stage for the next part of his captain's plan.

———

SIN COWE ISLAND

Nguyen's approach to Sin Cowe Island was more cautious, the danger in these waters was very real. They closed the island passing the rusting hulk of a Vietnamese Navy transport.

Nguyen didn't need to be reminded of the atrocity committed by the Chinese in 1988. They had slaughtered scores of his countrymen in a brief but bloody battle for control of the island.

"XO, come about and slow to five knots. Bring us to within three-hundred meters of the shore. We're going to take a closer look."

Nguyen scanned the isolated beach, alert for any sign of trouble. Sin Cowe was just one of a scattering of atolls bordering an area called Union Reefs. Over the years, the Chinese had invested a significant amount of effort and money to establish a substantive presence here.

Johnson Reef, ostensibly a fisheries logistic center, lay a short distance away. In reality, the center linked the PLAN's command center for the central Spratlys on Fiery Cross Reef and their outpost on Mischief Reef.

Hanoi insisted it still had a legitimate claim to the area despite its defeat in the earlier battle. The Vietnamese claims were tenuous at best, and they had no structures on any of the other atolls except for an abandoned lighthouse on Sin Cowe Island.

Nguyen concluded there was no evidence of Chinese troops on the atoll when a movement caught his attention. *A man running down the beach?*

Tien interrupted before he could confirm what he'd seen. "Captain, we have a contact bearing 120 degrees true."

"Repeat your last."

"Sir, we have a bogy making two-hundred and forty knots, altitude one-thousand feet."

"Distance?"

"Fifteen kilometers and closing."

"Light it up with the fire control radar. We'll permit one pass. If they come around for another look, we'll fire warning shots."

The aircraft came into view. Nguyen thought it might miss them altogether, but at the last moment, the plane altered course and flew over their masthead.

"It's an OV-10. Harmless."

"Perhaps, XO."

The OV-10 circled to begin another pass. It descended and began an approach that would take it down their port side.

The patrol boat's radar-controlled gun traversed drawing a bead on the aircraft.

He had a second to react. "Fire."

The gun spit out three rounds. Nguyen flinched at the sharp bark of the 76mm cannon even though he was prepared for the blasts.

The effect on the OV-10's startled pilot was more pronounced. He banked his aircraft in a steep turn, almost cartwheeling when the plane's wing clipped the top of a palm tree. The pilot recovered and clawed for altitude. He leveled off and headed south distancing himself from the hostile warship.

———

This brief engagement also terrified the unsuspecting soldier on the beach. Just moments before he was happily waving to the ship. Then he spotted the plane diving at him and heard cannon fire. He dove for cover, burying his head in the sand in a panicked act of survival. Pieces of palm tree cascaded around him, preventing him from observing any more of the engagement. He could only conclude his island was under attack.

Nguyen was not the only one tracking the AFP plane. The Chinese on Johnson Reef also monitored the OV-10's progress.

The Chinese operator was used to the periodic appearance of the reconnaissance plane and was jotting down a perfunctory note in his logbook.

There appeared to be nothing out of the ordinary until he glanced at his screen. The contact had disappeared from the scope. Puzzled by the anomaly, he adjusted the gain just as the watch officer seated next to him received a distress call.

"Command, command. I'm under attack."

"Attack? Who is this?"

"Corporal Chen, NCO in Charge, Sin Cowe detachment."

Incredulous, the officer replied, "Are you sure?"

"Yes."

"But why would someone want to do that? There's nothing there."

"How should I know? I'm here. Maybe they attack you, too."

The watch officer was at a complete loss for a rational explanation. He could only conclude the report was valid. He alerted the garrison's gun crews and picked up the phone to notify his commander.

"Colonel, this is the watch officer. We have received a report of gunfire from Sin Cowe. An unidentified aircraft is approaching. I've directed the gun crews to target the plane."

"Don't do anything until I get there."

"Excuse me, Colonel. We have a visual."

"Have you identified the aircraft?"

"Yes, sir. An OV-10. Probably from the 570th Composite Tactical Fighting Wing."

"Are there other contacts? The—"

A thunderous barrage of 37mm antiaircraft fire terminated the remainder of the commander's sentence.

"What are you doing?" the colonel bellowed over the din. "Cease fire. Cease fire."

The colonel ran to the control room and burst through the door. "Who gave them permission to fire?"

"Sir, the corporal believes he may have been mistaken."

"Corporal? What corporal?"

"The NCO in charge on Sin Cowe."

The commander shook his head trying to make sense of the chaos. "What does he have to do with this?"

"He called saying he was under attack."

"What exactly did he say?"

"Sir?"

The colonel looked at the radar officer. "What is it?"

"The corporal thinks the patrol boat was firing at the plane."

"What did you say? A patrol boat? What patrol boat?"

"I don't know, sir."

"Well, be sure to thank the corporal for that bit of clarity."

"Sir?"

"What the hell's going on around here? Get me headquarters on Fiery Cross Reef."

————

The pilot of the OV-10 skimmed over the wave-tops flying as fast as he dared. He was not going to stay in the area after receiving hostile fire for the second time in almost as many minutes.

"Cavite, Cavite. This is Scout Two. We have photographed a warship off Sin Cowe Island flying Chinese colors that matches the fishermen's description. It appears to be a Houjian class missile corvette, hull number N-603. We have taken hostile fire from the ship and the PLA installation on Johnson Reef."

Chapter Twenty-Five

COMCPACFLT HEADQUARTERS
PEARL HARBOR, HAWAII
07:00 MONDAY 24 MARCH

"Commander, you're gonna want to see this."
"Damn, Senior, I just walked into the room. How about, 'Good morning Commander, how was your weekend?'"

Mackenzie handed over the message folder. "Aye, aye, Commander. Good morning, sir. I hope you had a great weekend. You're gonna want to see this."

"I don't suppose it can wait until I pour my coffee?"

"Afraid not, sir."

"What do you have that's so all-fired important?"

"Things are heating up in the Spratlys."

Rohrbaugh took the folder and dropped into his desk chair. It contained the contact report from the AFP's Western Military District Commander and the intelligence department's analysis.

"Appears the Chinese can't leave well enough alone," Rohrbaugh commented after reading several paragraphs.

"Makes you wonder what's wrong with those guys. They're sure pretty slow on the uptake. You'd have thought they'd gotten the message."

"You'd think."

"What bothers me, Skipper, is they keep misjudging. One of these days they're gonna start something we won't be able to contain."

"Taking a pot shot at an OV-10 isn't such a big deal. Happens all the time—keeps the AFP from snooping around. What doesn't square up is the Chinese are raising hell. I would've thought they'd simply ignore Manila's protests or have some low-level functionary issue a denial."

"I'm impressed, Skipper. I didn't know you were becoming a beltway guy."

"Hardly, but I am learning to read between the lines."

"I'll bite. What're they saying?"

Rohrbaugh laid the report on his desk. "They didn't do it."

"Alright. Then, who did? It's tough to ignore the photograph of that corvette."

"The PLAN denies having a patrol boat in the area."

"Easy enough to say, sir, but we know the Chinese track record. They'll look you right in the face and lie if it suits them. Sounds to me as if they got caught with their hand in the cookie jar."

"Mac, let's think out of the box for a minute. Ever get detention for a fight the other guy started?"

"Yeah, really pissed me off. Especially when my dad found out and gave me a whipping when I got home."

"See where I'm going with this?"

"You've lost me, Skipper."

"What would the PLAN have to gain by pulling off another dumb stunt like they did with that other fishing boat?"

"Not much. If the Chinese didn't do it, who did?"

"The Vietnamese."

"That's just plain nuts."

"I'm not so sure. The Vietnamese can't be pleased that Beijing and Manila have begun exploratory talks on joint seismic surveys. If you were in their seat, what would you do?"

"I'd be looking for a way to stir up trouble."

"Exactly. And remember, the Vietnamese and PLA navies both have patrol boats based on the design of the Russian Tarantul class corvette."

"I hadn't thought about disguising their ship, Skipper. They just might be able to pull that off. Want me to work this with intel? Run a sanity check on your theory?"

"Yeah, that'd be good start."

"As long as we're on the subject of stirring the pot, aren't we looking at basing agreements for Cam Ranh Bay and Da Nang?"

"Yup, Admiral Cortez is scheduled to make a visit to Hanoi in the next week or two to lay the groundwork."

"I'm starting to get a bad feeling here, Skipper. It wouldn't take much to get in a fight we don't want. We've already had the P-8s."

"It may come to that if we don't play our cards right. The spark could be the PRC's new 'Law of Littoral Imperatives.'"

"Never heard of it."

"Came up in yesterday's morning brief. It codifies the changes in Chinese naval doctrine we've seen over the past year. Just a sec, I've got something."

Rohrbaugh pulled open a desk drawer and leafed through a series of green hanging folders. "Here it is. You'll love this:

'To ensure that the descendants of the Chinese nation will prosper and flourish in the coming millennium, it's imperative that we vigorously develop and use the oceans. To protect and defend the rights and interests of the reefs and islands within Chinese waters is a sacred mission.'"

. . .

"That's a load, Skipper."

"I'd say, but the folks at State and the Pentagon got really spooled up over the next section. The PLA pushed through the wording over the objections of the Ministry of Foreign Affairs. The Chinese are claiming all of the South and East China Seas. Every reef and island of strategic importance."

"That's just priceless."

"Actually, Mac, you've got it right. The PLAN has now defined a national imperative linking its mission to the economic wellbeing of the country."

"If that's the case, Skipper, then I'm placing my money for the OV-10 and fishing-boat incidents on the Chinese. They're sending a message to everyone in the region to stand clear."

"Valid point."

"Sir, the piece I don't care much for is the East China Sea. They've fired a shot across Japan's bow."

"They have, indeed. Time will tell how that piece shakes out. There's already a lot of bad blood between them. And speaking of bad blood, did you happen to catch the article in yesterday's *Star Advertiser* about the abuse the Japanese national soccer team took in Beijing? Made a Yankees-Red Sox game look like a picnic. Japanese team needed an armed escort to get out of the stadium."

"Poor form. What was it all about?"

"The Chinese are totally pissed about a new Japanese schoolbook."

"You're kidding. Right?"

"Straight up, Mac. The book minimized the atrocities the Imperial Japanese Army committed during World War II. Got the Koreans all worked up, too. Both countries are demanding a formal apology from Tokyo and demanding the textbook be withdrawn."

"So now the pot is being stirred up north. Seems to me,

the linchpin to containing the Chinese may be collaborating with the Vietnamese."

"Hanoi could be the key. There're a couple of scenarios unfolding. Depending on what shakes out, we'd be wise to look south for a containment strategy."

"What? South Vietnam? Again?"

"One of our scenarios is predicated on the PLA making a move against Japan. Either a grab for the Senkakus or Tokyo's new oil exploration rigs in the East China Sea. If that were Beijing's intent, it would make sense for them to create a diversion in the south."

Mackenzie's eyes drifted to the intelligence folder. "And if they continue to deploy anti-ship missiles to the Spratlys?"

"It will get ugly."

"Do we have anything in the works with the Vietnamese?"

"Funny you should say that."

Mackenzie stiffened. "What's up, Commander?"

"I've been tagged to go to Vietnam with a military liaison team. We're tasked with developing the framework for a Joint Forces Agreement."

Mackenzie covered his surprise. "Got a departure date?"

"The week after next. The team is going in-country following Admiral Cortez's trip. I don't have the specifics. There's a kickoff briefing scheduled for this afternoon. I'll have a better handle on what's going on after that."

"Pretty short-fused. This going to impact the work we're doing on the OPLAN?"

"This mission is tailored to fit."

"I'd think the ideal scenario would be for us to set up basing agreements with the Philippines, Japan, and Vietnam so we're positioned to strike from three different directions."

"You're on target, Mac. Manila is already working their options. While they're pursuing cooperative agreements with Beijing in fisheries and seismic studies, they're hedging their bets by keeping the door open to us."

"Balikatan?"

"Correct. The *Early Bird* had an interesting article several weeks ago excerpted from the *Manila Times*. Should be in my Philippine file.

Several of our guys deployed to Fort Magsaysay for the exercise and worked with the AFPs Special Operations Command. They traded notes with a Special Warfare officer who led the rescue operation of that hijacked fishing boat a couple of months ago. Kept his head under fire and got his people out. Name was Torres."

"Sounds like one of us. I'd like to meet him."

"We may get the chance. Got it. 'Balikatan Starts, New Venues Added.'"

"Don't keep me in suspense, Skipper."

"The press picked up on the inclusion of Palawan and Batanes and went after the AFP Chief of Staff. He responded with a 'No comment.'"

"Nothing to get worked up about."

"True, but the general shot himself in the foot."

"Oh, great."

"Yeah. When pressed, he added the emphasis of this year's exercise is to explore the range of possibilities of the Mutual Defense Treaty and Status of Forces Agreements."

"Nothing new there."

"Ah, don't be so quick to jump to conclusions, Mac. On the surface there isn't. But it does give the PLA a read on where PACOM is headed."

"How's that?"

"First off, the general noted the tie-in to the Mutual Defense Treaty and Status of Forces Agreements. I can tell you the Filipinos are focused on the security of their Malampaya and Reed Bank natural gas fields. And, keep this in mind. Because of the wording of our existing treaty, the fishing boat incident didn't trigger our involvement. That said, the open question is whether the defense of those gas fields would fall under the Mutual Defense Treaty. He stated this issue was not discussed in the exercise-planning sessions."

"Using your theory, the treaty probably was. Now, what about Batanes? I've never heard of the place."

"I had to look it up. It's a province north of Luzon. From a tactical perspective, it's ideal. We'll be able to stage clandestine ops once the infrastructure's in place."

"That being worked?"

"Yup, exercise Balikatan's Civic Action Programs provided cover for the Seabees. Usual stuff. Roads, couple of school-houses, medical clinic."

"Constructed for dual use, I suppose."

"Our intentions are always altruistic."

"Warms my heart, sir."

"You've always had such a gentle touch, Mac. By the way, the general also happened to roll this little grenade into the room before being hustled off the stage."

"Oh, Lord." Mackenzie said, bracing for the next piece.

"He said that Batanes was chosen as a venue because of its strategic location just two-hundred fifty kilometers from Taiwan and because it has served as a refueling station for U.S. forces."

"Damn, Skipper. Talk about poking a stick at a sleeping dog. The last thing we want is to get Taiwan mixed up in this. All hell could break loose."

"Admiral Lawson and the Secretary of Defense rolled over hard right when they read the excepts of the general's press conference. Went all the way to the White House."

Rohrbaugh grabbed his cover. "I've gotta shove off for the morning lineup. Go ahead and pull our files after you talk with Intel. I'll fill you in when I get back."

"Aye, aye, Commander. Good hunting."

"Yeah, right."

Chapter Twenty-Six

CAMP H. M. SMITH
HEADQUARTERS U.S. PACIFIC COMMAND
13:00 MONDAY 24 MARCH

Mike Rohrbaugh cast his eyes over the parallel rows of tables. He picked a seat near the front, pushed the adjacent chairs away to make more elbow room and dropped into a seat.

A series of events had occurred throughout the morning that accounted for the sour look on his face. He had cut his run short because of a sore hamstring, Kate had left for the mainland to visit her mom for two weeks, and he never did get his cup of coffee.

Underlying his discontent, he couldn't shake his sense of unease about the emerging trend of Chinese activity in the Spratlys. He heard the sound of footsteps and looked up to see an Air Force officer position himself behind the lectern.

"Good afternoon, gentlemen, I'm Major Frank Dowling with the J-31 shop. My brief will lay the groundwork to address the specific aspects of your mission to Vietnam. I'll focus on the strategic ramifications of recent developments in the South China Sea, not the tactical implications. That's your job, to integrate our strategic objectives into your CONOPs and OPLANs.

"Admiral Cortez is developing a balanced plan to address the immediate threat in the South China Sea and the long-term challenges presented by the PLA. The CONOP will define PACOM's mission to shape the security environment, develop flexible deterrent options, and the supporting infrastructure to execute them. And if it comes to confrontation, gentlemen, let there be no doubt we will dominate the battlefield."

Rohrbaugh grimaced. *Man, stow the rah-rah.* He looked around the room to get a read on the other officers. Nothing. He shrugged and turned his attention back to the brief.

"Keeping these points in mind," Dowling said, "let's take a look at the trend we've seen over the past six months. The PLA has continued to solidify and expand the capabilities of their existing bases. They have done so while establishing additional garrisons in the eastern Spratly Islands. As you see on this slide, their installation on Mischief Reef is within the two-hundred-mile EEZ of the Philippines."

Rohrbaugh looked up from his doodles to see what Dowling was referring to.

Downing pointed to another island. "They may occupy Nanshan Island, located due north of Mischief Reef. The island's only 580 meters long, but it has a small airstrip."

"Excuse me, Major," Rohrbaugh said. "A question."

"Rohrbaugh, isn't it?"

Rohrbaugh kept his face impassive. *How'd he know my name?* "Yes, PacFleet Special Ops. We identified Nanshan as a staging point if we target Mischief Reef. Do you have any hard intel?"

"Not at this time."

That's all he needed to know. "Thank you."

"Commander Rohrbaugh highlights a valid point. As it stands, the PLA will soon dominate our lines of approach. This is a good segue to my next point. Let me jump ahead a couple of slides. I want to touch on the documents underpinning the PLA's strategic planning.

"Your briefing pack includes copies of the salient points of Beijing's Law of Territorial Seas and Contiguous Zones and the recently promulgated Law of Littoral Imperatives. Besides providing the justification to implement measures aimed at neutralizing the forces of the Pacific Command and the Japanese Self Defense Force, these laws brush aside the national interests of the ASEAN member states."

Dowling paused. "Questions?"

None were forthcoming. "Suffice it to say, the intent of these Chinese laws is to codify their claim to the South China Sea and justify their use of force. We must not lose sight of the fact the PRC has adopted a strategic doctrine of power projection and sea control. The key point in our analysis of possible outcomes is Beijing has demonstrated a willingness to resort to armed intervention when it is in their interest to do so."

Rohrbaugh shifted in his seat and lifted his hand. "Such as the latest incident over Johnson Reef?"

"Exactly, Commander," Dowling responded, welcoming the opportunity to abandon his power point. "And, I'd add, the previous hostage incident."

Rohrbaugh kept his mouth shut. He didn't share Dowling's certainty about Chinese culpability in the fishing boat incident, but this was not the place or time for a debate on the merits of his ideas.

Dowling flipped through several pages of notes. "In a counterpoint to the PRC's ambitions in the region, the Vietnamese are pursuing development of their own offshore oil deposits. Washington is monitoring the situation because of the proximity of an American-Vietnamese joint venture. The American company is a start-up named Horizon Offshore Exploration."

"And this has created another flash point?" the Army officer to Rohrbaugh's left commented.

Dowling noted the time and chose not to elaborate. He needed to corner Rohrbaugh. There was a matter of such sensitivity that his boss, a Marine Major General, wanted to personally speak to the SEAL. "This is a good stopping point. We'll reconvene at 1345."

He stepped away from the podium and caught Rohrbaugh before he could make it to the head. "Excuse me, Commander. You have a moment?"

Rohrbaugh hesitated, worried he may have overstepped. "Sure, what's on your mind?"

Dowling gave no indication of what he might have thought of Rohrbaugh's concern. "The J-3 wants to speak with you after the brief."

"Can you tell me the subject?"

"Afraid not."

"You can't tell me? Or you don't know?"

"Both."

"Okay."

Rohrbaugh knew better than to press the matter, but his curiosity was piqued. He decided he didn't need to go to the head after all and reversed course back to the conference room.

———

Dowling reconvened the session fifteen minutes later. "There are political, security, and economic imperatives driving Tokyo, Manila, and Hanoi to reassess their relationships with the United States. Suffice it to say, the common link driving these countries is China."

"What about the Nationalists?" the Colonel asked.

"With the exception of Taiwan's nascent garrison on Ita Abu Island, they haven't been a significant player in the Spratlys. Driving our relationship is a change in Washington's view of our security alliance with Tokyo. That said, Seventh Fleet has begun exploratory discussions with the Japanese Maritime Self Defense Force to expand the scope of exercise Annual-Ex. PACOM is also pursuing the possibility of moving up the timeline for exercise Keen Edge. Beijing's reaction to these discussions will bear watching."

Rohrbaugh recalled what he'd read in yesterday's *Early Bird*. The news summary contained a clipping about China's Vice Premier canceling a scheduled meeting with the Japanese Prime Minister and returning to Beijing. The Xinua News Agency placed the blame for cutting short the diplomatic visit at the feet of the Japanese. Something to do with Japanese government officials visiting a shrine that the Chinese felt glorified Japan's militaristic past.

The old wounds from World War II are still festering, Rohrbaugh thought before picking up the thread of Dowling's presentation.

"...our main strike force elements would be tasked with neutralizing the PLA naval and air forces at their bases at Fenghuang, Yulin, Zhanjiang, and Harkou. Depending on the scope of the conflict, the Japanese navy would be called on to help contain the PLAN's submarine force. Those submarines, especially their diesel-electric Type 636 Kilo's, present the single greatest threat to our carrier strike groups."

Rohrbaugh nodded. Japan's participation with exercises Keen Edge and Annual-Ex, would not be lost on the Chinese and the PLAN had already begun to probe the JMSDF for any weaknesses in their ASW defenses. While he pondered what role, if any, the Japanese would play in an open confrontation with the PLA, a new slide appeared:

MISSION EXECUTION: PLA CHALLENGES

Downing pointed. "Our analysis indicates the Chinese have encountered significant tactical issues they must overcome if they are to realize their ambitions in the South China Sea. Our intent is to exploit these."

Rohrbaugh grunted in agreement. Their garrisons were small and widely dispersed and the PLA would be hard pressed to counter an external threat. This fact was pounded home to the Chinese after the AFP sank two of their patrol boats. Dowling's next point caught Rohrbaugh's attention.

"The other reality is Beijing's assertion of sovereignty over the South China Sea as defined in their Law of the Territorial Seas does not have validity. Article Eight of this law pertains. It's quoted on this slide. Please take a moment to read it.

"The People's Republic of China has asserted it retains the right to prevent the passage of vessels through its territorial waters and will order the eviction of foreign naval vessels. Foreign naval vessels, under this 'law,' must obtain Chinese permission before proceeding through the South China Sea and foreign submarines must surface and fly their country's flag."

"Bullshit!" erupted a voice from the room.

"Actually, those were Admiral Cortez's sentiments, although he expressed them in slightly different language," Dowling replied silencing the chuckles in the room.

"The Admiral has made it clear we will take whatever actions are necessary to comply with the President's directive that no country will threaten our right of free passage."

Dowling paused. "The PLA does not currently present a direct threat. They have, however, made significant progress in fielding an anti-ship variant of their CSS-5. This missile is projected to have a 1500-kilometer range and would place any carrier strike group operating within the South China Sea at risk. That said, they have three significant obstacles to overcome: a proven second stage re-entry vehicle with terminal guidance, penetrating sub-munitions for their warheads, and a lack of ocean surveillance satellites for targeting."

Rohrbaugh had heard the scuttlebutt about the Chinese missile, but it didn't address his immediate concerns. "Excuse me, Major."

Downing stopped. "Commander?"

"That's all well and good, but my planning is focused on the immediate threat."

"Understood. Analysis of satellite imagery and SIGINT suggests the Chinese have constructed at least one storage bunker and several launch ramps for their H-2 Seersucker anti-ship missile on Woody Island. They are supported by tracking and targeting radar installations on Rocky Island."

Dowling pointed out the locations with his laser designator. "Both of these islands are part of the Paracel group in the northwest South China Sea. Furthermore, we have evidence the PLA recently test-fired a C-802 tactical cruise missile from a site in the Paracels. The C-802 has both land attack and anti-ship capability. The PLA will, in very short order, have a credible offensive capability to interdict and destroy vessels transiting the international shipping lanes or attack static targets such as the Philippine base on Pagasa Island."

Before Dowling could continue, the conference room door opened and a khaki clad naval officer with four silver stars gleaming on his collars strode into the room.

"Attention on deck."

"At ease, gentlemen, please remain seated."

Everyone in the room ignored this polite request and came to attention.

"Major, may I take a few moments of your time?"

"Of course, sir."

Admiral Alberto Cortez, Commander, United States Indo-Pacific Command, took his station at the podium. "Please take your seats. I trust you are finding Major Dowling's presentation informative.

"My guidance to the Three was to put together a succinct presentation outlining the broader policy and strategic challenges we face in the theater. Your understanding of these fundamental issues will be of great value in your work with your counterparts in Vietnam. The personal working relationships you form with these officers will provide the critical underpinnings for our initiatives in the region. I expect you to be observant, noting the state of their morale, their leadership, equipment, and training.

"Let me share some of my observations on the region. The combination of old resentments, emerging economies, increased military spending, and the restructuring of the social order has created a dangerous brew. With the various nations in the region seeking to exert their influence and protect their national interests, a strategic convergence has developed with their goals and those of the United States.

"Your work will augment the Joint Chief's directive to increase the visibility and response time of U.S. forces in the Western Pacific. I expect you to frame your thinking within the context of restructuring the command and deployment of our forces.

"All of our indicators point to the same conclusion. If hostilities were to break out in the South China Sea, there will be little, if any, notice. There may be various scenarios such as an increase in small unit encounters, imposition of trade tariffs and counter sanctions, a ratcheting up of belligerent speech and threats, but in the end, the thrust of the sword will be swift, unexpected, and deadly. Major, you may now resume your presentation."

"Thank you, Admiral. Attention on deck."

Dowling wrapped up his briefing at fifteen-thirty hours and approached Rohrbaugh.

"Ready to roll?"

"Lead on."

"The Three's office is just down the hall."

"Good brief, Major. Name's Mike."

"Thanks. It's a different life up here with the staff."

"Yeah, tell me about it."

"In my real life, I fly Paveways for a living."

"You been to 'The Stan?'"

"Yeah. Twice."

"You?"

"I've been stuck at a desk for the past year." What Rohrbaugh didn't volunteer was what he had really been doing for the past decade including his three clandestine missions in northern Pakistan.

Chapter Twenty-Seven

DIRECTORATE FOR OPERATIONS
J-3 USCINCPAC
15:30 MONDAY 24 MARCH

Dowling stopped in front of the J-3's office and rapped on the open door. The red nameplate indicated the occupant was a Marine two star. "General, Commander Rohrbaugh is here to see you, sir."

"Enter."

Dowling escorted Rohrbaugh into the room and came to attention. "Will there be anything else, sir?"

"Would you ask the Captain to join us and secure the door as you leave."

The Marine waited until the door clicked shut before speaking. "Commander, please have a seat. Coffee, water?"

"No, thank you, sir. I'm good."

Rohrbaugh wasn't able to get a read on the situation and was further nonplussed to recognize an old shipmate enter through the side door.

"Good afternoon, General. Nice to see you again, Mike."

"You two know each other then. How come I'm not surprised."

"Yes, sir," replied the newcomer. "We've shared some interesting times together."

"I have no doubt. 'Interesting' covers a lot of territory."

"Yes, sir."

"Since no introductions are necessary, Commander, let me just say that Captain Kaukane has been working a special project."

A thousand questions spun through Rohrbaugh's mind, but this, again, was not the time or place to voice them. That would come later. The General's demeanor demanded he just listen.

"Admiral Cortez has cleared your participation with Admiral Morey. Admiral Morey is the only individual at PacFleet who is aware of the project and your involvement."

Pausing, the Marine looked at Rohrbaugh to emphasize the implications of his statement.

"Yes, sir."

"Good, we'll proceed. You've been selected to be part of a special surveillance and intelligence gathering mission code-named, 'Valiant Crane.' Captain Kaukane has been working the mission since its inception and will be your point of contact. I've asked him to provide you the thumbnail. Captain."

"Mike, elements of the mission team are already in transit. You will detach from your liaison team and lash up with them via an at-sea transfer."

Kaukane read the look on Rohrbaugh's face. "Question?"

"Negative."

Rohrbaugh cast a look at the General. The Marine's expression indicated he wasn't going to insert himself in the conversation.

"Your timelines are tight," Kaukane continued. "They're covered in the mission planning book we'll go over tomorrow morning. I can tell you, that once on site, the team's mission will have several components: mapping navigation points, oceanographic analysis, surveillance, and intelligence collection.

"The Chinese have several high-value assets in the area we want to exploit. The nature of the mission is such that certain elements are compartmentalized."

Rohrbaugh pondered Kaukane's statements. There were clandestine elements even he couldn't be brought in on. He wondered who else was involved in this operation.

"Thank you, Captain. I believe we have provided Commander Rohrbaugh a starting point to begin mapping out his mission."

Standing, the General ended the meeting. "Stay in touch."

"Yes, sir," the two SEALs responded in unison.

Rohrbaugh pulled up in the hallway. "Just what exactly have you signed me up for, old buddy?"

"Just looking after your welfare. The word on the street is you're pining away at your desk job. I thought you might be needing some excitement in your life."

"Thanks."

"Let me show you where I'm hanging my hat. You got anything online for tomorrow morning?"

"I'll clear my schedule."

———

COMPACFLT

"Any luck with the N-2 shop?" Rohrbaugh asked on returning to his cubicle.

"They're skeptical, Skipper," Mackenzie replied, "but I

think I've convinced them your theory warranted a deeper dive."

"That's a start."

"How was the brief?"

"Went well enough. Got our rudder orders. The CINC stuck his head in the door."

"Oh? What'd he say?"

"Gave the world view. My takeaway? The work we've been doing on 1729 is right on course."

"How about your detail to Nam?"

"Still tracking. The Air Force is going to check out the fields at Bien Hoa, Da Nang, Nha Trang, and Tan Son Nhut while the Navy focuses on Cam Ranh and Da Nang. I've got follow-up meetings scheduled for tomorrow morning and Wednesday to cover the details. Admiral Cortez'll be leaving next week to lay the groundwork."

"Got any specifics?"

"He'll be exploring opportunities for joint training, exchange visits, base sharing, status of forces agreements."

"Timelines?"

"We're looking at a several-year evolution."

"Judging on how things are shaping up, I don't think that'll cut it."

"I've got a hunch our trip will speed things up. We will have the camel's nose in the tent soon enough."

"You working an angle, Skipper?"

"Possibly."

Chapter Twenty-Eight

PACO MARKET
ESTERO DE PACO, MANILA
17:45 TUESDAY 3 APRIL

Lynne payed the cab driver and paused on the cracked sidewalk before making her way to the Paco Market a block away. She had dressed down for the meeting: sandals, jeans, blue-cotton T, her long auburn hair gathered into a ponytail.

Why Raul had asked to meet him at the market mystified her. But then, all of his communications of late were obtuse. Perhaps he wanted an update on her reporting of the Pagasa Island and P-8 incidents? Or something else?

She swiveled her head, surveying the decayed neighborhood. Hardly the quiet ambiance of the Manila Hotel or the safety of the Quezon City market. *Safety, that is, until that guy scared the shit out of me last month.*

She pressed her purse against her side, conscious of the pickpockets and thieves known to prowl the banks of the Estero de Paco, the listless tributary of the Pasig River that flowed into Manila Bay.

She startled at a shadowy form that ducked out of sight between two buildings. She gripped the clasp of her purse, fighting the temptation to pull out her canister of pepper spray. *Just because I'm being paranoid doesn't mean someone isn't following me.*

The government had invested a considerable amount of money to eliminate the squalor along the riverbank to no avail. Falling back into decay, shanties with rusted corrugated metal roofs once again spilled onto the sidewalk. A watcher could be anywhere.

She swatted away a mosquito and made her way across a crumbling concrete bridge. The smell of raw sewage rose to meet her. A printed sign tied to a paint-flaked pole caught her eye: *Bawal Magtapon NG Basora.* "It is forbidden to throw trash." Judging from the smell and the garbage caught on the exposed rocks of the dull-gray water, few paid attention to the sign.

She left the bridge behind and proceeded down the opposite bank lined by the remnants of old tropical plantings. A trio of smudged children in tattered clothing made their way toward her. She gestured the nearest away, admonishing him to go away and return to his mother. *"Humito ka sa akin. Umuwi ka san an mo."*

The startled kids parted, opening a passage as she continued on to her destination. The market, advertised as the centerpiece of the prior restorative efforts, was a disappointment. Three wide arches and two yellow pedicabs defined the front of the white-washed concrete block building. She made for the center arch and stepped around a burlap bag of Hog Grower Mash that sagged against a banner advertising a smiling Facebook influencer.

Ducking under a drooping black tarp, she entered the cavernous warehouse and walked down the central aisle counting the side-bays. She stopped at the third fronted by a four-tier display of gaily-colored children's clothing.

"Here."

She recognized Raul's voice and squeezed through a clutter of bargaining locals into a large room. Atencio was the only occupant. He rose to greet her, patting his lips with a ragged paper napkin.

He pointed to several oil-stained paper plates overflowing with pork and vegetable filled Lumpia and Turon Sagings. "Please," he said offering her a can of Coke. "These are the best in all Manila."

Lynne eyed the sweet banana and jack-fruit filled Turons and decided they could wait. There had to be another reason he had invited her to the market besides the food. She popped the tab of the Coke and took a seat in a white molded-plastic chair while studying Atencio's face.

"Ms. Lynne," he opened. "You are a keen observer and your reporting of the Pagasa Island affair have been most useful in articulating our government's position to those in the Washington establishment."

"You are too kind. I was only—"

"And you are too modest," Atencio interrupted. "My colleagues and I of the Government of National Unity movement feel you understand that the recent actions by Montalvo and his cronies at Malacalong Palace run counter to our country's long-term interests."

Lynne's eyes narrowed. *Had Raul just made an overt play for my support of his opposition?*

Atencio slid a thick envelope across the table. "You are in a unique position to help our country. Perhaps you will consider."

"I—"

He stood. "I will see you home. We wish that no harm will come to you."

Lynne stood, dazed, and followed him outside to a narrow alleyway. A black Toyota Avalon waited, engine running, guarded by two muscular men, one whom held open the rear door of the car. The Avalon was Toyota's most expensive sedan, not something a mid-range bureaucrat would have. Then she saw the conspicuous bulge under the guard's long sleeve Barong. He packed a very deadly weapon, a Uzi pistol favored by the country's security service.

Several youths hovered in the distance, having likely been chased away after pestering the guards about the name of the mobster who could own such a car.

She fingered the envelope, put it in her purse, and followed Atencio into the back seat.

Chapter Twenty-Nine

UNITED AIRLINES FLIGHT 869
SOCIALIST REPUBLIC OF VIETNAM
21:20 WEDNESDAY 23 APRIL

United Flight 869 descended through a layer of high cirrus clouds covering the South China Sea. Buffeted by moderate chop, the Boeing 767 completed a fifteen-degree turn to begin its approach to Tan Son Nhut International.

Rohrbaugh stirred in the cramped confines of his seat, jostled awake by the turbulence. A thin layer of scum coated his teeth and his mouth tasted like a mouse had died in it. He massaged his neck and pulled up his left sleeve. 2120.

A flight attendant completing her rounds stopped at his isle. "Water?"

"That would be great, thanks."

"Lemon?"

"I'll come get it," Rohrbaugh replied, hoping the lemon juice would dissolve the layer of glue covering his teeth. He eased out of his seat and followed her to the rear of the aircraft.

"First trip?" she asked.

"Yeah. I was just thinking. My dad deployed a couple times. A-6 Intruders. He spent the last three years of the war as a POW."

"Oh, I'm so sorry. Is he okay?"

Rohrbaugh didn't hear. "His RIO didn't make it. Hard to believe it's been over forty years. Things have changed. *Forrestal's* a tourist attraction in Texas and the *Oriskany* is an artificial reef off Pensacola. Dad ..."

"I understand. My mother was an attendant on the Trans World flights bringing the guys over. She can still hear the voices of the kids who didn't come home. She doesn't talk about it much."

"Neither did Dad."

They were interrupted as more turbulence shook the aircraft.

"It looks like we've encountered some rough air. I'd better take my seat."

Rohrbaugh settled in and fastened his seatbelt. He looked out the window. The appearance of twinkling lights below indicated they'd crossed the coast. The world below seemed peaceful—a different reception than his dad experienced.

His father never shared the stories about the years he spent as a POW in the Hanoi Hilton. He'd kept those memories locked up forever. Over the years, Rohrbaugh tried to break through this impenetrable barrier to release the demons. He never could.

The overhead speaker blared as Rohrbaugh wrestled with the memories.

"We will shortly be arriving at our destination. The local time is eleven fifty-five. Please ensure your seats are in the full upright position and your tray tables are secured."

United Airlines 869 touched down fifteen minutes later and taxied to the terminal, their arrival at the gate signaled by the impatient clicking of seat buckles. Rohrbaugh joined the other passengers jammed together in the aisle and shuffled off the aircraft.

He scanned the crowd in the reception area. Two tanned Caucasians with close-cropped hair stood off to one side. With them were several men wearing the distinctive dark mustard-yellow uniforms of the Vietnamese army.

"Must be our reception committee," Rohrbaugh commented to his teammates.

One of the men from the delegation confirmed Rohrbaugh's assumption. "Hawaii? Follow me."

Rohrbaugh and the others were ushered through an unmarked door into an adjacent room. Utilitarian at best, the room was empty except for a single table and several rows of chairs lined up along either side of the two longest walls. The obligatory picture of Ho Chi Minh gazed benevolently at them from across the far wall. Several stern officials were positioned in the center of the room behind a wooden table decorated with a pot of red-plastic carnations.

"Welcome to Vietnam, gentlemen. I'm Lieutenant Colonel John Taylor, the assistant military attaché at the embassy. I'll be your escort. You'll be meeting Colonel Meyer tomorrow. He motioned to the Vietnamese officer at his side. This is Senior Colonel Vu Tan of the People's Armed Forces of Vietnam."

Tan took a step forward.

"Good evening. Welcome to the Peoples Socialist Republic of Vietnam. I trust you had an uneventful flight," he said in passable English. "Before we continue on to Hanoi, our customs officials will be pleased to inspect your passports and ensure all of your travel documents are in order."

I'm also sure your comrades will be equally pleased to inspect our luggage, Rohrbaugh grumbled to himself. *Well, have at it in the name of peaceful co-existence.*

"We will depart for the capital as soon as we complete your paperwork. You will be staying at the Ministry of

National Defense guesthouse. This honor reflects the importance the government places on your visit to our country. The
government sees great value in promoting a harmonious relationship with the United States. There are certain elements
whose activity in the South China Sea has been counter to the
common purpose of peace, cooperation, stability, and development in the region."

Colonel Tan completed his prepared remarks and gestured
to the customs officers. "You will now be pleased to complete
our entry requirements."

"Happy to," Rohrbaugh replied. Bemused by the rigid
formality of the Army officer, he added under his breath to a
travel mate, "With any luck, he'll loosen up after a few beers."

Rohrbaugh knew from personal experience, the Ba M'Ba
33 and Tiger beers packed a punch. Bottled by the Heineken
brewery, Ba M'Ba was pretty good. He wasn't much impressed
with the Tiger that bore the unfortunate label "Tiger Piss"
bestowed upon it by the American troops who served here
during the war.

He fancied himself a beer aficionado and possessed an
impressive collection of foreign and microbrewery ales and
lagers. Kate indulged his hobby by permitting him to rack the
bottles in an unused bedroom in their quarters at Makalapa.
He was always on the prowl for a more suitable brew for his
palate than those plebeian offerings set out at receptions.

Colonel Taylor, whose focus remained on getting his
charges to the guesthouse, cut his musings short. "Right-O,
let's move along smartly, gentlemen. We don't want to be
keeping our hosts waiting, now, do we?"

———

HANOI
UNITED STATES EMBASSY
08:05

Rohrbaugh and the rest of the team were rousted out of bed the next morning and hustled off to the embassy to begin their day with the Country Team Brief.

The Deputy Chief of Mission led off explaining that recent events in the region dictated a more aggressive posture be taken to develop military and diplomatic ties with Vietnam. Rohrbaugh and the other members of the liaison team needed to be cognizant of the host nation's issues and sensitivities while conducting the business of their mission.

Rohrbaugh listened to the senior members of the embassy staff as they reviewed the salient points of their department's work. The team regrouped with Colonels Taylor and Meyer after a break for lunch to review specific aspects of the site visits scheduled for the next day.

Meyer wound up the discussions. "You've had a full day, but we've got two more events on tap before we can call it quits. A sightseeing trip and an informal reception. On the surface, they seem innocuous enough, but there can be some real danger if you don't pay attention to what you say."

"Remember," Meyer emphasized, "your every action is going to be scrutinized. We can't afford to have any slips of the tongue, offish references to the war, or rendering of political opinions. Let me very clear. There will be attempts to pry sensitive information from you. Remain alert. And, I should not have to remind you, do not overindulge this evening. John, you have anything to add?"

"This afternoon we'll be making what we, at the embassy, call the Great Victory Tour. It can be a little grating if you don't have the right mindset going in. Among other places we'll visit is the site of the old Ho Loa prison. It's better known to you guys as the Hanoi Hilton. Don't get angry or defensive..."

Taylor caught the look on Rohrbaugh's face. "Commander?"

"My dad was imprisoned there for three years."

"Oh, crap."

Meyer addressed the team. "Let me frame this differently. Listen to what our hosts have to say. Their words will apply to what's happening now, not what happened forty years ago."

"Ed, can I add something?" Taylor interrupted.

"Sure."

"Mike, it's probable the Vietnamese have done their homework much better than we have. We should presume they know your father was a POW. In fact, count on it. They'll be watching your reactions. The questions they'll be asking themselves will be: 'Can we trust this American? Will he have his own personal agenda that will compromise our goals?'"

"Understood."

Taylor worked through the awkwardness. "From past experience, we know the Vietnamese have designed this afternoon to serve as an ice breaker. Their intent is for you to get to know your escorts and work through any issues from the war. The returning vets have done very well with this, by the way. That, in fact, is the point of the side trip tomorrow."

"Good points, John," Meyer said. "I want to touch on one final item before we head to the bus. Tonight's reception is co-hosted by the PAVN and the Director of the America's Department of the Ministry of Foreign Affairs. The significance of the sponsorship by the Ministry is probably lost on you, but it impressed us. The reception speaks volumes about the emphasis the Vietnamese government has placed on your visit. Gents, you're high profile. Questions?"

Receiving none, Taylor set off for the door. "Let's mount up."

Meyer caught up with Rohrbaugh. "I'm sorry we bungled that. You alright?"

"Yes, sir. More of my own issues I've got to work through."

"Understand, you're not the first guy who's come through here who's been caught off guard. It can be tough. If you want to talk about anything, give me a ring."

"I'll let you know."

———

Rohrbaugh lay on his back resting while sorting through his feelings. The emotions of encountering the ghosts of his dad's past and those his own childhood compounded his symptoms of jet lag and fatigue from the day's meetings.

In the solitude of his stark room, he came to the realization he'd found a certain closure with his dad's death, discovering common ground with his Vietnamese hosts. Their fathers had fought bravely and many had died. They too had grieved and come to grips with the holes in their lives. They also understood when Rohrbaugh broke off from the group and stood in front of the wreckage of an A-6 Intruder on display in the Central Army Museum.

"Mike?"

A knock on the door accompanied the disembodied voice. "You ready to roll?"

"What we won't do for God and country," Rohrbaugh said with more enthusiasm than he felt.

Well, suck it up, old buddy, he told himself rolling off the bed. *Last event of the day.*

———

Receptions were trying affairs, but to Rohrbaugh's surprise, this one was proving to be an exception. However, his mind did drift during a conversation about the impact of Internet technology in the country. He looked around the room and saw an officer standing by the door dressed in the uniform of a commander in the Vietnamese Navy. The man was sipping a beer watching the foreign visitors, assessing them.

Rohrbaugh accepted another Ba M' Ba. He hefted it in a

salute to the naval officer and turned his attention back to the conversation that had drifted on to streaming services.

MINISTRY OF NATIONAL DEFENSE GUESTHOUSE
07:45 THURSDAY 24 APRIL

Oppressive, muggy air smothered the team as they began their mission in earnest. They were herded onto a Vietnamese Air Force plane and headed south. Their first destination; the old Marine firebase at Dong Ha, site of fierce fighting in the central highlands of the former South Vietnam. The excursion was planned to reinforce Hanoi's willingness to bury old animosities and foster a new sense of collegiality.

The team departed Dong Ha at mid-morning and proceeded to the deep-water port of Cam Ranh Bay. Rohrbaugh knew the history.

The base had been turned over to the Soviet Navy after the fall of Saigon as repayment for Vietnam's considerable war debt. The Russian presence also provided Hanoi leverage against Chinese expansion into the adjacent oil-rich basins of the South China Sea.

The subsequent collapse of the Soviet Union led to the breakup of the VietSovPetro drilling consortium and Hanoi wasn't positioned to defend their national interests after the Russian pullout.

Rohrbaugh caught himself watching the activity around the bay and turned to the escort officer.

"…and certain powers have since attempted to exploit this situation. I am certain you are aware of the impact these elements have on regional security. Yes?"

The officer already knew the answer to his rhetorical question and continued without pausing for an answer. "Our government has taken measures to counter these provocative elements, including soliciting the assistance of friendly nations who share our desire for regional stability.

"Another positive development has been the Foreign Ministry's efforts to encourage the formation of international partnerships to assist us in realizing the full potential of our offshore oil fields. The security of these basins and our exploration platforms in our coastal waters, of course, lie with the Navy."

Rohrbaugh's attention began to drift as the escort concluded his remarks with a surprise.

"Because our oil fields are of such strategic importance and their security is vital to the stability of the region, we have added an aerial inspection of the Bach Ho basin and several drilling platforms to your itinerary. Perhaps you know we have granted an American company, Horizon Offshore Exploration, the rights to assist in developing this particular field?"

"Whoa, this ought to be interesting," Rohrbaugh said to the Air Force colonel traveling with him. What Rohrbaugh didn't say was that the Americans were also planning their own tidy operation for Platform Ten.

He looked forward to the inspection, but his enthusiasm was blunted when he caught sight of the aircraft that was to transport them to the field.

It was a Soviet Mi-8. Those helicopters had been around since the 60s. Rohrbaugh sighed with resignation as he climbed aboard. He had no doubt the Mi-8 was older than him.

He took his seat and conducted a quick survey. The helicopter appeared to be in pretty good shape. At least there were no tin cans on the deck collecting hydraulic fluid. That was always a positive sign. He was further relieved when the Mi-8's rotors achieved full rpms, lifted smoothly off the runway, and proceeded over the coast.

———

PLATFORM NUMBER TEN
BACH HO OIL FIELD

A finger tapped Rohrbaugh's shoulder. He nodded and twisted to scan the sea below.

The helicopter slowed to a hover as it approached a rust-streaked drilling rig balanced on a steel latticework of four large pylons. The platform's outward appearance was decidedly low tech. He studied the structure.

The rig matched the pictures of Platform Ten, code named Blue Horizon. Any creature comforts were subservient to its primary function to tap into the oil-bearing strata below and to withstand the typhoons that ravaged the South China Sea.

The rig appeared to be non-producing. There was no torch of flame belching from the nozzle of the natural gas bleed-off line. More telling, though, was the dirty-brown plume staining the surrounding sea. The stain was composed of debris gouged from the ocean floor by a tungsten carbide drill bit cutting through the soft bedrock of the seamount.

Rohrbaugh studied the length of the plume drifting to the northeast, concluding that the prevailing current ran two to three knots. Docking the ASDS would be tricky even with the use of its side thrusters. Ideally, they should make their approach from the southeast instead of perpendicular to the prevailing current, but the depth of the water wouldn't permit it. They would approach from deeper water to affect the covert transfer of equipment to Blue Horizon.

He craned his neck to see if he could get a better feel for the approach they would make. There was barely enough leeway between the pylons. He couldn't see if there were any fenders. *That might be a problem.*

Rohrbaugh stored the thought and considered the positives. Platform Ten was ideal for its purpose. The rig was perched on the northwest edge of the Bach Ho seamount, a good five hundred yards from the nearest rig. Judging from the deep blue of the ocean, the mount had a steep drop-off. This would provide a safe operating depth for the *Jimmy Carter* in contrast to the shallower turquoise-colored seas southeast of the platform. He thought of the *Carter*. She was due on station near the Paracels within the day.

———

DA NANG

Rohrbaugh stepped onto the tarmac of the old American airfield at Da Nang. He hesitated while his eyes adjusted to the glare. In the distance loomed the edifice of Monkey Mountain guarding the northern approach to the deep-water bay. He only had a moment to note his surroundings before being ushered onward.

"This way, please. This way," urged his escort, pointing to a row of sedans lined up at the edge of the runway.

Rohrbaugh had barely settled in his seat before the door slammed. Their escort scrambled in the front seat and they roared away, leaving the others to catch up.

"Wonder what the hell's going on?" Rohrbaugh said to the equally puzzled Air Force colonel seated next to him.

"Guess we'll find out soon enough."

The sedans pulled up in front of the headquarters building of the Fifth Military Region.

"This way please. This way."

The escorts were very excited as they led the team past several saluting sentries to the office of Major General Danh Ngoc Loi. They were most impressed with the impromptu audience the General granted the Americans. He was a busy man and rarely spoke to outsiders. His willingness to speak to the Americans was a most magnanimous gesture.

The General wasted little time on perfunctory statements before conveying the startling news that the Ministries of Defense and Foreign Affairs had agreed to move ahead with direct military-to-military exchange programs.

The team had been briefed that the Vietnamese would take a nuanced approach to negotiations. Rohrbaugh recalibrated, caught off guard by the pronouncement. *There's nothing the least bit circumspect in the General's pronouncement. What prompted this move? Do the Vietnamese know something about the PLA's intentions American intelligence didn't? Likely. Could their urgency to formalize military cooperation be tied to a threat to their merchant shipping, or was more trouble brewing in the Spratlys? The Chinese couldn't be happy about being blamed for the latest fishing boat incident. Are they planning a counter-move?*

No closer to an answer, Rohrbaugh settled into his vehicle's seat to resume the window tour of the base. This was just as well, since they couldn't compare notes about the meeting until later. That would have to wait until they could speak without their hosts eavesdropping.

He listened to the escort officer's running narrative of the facility's history and realized that other than being of historical interest, the sites held no emotional impact.

The caravan passed the end of the runway and neared an arched gate with 'CAMP TIEN SHA' embossed in faded letters across its horizontal beam. The sign was a vestige of the American presence years before. The gate wasn't the only reminder of the Navy's past. The caravan slowed by a wide expanse of sandy beach.

"China Beach," Rohrbaugh's host commented. "It used to be a popular recreation area for your forces."

The conversation died of its own accord when the sedans slowed near a series of stone jetties. Tied up to one of these, a patrol boat.

"Can we stop a moment?"

"Is there something you wish to see?" the escort responded.

"The patrol boat. That's one of —"

"Ah, the ship I mentioned yesterday? I see she hasn't departed for its escort mission. HQ-371's commander is one of our most accomplished captains."

"Didn't he just return from a mission to the Spratlys?" Rohrbaugh asked, fishing for information to confirm his theory.

The escort evaded the question. "Our navy spends a considerable amount of time at sea. I'm afraid I am not familiar with the captain's orders." He cut Rohrbaugh off before he could ask another question. "Shall we return to the car?"

Rohrbaugh pondered the officer's oblique response and dropped the subject before he noted something else—a working party near the bow. Further down the hull, a painted rectangle in new haze-gray validated his assumptions. Unlike the Vietnamese Navy, the PLAN located their ship identification numbers below the bridge. The crew had just stenciled a new set of hull numbers near the bow.

"Well, I'll be damned."

"Excuse me?" the escort office said. "Is something wrong?"

Rohrbaugh caught himself. "No. Not at all. She's a very good-looking ship."

Chapter Thirty

THE WHITE HOUSE
10:25 TUESDAY 6 MAY

South Rock? Stuart sighed. He had multiple issues to address, but those in the South China Sea kept intruding. The feud between Manila and Beijing just wouldn't go away. He set the latest update on the incident near Scarborough Shoal in the outbox and called his secretary. "Mary Allus?"

"Yes, Mr. President?"

"Wasn't Bob Lawson on tap to meet with Justin this morning?"

"I believe so. Let me check. Yes, at 09:30."

"Would you round him up before he gets out of here? I'd like to have a talk with him."

"Can I tell him the topic?"

"Just say, 'I'd like to share a cup of coffee.'"

His finger lingered on the intercom, aware of the gossip floating around Washington. He was perceived as being too deferential to the wishes of the Chairman of the Joint Chiefs. He dismissed the thought and removed his finger from the button. They had known each other for over thirty years.

Stuart smiled as he recalled one his first memories of Lawson. Their relationship had been very different in 1978 when they first met at Naval Air Station Pensacola. He'd just received his commission from the Navy ROTC program at Ohio State. Lieutenant Robert Lawson was an instructor pilot assigned to Training Wing Ten.

He swung his chair around. His eyes came to rest on the glass case suspending his gold Naval Aviator Wings. His mind drifted to a cloudless September afternoon over the Gulf of Mexico.

———

He'd been in the front seat of a T-28 trainer, Lawson strapped in the seat behind.

He lined up for his approach and shot a nervous glance at the blur of approaching pine trees off his right shoulder. He dropped the flaps and reduced airspeed.

The aircraft slammed onto the runway for the third time that day. His head whip-lashed at the impact.

"Damn."

"Sorry, sir."

Lawson checked his instruments and verified their altitude. Assured, that for the moment at least, they were safe, he turned to glare at his student.

"Stuart, if you don't get your act together I'm going to unstrap my kneeboard and throw it at the back of your head. Focus on what you're doing, or you're gonna fly this aircraft into the ground, killing yourself and, more importantly, me."

Stuart knew better than to interrupt.

"Ensign, if you will recall," Lawson continued, "the intent of this exercise is to have the number of successful takeoffs equal the number of successful landings. Do you understand what you screwed up? If you can't get this right, I'm going to bust you out of the program."

"Yes, sir. I understand my error, sir."

"Let's come around and try again. Watch your rate of descent and airspeed."

———

Stuart's mind returned to the Oval Office. He reached out to touch the case with his wings. *It's a miracle I didn't kill us both.*

The door to his right opened and Mary Allus' head popped into view. "Mr. President? Admiral Lawson."

"Can you shuffle my schedule?"

"Already done. I moved your 1100."

Stuart glanced at the schedule and grunted at the name filling the timeslot. He would have preferred she had just canceled. "Thank you."

Mary Allus ducked out of sight as Lawson replaced her in the doorway.

Stuart stood and walked around his desk. "Throw your cover on the couch. You have time to catch lunch with Dianne and me?"

"You kidding? I'll make the time. Sure beats what I had in the works."

"And that was?"

"Six-inch tuna on wheat at my desk."

"I think we can beat that," Stuart said crossing to the door. "Mary Allus, can you let Dianne know Bob will be joining us for lunch?"

"Will do."

"You have your flag lieutenant in tow?" Stuart asked.

"He's hanging out in the Military Office with our driver."

"Good, figure they can catch something to eat in the mess. Coffee?"

"That'd be good, thanks."

"Make yourself comfortable. I'll be back in a sec."

Stuart disappeared into the pantry and grabbed two coffee

cups embossed with the Presidential seal. He topped them off from the pot the steward brewed earlier in the day.

"Try this," he said, handing a cup to Lawson. "I've got a connection with one of the small plantations on the Big Island. They keep me supplied with their Pea Berry."

Lawson took an appreciative sip and waited until Stuart settled into his chair before speaking. "What's on your mind?"

"The *Carter.*"

"Rohrbaugh's pickup went off without a hitch. We'll have confirmation on Valiant Crane within thirty-six hours."

"Tell me about South Rock."

"Turned into a Mexican standoff. The Chinese have deployed a number of paramilitary ships but have refrained from sending any warships. Makes sense."

"It does?"

"A Fisheries Department spokesman insists the incident was an unfortunate mistake about fishing rights."

"They expect anyone to buy that story?"

"That's what they're hoping. My cut? The PLAN had no idea those Chinese fishing boats were even near Scarborough Shoal when they were boarded by the Filipinos."

"I'm not convinced there wasn't intent."

"There's one positive. Their Coast Guard is now playing a significant role in coordinating the multiple agencies with conflicting jurisdictions scattered across the area. I can't recall them all, but they include Fisheries, Oceanographic, Border Control, Maritime Safety, and a bunch of local provincial vessels. They've lumped them all under the umbrella of the People's Armed Forces Maritime Militia."

Stuart recognized the implications. "Any one of them could trigger an incident that could spin out of control."

"Zhu and Xiao are in a bind. On one hand, they're trying to contain the situation with their paramilitary units to diminish the odds of a regional backlash. On the other, they've backed themselves into a corner with the territorial jurisdiction issue."

Stuart motioned to a green folder set amongst the clutter of his desk. "That's consistent with State's summary."

"Did Richard's summary happen to mention that a couple of days ago two Chinese ships made a high-speed run at a Filipino cutter near Second Thomas Shoal before breaking off at the last second? Generated a seven-foot wave. Injured some folks."

Stuart suppressed an epithet. "No."

"Their actions are all part and parcel of their 'Cabbage Strategy.'"

"Their what?"

"One of their admirals coined the term describing a strategy using an inner ring of fishing boats and an outer ring of warships to prevent resupply. Wrapping an objective in layers like cabbage leaves."

"Second Thomas Shoal? Isn't that where that small Philippine garrison is living on a beached World War II-era landing ship?"

"The *Sierra Madre*."

"Manila have any recourse?"

"Short-term, they could protest the incident under the International Provisions of Prevention of Collisions at Sea. Long-term, they may consider going to the UN's International Tribunal on the Law of the Sea."

"They have a case?"

"Doubtful. Beijing's already ignored the Hague's Permanent Court of Arbitration verdict that rules their claims in the South China Sea violate international law."

Stuart signed. "And Beijing continues to coerce most everyone in the region."

"While accusing us of sowing discord. That said, under UNCLOS, Manila could still try to site the sovereignty issue.

The Shoals are roughly one-hundred forty miles from Luzon. Well within their two-hundred-mile EEZ."

"They might have a better chance bringing the issue to the World Court for adjudication."

"Neither is likely to go anywhere. Beijing has no intention of backing down."

"You have timelines?"

"Xiao's not talking, but we've had back channel communication with the Deputy Chief of the General Staff. Army general named, Cheng."

"Good cop, bad cop?"

"I've heard he's aligned with Zhu, but you never know. DIA is pulling background."

"Speaking of UNCLOS, the VP's been doing some arm-twisting. We've been screwing around with this bill for over two decades. It's time to move it out of sub-committee for a vote on the floor."

"Agreed."

"Aren't you on tap to testify before the Senate Foreign Relations Committee?

"Next Wednesday."

"You think I'm pushing too hard?"

"No. The way things are shaping up, you don't have a choice."

"And if I make the wrong move, the country..."

Lawson held up his hand. Behind the question lay the real intent of the impromptu meeting. "You won't. And you don't have to do this alone. We've got your back."

"Care to check out the roses?"

Stuart pushed back from the desk and led the way to the portico. He stopped by the podium set up for an event later in the day and swept his hand over the expanse of green. "Did you know this entire area once housed the stables?"

"Explains why the grass grows so well," Lawson said with a grin.

"You would think of that."

"You're the guy who grew up on a farm."

"This one's my favorite," Stuart said pointing out a flower. "King's Ransom."

Lawson leaned over the yellow rose and gave it a sniff. "I need to get this one for Chris."

"Good move. Dianne will want to compare notes with her. She's been after me to get you guys down to Camp David for a long weekend."

"Just give the word. We'll crack open my new bottle of Scotch."

"Your usual firewater?"

"I'll have you know, it's a double-matured, eighteen-year Lagavulin. The Scots say, 'tis nectar.'"

"You've bought yourself an invitation."

"What are wingmen for?"

"Roger that."

Stuart placed his hand on Lawson's back to steer him toward the residence. "Let's get lunch. I'm starving."

Chapter Thirty-One

USS JIMMY CARTER SSN-25
SOUTH CHINA SEA
01:00 WEDNESDAY 7 MAY

The USS *Jimmy Carter* maintained neutral buoyancy two-hundred feet beneath the surface, her crew preparing for the next evolution of her top-secret mission. She'd completed her run through the Ryuku and Palawan Trenches the day before, then turned west to assume her current position between Fiery Cross Reef and Woody Island. She'd come to periscope depth shortly after her course change and rendezvoused with a fishing boat carrying mission commander, Mike Rohrbaugh.

Four dull thuds signaled the mission was underway. The latching mechanisms holding the submersible to the back of the *Carter* released their grip. No longer captive, the minisub lifted several feet off the deck pylons. The ASDS's pilot applied power to the thrusters and began a series of delicate maneuvers to position his vessel alongside the *Carter's* ocean interface hull module located aft of the sail.

. . .

"Free and clear," Ace announced.

"ASDS-1, 'Free and clear,'" the sub's operations officer echoed. "You have a 'go' to deploy swimmers."

"Wilco. Maintaining station. Preparing to deploy swimmers."

Ace alerted Rohrbaugh. "Y'all ready, Commander?"

"Affirm."

The first pair of divers from the eight-man detachment verified the oxygen/helium mix of their breathing apparatus. Each was a master diver with unique qualifications in the dangerous field of deep-sea diving. These men, like the SEALS, were a select few. Their work would become the source of legend if their mission was ever declassified—which was doubtful.

"Initiating egress."

The divers exited the ASDS's hatch into absolute darkness. They switched on their high voltage lamps. "We are positioned abeam of the payload aperture hatch. Ready for extraction."

"Roger that," the payload specialist aboard the *Carter* confirmed as he initiated the sequence of procedures required to open the cargo bay door.

"*Carter*, we have visual."

The first Towed Deployment Vessel carried three pieces of mission-essential gear: A remotely piloted underwater vehicle equipped with high-definition cameras, a suite of LED lights, hydraulic grabbling arms, a large reel of digital cable, and a sophisticated communications buoy. The second TVD held a featureless black oblong object twelve-feet in length and three-feet in diameter. This entity was known as "The Pod."

The Pod's design enabled it to eavesdrop on communications transmitted along undersea fiber optic cables. It performed this function by tapping into the amplification junctions used to boost the signals traveling along miles of cable. The Pod intercepted the cable's fiber optic light signals and converted them into digital signals to be stored for burst communications by the communications buoy.

The moment the two Navy divers had been preparing for had arrived. For the past two months they'd perfected the maneuvers necessary to transfer the TVDs from their storage bay on the *Carter* to link them in tandem to the minisub. Thirty minutes later, their task complete, the tired men entered the ASDS to begin their decompression procedures. The TVDs were secured to the ASDS, their electric systems activated, checked, and verified.

Receiving confirmation, the swimmers were back on board,

Rohrbaugh gave the go-ahead to begin the next evolution. "Ace, we're good to go."

"Roger that. I'll pass the word."

Ace selected a new channel and informed the *Carter* that all systems were 'Go.'

"We copy, DV-1. You are cleared to proceed. Rendezvous is set at this location for 0500 hours. Please verify your plotting data is downloaded in the inertial guidance system."

Ace punched a button on his console and gave a thumbs-up to his co-pilot.

"*Carter*, data is verified. We'll be able to find our way home."

Ace dove to their operational depth. He had little difficulty maneuvering to the location of the Chinese fiber optic cable mapped by the *Impeccable*.

The communications trunk's position had been identified five months earlier by the National Reconnaissance Office's Earth Imaging Satellite System. The satellite had locked in on a PLAN Yudian class cable-laying ship with real time imagery and transmitted the ship's precise location to the NRO. This data, and that from *Impeccable*, was loaded into the ASDS's inertial guidance system. Rohrbaugh now possessed the means to find the proverbial, needle in a haystack.

———

ASDS-1

02:37

Mission Specialist Charles Dane rolled his head to release the tension in his neck. He'd spent the better part of an hour hunched over a TV monitor searching the monotonous length of cable for a very specific object. Seven minutes later, his efforts were rewarded.

"Got the sucker."

Dane manipulated the toggle control to position the RPV's camera for a closer look. A few more taps positioned the platform over the target. "Sure enough, looks just like the pictures."

Rohrbaugh slid across the narrow bench to peer over Dane's shoulder.

Centered in the screen was the object of their search, an amplification junction of the Chinese sub-ocean laser communications trunk line.

"Ace, what's our depth?"

"Ninety-eight meters."

Rohrbaugh gave a thumbs-up to his crew. "Teams 2 and 3. Ready to roll?"

"We're set," the senior diver responded.

"Commence egress."

The four divers exited the hatch and made their way to the TOV where they unlimbered The Pod and maneuvered it to a position over the five-inch optical cable.

"Rendezvous effected. Initiating tapping protocol."

"Copy that. Sequence initiated."

Rohrbaugh kept to his schedule and allowed another fifteen minutes to elapse before alerting his fourth team. The intent of the staggered sequence was to prevent congestion at the tap site and reduce the likelihood of mishap. This team's job was to ready the communications buoy for deployment and connect its digital cable to the Pod.

"Team 4. Up."

The teams completed their tasks without incident and were soon inside the submersible. ASDA-1 assumed a course conforming to the prevailing undersea current while the divers recovered from their mission.

"Commander, we've reached the drop-off point."

"Release the Package."

Dane flipped open the red safety cover of the release button. He pushed the exposed toggle to the down position, sending a signal to the TDV, releasing the clamps holding "The Package."

The critical component was an extreme HF transmitter capable of sending billions of bits of encrypted data within milliseconds. The transmitter, contained within the buoy, permitted it to be deployed to the surface and complete the link with a stationary military communications satellite.

Dane completed his systems checks ten minutes after releasing The Package. "Commander, we have optimal deployment. All components are powered up and in a full-go status. The test transmission has been sent."

"Affirm," Rohrbaugh replied. "Ace, take us home."

"What the hell?" Ace shouted. "Commander, we're been lit up. Someone's tracking us."

Dane jerked upright. "How'd they find us? There weren't any reports of PLAN warships in the area."

"The Undersea Great Wall," Rohrbaugh answered. He redirected his response. "Ace, the Chinese are laying a system similar to our SOSUS array, but there hasn't been any intel to suggest they deployed it in this area."

Ace didn't need more. He questions could come later. "Up plane ten degrees."

"Up?" Dane said. "Is he nuts?"

Ace ignored the comment and started to prepare for an emergency blow. The action, used for an emergency assent, would forcefully empty the mini-sub's ballast tanks creating a huge amount of noise and surface turbulence. Exactly what you shouldn't do if you were trying to hide.

Before Rohrbaugh could respond, the blow commenced, then abrupted stopped only to be replaced by another sound as the vessel began to descend.

The entire sequence left him bewildered. A repetitive modulating noise that he could only describe as someone pounding on a Jamaican steel drum resonated through the hull.

"Commander, Ace explained, "we are now a gray whale that just happened to be bottom grazing. He came up for air, spouted a beautiful flume, and now is calling for a female."

Rohrbaugh gave his head a shake. "Well, I'll be damned."

Chapter Thirty-Two

BLUE HORIZON
02:10 THURSDAY 8 MAY

The ASDS-1's co-pilot scanned his oxygen and CO_2 scrubber indicator gauges. "How we doing, Skipper?"

"Ten minutes to the last navigation point. When we make the mark, I'll bring her up for a look around," Ace replied. "Time to give Rohrbaugh a heads up."

"Commander, Senior? Y'all still with us back there?"

The question was rhetorical. Rohrbaugh wouldn't have gone anywhere even if he'd had the choice. He and Dane were alone in the rear transport compartment preparing for the final stage of their operation. There was no further need for the Navy divers. They had remained aboard *Carter*. "Any indication we're being tracked?"

"Nothing. We're approaching our last marker and will come up to depth. Expect some turbulence."

"Appreciate the head's up. We'll secure the gear. Sure hate to come all this way and drop the eggs."

Rohrbaugh's eggs were well-padded crates of top-secret communications gear they were delivering to Blue Horizon.

The nature of their mission, so sensitive, even their arrival at the rig was on a "Need-to-Know:" basis." Only a select group of CIA Special Operatives remained on watch.

The operatives left nothing to chance. The sixty roughnecks, roustabouts, and riggers who comprised the actual working crew were asleep in their dorm. Like the crews of their sister rigs in the South China Sea, their wakeup calls in the morning came at 1030. They'd knock off at 2400. These blue-collar men and the two women on the rig were emblematic of America's backbone. They would fight to protect their beliefs and their countymen's backs.

The eighteen CIA and NSA agents assigned to the rig whose hours were decidedly different. The operatives did their best to blend in with their fellow workers. A casual observer would not be able to distinguish the two groups, but to the trained eyes of the professionals working the platform, something was definitely amiss.

The boss of the rig told the crew the Houston-based execs of Horizon Offshore Exploration wanted some of their new hires on- board for training so they could open up the new rigs.

"Maybe?" was the skeptical response. If these guys from HOE represented the future workforce not much, if any, oil would ever be pumped. In any event, the regulars were paid handsomely and had been told to keep their mouths shut.

More problematic to the security of the operation were the five Vietnamese nationals assigned to Platform Ten. Their presence had been part of the deal negotiated with VietPetro. Their leader, Minh Le Tran, seemed a good enough guy. He was a hard worker, spoke passable English, and he stayed out of the way.

Minh Le was on shore leave in Vung Tau, the coastal resort southeast of Ho Chi Minh City, this particular night.

The agents didn't have to worry about him or his comrades stumbling across their operation.

Ace set the minisub's inertial guidance system to execute a thirty-five-degree starboard turn. "Five, four, three, two, one, mark." He disengaged the autopilot and the submersible assumed its new course.

"I'll take her manually from here," he said. "Ten degrees up plane. Get the mast up."

"Mast up and locked."

ASDV-1's periscope broke the ocean's surface when they reached a depth of fifteen feet. Ace swung the optical sight down from its stowed position and looked through the eyepiece. He was offered a blurry view of the night sky before the lens cleared. He rotated the periscope through a wide arc examining the projected image. "Got it."

He manipulated the joystick, lining his approach to the six parallel lights defining the sides of Platform Ten's docking bay. A laser range finder provided him the distance. One hundred yards. "I'm bringing her up. We'll complete the run-in on the surface. Flash our recognition signal."

A moment later, he received confirmation. "Commander, we've good to proceed."

"Roger," Rohrbaugh acknowledged.

Ace noted some slippage from the prevailing current and engaged the sub's side thrusters. The remainder of the docking maneuver went without incident. He had Rohrbaugh's information to thank for that.

"Commander, you were right on the mark. Appreciate the assist."

"We clear to pop the hatch?" Rohrbaugh asked.

"We're secure."

Fifteen minutes later, they were submerged on a heading for their rendezvous with *Carter*. There had been no need to disembark. Rohrbaugh understood Platform Ten was linked to covert operations in the South China Sea, and the less he knew, the better.

This much he did know; Operation Blue Horizon encompassed the monitoring and transmission of data from the tapping pod his team just placed. It was also probable that agents were being run from the platform.

What he couldn't have known was the shroud of secrecy for the clandestine operations of Platform Ten had been penetrated.

Chapter Thirty-Three

VUNG TAU, VIETNAM
03:17 THURSDAY 8 MAY

Minh Le rolled over so he would not wake the sleeping form next to him. He studied her a moment before turning over on his back to stare at the revolving blades of the ceiling fan. He couldn't sleep. Monkey brain, he'd heard it was called. The voices in his head asking so many questions. His Tai Chi master taught him breathing exercises to refocus his mind so he wouldn't answer the monkeys. They weren't working.

He had first seen her shopping in the old Ben Ton Market several months before. Their first encounter had been awkward, but over the ensuing weeks, they spent hours together sharing their dreams.

She had brought such joy to his life, filling the void in his heart created when his family had abandoned him so long ago. He shared with her the pain he endured growing up as an orphan.

His companion was an empathetic listener and understood his feelings. Her family was of Chinese ancestry from the northern provinces and, despite being of the third generation, they still suffered from the wounds inflicted by racial discrimination. These she learned to bear, for she had suffered a similar fate. She, too, had been abandoned.

Her family was poor and they could not afford a daughter. Not only could her three brothers carry the family name, they could work. The answer to her father's troubles was straightforward. She was sold. At least, this was the story she told him several weeks after they'd met.

The final gesture forging Minh Le's bond was her offer to help locate his family. She wouldn't elaborate on how she could do this except to say she had sources within the Ministry. Exactly what Ministry, she wouldn't divulge.

Their evening together had started well enough. A shy kiss. Dinner. A few drinks at their favorite club. Then her questions about his work on Platform Ten became annoying. It was as if she cared more about the Americans than him.

Minh Le answered as best he could, striving to keep her happy. She had become so fickle. Their relationship had changed, but he stayed with her. She'd made him feel important. And, for the first time in his life, he felt valued in someone eyes.

Chapter Thirty-Four

MANILA
10:35 SATURDAY 10 MAY

Lynne shifted her box of groceries and pulled her purse within reach. She pushed around its contents, found her house key, and unlocked the door to her flat. She gave the door a kick, pausing at the threshold to survey the living room.

Everything was in its proper place. She threw the deadbolt and headed for the kitchen. She dropped her box on the dinette table and sorted through the produce before selecting a papaya. The fruit represented a small victory. She hadn't been to the Quezon City market since March when she'd been terrorized.

Lynne studied the fruit a moment, before turning her attention to the box. *What the hell?*

Wedged between a bunch of bananas and a newspaper-wrapped chicken was an envelope. *How'd that get in there?*

There was nothing remarkable about it—except her name inked on the outside. More curious than frightened, she slid the blade of a paring knife under the flap and extracted a folded sheet of notepaper. On it, a typed message:

. . .

Ms. Lynne, we have information of interest to you. Rizal Park, Valencia Circle. The Butterfly Pavilion. 1030 Sunday.

Lynne pursed her lips in consternation and turned the paper over several times. Nothing more. Nothing to indicate what information they had, who had written it, or whom she was to meet. Uncertain of the writer's intent, she pondered what to do before deciding to finish unpacking her groceries.

———

Lynne kept to her usual Sunday routine, breakfasting on a cappuccino and chocolate croissant. She felt at ease scanning her email, having convinced herself she would be in no danger. Then she spotted the note from her Bureau Chief. An attempted break-in.

She frowned, wondering if her sense of security was misplaced. She grabbed her purse and felt for the familiar shape of her pepper spray. She released the canister and set off for the bedroom assured by the sense of safety the spray conveyed.

She sorted through her cloths considering what one should wear for a clandestine meeting on a Sunday morning. She selected a tan pair of slacks, white cotton blouse, and suitable necklace. She tied her long auburn hair into a ponytail and slipped on her Prada sunglasses before looking in the mirror. She smiled. *La femme fatale.*

Lynne noticed nothing out of the ordinary on her drive across town to Rizal Park. It wasn't difficult finding a parking space on a side street near the Shell station. She locked the car, strode across Kawa Boulevard, and proceeded up Valencia to her rendezvous.

She slowed at the sight of an old man in a tattered coat sitting on a park bench reading the morning paper. *Harmless.*

A family passed, then a couple of street urchins looking for a handout. She reversed course, intent on returning to her car.

"Ms. Lynne?"

Lynne jumped at the sound of her name. She pivoted to locate the voice. A four-door Toyota with faded green paint coasted to a stop next to her. The rear passenger window was down.

"Would you join me, please?"

The door opened and the stranger moved to make room. Lynne hesitated, peering inside. The voice belonged to a middle-aged Caucasian male. Brown hair, average build. He looked vaguely familiar, but she couldn't place him. He gestured for her to enter.

Lynne pressed her purse against her side, backing away from the car. Her fingers tightening around the canister of pepper spray. She took another step back and bumped into something. "Excu—"

A rough shove sent her tumbling toward the car door. One of her shoes fell off before a powerful set of hands grabbed her under her arms, pulled her upright, and tossed her into the back seat. The shoe tumbled in after her. Lynne caught a glimpse of the assailant. *The old man?*

She screamed and grabbed for the doorframe. The stranger yanked her back. Struggling out his grip, she reached for her pepper spray.

"Ms. Lynne, that would be ill-advised," the man said. His eyes never left hers. "May I have your purse, please?"

The tone of the stranger's voice, commanding. Not a request. She clutched at the pepper spray. He pinned her arm and ripped the purse from her grasp.

He extracted the canister from her grasp and pitched it to the driver. "You won't be needing that."

The man rummaged through her purse and handed it back after finding nothing of interest. "Simply a precaution, Ms. Lynne. You have nothing to fear from me."

"God damn you!"

The man leaned forward and picked up her shoe, ignoring her expletive. "Perhaps, but I'm afraid there are others who wish to harm you."

Lynne glared at him, snatching her shoe out of the stranger's hand. A bead of sweat trickled down her inner arm. *What the hell was he talking about? What others?* "Who are you?"

"It's best you don't know."

"That's not helpful."

"True, but this isn't about me. It's about your friend, Mr. Atencio."

Her eye's widened. "Raul?"

"Are you aware your friend is watching you?"

She spun around, looking out the window.

Her captor waited until she turned to face him and answered his own question. "No, I suppose not."

"How do you know that?"

"It's my business to know such things, Ms. Lynne." The man's voice remained calm. "Don't you think it's ironic that Mr. Atencio has enlisted the assistance of the Presidential Security Group to trail you?"

Presidential Security Group? The guy in the market? Why would they do that? Oh, God. And, I thought it was someone from the embassy.

A hint of a smile crossed the man's face. It was all part of the game, the weaving of half-truths into a whole. The Agency's work served a larger purpose and that's what mattered. "Our problem is that Mr. Atencio is on the payroll of the Chinese Ministry of State Security."

Lynne slumped against the back of the seat. *Our?* Raul was

her friend. Or, at least she'd thought. *Is this why our last meeting was so strange. He was under surveillance. But by whom?*

"It makes sense now, doesn't it? Suffice it to say, you are now in a unique position to assist your government."

"I am?"

"We have certain information we would like to pass to Mr. Atencio."

Lynne collected herself. "What information?"

"It's best you don't know the details."

"But he's a trusted source."

"For whose benefit, Ms. Lynne? You'll soon learn you have no friends in this business."

"This business?"

"I'll summarize. It is best to trust the person you don't know than the friend you presume to know."

Lynne tried to process what the man said. "You're presuming I'll agree."

"We think you'll consider our offer. You possess certain talents…."

Lynne flushed, willing her voice to remain steady. "I see. And what is it, exactly, you want me to do?"

The man reached for a small package on the seat beside him and handed it to her. "Call Atencio and tell him you happened upon some information he will find of interest."

"That's it?" Lynne said, starring at the package resting in her hand, wondering why she had taken it. She threw it at his face. "No fucking way. You just kidnapped me."

His hand shot up and caught the package before it struck him. "You're free to go."

Lynne pushed open the door.

"I'd suggest you consider who is in the best position to protect you."

She turned back. "What if he asks—"

He held out the package. "Tell him you happened upon

some documents from the American embassy pertaining to the recent Chinese activities in the South China Sea."

"The incident at Pagasa?"

"Ms. Lynne, it is best this information is not compromised before reaching Atencio. Do you understand?"

Lynne accepted the package. "Can I read it?"

"I see we have arrived at your car." The man reached across Lynne and opened the door. "We trust you will not betray our confidence."

Chapter Thirty-Five

THE STATE DEPARTMENT
10:00 TUESDAY 10 JUNE

Adrian Clarke left his second floor office at precisely ten o'clock and walked to the adjacent conference room. He nodded to the two men who had accompanied him to Manila, Jim Crenshaw and the Marine Colonel from PACOM. An air of tension permeated the room. He braced himself before taking his seat. The strain wasn't about to get any lighter.

He extracted a folder from his briefcase and placed it on the table. "The President isn't happy. He's looking for answers, not excuses."

Clarke spoke with conviction. He'd been an indirect recipient of Stuart's displeasure when Valardi accosted him the day before, demanding answers as to why Beijing had been able to counter all of their policy initiatives. "Sean, let's begin with Vietnam."

"Prime Minister Tran confirmed he will be making an official visit to Washington later this year. Part of the package is a preliminary visit by their Prime Minister to the Asia-Pacific

Parliamentary Forum in Cancun next week. We're on tap to meet with him."

"Has this gotten out?"

"Yes."

"Any comments from Beijing?"

"They're spouting their usual bullshit."

Clarke bit his lip. He'd inherited Sean Waites, his Vietnam section chief, from another department in a lateral transfer and was looking for a way to move him out. He managed to suppress what he wanted to say in response to Waite's useless answer. "No doubt, although I thought they'd have been more circumspect. Has Hanoi countered?"

"They had a measured response. Tran rejected any suggestion the Vietnamese delegation would discuss how to contain the Chinese."

John Breckenridge shook his head. "Beijing won't buy."

"Hanoi is hedging their bets," Waites added.

Clarke scowled. "How?"

"A Chinese business delegation is on tap to visit Ho Chi Minh City."

"Do we know their agenda?"

"Shrimp."

"Shrimp?"

"That's their pretext."

Clarke wasn't satisfied. He turned to Breckenridge. "John, can you flesh this out?"

"We've had an ongoing dispute with China and Vietnam over shrimp imports that has been simmering for months. What lit the fuse was the recent jump in diesel fuel prices."

"What does diesel fuel have to do with shrimp?"

"Profit margin. The end result was the Southern Shrimp Alliance filed an anti-dumping petition with Commerce and the International Trade Commission."

"Are there other commodities we should consider?"

"Furniture, textiles."

"Your department is considering more tariffs?"

"Yes."

Clarke drummed his fingers on the table. They had been down this road before. Aside from alienating Hanoi, he knew tariffs were a dead end. He turned to Breckenridge. "John, we've been working for nearly a year now to open new venues for collaboration with the Vietnamese. It seems your policies are running counter to just about everything we've been trying to do."

Breckenridge's head snapped up from the briefing paper he'd been studying. He was still suffering the consequences of his reprimand from the computer incident and reacted to anything that suggested he wasn't exercising due diligence. "We're really getting beat up by the lobbyists and Congress."

"That's a given. We're going to have to offer up something concrete," Clarke said.

"The hell of it is, we'd be hitting the President's base in the South pretty hard. It's going to be a tough call for him to reconcile our recommendations with his domestic agenda."

"That's for the White House to figure out. Isn't it?" Jessica Auden interjected. The Japan section chief, she had gotten word of her boss's ass-chewing and had made it known she was more concerned about supporting Clarke, than Stuart's Southern constituency.

Clarke stiffened. He knew of his staff's antipathy toward Valardi, but he'd been around long enough to know that dealing with prickly bosses was part of doing business. He couldn't permit open dissension and made a mental note to speak privately with his section chief. He stopped any further discussion on the topic, redirecting the discussion. "Sean, you have anything else?"

"It may amount to nothing, but earlier this year, a Vietnamese company purchased several Russian-built minisubmarines to explore for red coral in the Spratlys. APEC was supposed to address their request, but they got bogged down squabbling about oil and mineral rights."

The Pentagon's representative, who had been content to remain silent up to this point, spoke. "May we back up a moment?"

"Certainly, Colonel," Clarke said, happy for the reprieve.

"There's more to the submarine issue. The Vietnamese Navy is preparing to accept several North Korean-built boats. Their support facilities are almost complete and the crews are completing their training."

"I can't imagine Manila getting worked up," Auden said.

Clarke parried. "What about the Chinese?"

"Beijing's linking the two."

"Seriously?"

"There's some logic to their position."

"We don't have any plans to intervene—do we?" Waite asked.

"The short answer is, no. The Pentagon has no desire to intercede in what is a regional issue."

Clarke picked up on the Marine's stilted response. "Could you amplify 'intercede'?"

The Marine evaded Clarke's question. "There are any number of options we could exercise. For example, we could reconsider our approach if there were an imminent threat to our national interests."

Clarke eyed his traveling partner from Defense. He couldn't read his face. He tried another tact. "What can you tell us about Admiral Cortez's trip to Hanoi?"

"He made significant progress in discussions pertaining to our use of Da Nang. He stressed an American presence could exert an important moderating effect on any further Chinese advances into the Con Song Basin."

"Anything else?" Clarke prodded, wondering what the Colonel wasn't saying.

"I don't have the specifics."

Clarke broke the following silence. "Ian, there are the recent developments in Manila. Can we continue to count on Montalvo?"

"The jury's still out," the Philippine expert, Ian Place, answered. "Things are getting interesting."

"I'm always leery of the word 'interesting' when it's used in this context. How interesting?"

"Montalvo may have the upper hand after calling a national State of Emergency to counter a possible coup. He ordered the arrest of several members of his cabinet."

"What the hell?" Crenshaw interrupted. "Did this just happen?"

"Yesterday. It's our understanding the Undersecretary for Policy, Florencia Cruz, and his Special Assistant, a guy named Atencio, are under house arrest."

"The charges?"

"Sedition."

The Marine arched his eyebrow at Crenshaw. "Well, I'll be damned."

Crenshaw nodded a reply, wondering if his back-channel source at the CIA was right about the agency's plans to enlist the services of the reporter in Manila. "You have any details?"

"We've been hearing rumors both Atencio and Cruz are linked to the Chinese Ministry of State Security."

Crenshaw cocked his head, concerned that sensitive details about his department's dark programs with the AFP would surface. "Any others?"

"None that I've heard about. Montalvo's still in control, but just."

"What about the Department of National Defense?" Clarke asked.

Crenshaw's right hand tightened around his pen. The last thing he needed was an entanglement with the Chinese he didn't know about. "The generals at the DND are supportive or neutral."

The Marine observed Crenshaw's white knuckles and weighed in. "They've remained engaged with PACOM negotiating a new agreement called the Security Engagement Board. It's co-chaired by Admiral Cortez and the Chief of Staff of the AFP.

"We're hopeful the SEB will provide us workarounds for the issues we've run up against in our deliberations. The agreements have been structured in such a way as to provide a mechanism to expand the provisions of the 1951 Mutual Defense Agreement to strengthen their position, vis-à-vis the Spratlys."

Clarke sensed Crenshaw was holding something back. "The Spratlys?"

"The AFP insisted. The SEB will have a broad mandate to address restrictions imposed by current Philippine law. The DND issued a statement saying the SEB will provide a consultative mechanism for cooperation for non-traditional security concerns including terrorism, maritime safety, and security."

Clarke tried another tact. "Ian, with Cruz sidelined, how do the provisions square with the Foreign Ministry's agenda?"

"Too early to tell."

Clarke reached down for his briefcase. Up to this point, he had concluded the meeting was going nowhere and was about to call it quits. Thinking better of it, he decided to give it one more shot. "What are your thoughts about the trade delegation the PRC is sending to Manila?"

"I'm for anything that helps the Philippine economy and stabilizes the country."

"I beg to differ," Crenshaw said. "I'd like to provide another perspective."

Clarke released his grip on the briefcase's handle. "Let's hear it."

"Far from moderating their relations with Manila, we feel the Chinese have reached the limit of their patience. Same goes with the Vietnamese, by the way. As long as Manila agrees with Beijing's proposals on joint development of energy and mineral resources, things may work out, but remember this. The Chinese have resisted any move for discussions on territorial disputes."

"But Beijing has acknowledged the Manila Doctrine," Auden countered.

"Yes, and the PRC has continued to refuse to even consider including the Paracel Islands in any negotiations. They have also dismissed all requests to dismantle their garrisons on Johnson and Mischief Reefs, and they have repeatedly blocked all attempts by Manila or Hanoi to raise these issues at the Asia-Pacific Parliamentary Forum. I don't see any improvement in the South China Seas. In fact, I believe all the indicators point to a significant crisis within the next six months."

"That's an ominous prediction, Colonel. Have you identified a specific flash point?"

"Up north."

The answer caught Clarke off guard. "Really? Where? All the turmoil's been to the south."

"We believe Beijing's testing the waters," the Marine replied. "Vietnam and the Philippines are small potatoes. The PRC's main focus has always been on Taiwan and countering our ability to intercede on the Nationalists' behalf."

"You're not suggesting the Chinese are prepared to go to war—are you?"

"Only if they're pushed." Crenshaw pushed aside the papers scattered in front of him. "Let me dispense with the innuendos and get to the point. Frankly, we believe Beijing is positioning itself to neutralize Tokyo and Washington economically while the PLA competes their preparations for military intervention."

Clarke silenced the agitated murmurs from around the table and addressed the committee member from Treasury. "Matt, the ball's in your court."

"John has connected the dots. His assumptions on the connectivity of the various factors are spot on. Oil is driving their industrial base and they're looking to the Spratlys for more."

"Hence, the genesis of the PLA's strategic doctrine."

Clarke listened to the exchange while beginning to formulate a cogent plan for his boss. "Then our best bet to reduce the risk of a military confrontation with Beijing is to structure our national security policy to address this imperative."

"And the hysteria from The Hill," Waite said.

"I would be hesitant to characterize legitimate national security concerns as hysterical," Breckenridge countered. "I'd like to comment from the International Security Affair's perspective. There was Beijing's unsolicited all-cash bid of 18.5 billion dollars for Unocal. I should also point out that CNOOC is now eyeing Lakeland Energy Corporation."

"Never heard of them," Auden said.

"I'd be surprised if you had. They're a small Denver-based outfit drilling in the Con Song Basin on blocks leased to them by CNOOC. The complicating piece is that Hanoi claims the same blocks. Several months ago, the PRC announced it would protect Lakeland's operations by force."

"You see a pattern here?" Crenshaw continued. "First Unocal and now Lakeland. The PRC wants a controlling interest of, or to buy outright, any company that has an internationally recognized presence in the Con Song Basin."

"Trojan horses," Waites answered.

Crenshaw nodded, "Correct. And the significance of these moves hasn't been lost on the Vietnamese. They've countered and partnered with an American firm, Horizon Offshore Exploration, to drill the same area."

"And that has not set well with Beijing," Clarke said. "Especially since Congress blocked the Unocal deal. Adding insult to injury, the uproar CNOOC's bid caused in Congress led to even more provocative posturing by the Senate and threats of trade tariffs."

Auden pulled off her glasses and dropped them on the table. "The PRC is financing fifty-percent of our national debt, for God's sake. And Congress wants to screw with them? That's insane! Think of the Unocal offer... Eighteen billion. Don't you think it's just a tad ironic that all the Central Bank of China had to do was liquidate a *fraction* of their holdings of U.S. securities and buy one of our biggest oil companies? And what about our monetary system if they sold off that eighteen billion?"

"Ironic isn't the word I'd choose to use," Crenshaw said. "Alarming doesn't even fit."

Clarke massaged the nape of his neck. There was nothing to be gained by belaboring the obvious. He changed the subject to address the wildcard in the region. "Hugh, what do you have for us on Taiwan?"

"Taipei's poked the skunk."

"The independence issue?"

"Yeah, the opposition party introduced a referendum seeking to change the country's constitution to set the legal foundation to break from the mainland."

The Marine groaned. "Why in hell would they do that?"

"We presume they're responding in kind to several actions by the Chinese."

"The White Paper on military preparedness, and an anti-secession law?"

"I'm not sure I want to read anything ominous in what you've said, Hugh. It sounds like a replay of the same verbal bombast we've heard before."

"Ordinarily I'd agree with you, Sean, but this time around the Taiwanese have said they're not going to send their representatives to the National Unification Council"

"There's more to this," Crenshaw said. "Taiwan occupies Itu Aba Island, a key piece of the strategic pie."

Clarke jotted a note to himself to find out what was so important about the place. "What's at stake, Jim?"

"Until recently, not much. There has only been a small Coast Guard garrison of some one hundred and thirty personnel conducting search and rescue operations. The Nationalists just upped the ante and announced a major project to upgrade an old airstrip."

"At the very least, their announcement has to be a calculated irritant," Auden observed.

Waite snorted. "So, we add Itu Aba to our growing list of weather stations, bird watching stands, and tourist attractions."

"Don't trivialize this," Clarke scolded. "The Nationalists are militarizing Itu Aba and not everyone in this room appears to appreciate the implications."

"Excuse me," Crenshaw interrupted. "We're staring at a dangerous situation. I'll reinforce what Adrian just said. Releasing a statement that we view the situation as 'a matter of grave concern' won't hack it."

Clarke held up his pen silencing the room. "I don't think any of us here have underestimated China's position on reunification, but Beijing has demonstrated a certain amount of ambivalence in their actions."

Crenshaw poured himself a glass of water before responding. "Not enough. I can tell you with complete certainty that unless the Nationalists abandon their plans to militarize Itu Aba Island, we'll be heading down the road to war."

Clarke almost choked. "What's that?"

Crenshaw jabbed his hand to emphasize his point, knocking over his water glass. Righting it, he flicked ineffectively at the water soaking his notebook. "The placement of air combat elements on Itu Aba Island will pose a direct threat to China's maritime security."

Clarke stared at the spreading pool of water. "We understand that, but you still haven't said what has gotten the Pentagon spooled up."

"The PLA is repositioning their forces to the coast. If diplomatic efforts fail, they will attack."

"But they've done this before in their training exercises," Turner protested.

"There are no scheduled exercises."

"They're bluffing," Clarke countered, not really believing it himself.

"Not this time. I'm not at liberty to discuss the details; however, there are specific indicators that distinguish a training exercise from those measures taken when you ramp up prior to commencing military action."

"You've seen these?"

"Yes."

"Oh, shit."

Stunned by Crenshaw's revelation, Clarke pushed away from the table and walked to the windows. He kept his back to the room struggling to collect his thoughts. After a long minute, he broke his silence and spoke to the window. "We're going to be here a while. We'll take fifteen minutes so you can call your offices." Turning to Crenshaw, he added, "Got a sec?"

When they were alone, Clarke lashed out. "God damn it. You blindsided me."

"Sorry. This information is tightly controlled. I'll probably get my ass chewed for saying this much."

Clarke resigned himself to this reality and uncrossed his arms. "It's going to get ugly."

"Yeah, I know."

Chapter Thirty-Six

COMPACFLT HEADQUATERS
09:35 MONDAY 30 JUNE

"Will the mystery guest please sign in?" Mackenzie said when Rohrbaugh surfaced after morning report.

"Give me a break. The Ops Boss held us over."

"Anything going on?" Mackenzie replied, not expecting much.

"Yeah, as a matter of fact, plenty. We've been directed to start bringing in selected augmenters for 519."

Mackenzie picked up a brass .50-caliber shell casing and rolled it around in his hand. "The North Koreans looking to set off another nuke?"

"It's the Chinese."

Mackenzie carefully balanced the shell upright on his desk. "I would have thought they'd leave the Spratlys alone for a while." Mackenzie stood and took a step toward their safe. "I need to dust off the Spratly pics?"

"It's not the Spratlys. It's bigger."

"Oh?" Mac dropped back into his chair. "What's happening?"

"Taiwan."

"Taiwan? The PLA's not thinking about crossing the Straits, are they? That's not a great idea."

"I suspect the Nationalists don't think so either."

"We have anything hard?"

Rohrbaugh closed the door to their office. "Imagery, intercepts, key indicators."

"This isn't adding up. There's been some mention in the message traffic of the Nationalists' intent to station Marines on Itu Aba. There's nothing to suggest we're about to go to war, for God's sake."

"Up to now, it's been compartmentalized. Some bright analysts with the National Intelligence Council and DIA who have access to all the pieces put things together. They set off the alarm with a report to the White House."

"How come the Chinese are so pissed?"

"I'll fill you in with what I know. There's more going on besides putting a few Marines on Itu Aba. The Executive Yuan and the Nationalists' legislature passed a supplemental budget for the Ministry of National Defense."

Mackenzie knocked the shell casing over sending it rolling to the floor. "A budget's setting this off? No way."

"There was a considerable difference of opinion on the wisdom of the appropriation. Up to now, the opposition had managed to keep the bill locked up in conference."

"I can't see how a budget bill ties in," Mackenzie said trying to wrap his head around what had just wiped out the start of a pretty good day.

"It falls under the category of: 'Be careful what you ask for.' Besides providing the funding for the airfield on Itu Aba, the supplement allocated money for the purchase of PAC-II anti-missile batteries and a squadron of old P-3C's."

"What's wrong with that?"

"Guess where that weaponry is going?"

Mackenzie took a shot at the answer. "Itu Aba?"

"Bingo."

"Makes sense, Skipper. They're dispersing their forces and expanding their defensive perimeter."

"There's nothing defensive about a P-3 looking around for something to sink. The PLAN is particularly sensitive to a Nationalist presence on Itu Aba because any anti-submarine assets based there can block their submarines' access to the South China Sea. And remember, Itu Aba sits squarely in the middle of a cluster of Chinese garrisons in the Spratlys. A strong Nationalist presence could neutralize the PLA outposts on Johnson Island, Subi and Mischief Reef."

"Point made."

"What the analysts are telling us is the Nationalists may have finally exceeded Beijing's level of tolerance. They've backed up their assessment citing a quote from Xiao in the *Global Times*."

Mackenzie rescued the .50-cal shell from the floor. "Crap."

"That sums it up. The situation can best be described as 'fluid.' That's why the boss is bringing in the augmenters for 519. The good news?"

"There's good news? My thinking is: 'If there's all this shit, there's got to be pony somewhere.'"

"The Three said we don't have a warning order. We're still far short of implementing phase one of the OPLAN."

"Well, I suppose that should be reassuring," Mac replied not feeling at all assured.

"There's an update scheduled at 1300."

"I'll start pulling stuff together." Mac set the shell upright on is desk. "If this turns to shit, we might as well be prepared."

He leaned over to spin the dial of their safe containing the OPLAN for a war with China, then paused. "I don't have a good feeling about this, Skipper."

"Neither do I, Mac. Neither do I."

FLEET INTELLIGENCE CENTER
13:00

Rohrbaugh stood with the others when Admiral Morey entered the Fleet Intelligence Center conference room. They were all surprised to see the other four-star on the island at his side.

The significance of Admiral Cortez's presence was not lost on the officers of Joint Task Force 519. If there had been any doubt in their minds about the seriousness of the situation in the Western Pacific, it was dispelled when Morey began to speak.

"There's been a lot of scuttlebutt concerning the intentions of the PLA. Our intent this afternoon is to put those rumors to rest. We cannot afford to waste time on speculation or running down false leads. Admiral Cortez?"

"This morning, I received an alert order from the National Command Authority directing me to increase the readiness posture of our forces. To that end, I have ordered the augmentation of the command staff of JTF 519. Admiral Morey has been provided guidance to initiate the planning process for his Commander's Estimate."

A sense of unreality swept over the room.

Rohrbaugh fixed his eyes on the COMPACFLT logo on the podium, his mind pummeled by Cortez's words.

"We must be ready to respond with the appropriate application of force to any of several scenarios that may play out. I have not received authorization to deploy our assets beyond augmenting your staff. The President's intent is to provide the concerned parties every opportunity to resolve this crisis by diplomatic means. To this end, he has dispatched a special envoy to Beijing in an attempt to defuse the situation."

Cortez consulted his notes. "Taiwan's ambassador was summoned to the White House this morning. The President informed him that yesterday's affirmation by Taipei of their intent to continue their Han Kiang war games was provocative.

The President made it clear that any action the PRC takes in response to Taipei's actions may not necessarily trigger our involvement under the provisions of the Taiwan Relations Act.

To ensure there could be no misinterpretation of his stance, Washington placed on indefinite hold any further transfers of military hardware to Taiwan.

That said, there is no ambiguity in Beijing's position in this matter. The PRC communicated to Taipei their planned war games will not be tolerated."

Rohrbaugh looked around the room to get a read on the body language of the other officers. Their eyes were riveted on the Admirals. He turned his attention back to Cortez.

"It goes without saying that the Chinese are monitoring our response to these events. Zhu has spoken with President Stuart and expressed assurances that the PLA will not take pre-emptive action if diplomatic interventions are successful. Therein lies the rub. If diplomatic negotiations are not successful, it is probable Xiao will be ordered to eliminate the threat.

"With that in mind, we are reviewing the impact Exercise Summer Pulse. We've made no secret of our intent to surge three Strike Groups to the Pacific in the next two weeks. Depending on which side of the fence you're sitting, the movement of our carriers could be seen as a deterrent or a further provocation.

"The PLA estimates that without intervention, the longest the Nationalists could hold out in the face of a full-blown invasion is two weeks. With that consideration in mind, they could be inclined to act before we are in a position to intercede.

"The Chinese have a number of options. As a prelude to a larger invasion, they could invade the Pescadores, or they could occupy Itu Aba. Without going into any further detail on these possibilities, we should review what we do know about the PLA's intentions."

"Thank you, Admiral," Morey said. "Commander?"

"Yes, sir. We are witnessing an unprecedented mobilization. The movement of the PLA's missile brigades, assault divisions, and naval and air units exceeds even their largest exercises.

"Particularly noteworthy has been the forward deployment of logistic support forces to their various staging areas near the PLA's airfields and ports.

"Another indicator that has not been triggered before is the movement of Class VIII medical material. On this slide, we have highlighted a casualty receiving station being assembled adjacent to this airfield. As you recall, the United States signaled its intent to strike prior to the onset of the two Gulf Wars by deploying our medical units."

Rohrbaugh studied the briefer. His jaw tightened at sight of the officer's scant row of service ribbons. He appeared devoid of any sense of the impact he was having on the war fighters in the room.

"The next two slides document the mobilization of the PLA's short and medium range missile brigades. We'll begin with the increased command activity of the Second Artillery Corp at Qunghe. In concert with this, we've identified five CCS-11 and CCS-15 tactical missile units of the Corps' 815th Brigade moving by rail to their prepared launch positions in Xianyou and Nanping. These are in addition to short-range missile brigades deploying to Yongan, Fujian, and Jiangshan Provinces. Each of these brigades has sixteen transporter/erector launchers with five to six missiles per launcher stored in hardened bunkers.

"This slide shows the 815th Brigade's headquarters at Leping. There has been a corresponding increase in SIGINT from this site that matches to their force movements. The Chinese have not begun activation of Unit 80301 and its intermediate-range ballistic missiles. This unit's sole purpose is to strike our bases in Korea, Japan, and Okinawa. The fact we have not seen any increased activity indicates the PLA is not preparing for a broader engagement at this time."

Rohrbaugh sat grim-faced while the Commander documented the mobilization of the PLA's main force units, but it wasn't until the end of the brief that the focus shifted to the South China Sea. The Spratly Islands were tacked on almost as an afterthought.

Rohrbaugh straightened. These islands held the key to containing the crisis. His eyes widened at the changes on Mischief Reef. The PLA had abandoned any pretext of disguising the intent of their installation.

In addition to a new pier, the Chinese had widened the existing channel into the lagoon. Several Fulin and Dayon class resupply ships anchored beside a new pier. A larger vessel with a bow ramp and helicopter deck was moored near a sandy beach on the northern side of the lagoon. Identified as a Yuting class LST, the ship carried two-hundred and fifty troops and ten tanks.

"Presumably, the Yuting has just offloaded construction materials," the briefer said, "but they could be staging an assault force in preparation for an attack on Nanshan or Pagasa islands."

Exactly, Rohrbaugh thought, but *the PLA missed their chance at Pagasa. With the upgrades to the defenses and the recent stationing of additional Philippine Army Scouts and Naval Special Warfare troops on the island, it'd be a pretty tough nut to crack. On the other hand, Nanshan would be a piece of cake.*

While Rohrbaugh pondered the implications, the briefer continued. "To the northwest, the Chinese have completed construction of an aircraft shelter at Subi Reef. The PLA has positioned two Z-9 helicopters, both equipped with the C-701 anti-ship missile. By establishing a forward perimeter on Subi, Johnson, Nanshan, and Mischief Reefs, they can counter those measures we would take to intervene. We'll now turn our attention to the PLA installations on the Paracel Islands."

Rohrbaugh rocked back in his chair. *Damn. That's it?*

The briefer paused for the slide to change to one of the Paracel Islands.

"This island group represents the keystone for the PLA's control of the South China Sea. Woody Island is the most significant with its 1,800-foot runway and hardened shelters for their Su-30 fighters. The arrows point to revetments for track-borne Hangqui-17 surface-to-air missiles. To complement these, the PLA has built a layered air defense system placing batteries of high altitude SAMs on Lincoln, Duncan, and Drummond Island.

"The most significant threat to U.S. assets, though, is the anti-ship missiles the Chinese have deployed over the past six months."

That statement caught Rohrbaugh's attention. He'd been concerned about this threat since he first reviewed the intelligence reports following the fishing boat incident. Taking on a Chinese infantry division or missile battalion was one thing. This was different. It was something a SEAL Team could do something about.

"We detected long range HY-2 Seersuckers on Woody Island some time ago, but the PLA has increased their numbers and has begun to install hardened shelters and launching ramps for a land-launched version of the C-802 anti-ship cruise missile.

"The Chinese have also begun construction of extensive installations on Drummond Island after connecting it with a causeway to Duncan Island and its port facilities. You can see in this picture the two ships tied up to the pier. One is a Dahzi class submarine tender. The other, a Yannan-class survey and research vessel.

"Supporting these various installations is a robust PLA presence on Rocky Island lying just to the northeast of Woody Island. This island is notable because it has the highest peak in all of the South China Sea. The Chinese have taken full advantage of this geographic feature by emplacing multi-antennae arrays, intercept and guidance, SIGINT, and EW systems."

Rohrbaugh thought that was very considerate of the PLA. With most of their electronic eggs in one basket, it wouldn't take much to take them out. But something didn't feel right. His gut told him they were not seeing the forest for the trees. He needed to understand the PLA's ultimate intent.

"Commander Rohrbaugh?"

Rohrbaugh turned. The voice belonged to a Lieutenant working his way toward him through the jam of officers waiting to exit the briefing room. The four braided blue and gold ropes looped over his left shoulder identified him as Admiral Morey's aide.

"Lieutenant."

"Sir, the Admiral would like a moment. Would you accompany me, please?"

The request didn't require a response, and Rohrbaugh dutifully followed the younger officer to the back entrance of the headquarters building.

The Lieutenant proceeded through a narrow passageway to the reception area of the command suite and disappeared around a corner into Morey's office. A moment later, he reappeared.

"Commander? The Admiral will see you now."

Rohrbaugh had never been in the office. He cast a quick look around. Pretty standard stuff for a four-star. The notable exception was a huge oil painting of Admiral Chester Nimitz, the Pacific Fleet's commander during World War II.

Morey looked up from the desk Nimitz had once used. "An extraordinary man."

"Yes, sir."

"Please have a seat."

"Thank you, sir."

"I'll get straight to the point, Commander. We're sending you back to the Spratlys."

Rohrbaugh stiffened. *What now?*

"Thanks in part to Valiant Crane and the tap your team placed, we know there is much more to the recent construction activity on Drummond Island than was presented at the brief.

"The intercepts have provided our analysts critical information linking the infrared and radar signatures from a geostationary NRA bird to the Chinese construction.

"There is a significant amount of work being done under the cover of darkness. The PLA's intent is to conceal that from our daylight optical surveillance. Do you recall the picture of that Dahzi class submarine tender tied up to the jetty at Duncan Island?

"Yes, sir."

"That ship has the capability to transport and handle special weapons."

The one-on-one, and Morey's demeanor, permitted Rohrbaugh to ask a question. "Admiral, do we have evidence these weapons have been offloaded?"

"Yes, but that's not the full picture. You have to have a delivery vehicle."

"Yes, sir."

"The question is; what's on that island? Are there HY-2's or have they brought in the C-802s? We cannot permit the Chinese to deploy either of these systems. If they were to do so, they would have overlapping fields of fire over the South China Sea's shipping lanes.

The PLA has adapted the Russians' tactics for salvo fire of these weapons. A launch of a cluster of eight of these missiles would be extraordinarily difficult, if not impossible to stop."

"Yes, sir," Rohrbaugh responded, realizing the implications.

"We need hard intel to validate our planning assumptions. You've been chosen to lead the mission to determine what the PLA is up to on Drummond Island. Your team will rendezvous with the *Carter* off Guam in five days.

"By that time, we will have real-time imagery to assist your mission planning. Once on board, you will receive your orders. If there is any way to disable those missiles without leaving a trail back to us, you will have authorization to do so. Questions?"

"No, sir."

"Although luck may have very little to do with it, I'll wish you good luck anyway."

"Thank you, sir."

Morey hit his intercom button after the door closed. "Please have Admirals Noland and Brewer step in."

The fleet operations and intelligence chiefs entered his office within moments of their summons.

"I suppose you caught Rohrbaugh leaving?"

"A man on a mission," the Fleet Intelligence Chief, Ralph Brewer replied.

"I just gave him his rudder orders. Now it's up to us to

provide him the means to execute them. Duke, have you greased the skids?"

"SPECWARCOM is on board and Group One is expecting his call."

"How about the *Carter?*"

"She'll be underway within twelve hours."

"Good. I want both of you to work this next piece with PACOM. We need real time high-resolution surveillance of the target. I can't be sending Rohrbaugh in blind. What about that Army Warrior UAV unit at Wheeler?"

"We checked," Brewer said. "The loiter time and range are not optimal. The Army informed us that to meet their mission programming parameters, we'd have to get the Ground Control Station and some fifty personnel out to Pagasa or Batanes Islands. Provided they would even grant access, there's not enough time to obtain permission from the Filipinos. Besides, the risks of disclosure are unacceptable. Remember that young ABC reporter snooping around after the P-8 incident?"

"We don't need that distraction. What's the alternative?"

"The Air Force's 12th Reconnaissance Squadron out of Beale Air Force Base operates the Global Hawks. They'd provide us thirty-five hours of loiter time and a twelve-thousand mile range out and back."

"What's the link?"

"The Defense Airborne Reconnaissance Office. The Joint Service Imaging Processing Center will process the imaging."

"What can we count on, Ralph?"

"I've been told the ISR package has the upgraded sensor suite and SIGINT capability."

"Where would they deploy?"

"Anderson. Roughly a two-thousand-mile flight to Drummond Island."

"Can we keep the mission's profile covert?"

"The short answer is, yes. We're looking at two thirty-foot

trailers for the Mission Control Element and Launch and Recovery Units, both of which can be set up in an empty hangar. The antenna for the satellite link can be placed next to the hangar without attracting much notice. The four UAV's can be kept out of sight by operating under cover of darkness. The other plus is C-17s fly in there all the time. They won't draw any attention."

"Lock it in. Can you give me an update on the Broad Area Maritime Surveillance system?"

"We're working our Mariner UAV."

"Figure I could count on you guys to be a step ahead of me. What else?"

"We're drafting messages to Dick Triebull at Seventh Fleet and Commander, Undersea Surveillance for your release."

"The taskers?"

"Dick will direct CTF-74 to deploy his boats to take up station off Zoushon and Yulin. COMSUBGRU-7 is an addee on the message."

"Their load-out?"

"Standard."

"We'll want mines."

"SUBPAC has that for action. They've alerted *Houston* and *Corpus Christi*."

"Good. Where do we stand with SURTASS?"

"*Impeccable* is closest to the Op Area. Our message to Commander Underseas Surveillance will task him to reposition her to keep tabs on a Kilo we know to be underway in the vicinity of Woody Island."

"We can't afford to have the Chinese stumble into the *Carter*."

"*Impeccable* had considerable success against shallow water diesels with her SURTASS during RIMPAC."

"Let's be certain they can translate that success into an intercept of a 636."

"Another ace up our sleeve is the new Integrated Underseas Surveillance System we strung along the PLAN's approach lanes. We're sending one of our guys to the IUSS Operations Support Det at Pearl City to look it over."

"What about LASH?"

"It'll be a good fit in the shallow waters of the Spratlys," Noland answered. "The system will detect any changes in UV and infrared signatures made by their subs."

"Get a message to COMPATRECON WING ONE and tell him to hang LASH pods under his P-8s. If he needs more of them or has any tech support requirements, get them out to him. Anything else?"

"I believe we've covered the bases."

"I'll let you guys go. Keep me updated."

Chapter Thirty-Seven

DRUMMOND ISLAND
00:35 SUNDAY 13 JULY

"Commander," Ace called, "we're nearing our last navigation point abeam of Duncan Island. We'll assume a course to the northwest to your drop point. ETA: five minutes."

Rohrbaugh acknowledged the timeline for their insertion on Drummond Island. "What's the battery status?"

"Holding their charge, Commander. We've got a good eighteen hours."

"We'll stage for egress," Rohrbaugh said. "I'll signal when we're locked in and ready to flood the chamber."

"Roger that."

Rohrbaugh felt confident the insertion would go without incident. Drummond was one of five islands of the Crescent Group, strung together by a shallow reef, Antelope, Robert, Prattle, Duncan, and Drummond lay along the rim of a dormant volcano. The deep central lagoon of this cauldron would provide a safe haven for ASDS-1. Ace would maneuver the sub past the unsuspecting Chinese by way of a deep channel between Duncan and Antelope islands.

"Ready up. Buddy check."

He would have preferred to have run at least one simulated mission, but the mission's short fuse precluded any run-throughs. Mitigating this shortfall was the precise mapping data and real-time streaming video fed to them by the Global Hawk circling overhead.

Rohrbaugh turned to his team leader, Chief Boson's Mate Wayne Tinsley. "Boats, you good?"

"Yes, sir."

"Let's get on it. Ace, we're entering the chamber."

"Sonar has confirmed our approach to the shelf, Commander. That'll place you at one-hundred feet for your egress, four-hundred yards from the beach."

"Boats, you lead," Rohrbaugh ordered. "I'll lock us in."

The five other men of Rohrbaugh's Direct Action Team squeezed by him to join Tinsley in the ocean interface chamber. Rohrbaugh followed, closed the watertight door, and opened the sea valves to flood the chamber. Cold seawater poured around him. He was never prepared for the shock despite the number of times he had gone through this evolution. The water rose steadily, engulfing his legs, surrounding his chest, enclosing his head.

Within moments the chamber flooded. Rohrbaugh released the latches securing the egress hatch and swung it open. He propelled himself into open water, looking up to verify his depth. A thin line of bubbles trapped by the hatch drifted to the surface.

He checked his pressure and depth gauges while waiting for the rest of his team to emerge. They were soon assembled, hovering in neutral buoyancy over the deck of the ASDS. He signaled Tinsley to close the egress hatch.

Rohrbaugh set a compass course for the south and settled into the SEAL's energy-conserving kick and glide technique. His team kept pace in a tight formation by his side.

The offshore current was minimal, and the team easily traversed the short distance to the shallowing waters leading to the beach. Rohrbaugh broke through the surface, motioning the team to hold in place at the edge of a coral head. Low tide had occurred at 2031 hours and they only had to contend with minimal surge. Clouds obscured the moon. The conditions were optimal.

Rohrbaugh grasped a rocky outcrop and scanned the shoreline. A thick patch of low-lying vegetation abutted the water's edge. "Boats, the beach is clear. Hold at ten yards."

The team exited the water near the clump of brush Rohrbaugh had spotted and slipped out of their scuba apparatus.

"Boats, get the gear concealed. Suarez take point."

Suarez led off, guiding the assault team around the base of the basalt mount in which the Chinese had carved a cave for their missile emplacement. He exited the dense vegetation and motioned to Rohrbaugh.

The ground before them was dotted with coconut palms. offering no concealment for their final approach. Tinsley pointed to the cave entrance.

"Guards?"

Tinsley held up two fingers. The PLA soldiers standing watch on either side of the cave entrance were backlit by a single bulb.

"Saurez, we're going to have to take them out," Rohrbaugh whispered. "Take left. I've got right."

Rohrbaugh dug his elbows into the sand to brace his rifle. Drawing a bead on his target, he completed his mental checklist. The distance between him and the sentry was minimal. He wouldn't need to compensate for wind drift or bullet drop. "On my count. Three, two, one."

Two simultaneous pops dropped the guards.

"Miller. Anthony. Cover us."

Rohrbaugh bolted across the thirty yards of open ground to the cave. He dropped to one knee when he reached the rock face and peered around the steel door into the emplacement. No sign of activity. He motioned to the nearest body. "Niles, prop that one up next to the entrance. Suarez, drag the other guy inside."

"Go."

The SEALs swept the void of the cave mouth with their rifles. Two C-802 cruise missiles resting on their cradles dominated the space.

"Holy shit, Skipper. Look at those bastards."

Rohrbaugh pointed to the nearest. "Boats, wire that one. I'll take the second. Niles, see if you can locate the warheads. They must have them secured in another area. Suarez, C-4."

The SEALs set to work affixing the two-pound blocks of explosives in a pattern around the missiles' fuel tanks. Next, they paired their charges to primer cord and blasting caps, wiring the entire array to a firing device.

Rohrbaugh turned at the sound of thudding boots. Niles. "Skipper, I've found them. There's a locked wire-mesh door back there with a couple of signs plastered on them. One's red, the other looks like one of those yellow nuke signs."

"You got the flex charge?"

"Yes, sir."

"Wrap the door. We'll blow it just before we set off the main charges."

"Skipper, I also found these," Niles said, handing Rohrbaugh a four-inch thick stack of tan jacketed books. "Look like some kind of tech manual."

"Let's see 'em."

"What do ya think, sir?"

"Niles, you've hit the mother lode. These alone are worth the trip. Hey, Boats?"

"Checking the batteries, Skipper."

"Listen up. We've got to get our asses out of here. Niles, set your timer for fifteen minutes."

"Set at fifteen minutes," Niles confirmed.

"Boats."

"Remove arming pins."

"Arm on my mark."

"Yes, sir."

"One one-thousand, two one-thousand, now."

"Armed," Boats barked.

"Rally up, let's get the hell out of here."

Rohrbaugh pulled up next to Suarez at the cave mouth. "Clear?"

"Yes, sir."

"Go."

The team retraced their steps, joined up with the other SEALS, and made their way to the beach. Rohrbaugh checked his chronometer. Two minutes until the charges were set to blow. "Get your gear on."

Rohrbaugh hefted his apparatus, twisting to align his scuba tank. A huge explosion rocked the island. The blast wave knocked him off balance, throwing him onto his right side. A stab of pain lanced through his shoulder.

Niles was the first to respond. "Holy shit! What did they have in there?"

"Damn," Suarez said, his head swiveling to check their perimeter.

"Boats," Rohrbaugh coughed. He rolled to a sitting position, cradling his right arm in his lap.

"Skipper?"

"I've dislocated my shoulder."

Tinsley edged over to Rohrbaugh's side and made a quick assessment. He'd seen this injury before. "I need to fix this."

"Yeah, thought so."

"It's going to hurt," Tinsley said.

"I know."

"Niles, help the skipper with his rig."

"What gives?"

"Dislocated shoulder. Secure him."

Niles handed his rifle to Suarez, dropped to his knees, and positioned himself to prevent Rohrbaugh from moving.

"Ready, Skipper?"

Rohrbaugh set his jaw in anticipation of the pain. "Do it."

"I'm going to put my foot in your arm pit and pull like hell."

"This is my second time."

"Alright, here we go." Tinsley placed his boot, grasped Rohrbaugh's hand, and began to pull with steady traction.

"Arghhh!"

"Hold on Skipper. It's beginning to give."

Several seconds later, Boats felt the joint pop into place.

"Damn, Boats," Rohrbaugh gasped.

"You can thank me later. I'm going to strap your arm to your side."

"How the hell am I supposed to swim?"

"You're not. I'm going to drag you. All you have to do is kick."

"Do I have a choice?"

"Suarez, grab the skipper's gear. Niles, help with his rig. Skipper, you have the signaling device?"

"In my kit."

Tinsley found the device and aimed it into the lagoon, squeezing off two long bursts of infrared light. He repeated the sequence three more times. At the end of the third, the receiver flashed in response to an invisible signal broadcast from the mast of the ASDS. He sent another coded signal and waited for the reply.

"Let's get wet. They're waiting for us at four-hundred meters, due north. Ace knows we have a casualty and will be

near the surface. Skipper, you'll feel better once we're underway. Remember, all you have to do is kick. I'll get you home.
You ready?"

"Yeah."

"Shove off."

Chapter Thirty-Eight

THE WEST WING
13:00 MONDAY 14 JULY

Bob Lawson strode into the Cabinet Room, intent on finding Sheldon Payne. He spotted him, talking with Valardi, and caught his eye.

Payne nodded. The last update he'd heard of Rohrbaugh's mission was an hour ago. The infrared sensors of the Global Hawk circling over Duncan Island had registered a huge explosion. "Richard, would you excuse us please?"

Lawson and Payne separated from the others.

"What do we have?" Payne asked.

"They're safe."

Payne's shoulders slumped, exhaling in relief. "Injuries?"

"None that we know of."

"And the target?"

Lawson scanned the room. "They're being debriefed, but it appears our suspicions were confirmed."

Payne saw Stuart enter the room. "He'll want to know."

Stuart crossed the room and steered Payne and Lawson out of earshot. "Have we heard anything?"

"We got them out," Lawson answered.

That's all Stuart needed. "Keep me posted."

The brevity of his response belied Stuart's relief at this news. The consequences of a SEAL team member being killed or captured by the Chinese would have been unimaginable. Over the past twenty-four hours he kept questioning the wisdom of authorizing the mission. It would be a few more hours until he learned if the results justified the risks.

The other staff in the room had observed the brief exchange, but Stuart didn't drop any hints about what was discussed when he began the meeting.

"Sheldon, what more can you tell me about this morning's confrontation in the East China Sea?"

"There's nothing new. All we've confirmed is a Chinese patrol boat opened fire on a Japanese trawler, killing a fisherman. They impounded the boat and detained the survivors charging them with poaching and border violations."

"Hardly worth killing someone for." Stuart said, his exasperation evident having to contend with yet another incident.

"No, sir," Payne said. "The Chinese have expressed regret over the loss of life. They're insisting the trawler was engaged in illegal smuggling and ignored orders to stop."

"Can we substantiate any of these claims?"

"No, sir."

Brown peered over the rim of his glasses at Payne. "Do you think Beijing was reacting in kind to Tokyo's actions several months ago?"

"Please refresh my memory."

"When the Japanese chased those Chinese protestors off one of their islands in the Senkakus."

"That's one angle." Stuart drew a Rising Sun on his notepad. "Bob, what's Tokyo's response?"

"For openers, the JMSDF dispatched two destroyers to the area."

"Have the Chinese countered?"

"No yet."

"Stay on top of it."

Lawson returned his look, affirming he would do just that. Assured, Stuart turned his attention to Payne. "Justin, do you see any linkage with what's going on between Beijing and Taipei?"

"I don't believe so, but there is one possible scenario. The Chinese may well be sending Tokyo a message to stay clear."

"I can't put much credence in that," Valardi said. "The Japanese government has already indicated they have no intention of getting involved in what they consider to be an internal Chinese affair."

"Justin, presuming Richard's presumption is correct, where's that leave us?"

"We're focusing on the threat to Taiwan."

Valardi snapped the top of his fountain pen back on and set it on the table. "Then I'll cut to the chase. Are we willing to go to war to protect the Nationalists?"

"That's a valid question," Brown said. "The reality is, we could lose what leverage we may have with either party."

"Exactly," Stuart concluded. "We have to develop the ground rules within which we interact with the Chinese and define what constitutes unacceptable behavior. We'll operate within that context."

Brown sought to frame the discussion. "So, what's unacceptable?"

"Taiwan declaring independence."

"We're talking about Beijing's behavior," Stuart replied. "But since this happens to be the crux of our immediate problem, let's pursue it. Beyond drawing a comparison with the Federal government permitting the South to secede, I don't want to spend time deliberating the merits of Beijing's position. That's a reality we must accept."

"Mr. President?"

"Yes," Stuart responded, wondering what Valardi had on his mind.

"Might I suggest we just let Mississippi go?"

Payne picked up on the quip and replied in his best southern drawl. "Sah, ah take great offense at yah suggestion."

Stuart let the laughter die down. "Despite the wisecrack, I'll draw on it to develop an analogy. Let's say the good folks in Jackson announced their intention to leave the union and negotiations failed to dissuade them. What would happen if we just let them go? Would Alabama and Louisiana decide to follow suit?"

"The domino theory," Valardi said. "Vietnam falls to the communists and so does the rest of Southeast Asia."

"Correct, and communism has very little relevance now compared to the threat posed by radical Islam. Political manifestos and allegiances will vary, but nations will ultimately act in their own self-interest."

"Then we need to work within that framework," Brown said.

"Let me toss this out. Would the balance of power in Asia shift if we changed our position and not oppose reunification of Taiwan with the mainland?"

Valardi warmed to the idea. "We already support Beijing's 'One China' and 'Three-Noes' position."

"Technically that's correct," Stuart said, "but you know full well our actual stance says something entirely different."

"We can't write off Taiwan," Payne countered. "We'd lose all credibility in the region. Y'all know the costs of abandoning our friends."

"All too true. However, I shouldn't have to point out we haven't always chosen the best of friends—have we? A policy based on pragmatism and self-interest instead of principle will leave a void that will ultimately lead to a bad outcome."

"I should note ASEAN has already written off the Nationalists," Valardi added.

"Perhaps," Brown replied. "There are no permanent friends in that alliance. The constant we should not lose sight of is their over-riding permanent national interests."

"We need to move on," Stuart said. "We don't have time to rehash old discussions. Richard, what do you have on the Philippines?"

"Montalvo's in serious trouble. He's in no position to provide assistance."

"Does he have any support?"

"Whatever he had is eroding. In fact, several members of his cabinet have indicated their intent to resign."

"How'd he respond?"

"Asked his entire cabinet to follow suit."

"Resign?"

Payne waved his pen in the air. "For what it's worth, sixty percent of the respondents in a public opinion poll released in yesterday's *Manila Bulletin* said he should quit. Montalvo didn't help himself by saying the Philippine political system was so corrupt it was impossible to be a politician and avoid being tainted."

Brown appeared to reconsider what he was about to say, then uttered, "He really said that?"

"Sounds a lot like Louisiana."

Stuart ignored Valardi's remark. "What is the AFP's stance?"

"They're not happy," Payne responded. "Publicly they've indicated they're willing to support the constitutional process."

"Rather a nuanced response, don't you think?" Gilmore added.

Brown rubbed his chin, pondering the implications. "And Montalvo's position on Taiwan?"

"He's got enough problems at home."

"I agree with Richard," Gilmore said. "We should write him off."

Valardi couldn't let that pass. "I didn't say that. We can't afford to abandon an elected Head of State."

"Sure we can."

Stuart wrapped the side of his water glass with his pen. "Gentlemen, we are not going there. What's being said in private?"

Gilmore peered at Valardi. "Depends on who you ask."

"Montalvo's new Foreign Minister said the government of the Philippines would prefer peaceful dialog to confrontation in the South China Sea."

Payne staked out his position. "The AFP Chief of Staff's not following that line. He's made an open break with the Foreign Ministry and released reconnaissance photos. These refute the Secretary's acceptance of Beijing's claim that installation on Mischief Reef is a fishermen's shelter. The photos were accompanied by a statement saying the AFP will increase its air and naval presence in the Spratlys to discourage Chinese fishing boats from violating Philippine territorial waters."

"A disconnect in Manila's senior leadership," Brown concluded.

"Find out who we can deal with," Stuart demanded.

"I have a sidebar from their Ministry that pertains," Valardi said. "A recent editorial in the *Manila Bulletin* pointed out that under the Mutual Defense Treaty of 1951, the Philippines is obligated to come to the rescue of the United States if our forces are attacked. The treaty covered both Taiwan and the Spratlys. A point we differ on."

Payne choked back a laugh. "Are you kidding me? What a great twist. 'The Mouse That Roared.'"

Stuart's face hardened. "We can all appreciate the irony, Sheldon, but let's keep focused, shall we? Bryce, you have anything on the PRC's proposal to explore for oil in the Spratlys in a partnership with Manila?"

"China Oilfield Services announced a contract to conduct joint seismic studies with Philippine National Oil and Petroleum. The Chinese will furnish the research vessel and the PNOC will provide boat guides and staff."

Stuart tapped his pen on the table. "Is there a direct impact?"

"No, sir."

"Do you concur, Justin?"

"Only for the short term. I'd be inclined to view this venture as a positive development if it weren't for the immediate crisis. My distrust of the PRC's ultimate goals remains."

"It does fit."

"How's that?"

"Implementing the provisions of the Declaration of Conduct of Parties in the South China Sea. Malacanang is playing this announcement for all its worth to deflect attention away from Montalvo."

"And Hanoi?"

"They've been more circumspect," Valardi answered. "This deal impacts their demarcation negotiations with Beijing to establish fixed borders."

"My understanding is these don't include maritime boundaries."

"Correct," Brown said. "The PRC has said it may be willing to consider that issue in the future."

"Where does that leave us?" Stuart asked.

"We're pursuing a number of initiatives to balance those Beijing has put forth. Hanoi's distrust of Beijing's ulterior motives will work in our favor."

Another thought crossed Stuart's mind. "Bryce, have we shut down Beijing's attacks on our computer networks?"

"Cyber-Security has them blocked. They've also implemented a disinformation program to feed the Chinese false information pertaining to our negotiations with Hanoi."

"Could backfire," Payne said.

"It won't hurt to have that rig from Horizon Offshore Exploration sitting right at the edge of the disputed fields," Breckenridge said missing both Payne's comment and the oblique look from Gilmore.

"PetroVietnam's cooperation with HOE has opened a number of doors for us. We've been able to expand our network with the Vietnamese-U.S. Friendship Association."

"Bryce?"

"Mr. President?"

"Is anything wrong?"

"Ah, no, sir."

Stuart turned his attention back to Breckenridge. There was no sense in pressing him. "John, are we any closer to establishing Permanent Normal Trade Relations with Hanoi?"

"Yes, sir. And the timing's good. I'd recommend forwarding the proposal to Congress."

"Get something over to Dan, will you?"

Jotting a note, Lantis nodded.

"Sheldon, what are we doing to firm up our relationship with Hanoi?"

"We've completed negotiations for a port visit to Ho Chi Minh city by the salvage ship, *Salvo* and the minesweeper, *Patriot*."

"I can't imagine those two ships providing much of a deterrent," Valardi said.

"I wouldn't be so sure," Stuart responded. "Beijing must take into account the ripple effect of any action they take to counter our presence in the region."

"The Japanese are watching these developments with considerable interest," Valardi said.

"I'm concerned where the Japanese will land," Brown added.

"We've made no secret of our intentions to revisit the Joint Declaration of Security," Payne said. "We're completing a top to bottom analysis of our relationship."

Stuart read Brown's face. "What else?"

"We must remain cognizant of the past and not condone actions taken by Tokyo that appear to be reconstructing history."

"Your point is not lost, but the way things are shaping up, we're going to need the Japanese even if they do have to stretch their definition of 'self-defense.'"

"I'll second that," Brown said. "My concern with the whole situation is Beijing may over react and leave the Japanese with few options."

"Or us, for that matter," Stuart observed. "We'll need all of our friends in the neighborhood, which brings me back to the Nationalists. Richard, the Taiwanese must understand they are placing themselves in an untenable position if they continue to pursue a policy of provoking Beijing."

"The rhetoric being spewed by the Nationalists' Defense Minister and Mainland Affairs Council about the passage of the PRC's Anti-Succession Law is not helpful."

"On a positive note, Beijing's new law does not stipulate any new conditions on negotiations for reunification."

"But it does contain language spelling out those requirements the PRC would have to meet before taking military action against Taiwan," Brown said.

"I'm not convinced that's such a bad thing. What are the operative paragraphs?"

"The law states that:

'In order to protect China's sovereignty and territorial integrity, the Cabinet and Central Military Commission will be authorized to execute non-peaceful means and non-peaceful measures if possibilities for a peaceful reunification should be completely exhausted.'"

"Then get them back to the negotiating table. And Sheldon?"

"Sir?"

"Make sure we've stopped our arms shipments to Taipei. Let them know in no uncertain terms they are not to militarize Itu Aba."

"Yes, sir."

"Justin, get with Richard and craft a statement. No, make that a stern warning to all of the various claimants in the Spratlys that the United States will not tolerate any interference with international shipping in the South China Sea. For the Chinese, that means we reject the provisions of their Law of Littoral Imperatives that are counter to international law."

Valardi twisted his pen top in consternation. "Beijing will not respond if they perceive we're not approaching them as an equal partner."

"I understand that, Richard," Stuart said. "Publicly, we will not take sides in any territorial disputes in the region. Those disagreements should be resolved under the provisions of the Manila Doctrine for the Conduct of Parties in the South China Sea."

"Beijing won't like that," Valardi cautioned.

"Then, what would you suggest? I want those people sitting around a table talking, not dragging us into a God-damned war."

"Nobody disagrees with you, sir."

"Quite frankly, Mr. President, the entire Taiwan issue is a Cold War anachronism," Brown interjected. "We must take the long view and reconsider our position."

"Go on."

"If we are to advance your agenda, we must have assurances from Beijing they will respond in kind to overtures from the Nationalists and they will not resort to armed confrontation."

"The first piece will be tricky," Valardi said.

"That's why you get paid the big bucks," Payne replied.

"If that's the case, State recommends we reject any further consideration of the sale of those F-18 fighter jets to Taipei. Can the NSC and Pentagon support this?"

Stuart answered for Payne. "Yes."

"Mr. President, we already have a quid pro quo relationship with the Chinese. They look to us to keep Taipei in check just as we have expectations that they will keep Pyongyang in the box. It's imperative we pursue the common ground with Beijing."

"Such as trade," Brown noted.

"We've got some work to do with Congress on the trade piece," Breckenridge said.

"Yes, we do. So, let's talk about our friends in the Congress for a moment. What are you doing at Commerce?"

"I've got a meeting set up with the chair of the Senate Foreign Relations Committee. He's got to stall in committee the proposed legislation calling for a 27.5 percent tariff on Chinese imports."

"Is that part of the Currency Exchange Rate Oversight Reform Act?"

"It is now. The good Senator from North Carolina just added it as a rider."

"A tariff will not be helpful. Dan, place a call to the chair of the Senate Committee on East Asia and Pacific Affairs and set up a meeting of the Congressional Executive Commission on China. Now is not the time for Congress to be stirring the pot.

"On that note, let's wrap it up," Stuart said, cutting off any further comment. "Sheldon, Bob, I'd like a few minutes of your time. Justin, you stay too."

Chapter Thirty-Nine

MORGAN CITY, LOUISIANA
20:36 THURSDAY 17 JULY

The heat of the day grudgingly released its grip on the small harbor as Thuyen Tran emerged from the engine room of his shrimp boat. A freshening breeze from the north-east provided some relief to the oppressive humidity. He arched his spine, stretching the cramped muscles in his back, and swept away the sweat dripping into his eyes. Like him, the vessel and its engine were showing the ravages of time and a hard life.

It had been a rough year for the shrimpers of Morgan City, Louisiana, and he was no exception. The catch from the Gulf of Mexico hadn't been better in years, but the price per pound was the lowest in decades. Everyone was having trouble paying the bills. The hundreds of pounds of Royal Reds his crew unloaded and iced down from their night of shrimping wouldn't cover the cost of fuel. He wondered if the President understood their plight.

Tran shrugged, dismissing the disturbing thought. He had learned long ago to accept the uncertainties of life. For now, he needed to secure his boat so he could join his family for a rare dinner together.

He paused and listened to the gentle sound of water lapping against the hull before surveying his vessel. The long booms of the shrimping rigs resembled the spires of a cathedral, the nets extending from their peaks like flying buttresses. The sight never failed to lift his spirits and he said a brief prayer to thank God for his bounty. He finished securing his vessel, leapt to the pier, and walked to his truck.

He quickened his pace. There was a letter from his lost son, Minh Le, lying on the cracked vinyl seat. For so many years he had not known the fate of his youngest child, and he was struggling with a flood of conflicting emotions.

He started the pickup's engine and pulled onto the lane leading to the highway. He reached out to touch the letter. Once again, he felt the burden of those chaotic days in May of 1975. Tears appeared, blurring his vision. He passed the old warehouse that served the marina. He didn't see the stranger watching from the shadows.

The questions he could never answer continued to torment him. He would never be able to blot out the memories of his family's flight from South Vietnam. A minor functionary in his fishing village, he was none the less terrified of being taken prisoner and interrogated by the vengeful Viet Cong cadre he knew would appear any moment.

The memories swept him back to that time of fear and uncertainty.

———

Tran suppressed his growing panic. He'd left his wife to gather up their three children and ran to their fishing boat to prepare it. Prepare it for what, exactly, didn't cross his mind. They just had to escape. He unscrewed the rusty cap of the fuel tank and plunged a stick into the opening. He pulled it out, scrutinizing the stain. Half-full.

The loud clumping of feet on the wooden pier interrupted his preparations. His wife, with two of their children, ran toward him.

"Where's Minh Le?"

"I couldn't find him anywhere. The soldiers said the village is going to fall. We must go."

He looked past his wife toward the shore. A group of soldiers burst out of the village, stripping off their gear, intent on commandeering a neighboring boat.

"But, our son?"

"God will protect him."

———

Tran's thoughts returned to the present. He couldn't believe God had answered his prayers. The letter represented such deep joy and healing: "Dearest father and family…"

His lost son worked as an engineer for a joint Vietnamese and American project to develop the Con Song oil basin. The employees could take leave each month in the resort town of Vung Tau and he'd met a wonderful girl from the northern provinces. She helped him trace his family's long journey to Louisiana.

He pumped his brakes as he neared the narrow bridge crossing the bayou. He smiled. The joy of meeting this young woman who brought his family together. How strange fate could be.

What?

Blinding light paralyzed his brain. He slammed on the brakes. The truck fishtailed out of control and careened into the wooden guardrail. With a splintering crash, it gave way. The old Ford pickup toppled into the water.

Silence enveloped the night. A darkened car approached,

its tires crunching softly on the gravel road. A man got out and walked to the shattered railing. He peered at the black waters below, then switched on his flashlight to sweep the crash site.

A faint haze of white dust illuminated the narrow beam of light focused on the truck. It was upside-down, cab submerged, the rear wheels rotating. The night air hung still as death.

———

VUNG TAU, VIETNAM
19:12 FRIDAY 18 JULY

A sense of foreboding swept over Minh Le for reasons he could not explain. The evening had not begun well, and Yamei just picked at her rice. She had said very little during dinner and when she did, her voice had an unusual edge.

Perhaps she had read his thoughts? She seemed to care for him. At least in the beginning, he reminded himself. But something had changed during the past several months and she'd become angry when he said none of the Americans on the rig was the least bit interested in meeting her friend.

He sighed and rehearsed the words he would say.

Yamei heard the sigh, and fixed her eyes on his. "Minh Le, it is time to dispense with pretense. I have grown impatient with your foolishness. Tell me what the Americans are doing on Platform Ten."

The steel in her voice took him aback. "I'm sorry, what do you mean?"

"You will tell me what the Americans are doing."

"But they are oil workers."

"Do not play the fool with me."

"I don't—"

"Do you not understand a simple question? You know much more about that nest of spies than you are letting on."

His jaw dropped. "Spies?"

"We have been watching you."

Minh Le swiveled his head around looking at the other patrons. "We? Who are you?"

"Is it possible you can be so naive? Don't you realize we know why you are there? Perhaps you will understand this."

"Understand what?"

"Shut up and listen. Your father —"

"My father? What are you saying? Yamei, you are confusing me."

"Your father is dead. He has met with an unfortunate accident."

Her words hammered at his brain. "Accident?"

"Yes. And if you do not wish any further misfortune to befall your family in America, you will cooperate."

Chapter Forty

REED BANK, THE WEST PHILIPPINE SEA
07:40 FRIDAY 18 JULY

The Philippine Navy Ship *Emilio Jacinto's* bow surged upward, driving against the swells of the approaching storm. The *Emilio* plowed into the leading edge of a squall.

Reyes couldn't see anything through the sheets of rain pelting the bridge windows. The ship corkscrewed to port and dropped with a nauseating lurch into a trough. He cursed under his breath.

They had been at sea for ten days, and he thought it shear madness to be conducting a routine area denial mission in these current conditions. But his opinion accounted for little. He had his orders from WESTCOM.

He wasn't privy to the details of his superior's reasoning. That was above his pay-grade. What he did know was the senior staff in Manila took a dim view of Montalvo's declaration proclaiming a joint exploration agreement between Philippine National Oil and China Offshore Services for the waters around Reed Bank. This could not be tolerated. Their agreement flew in the face of Manila's decision to name the waters surrounding the contested atoll the West Philippine Sea.

Reyes shook his head. *Screw them.*

Another swell rolled into the ship. He broadened his stance to compensate for the movement and addressed his Executive Officer, Lieutenant Lenny Santos. "XO, we're in for a pounding. Rig for heavy seas."

"Captain, I have a contact," the radar operator broke in.

"There can't be anyone crazy enough to be out in this weather. It's not land scatter?"

"No, sir."

A wall of gray water exploded over the bow enveloping the ship in spindrift up to the forward gun mount. Reyes squinted, trying to see through the haze blanketing the sea. *What's out there?*

The approaching storm churned the shallow waters surrounding Reed Bank, obliterating his few visual references. The *Emilio* could easily run aground on an unchartered reef. "Slow to five knots. Maintain our current heading."

The engine room telegraph rang out its confirmation and the *Emilio* slowed. Within moments, they broke through the squall line. "XO, station a bow-watch. I want a set of eyes forward."

"Target bearing five degrees. Distance four hundred yards," the OOD announced.

Reyes leaned forward, squinting to focus on the horizon. Dead ahead, he spotted the unknown contact. Streaks of rust stained the white superstructure situated well aft of the high forecastle. A Chinese fishing boat.

What the...? He couldn't believe his eyes. Strung out behind the trawler were at least three dinghies.

Reyes pointed to the distant ship. "XO, over there, just to port."

"What the hell are they doing out there? They can't possibly be working their nets."

Santos grabbed a pair of binoculars and handed them to Reyes.

Reyes studied the trawler. The captain of the trawler appeared to be calling it quits and retrieving the dinghies. "XO, we're going to close. Right, thirty-degree rudder."

"Right, thirty-degree rudder,' the helmsman echoed.

Reyes braced his legs as the *Emilio* rolled and veered off course.

"Mind your helm."

Puzzled, the helmsman looked at the rudder indicator dial and turned the wheel to bring the *Emilio* around to the proper heading. There was no response. He tried again. "Captain, she's not responding."

Reyes was focused on the response of the trawler to his approach and the matter-of-fact tone of the man's warning didn't register. "Say again?"

The helmsman stared at the Chinese ship looming ahead. "Captain, the rudder's not responding."

Reyes had no reason to question the helmsman. Something was very wrong. They were about to ram the trawler. "Sound the steering casualty alarm. Starboard engine, emergency back. After steering, rudder amidships."

Another wave pushed the *Emilio* back around, countering the measures Reyes had just taken. The distance to the fishing boat was seventy yards and closing. "All back, emergency."

His actions wouldn't be enough. They were slowing, but the *Emilio*'s momentum would carry her into the trawler. The unrelenting whoop of the collision alarm pounded his ears.

He caught sight of the helmsman out of the corner of his eye. The terrified man was about to bolt. "Stand fast, Mendoza. I need every man at his station."

Only a few yards separated the two ships. The impact would be just forward of the trawler's bridge.

Transfixed, Reyes gripped the handles protruding from either side of the rudder indicator consul. He could make out several faces staring in disbelief from the other vessel's bridge. One held a video camera. He heard their panicked shouting.

A belch of oily smoke erupted from the trawler's stack. A door leading to the deck flew open. Caught by a gust of wind, it clanged against the superstructure. Three men poured out of the door and sprinted toward the boat's stern.

Reyes tightened his grip. He had no time to question what they were doing. "Brace for impact."

A dull thud and the screech of iron-on-iron resonated across the water. He ran to the bridge wing, ignoring the slashing rain to examine his hull. The anchor appeared intact. A smear of dirty-blue paint was all the damage he could see.

The glancing collision forced the two ships apart. The trawler surged ahead, opening the distance. He gripped the railing. A ragged line of white-water loomed to leeward. Beads of sweat formed on his forehead.

Holy, shit. Just visible in the distance, the raging surf pounded the fringing reef of an atoll.

Reyes yelled to Santos over the roaring wind. "XO, do we have emergency steering?"

"Yes, sir. After steering confirms they can respond."

"You see the reef?"

"Yes, sir."

"Take the conn. We'll use the swells to help push us around. Hard left rudder."

Reyes was transfixed at the sight of white-water exploding over the reef. His mind registered the *Emilio* responding. She was swinging away from danger. They were on a heading toward open water and safety. His shoulders slumped in relief. "All ahead, full. Let's get the hell out of here."

Reyes scanned the receding rocks of the atoll. His relief was cut short at another sight. *Oh, crap.* He leaned against the railing. *The line securing them must have parted.* The Chinese dinghies were being swept toward the reef. They would all drown. *That's what they'd been doing. They cut the line and abandoned their own shipmates. Cowards.*

He ran back to the bridge and grabbed Santos by the shoulder. He pointed to the dinghies. "We've got to come around. Keep them to leeward."

Santos looked at the helmsman. "Mendoza, you good?"

"Yes, sir."

Reyes turned to Santos. "If we're lucky, we'll be able to heave them a line and secure the entire string. We'll only get one chance before they go over the reef."

"No sweat, sir," Santos replied seeking to calm the rest of the men on the bridge.

Reyes took a moment to get his bearings. *God, what a mess. The Chinese are going to raise holy hell. And what am I going to do with those fishermen? Provided I can even get them on board.* "XO, I'll guide you in. And XO…"

"Sir?"

"Secure that damn alarm."

Reyes turned his attention back to the dinghies. Santos was making a flawless approach. *Blessed Mother of God. We're actually going to pull this off.*

"XO, when we get those men on board, set a course for Palawan, Hulugan Bay. We'll ride out the storm there."

"What about them?" Santos said gesturing toward the fishermen bobbing in the dinghies.

"We'll dry them off and give them some of our stash of San Miguel."

"Works for me, Skipper."

Reyes smiled for the first time that day. "After we drop them off, I'm confident the Foreign Ministry will be able to figure out what to do."

Chapter Forty-One

UNITED STATES EMBASSY
MANILA
13:25 MONDAY 21 JULY

M arie Lynne made a quick mental note of her surroundings. She, and many of the other correspondents stationed in Manila, were packed into the embassy's small pressroom. They were anxious to learn Washington's comments about the rescue of the Chinese fishermen by the Philippine navy. Lynne smiled. Her friend, Captain Reyes, made the news again.

She listened while the press officer recounted what he knew of the event, but soon lost interest. The story didn't have enough substance to make it on ABCs international broadcast. She jotted down a perfunctory note and closed her iPad. Her mind drifted, dwelling on her evening's date with the cute expat. *His blue eyes*—

The grating of chairs on the wooden floors interrupted her musings. The briefing was over. She stood and made her way to the exit, exchanging pleasantries with the reporter from the *Manila Bulletin*. A hand touched her elbow.

"Ms. Lynne? Do you have a moment?"

Lynne didn't recognize the man. She glanced at her companion. "May I ask the subject?"

The man addressed the other correspondent. "Could you excuse us, please?"

When the reporter turned away, the man said, "We can't talk here."

Lynne nodded and followed the stranger out a side door. They wove their way through several narrow corridors and up a flight of stairs before the man deposited her in a windowless room.

"Where are—?"

"Please make yourself comfortable. Someone will be with you in a moment."

Lynne took a step toward the door. "I'm—"

The man closed it in her face.

What the hell? She grasped the door handle. It spun in her hand. She pounded on the door. "Hey, is anybody out there?"

There was no response. *Are you kidding me? I'm a prisoner?*

She pulled out her iPhone and pressed the speed dial. Nothing. She tried again. *Crap.*

Lynne dropped the phone into her purse. *Well, they can't keep me in here forever.*

She tapped her thumbs together and flicked her eyes around the enclosed space before ending up staring at a plain wooden chair. She looked at her watch. *Enough of the mind games.*

The door opened.

"You." She dropped into the chair at the sight of the stranger who'd accosted her in the park.

"Good afternoon, Ms. Lynne. I'm sorry to have kept you waiting. The briefing ended sooner than expected."

"What do you want?"

"To thank you."

"You just locked me in this damn room."

"Yes, that wasn't a good start. I'll have a word with my assistant."

"Seriously?"

"I couldn't be more serious, Ms. Lynne. Your assistance made it possible for us to intervene on President Montalvo's behalf and thwart a major initiative by the Chinese Ministry of State Security to destabilize his government."

"The box you gave me?"

"We're going to arrange for his release."

"Raul? I won't betray my friend."

"Friend? Please, spare me." He leaned forward. "Perhaps your relationship is more, shall I say, pragmatic—perhaps a financial one? Perhaps something in the order of twenty-thousand dollars."

"I didn't—"

"Yes, we know. We've tracked your accounts and there have been no large charges on your credit cards, major purchases, or evidence that you've opened an overseas account."

"You—"

"Certainly, you can't be so naïve as to think we don't have our own sources within Atencio's network?"

"Who?"

"I'm not at liberty to say, but with that in mind, we—"

Lynne stood to leave. "Not interested."

The man blocked the door. "Patience, Ms. Lynne. I will not keep you, but before you go, you may be interested in what I have to say."

"I'm listening."

"We'd like you to consider joining us."

"What? You're kidding, right?"

"We thought that would be your first reaction."

"My *first* reaction?"

"Yes. We believe you could be a valuable asset."

"Asset? Who the hell are you? CIA?"

"We've done a considerable amount of research, Ms. Lynne. Of particular interest is the time you spent at Subic Bay as a teenager when your father commanded the Naval Shipyard."

"Leave my father out of this."

"We have. His record is impeccable. What is pertinent is your work at the orphanage in Olongapo City. Your efforts were most commendable despite the radicalized Priest in charge."

"Father Diaz was a remarkable man."

"I don't disagree. The point is, you've made a remarkable connection with the Philippine people and learned a considerable amount about the Pacific region in your short time here."

"And?"

"And, we would like to provide you the opportunity to… No, I'll get straight to the point. You know as well as I, how much of what ends up in the news is just plain wrong or leaves so many gaps as to be worthless."

"Why should I want to do anything for you?"

"This is not about me. We're looking for what's not being said. There's much more you can do beyond providing thirty-second sound bites to your network. The danger is miscalculation by all parties, misinformation, and the manipulation of events."

Lynne stiffened, but inwardly she agreed. She had lost count of the number of times her material had been altered or cut out in its entirety. Before she could comment though, the man said something that stuck a cord.

"You're too good for that, Ms. Lynne. We can provide you the means to make a difference out here—just like you once did in Olongapo."

"Who are you?"

"Name's Jack. I'm the Station Chief."

"Okay, Jack. I'm still not convinced."

"At some point in your life, Ms. Lynne, you're going to

look back and think about what you've contributed. Have you made the world a better place? It's entirely your decision."

Lynne realized there was much she didn't know and likely never would, but she knew she could make a difference. She thought of Reyes and his crew repeatedly putting their lives on the line against overwhelming odds.

"Not good enough."

"Do you want money?"

"No."

"Then what do you want?"

"To make a difference. To protect the Philippine people."

"Notable goals, Ms. Lynne, but only if the Philippines doesn't become a vassal State. And to do that, we must disable Cruz's and Atencio's network."

"What's that say about us?"

"Not a damn thing. We're trying to prevent a war."

Lynne considered what she must do. "And if I say yes?"

"You won't be asked to do anything immediately. While we already know a great deal about you, you will still need to be vetted and go through the formal hiring process."

"Understood."

Jack extended his hand. "Welcome to the Agency, Ms. Lynne."

Chapter Forty-Two

THE OVAL OFFICE
07:00 TUESDAY 22 JULY

Stuart waved Gilmore toward the vacant chair beside Dan Lantis. "Morning, Bryce. What do we have going?"

"We need to review the latest developments in the Spratlys."

Stuart's jaw tightened. Despite the hour, he was already having one of those days when he asked himself why he had been crazy enough to want to be President. He concluded he was suffering from the delusion he could actually control events and make a difference.

Gilmore read the look on his boss's face. "The implications of the first could be significant, and the others—"

"Start with the first."

"A Philippine navy ship intercepted a Chinese fishing boat near Reed Bank and detained a number of the crew. The embassy was directed to acknowledge the event, but not go into the details."

"The same area where that Chinese patrol boat fired a round at that Filipino archeological survey ship?"

"The *Saranggani*. Had nine French nationals on board."

"Has Beijing reacted?"

"Not yet. Paris is really pissed, but the French can take care of themselves. I'm more concerned about the implications for Montalvo."

"Oh?" Stuart shifted in his chair. "How's that?"

"We have it from a trusted source that General Medeiros decided to take matters into his own hands and manufactured the confrontation to undermine Montalvo's efforts to engage Beijing."

Stuart stared at the wall over Gilmore's shoulder. "That may not be such a bad thing. We don't need another crisis, but I'm tired of waiting for him to get off his butt and make a decision on the new basing agreement."

"You thinking of pulling our offer?"

"No, but I am going to pull Richard from the Two-plus-Two negotiations in Manila. Clarke can go."

"That'll send a message, but this may not be the time to play hardball."

Stuart compressed his lips into a thin line. "Understood. What else?"

Gilmore paused. There wasn't any way he could make this any easier. "Valiant Crane may have been compromised."

Stuart removed his glasses and fixed his eyes on the DNI. "What's going on?"

"One of the Vietnamese nationals working on Platform Ten went missing. The authorities found him yesterday. Dead. We have reason to believe he was turned."

"Got a name?"

"Tran."

"I didn't think you had any of them on your payroll."

"We don't. Our operatives on the rig were suspicious when he began nosing around the restricted area asking too many questions."

"What's the connection?"

"There was a handwritten note stuffed in one of his pockets. It said he couldn't bear the shame of betraying his father and that he forgave him for abandoning him."

"You're losing me, Bryce."

"Tran was Hanoi's senior rep on the platform."

"Go on."

"And we knew he was orphaned at the end of the Vietnam War."

"How does any of this tie into Valiant Crane? There were thousands of orphans. Do we know anything about his father?"

"Nothing. Our background investigation of the victim did turn up something, though. He was left behind when his family fled Vietnam at the end of the war. We're presuming the family ended up in the U.S. or Canada."

"We don't know for sure?"

"No, but somebody does. A couple PRC State Security agents we'd been tracking in Louisiana just disappeared."

"Louisiana?" Stuart said, struggling to make sense of what Gilmore was saying. "What were they doing down there?"

"Remember when the FBI busted that Chinese agent in New Orleans?"

"Could be a coincidence," Lantis said.

"Perhaps. We're checking to see if there's a connection with the recent death of a Vietnamese shrimper with the same last name."

Stuart removed his glasses and rubbed his temple with the stem. "How could that possibly relate? Isn't Tran about as common a name as Smith?"

"It's a long shot, but we can't ignore blackmail."

Gilmore's answer didn't help, so Stuart took another tact. "You said Valiant Crane might have been compromised."

"Last week a Chinese Foreign Ministry spokesman released a statement citing a specific incident they could only have known about through our Valiant Crane intercepts."

"Couldn't they have found out through another source?" Lantis asked.

"It's possible."

Stuart considered the scenarios. "Have we detected any change in the PRC's communication patterns?"

"None."

"Alright, keep working it. And Bryce, I want to be notified immediately if there is any imminent danger to our people."

Gilmore gave an affirming nod.

"Is that it on the Spratlys?"

"No. We've got confirmation on the Drummond Island raid."

"Let's have it."

"We have intercepts from the Chinese referencing something they're calling the Assassin's Mace. We've linked it to the nuclear forensics we ran on the material collected by the Constant Phoenix flights."

"One and the same."

"There's no doubt. The Chinese pulled their people off the nearby islands and sent a HAZMAT team to Fiery Cross."

"Do they know we're behind this?" Lantis said.

"There's no indication they do, but if they figure out our Air Force WC-135 is flying air sampling missions, they could put two and two together."

"Good point," Stuart looked at Lantis. "Dan, tell Sheldon to recall the mission. I've got enough to convince me we've taken their nuclear card off the table. Anything else?"

"Something's going on in the Con Song Basin."

"Damn, Bryce," Stuart said sinking back into his chair. "You're killing me."

"Believe me, I wish it were better. The Vietnamese just lodged a protest with Beijing. They're demanding an explanation from the Chinese about the actions of one of their seismic survey ships."

"I knew about that. Sheldon briefed me. Vietnamese

gunboats forced the Chinese ship out of the area. Is Beijing prepared to do anything?"

"Until yesterday, I wasn't sure."

"What's changed?"

"The PLAN is preparing to arbitrate their claims."

"Interesting word choice."

"Indeed. Straight from the South Sea Fleet Commander. Beijing is putting the region's capitals on notice that any further interference in China's operations in the South China Sea will be viewed as 'irresponsible and reckless actions that will have grave consequences.'"

"Hold up a sec, I want Justin in here. Dan, would you ask Mary Allus to chase him down?"

While they waited, Stuart slid open his desk drawer and pulled out his bottle of TUMS. He shook out a couple pink tablets and popped them in his mouth. "What else have we learned?"

"Sheldon informed me the PLA is preparing to reinforce their outposts on Tizards Bank and Whitman Reef."

"Have—"

Before Stuart could continue, Brown appeared through the Oval Office's side door.

"Pull up a chair, Justin. You need to hear this. Go ahead, Bryce."

"Beijing is preparing to reinforce their installations in the Spratlys."

"I'm not surprised," Brown said. "The Chinese don't believe we can restrain the Nationalists. They're citing Taipei's Hsiung Feng II cruise missile and the rhetoric from the Nationalists' Democratic Progressive Party about promoting independence."

Stuart cocked his head. "The Nationalists? We were discussing the Vietnamese."

"The real danger is Taiwan," Brown replied.

"What's the Agency's read, Bryce?" Stuart asked.

"Taiwan could be the spark."

Stuart drew a counter-clockwise spiral on his notepad. "Justin, your recommendations."

"For starters, they have to cancel their Han Kuang exercise."

"And if they don't?"

"Then we could all be in for a great deal of trouble," Brown said.

"What's the script?"

"Defense of the main islands. Countering a Chinese blockade of Itu Abu."

"Do we know Beijing's intentions?"

"My bet is if the Nationalists don't change their posture, Beijing could well resort to force," Gilmore answered.

"I need to place a call to Zhu," Stuart said. "Short of someone doing something really stupid, we may still have some room to maneuver out of this mess."

Chapter Forty-Three

PACO MARKET
ESTEVO DE PACO, MANILA
18:23 WEDNESDAY 23 JULY

C uriously, there were few people on the street. Those remaining cast long waving shadows across the building fronts. Lynne suppressed a shudder. Even the urchins who had accosted her before were nowhere in sight. This was not what she had bargained for.

Jack's call had come as a complete surprise. The surveillance photos, bank statements, and other incriminating evidence left no doubt in her mind. Atencio was an agent for the Chinese Ministry of State Security.

The Agency had irrevocable proof of Atencio's and Cruz's complicity including substantiating the transfer of one million dollars from one of Beijing's shell companies in Hong Kong to the personal accounts linked to the two men. She was to ensnare Atencio and take down their network that had infiltrated the Lakas CMD party.

She only asked one question after Jack had detailed the

operation. "Does Montalvo know?" "Yes," was the cryptic answer. She should have asked more.

She ducked under the drooping tarp in front of the market and entered the empty warehouse. Her footsteps echoed within the cavernous space, the quiet unnerving after the riotous bargaining of the locals during her first visit. The few remaining vendors intent on closing up their stands cast her only a cursory look.

Her eyes came to rest on the four-tiered clothes rack, the gay colors dulled in the dim light. She exhaled. "Raul?"

"In here."

A single low-watt bulb illuminated the room. Her eyes accommodated to the dark and focused on Atencio. "I thought you were in—"

"They did not have enough evidence to detain me."

"Are you okay?"

Atencio studied her, then pulled up the left sleeve of his Barong.

She gasped at the angry circular burns tattooed along the length of his forearm.

"Let us just say that my release was predicated on pleading guilty to a contrived offense and by making a false statement implicating my associates."

"You were tortured."

"The turds of NICA and the PNP interpret the law differently than in your country."

Lynne knew of the accusations against the National Intelligence Collecting Agency and the Philippine National Police by multiple Human Rights organizations, but....

Atencio continued before she could reply. "In the coming days, it will come down to the survival of the fittest. I have survived and have unfinished business. The Chinese will—"

"The Chinese?"

"They too have tired of Montalvo and the meddlesome

Stuart blocking our attempts to secure a joint gas project and an agreement on joint fishing rights in the water we share with the Chinese people. Agreements that will ensure our country's future. Foreign Minister Yang Po was within a hair-breath of securing an agreement with Minister Cruz before we were arrested.

Lynne struggled to keep her face impassive. Her right hand unconsciously felt for the outline of the wire hidden beneath her belt. *I have to pull him out.*

Atencio followed her hand, his eyes hardening. He saved her the trouble. "Events are in play that within days will secure our rightful place in all of Asia."

Lynne sat immobilized, stunned at what Atencio then revealed of Beijing's plans, but it was his mention of Taiwan that left her shaken. Her fears of Armageddon were about to be realized.

Atencio shoved his chair away from the table, spilling the plate of lumpia onto the floor. "Unfortunately, it is with sincere regret…" He gave a sad shake of his head before continuing. "I once considered you a friend, but you will not be a witness to these momentous events as they unfold. The story of our struggle would have made you famous." He motioned to a darkened corner of the room.

Lynne's eyes darted to the corner. A man she hadn't seen emerged from the shadows.

"Yes, Ms. Lynne, you know…shall I say, where the bodies are buried and you must join them." He gave a jerk of his head to his accomplice. "Seize her!"

She screamed as the man grabbed her arms, forcing them behind her. Her plastic chair toppled with a clatter to the floor as he yanked her to her feet.

"Search her. She's probably wired."

Lynne gasped in pain. "Raul, what are you doing?"

"What I must." He searched her face, then whispered in her ear. "No one will come for you."

She let out a piercing scream and tried to twist free. The

other man ripped open the front of her blouse and forced his hand into her bra.

Atencio grabbed her around the waist, lifting her off the floor and slammed her down on the stained concrete, straddling her. "You may make this easy or not. It is your choice."

Lynne thrashed out with her legs, twisting out of his grasp. "You bastard!"

The roar of automatic weapons gunfire erupted from the alleyway before either man recovered. The side door of the room burst open. A man clad in black tactical gear swung his MP-5 at Atencio's accomplice cutting him down with a lethal head shot. He changed his aim point.

Atencio struggled to his feet, pulling Lynne in front of him.

Two more men sprang into the room, the second covered by his partner's shoulder. The first sprinted forward and flattened both Lynne and Atencio with a fierce cross-body block.

Lynne untangled herself and rolled away. She recognized her rescuer's face. "You?"

"Yeah, the market place." He offered his hand and helped her up as his partner bound Atencio's wrists and ankles with flexicuffs. He smiled. "I also played tight end in college."

She tried to collect her wits. She recognized the partner. *The old man?* "How did you know?"

"Counter-surveillance," he said, leading her to the door. "We gotta get you out of here. You can thank Jack later."

Chapter Forty-Four

THE FAIRMONT HOTEL
13:35 FRIDAY 25 JULY

D an Lantis tried to ignore the incessant chatter emanating from one of his luncheon mates. He was about to silence the man when a Secret Service agent approached.

The agent leaned forward and spoke quietly to him. "There's a call for you, sir. You'll need to take it in the van."

Lantis folded his napkin, hoping the others didn't notice the tremor in his hands. Despite eighteen months on the job, these calls were something he hadn't grown used to. The White House Communications Office wouldn't call just to inquire if he was having a nice day.

He was escorted to the Fairmont Hotel's basement parking lot and ushered inside the communications van where he was handed a red-colored handset.

"Lantis."

Grim faced, he listened to the report. "Yes, yes. Do we know any more? No? Thank you."

He replaced the receiver and addressed the Army Warrant Officer seated next to him. "I need to speak with the Secretary of Defense."

In a moment, the officer handed him the telephone. "Mr. Payne, sir."

"Sheldon? This is Dan. Have you heard?"

"Our information is pretty sketchy."

"Any signs of a Chinese response?"

"Possibly. I've just been passed a FLASH message transmitted by the *Victorious*. She's *Impeccable's* sister ship."

"What's she doing out there?"

"Recording the acoustic signature of the PLAN's new Jin class ballistic missile submarine. They were intercepted by a Chinese destroyer south-east of Hainan Island and forced to alter course."

"Can they do that?"

"There wasn't much the Master could do. We've directed him to leave the area."

"Can we get air cover?"

"That's the President's call, but Seventh Fleet has alerted *Washington* to put a package together."

Lantis checked his watch. Nearly two. "We're scheduled to return to the White House."

"I don't know the President's schedule, but we need to meet."

"Gotta go. He's here."

"I saw you get pulled out," Stuart said as he approached the van. "Anything serious?"

"The Pentagon just received a FLASH message from the *Victorious*. She may be in trouble."

Stuart pulled up short. "What happened?"

"A Chinese destroyer forced her to break off surveillance. Sheldon believes it's connected to the Nationalist's Han Kuang war games."

Stuart threw his overcoat into the back seat of 'The Beast.' "Ride with me.

"This fits with what the CIA fed us from Manila."

"Lynne?"

"Yeah."

"We'll talk on the way back."

Chapter Forty-Five

THE SITUATION ROOM
18:00 FRIDAY 25 JULY

S tuart took a moment to gauge the mood of his staff. His
eyes came to rest on Valardi. Richard's face was drawn,
ashen. The other's appeared to be holding up better. "Sheldon, bring us up to speed."

"At 1300 hours local, the Nationalists fired four Patriot
missiles. Three of these hit target drones representing PLA
aircraft. One missed. They followed the missile test with jet
interceptor exercises conducted near Chinese airspace."

Valardi stirred. "Don't you think that's unnecessarily
provocative?"

"I'd venture to say that will be Beijing's response. A
miscalculation could prompt them to strike," Payne answered.

"What about —?"

Gilmore wasn't in the mood for questions from Valardi
and cut him off. "We may have already seen it."

What color was left, drained from Valardi's face. "Seen
what?"

"The initial reports we've received from Beijing and Taipei

are mixed, but it appears one or more Chinese fishermen have been killed off Quemoy Island."

Brown looked up from his laptop. "That fits with a report that just came across on ABC. The Chinese are claiming the slayings were the result of an unprovoked attack."

"You're ahead of me," Gilmore said. "What do you have?"

"ABC is reporting Taipei's Maritime Patrol Directorate General released a statement saying he was not aware of any boarding incident off Itu Aba Island and if that were the case, it had to be the work of Vietnamese pirates."

Valardi recovered enough to pose a question. "You believe him?"

"They're covering," Brown answered.

The certainty of Justin's response surprised Stuart. "Really?"

"Their statement also said that criminal elements have been cutting the nets and seizing the catches of Taiwanese fishermen near Macclesfield Bank. Perhaps the Chinese vessel was attacked by them."

"Macclesfield Bank?" Gilmore said. "Where the hell is that? I thought the Chinese said Quemoy Island."

Brown held up a hand. "Hang on until I finish reading. Okay, the Nationalists just issued a retraction. They're now saying their first report was in error. The fishermen off Quemoy were using explosives to fish in violation of established agreements."

Valardi, like everyone else at the table, was scrambling to piece things together. "At least that's plausible."

"The report we received at Langley said the fishermen ignored an order from a patrol boat enforcing the exercise restricted zone to stop and leave the area. When the sampan refused to acknowledge, warning shots were fired."

"That's probable," Brown admitted.

"One of these rounds could have hit a fisherman," Payne added.

Stuart shook his head. "Are we sure we're talking about a sampan and not a Chinese naval vessel?"

"That's a possibility, sir," Lawson said.

"God damn it, then what is all of this about Macclesfield Bank? I thought we were talking about Itu Aba or Quemoy Island?"

"Yes, sir. The Macclesfield Bank is almost equal distance between the PLA's installations on the Paracels and the AFP base on Pagasa Atoll. Itu Aba Island is about one hundred miles south of Pagasa."

"Bob, Itu Aba is a long way from Quemoy."

"Over five hundred miles, sir."

"This is hardly the time to not have our facts straight. Somebody get me a damn map."

Lawson knew the President rarely swore and sought to calm him. "I suspect Beijing is just as confused, sir."

"That's my point," Stuart said as Payne spread out a chart of the South China Sea on the conference table.

Have we heard anything from the Chinese Embassy?" Stuart asked.

Valardi looked around the table and answered for all of them. "No, sir."

Brown shifted through a pile of intercepts and pulled one. Stuart looked at him. "Go."

"Following the Nationalist's report, a Foreign Ministry spokesman said that when the fishing boat attempted to leave the area, bandits opened fire and boarded. The spokesman said the Agricultural Ministry has jurisdiction of the fishing grounds near Itu Aba. They're dispatching several vessels to investigate."

"We're looking at two separate incidents," Gilmore concluded.

"Maybe there's only been one?" Brown replied in the silence following Gilmore's statement.

"Maybe three," Valardi said.

Stuart slammed his fist on the table. "Nobody knows what's going on. How am I supposed to respond to this mess?"

Payne interceded. "We should look at the Agricultural Ministry piece, Mr. President. I suspect the Chinese will be sending something considerably stronger than a Ministry vessel. Bob, do you have any reports of ship's movement by units of the South Seas Fleet?"

"No, but we've got another satellite pass coming up. We'll know more after that."

Payne knew Stuart wouldn't be happy with the answer. He needed answers. "Bryce, what about our Valiant Crane intercepts?"

"There's been an increase in coded communications consistent with a heightened alert status."

"Any specifics?"

"Nothing we've been able to decipher, Mr. President."

That response prompted Lawson to consider something else. "Have they changed their encryption codes?"

"No, but they are doing something we haven't seen before."

Stuart picked up on where Lawson was going with his question. "Something to do with their comms?"

"Yes, sir. Several months ago, the Chinese implemented a program called the Blue Network Project. It's an open satcom network with their garrisons and ships in the Spratlys similar to our Armed Forces Network."

"And?"

"Several hours ago, they stopped their regular programming and began encrypted communications."

"You think they're ramping up in preparation for a strike?"

"That would be a valid presumption, Mr. President."

"I still can't believe the Nationalists would be so provocative," Valardi said. "Could the two events be coincidental?"

"Possible," Brown replied. "Regardless, these incidents indicate one of two things, neither of which is good. They were either deliberate, or they've lost control of the situation."

"I agree," Stuart said. "The situation appears to be deteriorating into a worst-case scenario."

"Mr. President?"

Stuart looked across the table at Gilmore. "Yes, Bryce."

"Taipei has said they would not condone the activity of criminal elements within its territorial waters. I wouldn't be surprised if they don't dispatch a couple Coast Guard cutters from Itu Aba to investigate."

"I don't like the sound of that," Payne replied. "Their use of the phrase 'criminal elements' refers to the PLA. And territorial waters, that's another 'in your face' directed at Beijing. Sending military vessels to investigate? These are all elements that will result in a confrontation."

"Bob, do you have any sense how the Chinese would respond if they choose the military option?"

"Yes, sir. We've gamed it out. But, that said, I'm not convinced Beijing is prepared to go that route."

"This would be a political, not a military decision," Valardi said.

Stuart wasn't so sure. "But if Xiao is calling the shots?"

Lawson overlooked the metaphor. "Our best estimate is the PLA will be prepared to mount an invasion of Taiwan within the next few days."

"Would they strike the main islands?"

"They can exercise any number of options short of that, provided they are given the go ahead by their senior leadership," Payne answered.

Stuart wasn't satisfied. "What's their objective?"

Payne deferred and looked to Lawson. "Bob?"

"I'd be looking at the Pescadores."

"Why?"

"They're a soft target and it would make strategic sense."

"How's that?"

"Besides requiring only a small commitment of forces to obtain their objective, the invasion would have minimal polit- ical ramifications for Beijing."

"Although they're being pushed to the limits of their toler- ance, the Chinese will not commit their forces until they have a clear political advantage," Brown said.

Valardi took advantage of the opening to insert a ques- tion. "What would that be, Justin? They won't be able to get much leverage by claiming to be the aggrieved party."

"My cut is the majority of the UN General Council will be looking for an excuse to ignore the entire situation or to side with Beijing."

Stuart looked at the spiral he'd drawn. "I'd prefer not to believe that."

"Oh, there may be some muted protests to maintain appearances," Valardi replied, "but privately, most of the world will not be interested in confronting China. They will take the position that the PRC's actions were a reasonable response to Taipei's provocations."

"I'll second that," Brown said. "My staff ran several scenarios based on outcome analysis. We've concluded that in the event of a limited regional dispute, the world's leaders would say the Chinese were settling accounts on a limited regional dispute. It would not be worth endangering their long-term political and economic ties with Beijing."

Stuart nodded and retraced his spiral. "Where else could they go, Bob?"

"Itu Aba. Taipei may have provided the PRC with the rationale they've been waiting for."

"Unacceptable," Valardi said.

"If Beijing were successful, it would give them control over the entire South China Sea," Payne added.

"Richard, can you say with certainty Beijing understands our position on Itu Aba?" Stuart asked.

"Only within the context of our previously stated position on the region."

"Not good enough," Stuart said. He knew it wasn't Valardi's fault. It wasn't anyone's fault. The decision would be his alone. He reversed the direction of his pen and rapped its tip at the center of the spiral. "Justin, how much time would you give us?"

"Forty-eight hours, max."

"Richard?"

If Valardi was upset by Stuart's earlier response, he didn't let on. "No more than that."

"Sheldon?"

"Forty-eight sounds good, sir."

"We have to move," Stuart said. "Justin, sit down with Richard and draft the position paper. And Justin, I need to talk with Zhu."

"I'll set it up," Lantis replied.

"Bob, call Admiral Cortez. Tell him he has his alert order, hard copy confirmation to follow."

Lawson reached for the secure phone at his side. "Yes, sir."

"And, Bob, what's *Victorious'* status? As much as I'd like to have the intel, it's not worth putting her at risk."

"Hold one," Lawson said to the officer in the Pentagon's command center. "She's safe, sir. Once she turned, the PLAN broke contact."

"Okay, continue your call. Sheldon, where's the *Washington?*"

"Off Okinawa. The Strike Group's been conducting a scheduled exercise with the JMSDF."

"ANNUALEX?"

"Yes, sir."

"They are not to do anything that could be interpreted by the Chinese as a move toward Taiwan."

"Those are our orders, Mr. President," Lawson affirmed.

"How about ocean surveillance? Can we extend our coverage to see what's happening around Macclesfield Reef?"

"We'll reposition a satellite," Payne responded.

"Keep me appraised. And Dan, one final thing. Round up the Congressional leadership. I have to bring them up to speed."

"On it."

"Thank you, gentlemen. We'll reconvene at 0730."

Chapter Forty-Six

THE OVAL OFFICE
07:50 SATURDAY 26 JULY

Stuart strode into Oval Office, conscious he was late. "Good morning, gentlemen. If you need more coffee, get it now."

The only one to take him up on his offer was Gilmore. He wanted a cigarette, but settled for his third cup of caffeine. Stuart waited until he was back in his seat. "Justin and I were in the command center. We have a lot to go over."

"Mr. President, were you able to speak with Zhu?"

"Frankly, I'm not pleased with how things went. He told me the United States should exercise self-restraint and refrain from aggravating the situation."

"*We* should exercise restraint?" Valardi commented a bit too loudly.

"Permit me to finish, Richard."

"Ex…excuse me, Mr. President," Valardi stuttered, taken aback by the rebuke.

"I insisted our sole interest was to maintain peace, and resorting to force would not serve either of our countries' self-interest. He responded by asking: 'Peace and stability on whose terms?' Justin, you have the rest."

"Yes, sir. He said there were 'certain elements whose actions in the South China Sea have been counter to the common thread of peace, cooperation, stability, and development in the region.'"

"The Party line," Valardi ventured. "Did he provide specifics?"

"He provided two, both of which caught me off guard. That will not happen again. For starters, he read from yesterday's *Asian Times* quoting the Chairman of the Senate Foreign Relations Committee. The Senator from Alabama said the Senate was unwavering in its support of Taiwan and authorized the sale of two Osprey class mine sweepers to Taipei."

"How the hell did that get out? That's just pouring gasoline on the fire for God's sake!" Payne exclaimed.

Stuart's face darkened. "I said there were to be no further deals with the Nationalists. I thought I'd made that point abundantly clear."

"Mr. President?"

"Yes, Dan?"

"I have something that pertains," Lantis said.

"Go ahead."

"The mine sweepers were buried in a draft bill approved out of committee and sent to the floor for a voice vote."

"When do I meet with the Congressional leadership?"

"Eleven."

"I'll deal with it, then. Bryce, my next surprise falls in your court."

"Sir?"

"What can you tell me about our contingency plans with the JMSDF showing up on the Internet?"

"We've been working with Naval Intelligence and Cyber Security, Mr. President. The JMSDF confirmed the source.

One of their people. He had the material stored on his personal laptop and screwed up using a file sharing program."

"Has there been a network intrusion?"

"No, sir," Gilmore replied hoping that was indeed the case.

"What was in the files?"

"The damage assessment is ongoing, but it's my understanding there were some three thousand documents."

"What the hell!" Stuart said.

"Mr. President, I can provide some details," Payne said. "They mostly pertain to Korea. However, there were some operational plans outlining in general terms our combined response to a Chinese incursion into the Senkaku Islands."

"Anything damaging?"

"No, sir. Most of the documents were classified confidential or secret. Our analysts have concluded there was little information the Chinese didn't already know or could not have reasonably surmised."

"Any TS?"

"No, sir."

Gilmore was certain there hadn't been a breach in the firewalls, but he did have an explanation. "Mr. President, Zhu may have been referring to something else."

"Oh? What makes you think that, Bryce?"

"The security breach happened nearly six months ago. It came to light after someone leaked the incident to the press. My concern is they may have penetrated one of our electronic surveillance operations."

"The Minh Le guy?"

"No, sir. We picked up an intelligence analyst who tipped them off."

"Should we shut down Blue Horizon?"

"Not yet, but we've got to keep our eyes open. Xiao said there was too much intelligence gathering and the situation was 'very dangerous.'"

Payne frowned. "We're in receipt of a message from Hanoi's military attaché saying the Chinese have blockaded one of their rigs in the Wan Bei 21 Block and intercepted a supply vessel."

"Any shots fired?" Stuart asked.

"Unknown."

"We're working to connect the dots," Gilmore said. "The PLA may have presented the Vietnamese an implicit threat or they could have applied direct force. A threat would be more probable. Our operatives on Platform Ten reported hearing a Chinese research ship firing 100mm shells into the water while supposedly conducting a seismic survey."

"They're that close?" Valardi asked.

"Ten miles."

Stuart considered the implications. "Besides the noise, have the Chinese said anything?"

"They've responded to Hanoi's protest by saying the activities of VietPetro are illegal and must cease immediately. They went on to say if they did not stop, the government of Vietnam, and those supporting them, would be held accountable for any ensuing consequences."

"I presume they're talking about us," Brown said.

"That's our take," Gilmore confirmed. "The statement went on to say VietPetro and HOE have encroached upon China's maritime interests and Hanoi's stance is not beneficial to stability in the Spratly Islands."

"Beijing's upped the ante."

"Yes, sir."

"That's all I need to know. Bryce, prepare to get our assets off Blue Horizon. I can't offer them any protection, but overriding the imminent danger is the imperative to keep tabs on the Chinese."

"Mr. President?" Lawson said. "There's another development."

Stuart recognized the tone in Lawson's voice. "Go."

"We've been tracking one of their nuclear submarines. It left its homeport in Ningho three weeks ago on an extended duration patrol. After operating near Taiwan, it transited into the South China Sea where the *Victorious* picked the sub up before it changed course for the northeast and passed over our SOSUS arrays in the Palawan Trench. Once she entered the Pacific, *Honolulu* trailed her to Guam and back to a position south of Okinawa. The JMSDF went on alert after the sub ventured into Japanese waters. They prosecuted until the sub altered course toward the East China Sea."

"Premier Norita brought this incident to my attention when I spoke with him," Stuart said. "He's demanding an explanation from Beijing."

"All of these events are more than mere coincidence. They must be linked to a broader plan," Gilmore said.

"Perhaps. The Chinese responded by accusing the Japanese of sensationalizing their allegations and that it would not be appropriate to answer a random supposition."

"There was nothing ambiguous about the response in Japan," Gilmore said. "A member of Tokyo's Diet said the Japanese people would never be bullied. He implied that Japan's reserve of plutonium could be used to produce nuclear warheads."

"I'm sure Norita will put a stop to that nonsense," Stuart said.

"It didn't take long for Beijing's Foreign Ministry to respond," Valardi said. "They issued a statement saying that any reference to the use of nuclear weapons contradicts the shared desires for peace and friendship between the Chinese and Japanese peoples."

"Very nice of them," Payne said.

"I wonder what they will have to say about their damn sub shadowing the *Washington*," Payne added.

"Bob, what's he talking about?"

"We received a report from Seventh Fleet early this morning, Mr. President."

"Fill me in."

"A S-3 Viking spotted a Song class diesel boat on the surface some fifteen kilometers from the Strike Group. The sub was likely maneuvering to conduct interdiction and surveillance ops."

"How'd they get so damn close? Did we even know it was shadowing the Strike Group?"

"No, sir."

"Why not?"

"The Strike Group was not conducting anti-submarine ops at the time sir. This particular phase of ANNUALEX was not scripted for them."

"When's the exercise scheduled to wrap up?"

"Tomorrow."

"Don't wait. Call them off and have Seventh Fleet put CTF-77 on alert."

"Yes, sir."

"Wasn't she within range of the sub's cruise missiles?"

"Yes, sir."

"They have to surface to fire them, don't they?"

"No, sir. The 091s can remain submerged. We have observed them come to periscope depth, presumably for targeting."

"Do you think they could have had an engineering casualty forcing them to the surface?"

"That's our working assumption. The Songs have a history of mechanical problems. We can't see any reason why they would have surfaced with the sea state so high. They were really getting rolled around."

Valardi frowned. "This doesn't add up. Why would the Chinese take the risk?"

"You won't get any argument from us on that point," Payne said, "but we have to consider the Chinese weren't planning on being discovered. Our threat assessment suggests PLA airborne forces are preparing for an assault on Itu Aba."

"Have you identified the specific units, Bob?"

"Yes, sir. The 135th Regiment of the 45th Airborne Division is already staged. They could be airlifted in IL-76's with several hours notification. We believe the 133rd Regiment is being held in reserve, and we've verified the 164th Marine Brigade as the follow-on unit."

"A significant force. What else could they have in mind?"

"What if they're eyeing Pagasa?" Gilmore asked. "If they're determined to go that route again, it'll be difficult to stop them."

"The worst-case scenario is, once Beijing has weighed the risks and decides to grab Itu Aba, they'll take measures to consolidate their hold on the entire South China Sea," Payne said.

"They may have already moved to a higher alert status," Brown said. "Several hours ago, Beijing announced a public state of emergency. They've restricted all movement by foreigners in their coastal provinces and access by external news organizations."

"The Foreign Ministry has also denounced U.S. support and arms sales to Taiwan as a gross interference in Chinese affairs," Payne added.

"I have more on that, Mr. President."

"Yes, Richard?"

"A Foreign Ministry spokesman quoted Zhu as saying the Chinese people would do their utmost to strive for the peaceful resolution of this crisis. He went on to say the People's Republic of China would not permit the continued sponsorship by the illegal government in Taipei of terrorists targeting innocent fishermen and ended by saying that to ensure the security of the homeland, the People's Liberation Army would immediately conduct defensive maneuvers.'"

Stuart shook his head. "That doesn't sound like Zhu. Was there anything else?"

"Yes, the rest of the statement read:

'We are a threat to no nation. Our military is defensive and we have no history of invading other countries, but let me be very clear on one point. China is prepared to respond with various levels of force if our level of tolerance is exceeded.'"

"Hold up."

"Sir?"

"This is being driven by Xiao."

Brown tossed his notebook on the coffee table. "I suspect there're any number of Beijing's neighbors who would beg to differ on the first part of that statement. Sheldon, correct me if I'm wrong, but the PLA has conducted offensive operations against Korea in '52, India in '62, Vietnam in '75, and India again in '79 and '20."

"You missed one, Justin. They also fought the Russians along the Assuri River in '69. I would also point out Zhu's—"

"Or Xiao's," Stuart said.

"Or Xiao's choice of the word 'nation' in his comments is worth noting. Beijing does not recognize Taiwan as a nation."

"The wording isn't accidental," Valardi acknowledged. "Something's happened."

"Richard, contact the embassy and find out what's going on in Beijing. This situation is spinning out of control. We must presume the PLA is using their defensive maneuvers to mask final preparations for an assault."

"We believe that's their intent," Lawson confirmed.

"Will they push beyond Itu Aba?"

"There's a high degree of probability they'll attack the Pescadors, Mr. President."

"Any others?"

"We can't dismiss Pagasa. We'll have something more definitive by this afternoon."

"Bob, is that island north of Mischief Reef at risk?"

"Nanshan? If Beijing has made the decision to occupy Itu Aba, it would make sense for them to complete their occupation of the Spratlys. We have confirmation that elements of the Chinese Marine's First Brigade were transported to Hainan Island and are preparing to embark on amphibious ships of their Independent Landing Ship Regiment."

"Can we get the AFP on board?"

"Yes, sir."

"Have Admiral Cortez get on the horn and explain the situation to their Chief of Staff."

"What about Montalvo?" Valardi asked.

Stuart paused, massaging his chin in thought before replying. "I just don't know where he'd come down. In any event, this is moving too fast. We have to move without him."

"We already have components of Expeditionary Strike Group Five engaged in training exercises with the Filipinos," Payne said before Valardi could respond.

"Who's it built around?"

"*Boxer* and the 15th Marine Expeditionary Unit. PHIBRON 8 is the command element. We could provide an immediate assist to Manila under the guise of supporting the Philippine Navy."

"What's our cover?" Stuart probed.

"We've caught a break. The AFP already put out a press release saying that elements of their Special Ops team would be integrated with the Marines and conduct a mock raid on an island west of Palawan province."

"I want Marines on that island within twenty-four hours."

"Yes, sir."

Stuart felt good about the decision but wanted to hedge his bets. "Bob, what else can we do?"

"We can offer the AFP our amphib assets to transport their 3rd Marine Brigade and 2nd Scout Ranger Battalion to Pagasa."

"Alert PACOM. If the Chinese are intent on tangling with the Nationalists, I want to limit the collateral damage by sending a message that we also have a level of tolerance that should not be tested."

"Mr. President."

Valardi's voice had a pitch that set Stuart on edge. "Yes?"

"Listen to us. Are we seriously discussing war with China? There can't possibly be any good outcomes."

"Explain that to Beijing," Payne said.

"We shouldn't suffer from any delusions about our capacity to predict the ultimate outcome of such an action."

"I don't see how we're complicit."

"I understand that, Sheldon," Valardi countered. "Do you have an alternative?"

"I spoke with Taipei's Defense Minister yesterday," Payne said. "I told him he'd be well served to suspend his war games, and if he didn't, he'd have to deal with the consequences."

Valardi recovered. "How'd he respond?"

"Said that his government would consider our request."

"Are you sure he understands I have no intention of intervening militarily short of an all-out invasion of the main islands?" Stuart said.

"I emphasized that point."

A clicking noise prompted Stuart to look at Valardi. He was fidgeting with his pen. "Richard?"

"Taipei's Foreign Minister informed me the Chinese have not acknowledged their apology over the loss of life, or their overtures to discuss any misunderstanding."

"Preconditions?"

Beijing hasn't said anything."

Stuart threw up his hands. "Why shouldn't I be surprised? That's keeping to form. The last time I spoke with

Zhu, he wasn't interested in discussing my point of view either."

Valardi grimaced. "Do you think he heard you?"

"If he's out of the picture, what he thinks is irrelevant," Stuart answered.

"There is one point we shouldn't overlook," Brown said

"What's that, Justin?"

"Aside from pushing a sequence of moves calculated to rattle the governments in the region, the PLA hasn't attacked anyone."

"Yet," Payne observed.

"Perhaps Xiao is just playing a calculated game of chicken and wants to see how we respond?" Valardi replied.

"That's unacceptable. We've been down that road before."

"True," Valardi acknowledged, "but the stakes haven't been this high. I don't think we should be operating under any allusions as to what the Chinese want. Beijing has been very clear on this point. We can choose to ignore their words at our own peril."

Stuart relented, admitting Valardi's point. It would be foolish to abandon the possibility of a diplomatic solution. "Can we get them to the table?"

"Not very likely if Xiao is behind this," Payne responded.

Valardi snapped the cover back on his pen. "That's our problem. Beijing isn't interested in talking."

"We may have caught a break," Payne said.

Stuart wasn't sure he'd heard correctly. "A break?"

"There's been a lot in the media about Japan's reaction to the Chinese nuclear sub," Payne replied, "but no one seems to have the slightest clue about what's going on out there."

"True," Lawson said, "nobody appears to have connected the dots."

"What's your point, Bob?"

"If we have to resort to the use of force, we may be able to apply it in such a way that only impacts the PLA."

"And?"

"If they don't talk and we don't have a leak, no one will be the wiser."

"Is that possible?"

Valardi had no idea what they were talking about. "I'd appreciate knowing what Sheldon's working on."

"Okay, but briefly."

"We have a number of contingency plans Admiral Cortez has been working at PACOM. One of those involves the use of our special op forces. If called on, they would execute a low visibility mission to strike selected strategic targets to inflict maximum damage to their command and control infrastructure."

"My God, Sheldon. Are you talking about a pre-emptive strike?"

Stuart clenched his fist. "No, he isn't."

"It would be prudent to consult our allies," Valardi said.

"No. It's my decision. I don't want this, but if we're forced to act, we're damned well going to win. The Pacific will not be lost on my watch. Is that understood?"

Valardi began to object, but had run out of things to say. "I understand, Mr. President."

"Richard, find out what's happened to Zhu. If he's no longer in control, a diplomatic solution to this crisis may well be off the table. And Bob, I want somebody I can trust to keep an eye on the Nanshan Island mission."

Lawson went through the list of possibilities in his mind, settling on one. "If we can get that SEAL who led the mission on Drummond Island, I'd send him."

"Rohrbaugh, wasn't it?"

"Yes, sir."

"See what you can do."

Chapter Forty-Seven

U.S.S. BOXER LHD-4
NANSHAN ISLAND
06:35 SUNDAY 27 JULY

Mike Rohrbaugh navigated his way through the passageways leading from the command center of the Expeditionary Strike Group to the well deck of the USS *Boxer*. He had just reviewed his orders with the other officers at the confirmation brief, providing them an explanation for the sudden change in their exercise. They had given him the call sign 'Eyes One' in recognition of his new role.

The Certification Exercise had been scripted to be a combined training evolution with the Philippine Special Forces, but the script changed. The grunts of Kilo and Lima Companies, 3rd Battalion 4th Marines he encountered on the well deck were pushing 5.56mm rounds into their magazines. Not a normal procedure for a practice assault. Bathed in diffused red light, they appeared to be indifferent to the dull rumbling of their landing crafts' idling engines in the cavernous space.

The younger Marines clustered together making small

talk, an action betraying their nervousness. Their NCOs were more circumspect. Most had at least one combat tour in Afghanistan and wondered what was up. They had hit their racks expecting to wake up and spend the day crossing off another block on their exercise. The day's schedule hadn't included live fire.

"Gear up, Marines," the company Gunny bellowed. "Get your lazy butts off the deck and form up over here. The Captain's got something to say."

Rohrbaugh smiled and wove his way through the mass of men on his way to the flight deck. The Marines were in for a big surprise. He'd been surprised when he learned what they were to do.

He encountered the watertight door leading to the deck and gave an upward heave to the lever arm. He swung the door open and stepped into the morning light. The sun backlit the four CH-53E heavy lift helicopters of HMH-463 that would transport the initial assault force to Nanshan Island.

A pair of Super Cobra helicopter gunships spotted on the flight deck just forward of the 53s would serve as their escorts. Rohrbaugh was thankful he'd never have to be on the receiving end of their fire. The air detachment personnel had things well in hand. His thoughts turned to the person who greased the skids for his orders.

He'd barely stepped foot on O'ahu when he was handed a one-way ticket on a civilian airliner headed for the Philippines. Landing in Manila, he was whisked to a two-engine military plane that flew him to an isolated airfield on Palawan Island. There, a waiting Navy helicopter ferried him to the *Boxer*. Whomever wanted his eyes on the ground wielded a considerable amount of clout.

"Impressive, aren't they?"

"Yes, they are," Rohrbaugh replied without looking at the

speaker who'd appeared at his side. He fixed his eyes on the other two amphibious ships of the Expeditionary Strike Group. The *Fort Fisher* and the *Denver* carried the other elements of Three-Four's combat and support elements that would follow the assault wave. "I see you found your way to daylight."

Lieutenant Angelo Torres, Philippine Navy Special Forces, didn't skip a beat. "Part of my escape and evade training."

Rohrbaugh relented and extended his hand. Torres' grip was strong, assured. "I was briefed on your rescue mission. Strong piece of work. Welcome aboard."

"This time around, I hope our reception won't be so exciting," Torres yelled over the mounting noise of the helicopters' engines.

"Roger that," Rohrbaugh replied.

The two men stood apart keeping their own council until Kilo company's Marines poured out of the superstructure and began to form up on the deck.

Rohrbaugh slung his rifle and pointed to one of the helicopters. "Time to mount up. Empire One, Kilo's company commander, is in the first bird. We're riding in that one, Dash Two."

Torres spun his forefinger over his head mimicking a rotating propeller to alert his men. "Saddle up."

The assault force gave a wide berth to the whirling blades of the tail rotors and filed up the ramp of their helicopters. The noise was deafening.

Rohrbaugh's 53 crew chief pointed to the canvas benches lining each side of the aircraft, then handed him a handset plugged into the helicopter's internal communication system. He stepped aside to watch the twenty Marines of Second platoon, Kilo Company, fill the remaining seats.

A moment later, Rohrbaugh felt the rotor blades' torque rock the aircraft. He turned and gave Torres a thumbs-up as the aircraft lifted off the deck. They would be over Nanshan Island in a matter of minutes.

"Pegasus flight! Break Right! Tracers 3 o'clock! Break right!"

Rohrbaugh braced at the warning transmitted through his headset. A number of Marines on his side of the aircraft weren't so fortunate, and tumbled out of their seats.

"Deuce's losing power. Smoke's coming from his starboard engine," the pilot shouted. "Shit, they've taken rounds. He's trying for that clearing on the far side of the runway."

Rohrbaugh did a quick assessment and yelled back. "Can you patch me through to Empire One?"

The pilot pointed at Rohrbaugh's handset.

"Empire One. Empire One. Eyes One." Rohrbaugh repeated the call. "Empire One. Eyes One."

"Copy, Eyes One."

"Empire One. We will take the hostiles."

"Copy that, Eyes One. You're engaging the hostiles."

Rohrbaugh keyed his handset to alert the pilot. "Did you spot them?"

"Concealed position to the right of that concrete building."

"Can you set down?"

"Affirm," the pilot said swinging the 53 around so his right door gunner had a clear field of fire. The gunner didn't need to be prompted. A stream of spent .50 caliber shell casings rained down on the floor as the heavy machine gun's rounds swept the area.

"Deuce is down," the pilot yelled. "I've got Marines egressing the aircraft."

"Roger that," Rohrbaugh acknowledged over the words of his pilots verifying there were no obstructions in their landing site; 'Clear right. Clear left.'

The 53 settled firmly on the ground in a cloud of dust and

flying debris. Rohrbaugh grabbed the shoulder of the Marine platoon commander.

"Join up with your skipper. Torres and I will engage the hostiles."

The Marine darted a quizzical look.

"We don't want Marines killing Chinese. This exercise is going to shit. It's going to be easier to explain if the Filipinos are defending themselves."

Rohrbaugh thought they might have a chance to contain the situation until he saw one of the Cobra gunships unleash a torrent of 20mm cannon fire at the anti-aircraft gun site. The gun emplacement vanished in the hail of fire. Hovering over Deuce's helicopter, the other Cobra's nose turret traversed to the same target.

"Go, go, go," Rohrbaugh yelled pushing the platoon commander toward the 53's rear ramp.

"Everyone dial in," Rohrbaugh screamed over the mounting noise. "We gotta move."

The Marines poured over the ramp, deploying in an assault formation. The eleventh man out screamed, staggered forward several steps, and fell to the ground.

"Man down."

The platoon's corpsman dropped next to the fallen Marine, tore a tourniquet from his Unit One and tightened it around the Marine's thigh.

Muzzle flashes twinkled from the tree line. Rohrbaugh dodged around the two men and sprinted toward his objective giving them only a glance. It was obvious the Navy corpsman had done this before.

Rohrbaugh swiveled his head and spotted Torres. "We're going to take down that position."

A rocket propelled grenade exploded, showering them both with dirt and a spray of shrapnel. Torres leveled his rifle, emptied one magazine, and slammed in another.

A second grenade detonated with a thunderous boom.

The shockwave slammed into their chests, knocking them both off their feet. Dirty-brown smoke from the round's impact hung suspended in the air.

Torres reacted first. "Contact right. Counter fire." Coming to a knee, he tore a grenade from his web-belt. He lobbed it at the concealed gun position and charged.

Rohrbaugh shook his head to clear the ringing in his ears. He pulled himself up and took off after him. *Crazy son of a bitch.*

One of Torres' men spun, clutched his abdomen, and went down writhing in pain. Rohrbaugh slowed, grabbed the soldier's leg, and dragged him out of the line of fire. Sliding down next to Torres, he turned the soldier on his back to apply pressure to the wound. "Hang in there. You're going to make it."

Torres opened his mouth to say something, but before he could, the structure in front of them erupted in a ball of fire.

"You got him?" Rohrbaugh asked.

"Yeah."

Rohrbaugh inserted a fresh magazine in his rifle and sprinted, zigzagging his way across the runway. He pulled up at the sight of utter carnage. The twin rotor blades of the Cobra whipped the air above him, the only sound.

He heard the isolated pops of a rifle. Movement. Voices calling out to their buddies.

"Commander?" We've got one over here," Torres said pointing to a bloodied body.

Rohrbaugh looked at the PLA soldier and turned away. The Chinese infantryman wouldn't make it. *The guy's only a kid. Crap. Why'd they have to fire on us?*

Rohrbaugh sat down on a wooden crate of anti-aircraft ammunition. He reached into the pocket of his utility jacket and pulled out a couple of cigars, beginning his ritual to decompress. There was nothing here to celebrate. His hands started to shake. He hadn't noticed the holes—or the dents in the ceramic plates of his body armor.

Torres approached, eyes white against his blackened face. Rohrbaugh clutched the two cigars and took a deep breath. "How's your man?"

"The corpsman thinks he'll make it." Torres looked up at the sound of a helicopter lifting off. "Flores was with me on the other op. Guy can't catch a break. He took a round there, too."

"You okay?"

"Yeah…think so."

Rohrbaugh slipped the wrapper off one of the cigars and offered the other one to Torres. Rolling his cigar in his fingers, Rohrbaugh applied a flame and took a long draw. He exhaled through pursed lips and studied the cloud of smoke. *Fuck, now what?*

A squad of Marines approached and began to poke around the wreckage. Rohrbaugh took another pull on his cigar and crushed it out. *I sure hope there's a plan, because someone higher than my pay grade is going to have to sort this mess out.*

Chapter Forty-Eight

BLUE HORIZON
THE CON SONG BASIN
01:37 MONDAY 28 JULY

The two American operatives standing watch on Platform Ten were wide-awake despite the hour. They were monitoring the communications and radar signatures of the two PLAN warships that had been harassing the Vietnamese for the past several days. There wasn't anything noteworthy to enter in their logs until 0130, when the Chinese linguist detected a change in the radio traffic between the PLAN ships.

"They just went secure."

"They sure made a big show of leaving the area yesterday afternoon," his partner responded. "Wonder what's up?"

"Yeah, I ... What the...? Hey, check this out."

"What do ya have?"

"Wait one," the linguist replied pressing his hands against his headphones. "Somebody else just came online. There's a third ship out there. You have anything on your screen?"

"You're right. I've got the signature of a Snoop Tray target acquisition radar."

"They've been pinging these rigs ever since they got here, but we haven't seen this pattern before. We miss something?"

"I doubt it. I'm wondering why they're targeting these platforms. The Vietnamese aren't even aware the Chinese are hitting them."

"We passed all of this along to Washington," the linguist said. "They came to the same conclusion we did. Practice."

"Yeah, but we did kick around another scenario. We're going to be in serious trouble if they're on to us."

"We're still sitting here, aren't we? I'd figure we'd have been pulled out if there was a serious threat."

"Since when have you trusted anything coming from the Beltway?"

"Good point."

"I've got a bad feeling about this. Why something new and why in the middle of the night?"

"Pass me that book over there, would you? It's time we identify the source."

"What is it?"

The linguist didn't answer for a moment while he flipped several pages back and forth. "Wubon class diesel boat."

"A God-damned submarine?"

"Yeah, it's a modified version of the Russian Romeo. Carries six cruise missiles similar to our Harpoon."

"You don't think—?"

"Are we transmitting?"

"We are now."

A brilliant flash erupted from the direction of the nearest Vietnamese drilling platform at the same moment their burst transmission was sent to the military communications satellite circling overhead.

The report of a huge explosion reached their ears within a second.

"Oh, shit!"

The companion explosion extinguished both of their lives before his partner could reply.

———

The Chinese missile traveled just below the speed of sound, crossing the short distance between them and the submarine in less than a minute. The men of Blue Horizon didn't stand a chance.

Its mission complete, *Wuhan* 351 slipped beneath the waves and set a course for its homeport.

Chapter Forty-Nine

THE SITUATION ROOM
09:17 MONDAY 28 JULY

All conversation in the Situation Room ceased when Stuart strode in. The expression on his face required no explanation.

"Gentlemen, the situation in Southeast Asia has taken a turn for the worse. The PLA has removed our last options to resolve this crisis."

Valardi closed his laptop with a soft click. "What's happened?"

"This morning, cruise missiles fired from a Chinese submarine destroyed Platform Ten and an adjacent Vietnamese drilling platform in the Con Song Basin. The preliminary reports from Hanoi indicate there are no survivors."

Valardi blanched. "Are they sure?"

"The Vietnamese are preparing to conduct search and rescue operations."

"Perhaps they're mistaken," Valardi implored.

Stuart's jaw tightened. "I asked. At 0133 hours, NSA received a burst transmission from Blue Horizon indicating they were under attack by cruise missiles fired from a Wubon Class Chinese submarine. There has been no further contact with the rig."

"Do you think the attack was in retaliation for our raid on Nanshan Island?" Brown asked.

"Possible, but that would be pretty short-fused. I'm not sure the Chinese could pull it off," Payne responded. "My bet is the attack was already in the works."

"Premeditated?" Valardi asked, not wanting to believe what he'd heard.

"Yes."

"Do we have anything on our people?" Brown asked.

"It's three in the morning," Gilmore said.

Valardi turned to Stuart. "Were you able to contact Zhu?"

"I was informed he was unavailable."

"Did they provide an explanation?"

"No."

"Shall I try Premier Yanglin?"

"I'll place another call in an hour. Right now, we need to review the bidding. Sheldon, you lead off."

"We could see a preliminary strike by PLA tactical aircraft and missiles within two to three hours followed by their main force units within twenty-six."

"Dawn tomorrow? Why the delay?"

"Same tactics we'd use. Their initial attack will be designed to take down the Nationalists' air-defense system."

"That'll buy us some time," Gilmore said.

"Precisely."

"Is there any indication they're prepared to use their anti-satellite weapons?"

"No, sir. But if taking out Platform Ten is a prelude to a strike on Taiwan, I wouldn't dismiss the possibility of a cyber-attack on our command and control systems."

"I'm operating under the assumption the Office of National Counterintelligence has that covered."

"I wouldn't want to presume anything," Gilmore said. "You remember those cyber-attacks on Commerce last January?"

"Your point?" Payne asked.

"They were sending a message. The hackers left a tell-tale marker behind they knew we'd find."

"Why would they do that?" Valardi asked.

"A warning. They were saying our firewalls are vulnerable."

Stuart glanced at Payne. He looked vexed. "Bryce, put all the appropriate agencies on alert."

"On it."

"Now, what about Valiant Crane."

"We're still getting intercepts," Gilmore answered. "We switched to our backup system to relay the transmissions after Blue Horizon went down."

"What are we hearing?"

"Their communications are consistent with Sheldon's assessment. We're looking at a probable onset of hostilities within the next twenty-four hours."

"Our analysis suggests the PLA may confine their operations to Itu Aba."

"We will not permit that. I will not permit that. And the murder of sixty Americans will not go unanswered."

"Yes, sir."

"Mr. President?"

"What, Richard?"

"We have to presume he's no longer in charge."

"Zhu?"

"We know Xiao and certain senior elements within the PLA aren't pleased with the reformist movement in China. And, Zhu didn't help his cause any last week when he ousted a senior Politburo member closely linked to Xiao's faction."

"We've been hearing rumors of a power struggle within

the government," Gilmore confirmed. "The Minister of Public Security has aligned himself with Xiao's faction."

"You're suggesting Xiao took pre-emptive action before their fall elections?"

"It fits," Gilmore said. "NSA picked up something odd while monitoring China's Internet. The bulletin board of the search engine Baidu shut down right after reporting troops and armored personnel carriers moving toward Beijing."

Valardi understood the connection. "I need to call Yanglin."

"I concur," Gilmore said. "Our analysts feel he's no more than the general's puppet. If he's moved from his traditional role to one as principle spokesman for national affairs, we'll have strengthened our case."

"Make the call. And see what the embassy comes up with," Stuart ordered. "I'll try Zhu again."

Stuart paused. "I also want to pose a question to all of you. Why did the Chinese destroy the Vietnamese rig?"

"Could have been accidental," Brown ventured.

"We feel that's remote," Payne said.

"Do you have another explanation?" Stuart asked. "Seems to me, destroying an oil rig is far out on the edge of rational behavior."

"Perhaps, but if we look at the PLA's action within the context of—"

"What have the Vietnamese done, for God's sake? I haven't heard of them blowing up any Chinese."

"That's correct to a point, sir," Payne said, "but we know there's been a turf battle on maritime boundaries and Hanoi has been renovating that old airfield on Spratly Island.'

"There's something else," Lawson said. "I didn't pay much attention to it at the time."

"Could it explain what's going on?"

"Three months ago, Manila accused the PLAN of boarding a Filipino fishing boat and roughing up the crew.

The next day they demanded an explanation from the Chinese for shooting at a Filipino Air Force reconnaissance plane."

Gilmore reached for his breast pocket and pulled out a packet of Marlboros. He tapped out a cigarette. "I recall that."

"Sounds like a reasonable reaction from the Philippine government," Valardi observed.

"It was," Lawson said, "except the Chinese were innocent. They were set up."

"By who?"

"The Vietnamese. It was one of their patrol boats."

"I've heard enough," Stuart said frowning at the cigarette dangling from Gilmore's mouth.

"The reality is Zhu may be gone and we don't know who's running the government. What I do know is the PLA killed over sixty American citizens and is preparing to strike Itu Aba within the next twenty-four hours.

"Richard, you find out what's going on in Beijing. Establish contact with their Foreign Minister. Justin, share anything they have with State. Dan, contact Treasury and finalize our contingency plans in case Beijing chooses to play hardball with the $340 billion in U.S. Treasury Bills they hold. Sheldon, Bob, please join me in the Oval Office."

Chapter Fifty

THE OVAL OFFICE
16:50 MONDAY 28 JULY

Stuart reacted to the sound of Bob Lawson entering the Oval Office. He didn't wait for him sit. "Have we located the sub?"

"Yes, sir. It's being prosecuted by one of our P-8s."

"Where is it?"

Lawson dropped into the armchair next to Payne. "Running deep at thirteen knots. They're tracking east of Hainan's three-hundred meter shelf."

"How'd we find it?"

"We anticipated they would head for home and laid a line of sonobuoys across its projected course. The P-8 dropped directional frequency and ranging buoys."

"And the *Honolulu*?"

"She's proceeding south from her patrol area off Linghui. She'll be positioned to intercept within six hours."

"Order the P-8 to lay a field of active buoys and ping the hell out of them."

"You want us to go after them?" Payne asked.

"I want those bastards to sweat."

"Yes, sir. We'll order the P-8 to turn them toward the *Honolulu.*"

"Any contacts near the *Washington?*" Stuart asked.

"We tagged a Kilo when it passed over our SOSUS array. *Corpus Christi* has a solution and can take it out any time we want."

"I don't want to wait. Force that sub to the surface. He can take any action necessary, short of sinking it."

"Should I authorize the use of the MK11 depth charges?"

"Yes, but make sure they drop them well out of crush range."

"Yes, sir. We'll prepare a list of options for your approval."

"How soon can you get them to me?"

"Within the hour."

Stuart nodded his assent. "Sheldon, what's the status of the other components of Blue Fury?"

"Admiral Cortez reports he's ready to go. *Ohio* has downloaded her targeting data and is transiting the Palawan Trench. Her Tomahawks will take down every Chinese installation in the Spratlys."

"She alone?"

"No, sir. *La Jolla's* riding shotgun."

"What are our alternatives to minimize loss of life?"

"We have two delivery systems loaded on the B-2s flying out of Whitman Air Force Base."

"Are they in the air?"

Lawson looked at his watch. "They launched twenty minutes ago. They're taking the southern route. It's longer, but we want to avoid the Russian air defense radars covering Alaska."

"Good. Sheldon, you were about to say something about delivery systems."

"Yes, sir. One is the CBU-107."

"Freshen my memory."

"It's loaded with tungsten and steel penetrators designed to take out soft above-ground targets. Radar, fuel tanks, generators."

"Sounds like high-tech shrapnel," Lantis said, entering the room.

"True enough. They'll be pretty tough on any Chinese who happen to get in the way."

Stuart waved Lantis to the couch. "You mentioned two delivery systems. What's the second?"

"Our electromagnetic pulse weapon. We can fry all of their electronics within a several hundred-yard radius beneath the detonation point. The B-2's delivery vehicle is a modified JDAM."

"I recall the weapon is also configured for our cruise missiles."

"The *Ohio* carries four."

"Do you have a plan to use them?"

"Yes, sir. They're our weapons of choice for the initial strike. The *Ohio's* are targeting the Chinese installations on Subi, Johnson, and Mischief Reef. The B-2s will blanket Fiery Cross, Woody, Duncan, and Rocky Islands."

"Should we deactivate The Pod?"

"No, sir. We want to leave it up to monitor Chinese communications. It'll give us feedback on the mission and how fast they recover—if they can."

"Are we prepared to block their attack corridors?"

"The B-52's of the 23rd Expeditionary Squadron at Anderson are ready to go. They're carrying a mix of Quick Strike and moored mines. We've also ordered Seventh Fleet to surge his boats."

"And the *Washington*?"

"The Strike Group—"

The sound of an opening door stopped Lawson in mid-sentence. "Excuse me, Mr. President."

Stuart scowled, wondering what could be so important. "Yes, Mary Allus?"

"President Zhu is on the line, sir. Are you available to take the call? The operator says you won't need a translator."

"Yes," he responded, his mind in turmoil. He looked at the desk clock. Just after five in the morning in Beijing. "Yes, of course. Please put him through. Dan, the other line."

In a moment, the light on the phone console blinked. Stuart lifted the receiver. "President Stuart. Good morning, sir," Stuart replied to Zhu's greeting. "I'm quite well, thank you. I was concerned you were not available to take my call yesterday... Oh? What happened? Yes, I understand. And you're confident you've contained the situation? And Xiao? I can appreciate that. President Zhu, to have any party resort to the use of armed force would indeed be very unfortunate. Yes, our two nations cannot afford..."

Payne and Lawson leaned forward listening to Stuart's side of the conversation, trying to piece the fragments into something meaningful. Whatever had happened, it didn't sound good.

Dan Lantis, on the other hand, was more fortunate. He had picked up the line the instant Stuart picked up his receiver. Establishing eye contact with the other two men, he flashed them an 'Okay' sign.

Payne wasn't convinced. He pulled a copy of his appointment schedule from his suit pocket. He tore out a page and scribbled a note. 'I don't trust him. We only have one shot—the clock's running.' He leaned over and handed it to Lantis.

Lantis scanned the note, raised an eyebrow, and took a step to place it next to Stuart's phone.

Stuart picked up the scrap of paper while he responded to Zhu's explanation of the PLA's actions. "Yes, I agree, sir. Any loss of life, be it your fishermen or our oil workers, is most unfortunate."

He scanned Payne's note and nodded. His voice hardened.

"No sir, you know as well as I, the explosions on the drilling platforms were not accidental. Yes, we are tracking the submarine that carried out the attack".

Payne and Lawson exchanged looks. The President should not have divulged that information. They shook their heads and turned their attention to the one-sided dialog.

"And do I have your complete assurance the men responsible will be held accountable? Yes, that would be a positive development. Yes, Taipei's actions are ill-advised. Good."

"May I suggest we include follow-up discussions on the demilitarization of the South China Sea as an integral component of our discussions?"

Stuart paused. He needed to give Zhu something. "Your proposal at the East Asia Summit for multinational input to define the disputed areas could provide the foundation. Yes, we're in agreement, then? We can build on that to pursue the implementation of a Regional Code of Conduct. There can be no further deployment of armed forces by any party. I would also suggest PetroChina delay its seismic surveys of the Houquang Trough."

"Yes, I understand an American oil company has agreed to provide a deep-water drilling rig. We will discuss the implications of this collaboration with the American firm. We should explain in our joint announcement our intent to curtail further exploration in the field until the drilling rights are clarified. I agree."

"Elevating our deliberations to Ministerial level would be most productive. Secretary Valardi will be in contact with Vice-President Li later today.

"Yes, sir. It was a pleasure speaking with you again. May I call you later today? Yes, thank you. Goodbye."

Stuart exhaled before speaking. "Sheldon, your clock has slowed. We have our opening."

"What happened?" Payne asked.

"Richard had it right. Zhu didn't go into details, but Xiao

and Yanglin attempted a coup. Loyal elements of the military intervened. Bob, your gut feeling on Cheng was right on. Zhu mentioned his role in securing the capital."

"Thank God."

"Yes, Sheldon. We should indeed thank God. We were going down a path we didn't want to travel."

"So those reports on the internet about troop movements in Beijing were valid," Lawson said.

"Appears so."

"Sir?"

"Yes, Bob?"

"Did Zhu say what the PLA's doing to recall their units?"

Stuart rocked back in his chair. "Oh, hell. I didn't even think to ask."

"My greatest concern is they won't be able to contact all of their subs."

"The 'Fail-Safe' scenario?" Payne asked.

"But haven't we accounted for all of them?" Stuart said.

"That's not the problem, sir. If one of their subs presses home an attack, we'd have no choice but to defend ourselves. *Washington*'s at greatest risk."

Stuart massaged his temples. "Then my orders stand. Force that Kilo to— Bob, you've got that look."

"The Strike Group needs to disengage. If *Corpus Christi* determines the Kilo breaks off, we have a good chance of diffusing the situation."

"And if it doesn't?" Payne asked.

"Then, I'm not going to risk any more American lives," Stuart answered.

"Understood."

"What about the Wubon? The longer we keep the P-8 on station, the greater risk to the aircrew," Payne said.

Stuart's fists tightened. "I don't want the PLAN to suffer from any delusions their submarine force can stand up to us."

Payne and Lawson didn't respond.

"Bob?"

"We've made our point with the Wubon. I'm confident everyone on that sub knows their fate if we decided to engage. That, and we don't want to tip our hand on what we can do."

"Sheldon?"

"At this point, any action we take must be defensive."

"Bob, can we get word to *Honolulu*?"

"Yes, sir."

Stuart tapped his fingers on his notepad. "Alright. Get them out of there."

"That's the right call, sir."

Stuart stood. "Bob, get hold of Admiral Cortez. Sheldon, you need to stay. Dan, round up Richard. He's got some work to do. We need to give Zhu something. I want him to work a joint statement with Beijing stating our shared commitment to the Trans-Pacific Free Trade Pact."

"We'll need to put something together for the press to explain why the hell we increased our alert status," Payne said.

"That and putting something out about what happened on Nanshan Island," Lawson added.

"Not yet," Stuart said.

"What about that reporter in Manila? Lynne," Lantis countered.

"Lynne?"

"Yes, we got some good reports from the guys at the embassy. She should be able to spin it."

Stuart jotted down her name. "Okay, fill her in."

"On it."

"I'll get my Public Affairs office to work something up," Payne said. "They can craft the release to fit what we already said about the planned exercise to surge our Strike Groups."

"Have I missed anything?"

"What about bringing Rohrbaugh in?" Payne said. "I've got a spot open on the NSC. Deputy Director for Political-Military Affairs."

"Let me think on it," Stuart said while drawing a clockwise spiral on his notepad.

"I'll get you some background."

"Are we good, then?"

"You've got it covered," Payne responded.

Stuart allowed himself to smile. "Then gentlemen, we're in a whole lot better shape than we were about thirty minutes ago."

"Sir?"

"What's on your mind, Bob?"

"I wonder if anyone but us will ever know just how close we came."

Acknowledgments

I was most fortunate to benefit from the support and assistance of many individuals while writing *Flashpoint*. Foremost was my wife, Christine, who stood by my side during the entire process and would stave off my moments of panic and retrieve entire sections of manuscript that would seemingly disappear from my computer.

I still smile at my oldest daughter, Jennifer's red-penned edits of my first draft highlighted by "The Dreaded Awk" inscribed in the margin next to a particularly awkward paragraph. A special note of thanks is due my youngest daughter, Michelle, for her advice on developing the persona of my primary characters and her husband, pilot and warrior Major Brian Spillane, USMC. Brian provided the force of realistic dialog in crafting the Marine aircraft sequences.

In the small world category, I contacted my old command's Public Affairs Officer and Outreach Department at Commander, U.S. Pacific Fleet Headquarters in Honolulu, Captain John (Marvin) Gay, USN. In an incredible coincidence, we both served together on the USS *Blue Ridge* many years ago. He, in turn, linked me with the Fleet's Director of Operations, Captain John T. Pitta, USN.

A special note of thanks is due Captain Pitta, an F/A-18 pilot, who 'ran a sanity check' of my air-combat chapters and dragged me into the 21st Century. In his review of my air-combat chapters, Captain Pitta noted the 'excessive cockpit chatter' which I'd taken liberties. The chatter is excessive and a realistic portrayal of the communications of the air-combat chapters is, yup, secret. A prior commander of VFA-143, flying off the USS *Eisenhower* CVN-69, he has over 3,500 flight hours and 954 carrier arrests. It is to such men and the women of the United States armed forces that I dedicate this book. I am truly privileged to be flying in such rarified air.

Mr. Rick Ludwig was my primary reader for my manuscript suggesting many ways to tighten up my narrative and provide depth to my characters. I am indebted to Savannah Thorne who edited my final manuscript providing valuable insights, especially as they pertained to the character, Marie Lynne and to Ms. Alice Bernhardt for her formatting skills. And, finally, because one can really "tell a book by its cover," I am indebted to Maria Novillo Sararia, BEAUTe-BOOK, for her outstanding cover design that captures the essence of *Flashpoint*.

Finally, I must acknowledge my publisher Mr. William Bernhardt, best-selling author, teacher, and mentor. Without him, the release of this novel would not have been possible.

About the Author

Kenneth Andrus is a native of Columbus, Ohio. He obtained his undergraduate degree from Marietta College and his doctor of medicine from the Ohio State University College of Medicine. Following his internship, he joined the Navy and retired after twenty-four years of service with the rank of Captain.

His operational tours while on active duty included: Battalion Surgeon, Third Battalion Fourth Marines; Brigade Surgeon, Ninth Marine Amphibious Brigade, Operation Frequent Wind; Medical Officer, USS *Truxtun* CGN-35; Fleet Surgeon, Commander Seventh Fleet; Command Surgeon, U.S. Naval Forces Central Command, Desert Shield/Desert Storm; and Fleet Surgeon, U.S. Pacific Fleet.

He now resides with his wife in Honolulu, Hawaii.

Made in the USA
Middletown, DE
27 October 2020